LYRA FORGER

HOUSE OF YDRIL

THE ORIGINALS OF GRIMM ACADEMY

House of Ydril

The Originals of Grimm Academy series

All rights reserved. This book or any portion thereof may not be reproduced or used in any manner whatsoever without the express written permission of the publisher except for the use of brief quotations in a book review.

This is a work of fiction. Any resemblance to actual persons, living or dead, or actual events is purely coincidental.

First Edition 2023

Cover design: Artscandare

Copyright © 2023 Storycraft OÜ

LYRAFORGER.COM

All rights reserved.

Did you hear the one about the book that was so hot, it set off the fire alarm?

Hey there, lovely lady! Before you start reading this steamy book, I want to give you a heads up about some potentially triggering content. This book is meant for those who love spicy stories, so if you're not into **explicit sex scenes and mature themes**, then this might not be the book for you.

Now, let's get to the fun stuff. **This book is hot, hot, hot!** It's got more passion than a telenovela and more steam than a sauna. If you're a fan of strong female characters and intense romance, then you're in for a treat. But if you're easily triggered by explicit sex scenes and mature themes, then maybe take a deep breath and consider reading something a little less... spicy.

Here's a list of triggers you should be aware of:

- Explicit sex scenes

- Mature themes

- Strong language and adult content

- Nudity and sexual situations

- References to BDSM and kink

- Violence and action scenes (although nothing too graphic)

So, if you're ready for a wild ride, grab a glass of wine, get comfortable, and get ready to enter a world of passion and adventure.

This book is not for the prudes, but for those who like it sizzling, it's the perfect read.

CONTENTS

Grimm Academy Map	VIII
1. Chapter 1	1
2. Chapter 2	8
3. Chapter 3	11
4. Chapter 4	15
5. Chapter 5	23
6. Chapter 6	32
7. Chapter 7	43
8. Chapter 8	55
9. Chapter 9	61
10. Chapter 10	65
11. Chapter 11	72
12. Chapter 12	81
13. Chapter 13	93
14. Chapter 14	105

15.	Chapter 15	114
16.	Chapter 16	125
17.	Chapter 17	135
18.	Chapter 18	151
19.	Chapter 19	155
20.	Chapter 20	161
21.	Chapter 21	168
22.	Chapter 22	178
23.	Chapter 23	183
24.	Chapter 24	195
25.	Chapter 25	208
26.	Chapter 26	214
27.	Chapter 27	221
28.	Chapter 28	229
29.	Chapter 29	239
30.	Chapter 30	245
31.	Chapter 31	255
32.	Chapter 32	265
33.	Chapter 33	271
34.	Chapter 34	279
35.	Chapter 35	293

36.	Chapter 36	305
37.	Chapter 37	314
38.	Chapter 38	320
39.	Chapter 39	331
40.	Chapter 40	340
41.	Chapter 41	356
42.	Chapter 42	366

Grimm Academy
The Castle That Isn't
Lycan Forest
Arena
Lycan Tower
Greenhouse
Ydril Tower
N
W
E
S
Lake
Lilith Tower
Graveyard
Grimm Tower
Grounds Map

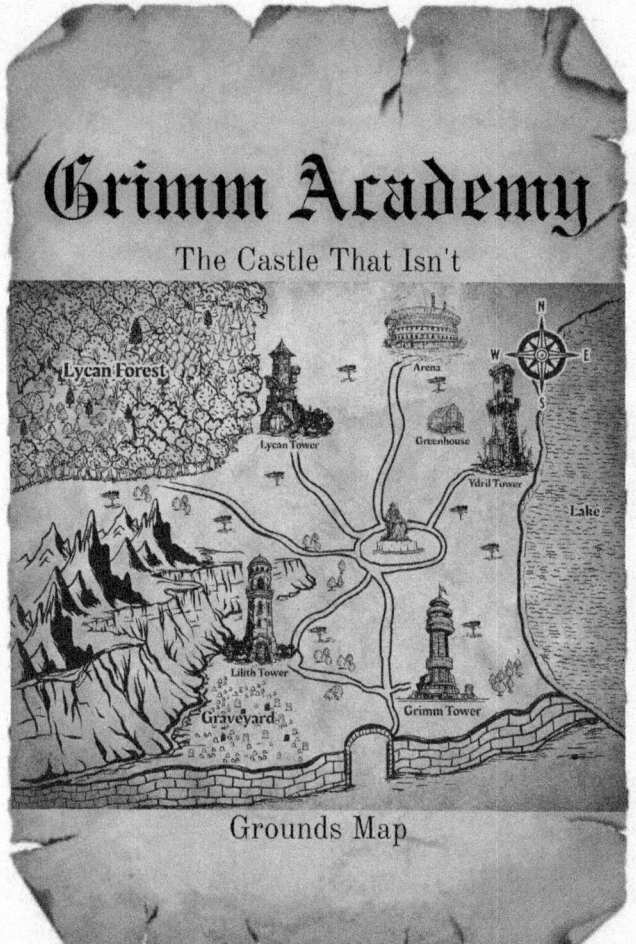

Chapter One

Whenever I look out the window onto the darkening street outside, I shudder because I imagine seeing the man from last night. If *man* is the right word. Probably not.

So even though I'm supposed to finish my report, I just keep glancing at the clock above my desk, waiting. I have the office to myself and that's something I usually enjoy. But today, it just makes me feel... exposed. Vulnerable.

For fuck's sake, Quinn, I tell myself as I let out a sigh, lean back in my chair and put my boots on the desk. Just push through it. You've had creeps trying to stalk you like this for as long as you can remember.

But this is different. "Tomorrow. Eight thirty PM," it says, in elegant cursive, on the note I found on my doorstep last night. I don't have to take it out again to check. The words have been seared into my brain.

I use one of my old tricks. Being a social worker's right hand is never particularly joyous, but it usually gives me such focus. Working on helping kids avoid the suffering that I myself had to go through, bouncing from one foster home to another and feeling like there's no place in this world for me at all? What could be more important than that?

So I grab the folder with the case I'm supposed to write a report on and force myself to look at the photos inside.

The bruises on the little girl's arms and back, the listlessness of her eyes, the way she huddles so as to make herself invisible. Things like that make for very good reasons to keep pushing. To make nice with the parents even when I want to rip their throats out. To write yet another support plan and watch it never be carried out.

But right now, there seems to be nothing I can do to take my mind away from the man.

Goddamn it. I let out a sigh and throw the folder back onto the desk. I turn to look out the window, trying to retrace my steps, again, to figure out who he could be and what he could want from me.

But right up until it happened, yesterday was as uneventful a day as any other. After work, I met up with Lisa and we went straight to Noxus. She'd just gotten a promotion and I wasn't going to let her *not* make a big deal out of it. The night was pretty warm considering it's almost September, and the bar was as deliciously loud and dark as ever, packed to the brim with struggling start-up owners and tattooed outcasts. Just my type of company and just my type of place.

Of course, like any smart, dirt-poor twenty-one-year-old, I immediately got to work on wasting all my money on… well, getting wasted.

That definitely wasn't such a good idea. At one point, the alcohol in my blood made the stuffy bar air nearly impossible to bear. I just had to go outside so I elbowed my way to the backdoor, the one that says Private on it. What can I say? I'm a regular.

When I finally threw the door open and barged onto the poorly lit back alley, all I could feel was relief.

That's when I saw the man. He was standing only a few yards from me, so still he could have been a cutout. I couldn't see his face because the streetlight was illuminating his back, but I could tell he was looking straight at me.

For a second, despite his ankle-length black cloak, I thought it was the self-important dude that had been trying to get me to talk to him all night. But this man's vibe was something else.

It made me suck in a breath. I've tasted enough danger in my life to know it when I see it. Add to it the fact that lately, there have been reports of the Originals breaking the Treaty...

Not taking my eyes off the man, I took a step back towards the bar. It was a small one, but it didn't escape him.

Like a shadow being sucked in my direction, he appeared only a few feet in front of me. For a second, I felt unable to move, my heart breaking into a painful gallop. I could finally see her face.

Yes, it was a her, not a him. Sharp, her features were so fucking sharp, but her eyes were even more terrifying.

They were the eyes of a predator. And as her lips curled into a smile, she reached for something in her pocket.

That's when I finally snapped out of it. Keeping my eyes on her, I mustered all my courage, jerked the door open and darted back into the bar.

She didn't follow me. I had the weirdest feeling that I was being toyed with. By the time I found Lisa, I was panting, eyes rounded with fear. I chalked it up to being drunk and told her I wanted to go straight home.

And I did. Only to find the note waiting for me on my doorstep.

So here I am, trying not to lose my mind after a long, sleepless night and almost an entire day spent glancing at the clock, waiting.

It's so close to striking eight. Eight PM is when I usually leave the office, go straight to my apartment and binge my favorite shows until it's time for my midnight run. It's the only thing that can put me to sleep.

But today doesn't seem like a good day to do what I normally do. It's that woman from last night, she's the one who left me the note. I just know it in my bones. And she obviously knows where to find me. So who can say she doesn't have a notebook with my comings and goings scribbled in it?

The clock finally strikes eight. It's time to go home. I breathe a sigh of relief and start panicking at the very same time. If that's even possible. I try to force out a laugh, but it's really not funny.

So I just throw on my jacket, get all my shit from the office and leave the building. It's practically falling apart, that's how little funding we get to keep it going. Usually I don't give a flying fuck, but today it just gives me the creeps.

Of course, it doesn't help that it's already dark outside and that there's barely anyone on the street.

Trying to avoid being murdered by some vampire stalker, I choose to go to the part of the city I usually ignore. The posh street that's all luxury stores and fancy restaurants.

When I finally get there, I find a crowded spot around an ornate fountain and throw myself on one of the freshly painted benches. I glance at my watch. And just as I my eyes land on its face, 8:29 changes to 8:30.

I look up, but nothing happens. There's a lot of people rushing past me, but no one gives me so much as a glance. I let out a breath I didn't even know I was holding in.

It's at that exact moment that I hear it. Music of the kind you rarely hear on the streets. It reminds me of an opera I once went to. But it's not that which throws me off. It's the fact that it's somehow managed to drown out all the other sounds. The people's chatter, the sound of water gushing from the fountain, the honking of cars from a nearby street.

I don't even manage to look around for its source before it happens. My body starts acting of its own accord, making me get up and start walking, away from the fountain and straight towards the little convent, the only building on the street that doesn't look modern.

My mind is buzzing. I'm reacting to the sound in a way that I've never reacted to any sound that came before it. If someone looked at me right now, they'd think I'm just a tourist taking a leisurely stroll, finding herself fascinated by Gothic architecture.

On the inside, I'm fighting the onset of a panic attack. And as I'm slowly approaching it, I'm looking up at the stone lace adorning the convent, but I'm only doing it because I'm looking for clues.

It's a lesson I've learned early on. You never know what piece of information might mean the difference between life and death.

But as soon as I find myself in front of the convent, I realize it isn't this building I'm being led to. The alley between the convent and the fancy apartment complex right next to it is narrow and dark, but there's someone waiting there, holding some kind of flute to their lips and using it to play that strange music with which it all started.

I don't even have to see her properly to know that it's the woman.

But the trick is, I find myself unable to stop walking straight towards her. My steps are small and measured, but my heart is making up for it, threatening to erase me from existence with its violent pounding. I know that a vampire doesn't really need blood to live, but some still drink it, either to get a boost in power or, well, to get off. Which does *she* have in mind?

As soon as I find myself in front of her, the woman stops playing. I urge my body to run the hell away, but it doesn't listen.

"Hello, little mouse," I hear her smooth, deep voice break the silence. She gives me an amused look. "We've had our fun, but playtime is over," she says as she takes me by the upper arm, her touch making me instantly nauseous.

CHAPTER 1

My eyes rounded with fear, I see a black hole form where she touches me. The world around the hole starts slowly spinning, until it gets sucked into it in a single, violent jerk.

Chapter Two

I wake up somewhere bright and warm, my head swimming. I barely have time to register that I'm lying in a bed before my entire body starts convulsing. I lean to the side to throw up and find a metal basin placed on the polished stone floor beside me.

As soon as I'm done puking my guts out, I push myself back up and check the state of my body. I'm not tied down, I don't seem to be injured and I'm still wearing my clothes. I breathe a sigh of relief.

But there's still no reason to celebrate. I nervously glance around the room, but all I see are rows of empty beds. I'm alone, there's that at least. The woman who took me is nowhere to be seen.

As the memory washes over me, the memory of her appearing out of thin air, my heart skips a beat and I realize I still have to make it quick.

Trying not to make a sound, I carefully get up off the bed, looking for the door as I do it. I seem to be in some sort of hospital, but it's unlike any hospital I've ever seen. The ceilings are so high, the distance makes me nauseous. The windows have stone lace on them, just like the Gothic convent I just came from. And the beds stretching in rows all around me seem modern, but not much else does.

As I tiptoe to the huge double door, my eyes land on a weird metal contraption placed beside one of the beds. It looks like a miniature water slide, but instead of water, there's foul-smelling vapors traveling up and down its spiraling length.

If I didn't know better, I'd think I got myself kidnapped to one of the First Cities. There's not a lot of them these days, given that the Originals and us humans are mixing at record speeds, but even I know of a couple by name.

I'm almost in front of the exit when a door on the other side of the room flings open. I freeze, but I don't turn around. I just crane my neck, letting my eyes dart to the source of the sound.

A young man is walking straight towards me. His features are delicate, he's wearing a white robe and he's carrying another one of those metal basins in his hands. I turn around, frowning.

"Top of the morning to you," he chirps out as he stops beside my bed and bends down to replace my basin. "Feeling better?"

"Where am I?" I ask, fighting to keep the anxiety out of my voice.

"You're at the Academy," the young man replies as he straightens up, a frown forming on his face. "Do you know what year it is?" he asks as he rushes to feel my forehead.

I slap his hand away.

"Twenty twenty-three," I blurt out. What the flying fuck is going on here?

"Oh, alright." He breathes out a sigh of relief. "You did take it harder than most students, so you had me worried for a sec. Was this your first time traveling by the Pull?" he asks as he peers into my eyes intently, as if doing a check-up.

"I don't know what that is," I mutter. But I have more pressing things to find out. "Where's the woman that brought me here?"

"The Pied Piper?" he asks, letting out a chuckle and waving an arm around. "She's a very busy person. But don't worry about it, you'll have one of the students show you around."

"Show me around?" I snap at him. "What the fuck do you all think you're doing? If you think I'm just going to stand around and let you keep up with this sick joke..."

The young man throws me such a surprised, sad look that I instantly regret my outburst. He takes a step back, his face tensing up right before my eyes. He seems to be fighting not to show how much I've offended him. "You're fae-blooded and you're twenty-one. We're only doing what's required of us by the Law."

I let out a laugh. "Fae? Look, dude," I start, raising my eyebrows in amusement, "the only supernatural thing about me is how much chocolate I can eat in one sitting. So I think you've made a mistake."

I turn to grab the door handle.

"That's not possible," he replies dryly. "If you weren't one of us, the Pied Piper wouldn't have been able to use the Flute to get you here in the first place."

My hand is left hovering above the handle. I turn to face him again. I can feel my eyebrows pulling down into a frown, but I can't do much more than blink at him stupidly.

Chapter Three

I can't seem to wrap my head around it. It's been an hour since I was discharged and told the student in charge of showing me around will be waiting for me at the Brothers' Grimm statue. I still haven't found it, mostly because I keep stopping every time I pass a mirror.

Under any other circumstances, if somehow I found myself in The Castle That Isn't, more commonly referred to as Grimm Academy, I sure as hell wouldn't feel the need to look at my own stupid face. I'd probably be running around, scrambling to take in as much of my surroundings as I can. The ancient tapestries on the stone walls, the gargoyles staring at me from every corner, the views from the windows that shouldn't even exist... because we're underground, for fuck's sake. For the most part, at least.

But it's not exactly the right time for me to do any sightseeing. I've just had my entire world shattered, after all. So I do it one more time. I stop in front of a very old-looking commode in the gazillionth hallway I've entered since I left the hospital wing.

Of course, the face staring at me from the ornate silver mirror hanging above it is the exact same face I can see in my bathroom every morning. Still, and I don't know if it's because I've started losing my mind or what, I start to see why someone might think I'm a fae. Sure, I'm curvier than they normally are. But my jawline is sharp, my eyes are large and I have that heart-shaped forehead.

So do a lot of humans, Quinn, I tell myself as I let out a frustrated breath. It's easier with vampires and shifters. Physically speaking, faes and regular people can easily be mistaken for each other.

But how many regular people spend their entire lives feeling like fish out of water among others? I guess I always assumed I felt that way because I was an orphan. And now, now I don't really know what to think anymore.

I make myself snap out of it and keep walking in the direction of the Main Hall, following the instructions the young man gave me. At first, the hallways were mostly deserted. I guess not a lot of students end up in the hospital on the very first day of school. But then the hallways become wider and I start seeing a lot of them, strolling around and cracking jokes, as if this was all perfectly normal.

It is to *them*, I remind myself as I try not to stare. I've seen a couple of shifters before, but other than that, I've had no contact with any of the royal bloodlines. I know enough to be able to assume that the young man from the hospital was a fae, but so am I. Supposedly.

I do manage to keep myself from staring, at least until I see one of the shifters, well, *shift*, right before my eyes. I suck in a panicked breath and force myself to keep walking as I watch the giant snake wrap itself around a stone pillar. Of course, no one else bats an eye.

The shock I'm feeling almost makes me miss it. But as soon as I turn the corner, there it is, smack in the middle of what looks like an entrance hall. The statue of the brothers who first revealed the Originals to the world. It's so large and imposing, showing the two of them holding actual balls of light in their palms, that I get a bit mesmerized by it despite my current state. I walk up to it and read the inscription. *Jacob and Wilhelm Grimm, 1847.* That's all it says, but of course, everyone knows who they were and what they did. The two brothers responsible for the Unveiling, the biggest event in world history in at least the last two centuries. The day when the veil fell and the Scions were made aware of the existence of the Originals.

For one long moment, I just keep staring at the statue, trying to picture what it was like. To find out that the creatures from fairy tales were living and breathing beings.

Then, curiosity gives way to uneasiness. I've found myself in a world I know next to nothing about.

Whatever I do, I can't let myself forget that.

Can I even be sure that it's true? That the Concordium is still a thing? I glance around, making sure the student assigned as my tour guide isn't already looking for me. Then I take a seat on the upper of the three steps leading to the statue and I whip out my phone.

I do a quick search, using 'breaking the Concordium' as the keyword. It feels weird because this pact is something I've always known about, but it was never of any actual interest to me. And there's not a lot of results, but one of them is fairly recent. News of a shifter who refused to enroll in his academy because he believed education equaled brainwashing. The sentence passed? Death by Mind Magic.

I feel myself shudder, my mind threatening to stop keeping panic and despair shoved away for when they're more convenient to deal with. But just as I open up my social media to see what Lisa's up to, trying to find comfort or at least a shred of sanity in my usual tricks, I feel someone's eyes on me.

I look up and find a strange girl standing only a few feet away from me. "You Quinn?" she asks as she tilts her head in a questioning way. Her body is toned, tattooed and tan, while the hair is blonde streaked with the purest white I've ever seen. A shifter, I'm almost sure.

I barely manage to nod in reply to her question before she slides closer to me, her eyes growing wide. "I heard you were brought here by the Pied Piper herself. You need to tell me all about that."

I raise my eyebrows, throwing her an amused look.

"Oh right," she says as she takes a step back, looking away for a second as if she's embarrassed. "My name is Nuala and I'm supposed to show you around."

For the first time in what feels like forever, I let out a chuckle. There's palpable tension in the sound. After all, I haven't exactly had time to process everything that's going on, let alone figure out whether it's good or, um, catastrophically bad. But at least I think I could like this girl.

Chapter Four

"So it's not something that normally happens?" I ask Nuala as she leads me through a huge archway behind the statue and into the biggest room I've ever laid eyes on.

"A Pied Piper personally coming for students?" she says, craning her neck to look at me. She laughs, the sound both deep and flowy. "Not since, like, the nineteenth century." She pauses, frowns and then shakes her head vigorously. "Yeah, since the Unveiling. So this here is the Main Hall," she adds in her formal tour-guide voice as she stops to let me take a look around.

Don't mind if I do, I think to myself. It's loud and packed with groups of students who all seem to be busy catching up with their friends after the summer break. My eye is drawn to so many different things at once that I can barely register anything in particular. Weird statues lining the walls, some of them covered in moss even though we're inside. Animals, large and small, climbing the colorful couches and armchairs everywhere I look. And let's not forget the piles of old books everywhere around us. I drool a little.

"It's where we come to hang out," I hear Nuala say, "although there's a lot of common rooms, too. But this one seems to be everyone's favorite."

"Uh-huh," I nod, my eyes fixed on a couple of students sitting at a low table, all staring at a metal cube levitating in the air above them. As I watch it, the cube shifts into a spiked ball and I see one of the students lean back in his chair with a smug smile on his face. But almost instantly, the ball turns back into a cube and I hear that same student curse loudly, wiping blood off his cheek.

Nuala's voice snaps me out of my trance. "I think you'll have a lot of fun here." She's leaning in so I can feel her breath on my skin. "But if someone asks you to play a game with them..." She pauses and I turn to look at her. "You better think twice before you say yes."

I raise my eyebrows slightly, but she just gives me a shrug and keeps walking. "Chop, chop," she chirps out, "I have a lot more to show you."

I don't protest. I just pick up the pace and patiently let her lead me through a million more hallways as she explains where most of my classes will be held, where I can get books, what professors to avoid and so on and so forth.

At one point, after she tells me I *really* have to try the cafeteria cheesecake for the millionth time, I feel the urge to stop her. We're in the middle of a wide hallway with rows of double doors, the classrooms behind them still empty. "I'm sorry if this is rude, Nuala, but I think there's someone in this castle, someone in charge of student selection, who thinks I have a *much* fatter wallet than I actually do."

She quirks an eyebrow at me and then lets out a laugh. "You don't pay for this yourself, silly."

I just blink at her stupidly. Back at the center, we can't even make sure all the kids have roofs over their heads. And here, it's 'Let them eat cheesecake' day, every day.

Of course, Nuala has no idea what's going through my mind. And she seems to have agendas of her own. "You know, it just crossed my mind..." She throws me a hopeful look. "You probably don't want all this info being forced on you on your first day here."

I hesitate. The more I learn about this place, the better my chances of surviving it. The Castle That Isn't has a certain reputation and I'm far from fitting right in.

"And I've no idea how much you know about the Academy," Nuala interrupts my train of thought, using the same gently persuading tone, "but it's fucking huge and it never stops changing. Trying to give you the full tour is kind of pointless. But of course, if that's what you want..."

I almost burst out laughing, that's how funny the look on her face is. It's like she's bracing herself for hearing me say yes and trying not to look too sour about it.

"If you'll just show me the Towers," I say with a smile, "we can call it a day. I've read lots about the castle in, well, human magazines."

She throws me a dazzling smile, her face visibly relaxing. "Oh, you have to tell me all about those."

I smile back, feeling actual excitement about seeing with my own two eyes what us humans generally only ever get to see in photos.

Us humans?

I shake my head as I follow Nuala back to the entrance hall. Right opposite the archway leading into the Main Hall, I spot what seems to be an elaborate brushed-brass lift.

How the fuck did I miss this, I think to myself as we walk up to it. But it's really no surprise.

"This," Nuala turns to say as she presses one of the million buttons to the side of the lift, "is something they installed right after the Unveiling. It's clumsy, I know," she chuckles as we enter and she presses another button, "but the Architect at the time was kinda obsessed with all things human."

Just as I open my mouth to tell her none of this could ever seem clumsy to me, the lift opens and I suck in a breath.

As soon as we step out of it, the Elevator disappears and we find ourselves outside, the deep, dark forest looming from the horizon as I take in the garden overgrown with moss, reeds and prickly bushes. There are gravel paths leading to its center, where I see a solitary stone statue that I recognize from photos. It's the statue of Dame Gothel, one of the most famous Originals of all times, her long cloak and wild hair made to appear as if they're billowing in the wind.

But of course, what draws my attention are the Towers themselves, the only part of the castle that's not underground. Plenty of distance between them, they shoot up into the darkening sky as if they were three enormous fingers threatening to pierce it.

"Lemme guess," I say, raising my hand to point at the one nearest to us, the one leaning dangerously to one side, all covered in vines. "*That* is the House of Ydril."

"Yep," Nuala nods, shifting from leg to leg as if she's having trouble staying in one place. "That's yours." She turns slightly to the left to point at the one with a surface so smooth, it seems to reflect light. "That right there is the House of Lilith," she recites, "and the one bordering with the forest is the House of Lycan."

As she says that, my eyes sweep up and down the tower that looks the oldest, probably because of all the rough stone.

"That's yours?"

She nods.

"You know," I say, smiling as I turn to look at her, "you look like your animal would be something really fierce."

And I don't expect her to shift to show me, but I definitely don't expect to see her frown at me. As if I'd just offended her.

"I think we better get going," she says flatly. "The opening ceremony should be starting soon."

I open my mouth to say I'm sorry if I was rude, but my eyes catch a strange movement to our left. I snap my head in its direction and I see a guy being spit out of a hole that looks just like the one I got here through.

It's just that, unlike me, he deftly lands on his feet and keeps walking with his hands in his pockets the entire time. Dammit.

Just as I'm about to turn to Nuala to recount what the Pull did to *me*, I recognize him.

"That's not..." I break off, unable to tear my eyes away.

"Andreas Faust?" she finishes my sentence in a voice that's barely above a whisper. "It sure is."

And the fucking prince doesn't stop walking, his movements smooth and controlled. But now I see that he's looking straight at me, as if he'd heard our little exchange loud and clear, even though there's quite a bit of overgrown garden separating us.

Because he did. Because he's a vampire, for crying out loud. Maybe he doesn't shy away from the Sun, as people thought in the good ol' days, but he definitely has heightened senses.

His eyes still on me, I realize my heart is pounding wildly and I can feel tension emanating from Nuala as well. Fucking hell, have I just done something stupid?

He breaks eye contact and disappears into the castle. I let out a breath I didn't even know I was holding in.

"Wow," I hear Nuala say and I turn back to her only to see her blushing from head to toe, "I didn't expect to see him without the usual entourage."

With that, she moves to lead me back into the castle. But my mind is still on the prince.

"He's not a student here, is he?" I ask as I rush to catch up with her.

She walks into the Elevator and presses a button. When she looks at me again, a slight frown is scrunching up her forehead. "I thought everyone knew he was enrolling. It was all people talked about the entire summer." She gives me a smile as she walks out of the Elevator and back into the entrance hall. "Even now, the tabloids won't leave it alone."

CHAPTER 4

I look up and almost let out a laugh. I haven't even noticed them because I was so focused on everything that makes Grimm Academy out of ordinary for someone like me, but there's more than one huge screen hung above us.

The sound is muted on all of them. But two out of four are currently dedicated to the prince. They're switching between photos of the Academy and photos of *him* in his perfectly tailored suits.

And there's strips of text below them, but my mind barely registers them. I'm too shocked to learn that my high-school celebrity crush, the vampire prince and heir to the throne, will be attending the Academy with me. An image pops into my mind, of all the posters of him I kept hidden beneath the mattress in my room.

"Anyway..." Nuala snaps me out of it by tugging at my sleeve, making me turn to look at her. "The opening ceremony is about to start." Giving me a little smile, she motions at the archway opposite to the one leading into the Main Hall.

"Oh fuck." I slap myself on the forehead. "You did mention it earlier."

"It's no reason to get your panties in a bunch," she says with a laugh. "It's basically dinner. But I do hope you enjoy it." And with that, she waves, turns on her heel and starts walking away.

It takes me by surprise, the abrupt way she ends our little tour. But she probably has her friends waiting for her to join them at the ceremony. So I shrug it off and start making my own way there, feeling like fish out of water as I walk past tattooed shifters, raven-haired vampires and faes who've probably known they're faes their whole fucking lives. God damn them.

But as I go through the archway into what seems like a giant dining hall, I almost have to raise my hand to shield my eyes. Outside, it's already dark. But in here, the light is reflecting off both seen and invisible surfaces. Ornate metal. Polished stone. Lacquered wood. Despite its enormity, the room is steadily filling up, the murmur of the students taking their seats creating a soft, feverish music that perfectly reflects how I'm feeling.

I guess I'm a fae now, I think as I look for a seat. And that has a lot of implications, a lot of which I can't even be fully aware of yet. But it also means a lot of unexpected possibilities.

Chapter Five

I find a seat close to the exit. I don't know what kind of danger I'm expecting, but it's better to be safe than sorry. I throw smiles to everyone around me, but only a couple of students at my table smile back. One of the girls even frowns. Oh well, you can't please everyone.

With the corner of my eye, I see Nuala sitting alone. Now that she's not giving me the tour, she seems different. As if she's trying her hardest to stay invisible.

I'd know. It's basically all I did when I was still in the foster system. And it makes my brain want to poke around hers in search of possible reasons, but I force myself not to think about it. It's a habit of mine. To make other people's problems my own. And it's a welcome thing when I'm at work, but when it comes to my personal life, it's not necessarily, um, good.

To distract myself, I turn to look around. The dinner hasn't started yet so I have some time to take in my surroundings. Besides the long tables the students are sitting at, there's one placed on a podium at the front of the hall. It's still empty, but it's obviously there for the professors and the faculty. Above it, there's a flag with the Academy's crest flapping in the breeze. It's full of detail and I can barely make anything out.

My eyes sweep over the walls around me. I see the other crests, too. The crests of the three royal bloodlines. There's the House of Lycan, the full moon with its two halves, one light and one dark. Then the House of Lilith, the black cross fitted inside a simple circle, the circle of life.

But when my eye finally lands on the crest of the House of Ydril, something stirs deep inside me. Of course, I've seen it a gazillion times before, the wide open eye shaped like a triangle. But the corners of the flag on which it's depicted are adorned with birds. Tiny black ones. And it's those birds that make me feel… something.

I squint, trying to bring back a memory I didn't even know I had.

I only snap out of it when I hear a murmur rise from all around me. I crane my neck in the direction of the archway, where I see the prince himself glide into the hall. Except now, he's not alone. He's surrounded by girls and guys dressed in the latest fashion, looking around as if they own the place.

What catches my eye as they walk is that they're all trying to get *his* attention, especially the women.

Can't really blame them. I used to spend hours staring at his photos and repeating his name to myself. Andreas Faust. Andreas. Faust. Until I could no longer tell the difference between real life and fantasy. And he's even more eerily handsome in real life. My eyes are struggling to take it all in. The chiseled jawline, the porcelain skin, the thick black hair. Even the long, elegant muscles straining his sharp suit. But it's his eyes and the way he carries himself that I think keeps his cohort and everyone around him under his spell. There's an air of bored privilege about him, that's for sure. But then there's also something else, something I can't put my finger on...

I'm so absorbed in watching him that I almost miss the whole thing. When the prince and his company reach the only empty front seats, I see a posh vampire dude with long sideburns come out of nowhere, placing his hand on the chair that the prince was just about to claim.

There's a stir in the crowd and I see one of the girls walking with the prince take a step forward, warning, "Don't do it, Leo."

But Leo doesn't even acknowledge her. His lips curling into a smile, he addresses the prince directly, "I think you'll find more empty seats to the back."

I hear so many breaths being drawn in, the sound echoes. Shit. This might get ugly, I think as I grab onto the edge of the table.

For a second, the prince just stands there and stares at the guy as the entire room waits for his reaction with bated breath.

Without taking his eyes off him, he takes one deliberate step back and I breathe a sigh of relief.

The very next second, he disappears.

Confused, I get up and look around, along with everyone else. And only once I see him crouching over the guy, who's now lying on the ground, do I realize that that's not what happened. He didn't disappear. He's just abnormally fast, so fast my mind couldn't even register his movements.

What snaps me out of it is the low groaning that comes out of Leo's mouth. I lean forward, my heart starting to pound when I see that the prince is keeping his arm twisted in a fucked-up position. He bends closer to him and whispers something into his ear.

"Fuck you," I hear Leo snap back at him.

With the corner of my eye, I see people glancing at each other as an actual scream comes out of the poor dude's mouth.

It's then that my instinct overtakes me. Before I even realize what I'm doing, I'm getting out of my chair and charging straight at them.

"What the fuck do you think you're doing," I snarl as I stop right before him, my hands balled into fists.

He slowly gets up and throws me an unreadable look, letting a few of the others grab Leo and lead him away. He's so tall, I have to look up to meet his eye.

"I could ask you the same question," he says flatly. "Addressing a prince without being formally introduced."

I have to fight the shivers that his voice sends down my skin. It's smooth and thorny at the same time.

"I don't see a prince, I only see an asshole," I snap at him, though my own voice is barely above a whisper.

For a second, there's a flash of surprise in his eyes. He doesn't move, except for the tiniest flick of his hand as he motions for one of his minions to come close. The guy rushes to him and whispers something in his ear. I think I hear the word 'human' being spoken.

His eyes still locked on mine, the prince frowns, stays still for a second and then lets out a scoff. His lips curl into a smile as he says, "I guess being raised by humans makes one stupid."

"What did you just say to me?" I hear myself raising my voice, but at the same time, there are so many gasps coming out of the mouths of the people around me.

He pays them no mind. "Here, let me make sure you hear me this time." He leans in so his lips are almost touching my ear. I shudder. "You're not among the Scions anymore. You better learn how things work here." He drops his voice to a whisper. "And you better make it quick."

The look on his face when he pulls away from me is, once again, unreadable.

It pisses me off so much, that he's nothing like the man my high-school self dreamed him to be. I open my mouth to tell him off, but then his eyes dart over my shoulder and to the front of the hall. Noticing students rushing to their seats, I crane my neck and I see the Pied Piper staring the two of us down.

The woman who kidnapped and brought me here. The vampire who's apparently the Academy's current Pied Piper.

She doesn't say anything, but I sense the prince tense up beside me. He quickly pushes past me and walks straight to the seat that Leo wanted for himself. I follow suit, returning to my own table.

When I look at her again, I see the Pied Piper gliding towards the table on the podium at the front of the hall. I breathe a sigh of relief.

I'm so shocked to see her again, I barely register the people who I can only assume are professors filing into the hall after her.

And I guess I should feel lucky that I've managed to come out of this unscathed, but I just feel like an idiot.

Even without the creepy back alley serving as the backdrop, the Pied Piper's presence sends shivers down my spine. As she glides up to her seat, a tall chair made out of wood and bone, I watch the hem of her charcoal cloak glide across the polished stone. She's sharpness, boldness, elegance all at once.

While the rest of the professors take their seats, she remains standing in front of her place setting. She doesn't have to say or do anything to silence the chatter. As soon as she reaches for the tall glass filled to the brim with what seems to be some kind of reddish champagne, everyone goes silent.

I notice the same glass with the same liquid appear in front of me. Then her clear, commanding, slightly bored voice fills the room, making me shudder a little.

"This is the third year I've had the privilege to address you all at the start of the year," she drawls as her mesmerizing eyes sweep over us all. They don't linger on me, which makes me at the same time relieved and disappointed.

"And I know you'd gladly listen to me for hours," she continues, making quite a few students chuckle, "but there's really only one thing I have to say to you today."

When she pauses, there's such silence, I could hear a fly.

"The blood gin is supposed to be excellent," she says, raises her glass and downs the whole thing.

Almost instantly, the students start clapping and cheering, following suit with their own drinks. I don't even raise my glass. I'm simply too stupefied.

Almost as soon as I found out who kidnapped me, I looked for information on her online. Johanna de Groot. She seems to have been many things throughout the course of her long life. The solemn heiress to a sixteenth-century nobleman. The woman who tracked the Mad King Aeres' army down, ripped all of their throats out and bathed in their blood... Stuff like that.

And here she is, the 127th Pied Piper cracking jokes at the opening ceremony.

As I watch her take her seat, I down my own blood gin and instantly regret it. I feel drunk, but it can't be. I've barely had two fingers of this shit.

Still, the world around me suddenly has that veil of softness drawn all over it. And I feel the familiar mix of excitement and longing flooding my senses.

I want to eat everything there is to eat, and then some. I want to take some more blood gin and go wandering around the castle until I know every nook and cranny. I want to climb to the top of its highest tower and yell 'What the fuck is going on'.

I only do one of those things. As soon as the food starts appearing on the table in front of me, I start eating like crazy. I don't even care that everyone seems to act as if I'm some pariah. Because Nuala was right. The Grimm Academy cheesecake is the best damn cheesecake I've ever had.

By the time dinner is over, I'm drunk, stuffed and sleepy as fuck. Some stuck-up fae-blooded girl comes to my table and waves me over as if I'm an animated piece of luggage. I throw on my warmest smile and I push myself out of my chair.

"Come, I'll show you to your room," she says when I finally manage to stagger to where she's waiting for me.

"You're like an angel sent from heaven," I chuckle, thinking I might even be able to fall asleep without my run.

The girl throws me a half-disgusted look. "Angel? Cringe."

"Wow," I drawl. "No angels then. Gotcha."

The girl just rolls her eyes and keeps walking, but she cranes her neck a little to add, "I'm also supposed to tell you that someone left some stuff for you in your room."

"Stuff? For me? Who?" I ask, frowning and trying to suppress a burp.

"Your parents? Your second grade Maths teacher?" she recites as she shoots me an annoyed look. "How the hell am *I* supposed to know?"

Parents. It's the only word that sticks with me, leaving me breathless, speechless. And by the time the girl leaves me in front of my room, the entire world around me is spinning in one continuous, slow motion that makes me sick to my stomach. All my life, I've been alone, bouncing from one foster home to another. But it's also true that all my life, I'd thought that I was human.

Apparently, I'm not. And it seems safe to conclude that my parents weren't either.

Or *aren't* either.

Because if everything else was a lie, maybe the bit about the dead parents is, too.

Chapter Six

I scoff as I fling another useless book at the wall of my room. It's been three weeks. Three fucking weeks since I first walked into this room and found a bunch of crap that I first believed, no, *hoped* to be some kind of treasure. Legacy left to me by my parents.

That hope didn't grow smaller even after I asked around and found out that it was all sent to me using untraceable magic. Not even after I realized that there really is no note, no signature, nothing. But now, now that I've gone through it all only to confirm that it's just a whole shitload of books...

I keep sitting on the floor, throwing daggers at them.

Now, my room is cozy, cozier than any room I've ever slept in. The bed looks like it may as well be from the sixteenth century, but the mattress is brand new. There's a TV hung on the wall opposite to it and I even have my own bathroom. Add to it the view of the overgrown garden from the window behind the armchair and you get everything a girl could ever want in a room.

But it's small. And the tall piles of books lying around make it so I can't take two steps without stubbing my toe on one of them.

Of course, that's not what's actually pissing me off. I've lived in houses with locks on fridge doors and I haven't been this fussy about it, I reason with myself as I push off the floor. I pick up the innocent albeit shabby volume I just took it all out on. Crouching, I take it in my hand and stroke its silver-embossed title. *The Second War of the Elements*, it says.

I scoff. If nothing else, I can be sure that none of this was sent to me by anyone I know, even if they did manage to get their hands on powerful, untraceable magic. Lisa would've told me when I asked her. Marlene? My boss ain't got time for anything other than work. And the rest... Well, let's just say my former foster parents are much better at taking than giving.

I let out a sigh and look out the window. It's haunted by a lot of bad memories, but I still miss my old life, at least what I made of it after leaving the system. Going for my midnight runs. Doing actual meaningful work instead of attending classes about magic I can't even use. Going for drinks with Lisa instead of just texting as I waste away alone in my room, no actual connection to anything or anyone in my new 'home'.

Which also means I've no one to help me figure out who the fuck sent me these mystery books.

I stand up and turn on the TV. I throw myself on my bed, deciding to spend the remaining time before the first class of the day distracting myself from everything that's slowly driving me crazy.

Remote in my hand, I start flicking through channels like crazy. Nothing seems interesting enough to tear my mind away from my ruminations. Until I pause on OTV. It's one of the human channels dealing exclusively with the Originals. Famous Originals, that is. They couldn't care less about the regular shifter, vampire or fae.

And of course, who looks at me from the screen? Andreas Faust himself. Or the Dark Prince, as the tabloids like to call him.

I listen to the newswoman reporting on his latest comings and goings. "...seen walking out of the Academy grounds for some fresh air."

For crying out loud, why are they all so fucking obsessed with him, I think to myself as I squint to take a better look. But the photo they're showing right now is too grainy, so I pull out my phone to look for images online.

Back in the days of my own obsession, when I still had the posters, sometimes, I'd focus on his lips because they looked like someone took a lot of time sculpting them to perfection. Other times, I'd focus on his hands, especially when the fingers would be caught running through his hair. And from time to time, I'd even take the time to scrutinize his perfectly tailored shirts and waistcoats. He seems to still love *those*.

But these days, more often than not, my eyes stay fixed on his. It's that look in them that I have to blame for it, the look that left me utterly confused when I found myself standing in front of him for the very first time.

I know people. I'm used to putting together an entire character assessment from the tiniest glimpse of contempt in the corner of the mouth, or the slightest nervous movement when someone's name is mentioned.

He gives me nothing. Except for the overwhelming urge to know more, apparently.

One I'm not stupid enough to act on, of course. He's not just a vampire,

But I honestly don't mind that it's powerful enough to help me waste more than enough time before my class starts.

Because, by the time I tear my eyes away from his photos and glance at the clock above my desk, I'm already three minutes late.

Fuck, fuck, fuck. It's really not okay that you're doing this to yourself, Quinn, I scold myself as I fling the door open even before I've finished pulling my sweater over my head. Professor Gamal hasn't exactly warmed up to me, even without me disrespecting him like this.

Walking as fast as I can without breaking into a sprint, I nervously fidget with the runes around my neck. By the time I'm barging into the classroom, everyone else is seated, the scrawny Professor Gamal's voice already scratching at my ears. "Who can tell me which set of Runes is the trickiest to control?"

He barely finishes the sentence before his eyes dart to me trying to sneak into one of the rows of seats facing his pulpit. "Ah, Miss Longborn. Proving that the early bird indeed does catch the worm."

I fight to keep my face expressionless as I sit down. "I apologize for being late, Professor."

"Apologies mean little when one has so much to catch up on," the professor says, referring without a doubt to the fact I haven't been able to answer any of his questions so far. "Well?" he asks, his eyebrows slightly raised.

"Um," I start, listing the different types in my mind in search of some logical answer. My hand darts to my own set. "Maybe the Creator's Runes?"

"Maybe?" the professor repeats after me as he looks at me from under his bushy eyebrows. "Is that the best you can give me?"

"I think it would make sense," I start, fighting not to get discouraged by the mocking chuckles the other students let out. "I mean, considering that they contain Genesis, the rarest and trickiest of all seven runes." At least that's what it said when I looked them up after my ceremony.

I breathe a sigh of relief when I see the professor nod, however hesitantly. "It would make sense, yes. And maybe it *would* be the correct answer, if there wasn't such a thing as the Keeper's Runes. After all, they're the only ones that contain all seven, *including* Genesis."

He turns back to the rest of the class as he goes on to explain the mechanics and characteristics of the Keeper's Runes. I seem to be off the hook so I let myself breathe.

But all I can think about is how much I'm struggling with my own set. My hand darts to it once again. I look down, but nothing's changed.

A week after my arrival, and in a pretty unceremonious manner if I may say, I've been given a set of three stone beads, the kind that the majority of faes have.

The only problem is...

The majority of faes get theirs when they're five years old and they almost immediately bond with them. And not just that, they very quickly manage to use Sight to unlock the first rune. So by the time they're at the Academy, they can already do stupidly amazing shit like blocking a Fire attack by conjuring full-body armor using only Earth.

At least that's what *that* girl did, the one sitting two rows in front of me, passing notes with the two students I always see her with. Zelda, a grumpy-looking vampire girl that always has headphones on, and Harry, a seemingly chirpy but violent shifter with tattoos on his neck.

And then there's their ringleader, Sarya, who apparently notices me looking and cranes her neck, her golden eyes slowly narrowing. She always has her dark hair braided and wears what I can only describe as flowy overalls. But that's where the delicate shit stops, because her entire body is covered in painful-looking piercings and scars.

I manage not to look away too quickly, but Sarya's stare still makes me squirm in my seat. Once she finally turns back to the front of the classroom, I breathe a sigh of relief. All three of them are sitting sedately at the moment, but when there are no professors around... They're practically bullies with powers.

If they tried to use them on me? I'd have to literally run for my life. Because although it's been more than two weeks, I still haven't even managed to figure out how to use Sight, let alone bond with my runes and actually start using them.

As soon as the class ends, I jump up off my feet and rush out of the classroom, heading straight for the cafeteria. As I walk away, I look over my shoulder a couple of times, making sure Sarya didn't decide to make me into her plaything for today.

When I finally get to the cafeteria, the huge hall is already crowded. It's past two o'clock, the time when most students come to have lunch. There are crowds around the fountains, everyone elbowing to get their glasses refilled with one of the many flavored sodas. I go straight for the counters where they normally keep pizza and other fast food.

But instead of pizza, my eyes go straight for the far corner of the room, where I hear a familiar voice rise above the chatter in the room. "And what am I supposed to tell Professor Ceallaigh?"

At first, I don't see her from all the students gathered in that part of the cafeteria. But then a few of them walk away and there she is. Nuala, getting red in the face, her hands balled into fists as she gets in the face of some scary looking shifter.

"That's your problem, not mine," he snarls at her. "I'd rather have a filthy Scion on my team than you."

I press my lips tight, feeling as if I'm eavesdropping on a private conversation.

"Fine," Nuala snaps, "I'll just do it by myself then."

And she turns on her heel and starts walking away, headed straight for where I'm standing.

I quickly look away, planning to pretend I didn't notice her.

But not before she catches my eye and gets even more red in the face. She tries to rush past me. And it's at that moment that I change my mind.

"Hey," I call out to her.

She stops and shoots me a defensive look. I know her enough to be aware of the fact that she doesn't want to be seen as a victim.

"Would you help me understand something?" I ask.

She raises her eyebrows slightly, the red in her face growing fainter.

"There's, like, every type of food here," I say as I motion at the counters stacked with pot roasts, breakfast burgers and pies. "But what about chocolate? How exactly are we expected to survive?"

For a second, she just blinks at me, before her mouth cracks into a smile and she motions for me to follow her. Without a word, she leads me to one of the glass cases that are always empty. But as soon as we come close, they appear. Rows upon rows of all sorts of chocolate delicacies, from delicate truffles to slices of layered chocolate cake.

"What the fuck?"

"It's the work of this guy who, well, really likes chocolate," Nuala explains. "The faculty has given up on trying to make him stop. He just always comes back and uses little tricks to make people blind to what's in this case."

I can't help but laugh. "My kind of person," I say as I open the case, grab the first plate I see and pile it high.

Nuala just watches me with an amused look on her face. "Have you already had lunch?" she asks when I'm done.

"Nope, this will be it," I grin at her. "What was that fight all about?" I ask innocently as I start for the nearest empty table.

For a second, she just keeps standing there, giving me a hesitant look. Then, as if her body is released from some bond, she joins me, taking a seat across from me. "It's nothing, really. We have this group assignment and we're fighting about who gets to do what."

My eyebrows shoot up before I can stop them. A straight-out lie, really? I clear my throat and choose not to acknowledge it. The road I pick is one that's a bit more winding. "Tell me about it. But at least you're not being shunned by everyone for being the absolute fucking worst," I finish with a laugh.

"What do you mean?" she asks, leaning in as a spark of interest shows up in her eyes.

I let out a sigh as I take my runes in my hand and lift them up for her to see. "This is my first contact ever with something like this. And I've no idea what I'm doing. And it doesn't make it any better that the students here have decided I'm untouchable."

"Untouchable? How so?"

I smile a bit because she's obviously relaxing. "I guess there aren't that many people here who've been raised by humans."

"No, I guess not," she purses her lips, thinking. "But still, that's fucking stupid that they're shunning you because of that."

I don't say anything straight away. I can feel that the pause is pregnant. I just wait to see if she's going to confide in me.

And she does. "I know how it is. That situation back there," she says as she motions at the back of the cafeteria with a guilty look in her eyes, "it wasn't about the assignment we were given."

"Really?"

"Yeah. We were divided into groups, but my group doesn't want me working with them."

"How come?" I ask, using my gentlest voice.

She opens her mouth and immediately closes it, shaking her head. "I guess they're intimidated by all this awesomeness," she says as she gestures at herself. "Who wouldn't be?"

And it's obvious she's not telling the truth, but I decide not to push it. I just give her a chuckle and change the subject.

"Hey, do you know if the Academy keeps records of the stuff that people leave here?"

Nuala thinks for a second. "Not sure, but what do you need *that* for?"

"It's grasping at straws really." I hesitate in between bites of the deliciously decadent chocolate cake. "I've had some stuff left to me here at the Academy. But they came with no note and there's nothing there that I could use to identify the person, or people, who left it to me."

"Hm." She reaches out her hand and takes a chocolate truffle from my plate. I smile at her, pushing the plate to the middle of the table. "There's the Archives. Maybe you could ask there. I can come with you if you want."

For a second, I just look at her, surprised that a single sentence could make me feel this warm around the heart. That it could make all this so much less frustrating. "That would be great!" I finally say. "How about tomorrow?"

"Tomorrow?" She almost chokes on that little bite of chocolate she took. "I don't think anyone from the faculty will be working tomorrow."

"Really?" I raise my eyebrows. "How so?"

She just looks at me for a moment. Then her eyes widen and she lifts her palm to her forehead, saying in a hushed voice, "Of course *I* was supposed to tell you."

"Tell me what?" I demand, my eyebrows pulling down.

"Tomorrow," she starts, still making a face to convey how sorry she is, "we're all required to show up for the Selection for the Trials."

Chapter Seven

The next morning, I wake up with a spring in my step. Sure, I'm about to have some tree decide whether I'm worthy of participating in what everyone just calls the Trials. Nuala told me it's this tournament spread throughout the school year. And there's no prizes and the whole thing tends to get out of hand, so much so that students sometimes get killed.

But it's not like I'd ever be selected for something like that and this just happens to be the first day since I got here that I don't feel all alone. So as I walk out of the castle, I'm practically skipping.

All Nuala told me was to find the statue of the Frog King and follow the path that runs along the brook until I see the Tree. Normally, I'd probably have a lot of trouble with that. But I just follow the people, thinking if we're all required to participate, there's no other place they could be going to.

Of course, I'm right. The little groups of students lead me straight to this enormous tree by the spring, where there's already a huge crowd. It's colorful but orderly somehow. It's only on second glance that I realize it's because it's very structured. There's the Pied Piper to the left of the Tree, towering over other professors, some standing still and some chatting casually. And then there's the audience that's made up of, I don't know, parents? Dignitaries? I've been reading like crazy, but looking at them sitting there in their lavish outfits just makes me acutely aware of how little I still know about the Originals' culture.

Still, even if I didn't spot Nuala waving at me, I'd know where to go. The students waiting to get tested are forming a line that runs along the side of the brook, most of their faces alive with excitement.

I walk up to Nuala with a smile on my lips. "I don't know about you," I start as I stand to wait next to her, "but I think this whole thing is barbaric."

She raises her eyebrows as she awkwardly pats me on the shoulder. "It hasn't even started."

"Yeah, but making us get up before nine…"

She chuckles. "I thought you Scions all work from nine to five."

I let out a laugh, letting my eyes sweep over the crowd. "That's just a song, Nuala. But now what?"

On closer inspection, I see that the crowd is made up of both students and professors.

"Now we wait."

"Alright," I say, watching the others exchanging tense little comments as they shift from leg to leg.

It makes me pity them. Whoever gets selected won't be able to refuse to participate. Of course, after Nuala told me that, I went online to check if it was really true. That they can just force you. But it is. There's a heated discussion about the ethics of the whole thing. Like, is it okay to put students in potentially deadly situations without their consent? I myself would say hell no.

But I wasn't in the least surprised when I saw one old interview with the current Pied Piper, then Professor of History Johanna de Groot. The conversation mostly revolved around politics. Whether the Scions should be scared of the Originals after the so-called Blood Moon Incident. Whether the Originals are using their powers to steer elections in directions that are favorable to them. And so on and so forth.

But at one point, the journalist asks Professor de Groot if she thinks the Trials should be banned. She laughs. Of course she does. And then she says, "I don't think we were ever more in *need* of the Trials than we are now. And anyone who says otherwise doesn't understand the true nature of our two worlds intertwined."

It's a cryptic answer, for sure. And I have no idea what to think of it, at least for now. My instinct still tells me it's a stupid, barbaric thing, but hey, it's not like anyone's asking me.

Still, I'm not in the least bit afraid or tense about it, like everyone else seems to be. And it's not because I'm stupid. Just yesterday, I've read enough records of gruesome ways in which students get hurt or killed in the Trials.

No, it's simply because I know there's no fucking chance in hell I'll ever be chosen. It's only for the worthy. And so far, the only thing I can use my runes for is breaking up the monotony of my outfits.

"What exactly are we waiting for?" I turn to ask Nuala.

It's at that exact moment that I notice a stir among the crowd.

"Him," Nuala whispers in my ear. "We're waiting for him."

But my eyes have already been drawn in his direction. It's the prince Andreas Faust in the flesh, slowly making his way to where we're standing and stopping to greet the people in the audience.

"Oh, for crying out loud. Does everything around here revolve around the Little Prince?" I ask, mocking the Dark Prince nickname.

I hear Nuala let out a weak laugh. "No," she says, "not him, his uncle Baldor."

It's only then that I notice a tall, gray-haired man walking next to him. He has a lavish cloak thrown over his shoulders, the left arm clad in some kind of armor and the hand resting on an ornate walking stick. As he approaches, everyone scrambles to get up and bow to him, even more than his nephew.

"He's the Regent," Nuala leans in to explain. "The one in charge of things until the prince turns forty."

"Why forty?" I ask, but I don't turn to look at her.

"That's when the Originals come of age."

"Mm." I keep staring at the royal duo until they've almost reached our line. At one point, I see the prince notice me, but choose not to acknowledge it. Taking my cue from him, I focus all my efforts on avoiding his eye.

But in doing that, I catch his uncles'. The two of them are just about to walk by when Faust Senior notices me and stops. A frown forms on his forehead. His nephew squints, his eyes darting between the two of us in what seems to be confusion.

Then, to my surprise, the uncle takes a step towards me and lowers his upper body in a ridiculously formal bow. By the time he straightens to look me in the eye, I feel countless pairs of eyes on us and I've no idea if I'm supposed to bow as well.

"Young lady, why do you look so familiar? Have we met?"

"I hardly think that's possible, uncle," his nephew answers in my stead, his voice smooth and bored, as if he wasn't caught by surprise just a second ago.

I turn to him. But he's not even looking at me as he adds, "Until a month ago, the *young lady* hasn't spent any time around us."

I feel myself start fuming. Where the fuck does he get off?

"That's true, Your Majesty," I say in the warmest yet most solemn tone possible, but I'm making sure I'm only looking at the uncle. "And it's my own misfortune, to only now be acquainted with someone such as yourself."

I notice the darling nephew's eyes dart to me and linger, but the uncle lets out a delighted chuckle.

"Does that mean that you've been raised among humans?" he asks. To my surprise, the tone is perfectly normal. Welcoming even.

"Yes, she has," the prince drawls as his eyes avoid mine, sweeping over the crowd instead. "And I know what you're thinking, uncle, but there's no chance you'll see her fighting in the Trials. So there's really no point in us wasting our time here."

"Yes, make haste," I reply flatly, with only a touch of mockery in my voice, even though I'm downright fuming as I watch him turn to keep walking.

But his uncle stops him with a glare. He turns to me and says in a warm but scolding voice, "I apologize for my nephew's behavior. Despite all the effort I put into his education, I apparently failed to teach him basic manners."

Faust Junior scoffs, turns back and looks straight into my eyes. For a second, I freeze, not knowing what to expect.

One corner of his lips curled into a sexy smirk, he dips his head and slowly bows with his hand sweeping forward in a single exaggerated, smooth movement. For a second, my heart stops beating entirely, until it starts again with a violent pounding.

"Now, was that so difficult?" I hear his uncle say as he turns to give me a smile and another curt bow himself.

I'm still breathless, dizzy from staring straight into his nephew's eyes for so long, so I only manage to nod back before the two of them take their leave, the prince joining some of his groupies to the front of the line. Of course, no one bats an eye.

In the meantime, Faust Senior makes his way to the Tree. Now that I give it a closer look, I see that its bark has elaborate carvings in the shape of the crests of the three royal bloodlines.

The uncle nods to the Pied Piper and the rest of the professors, turns to the audience and clears his throat. Instantly, all the chatter dies down. I guess he'll be the one giving the speech.

"I have always found it fitting..." He's smiling, but his voice is carrying a touch of nostalgia. "For the Selection Day to be on the day of the Fall Equinox, a time when Darkness starts encroaching on the land of Light."

He pauses for a second and all I hear is absolute silence. When he speaks again, his voice is filled with pride. "After all, that is what we Originals are. The Divine's persistent struggle for life."

Using his walking stick, he leans forward a little and raises his eyebrows at the people listening to him with bated breath. "And once a year, we get the opportunity to display our power to the world and convince it, once again, of our imminent victory against Darkness."

I can feel he's got everyone around me mesmerized. And I can't blame them, the man has a presence.

"Therefore," he says, raising his voice as he teases the anticipation, "there is only one thing I have to say to you on this grand, auspicious day…"

There's a silence filled with excited tension.

"Bring your Academy, your bloodline and yourself *honor*."

The crowd breaks into thunderous clapping.

"Wow," I lean to whisper in Nuala's ear. "So dramatic."

But she just throws me a smile as she joins in, clapping just as furiously as everyone else. And I guess we're no longer waiting for anything, because the student that's first in line, a vampire girl with a pixie, moves and walks up to the Tree.

After a moment of hesitation, as the crowd draws in a breath, she places her hand on the carvings on the bark.

I stand on the tips of my toes to see what happens.

Nothing.

After a few moments of silence, the girl lets her hand drop to her side and turns on her heel with a devastated look on her face.

There's no reaction from the crowd but a few sympathetic looks. "What's going on?" I ask Nuala.

"She wasn't chosen."

"And she's disappointed. I'd think she'd be relieved."

"It's a great honor," she tells me with a shrug.

But the next student is already in front of the tree. Not chosen.

Then another one. Not chosen.

Not chosen.

And so on and so forth, until Sarya walks up to the tree, throwing a smile at the rest of her trio over her shoulder.

"Ugh," Nuala says. "A Viper."

"What's that?"

She snorts. "It's not a 'what'." She points to Sarya and rolls her eyes. "The Vipers are this clique whose members just happen to win the Trials *every single year.*"

I open my mouth to ask how, but I notice a stir among the crowd. I turn to look at Sarya, who's already placed her hand on the carvings.

And they're glowing. It's a bright blue light that wraps itself around her wrist and then disappears. But when she turns around, it looks like she has a new tattoo where the light touched her skin. A thin, dark circle.

"And what's that?" I whisper to Nuala without taking my eyes off the girl's hand.

"That's the mark of the Bond," she leans to whisper back. "When you're chosen for the Trials, you basically sign a contract you can't get out of."

"Holy shit," I blurt out. "So that's how they make sure you participate?"

I turn to look at her, but her eyes are still fixed on the procession. She doesn't say anything, she just nods, looking tense as fuck. Maybe she actually cares about this.

"Maybe it's a good thing then," I start, staring at her so she'll look my way. When she does, I throw on a grin, adding, "That I'm so useless at this whole 'being an Original' thing."

She does laugh, but it doesn't reach her eyes. Wow, this must be a huge deal.

I watch as some of the other familiar faces get chosen. Harry. Zelda. Even Leo, who turns to the crowd to get an applause, his eyes stopping on mine for a second.

And even though most other students seem to just want to get it over with, it's all taking such an incredibly long time. And just when I think I'm going to blow my brains out, there's another stir in the crowd. It's him, it's his turn, I know it even before I turn my eyes back to the tree.

I'm right, of course. I can't help but stand on the tips of my toes again, moving my head left and right to get a better look at him.

He's taking his time, walking up to the tree as if he's the only one there, as if there aren't a whole bunch of people still waiting for their turn. I hate him for it. But I also don't mind getting a better look at him. It's so simple, the way he's dressed, but it oozes luxury and elegance. Just like his entire presence, every move of his toned but slim body.

Even the way he places his hand on the tree is regal. He makes the act a lot more solemn, a lot more suspenseful than it was with the other students. I can't help but draw in a breath.

And just as I thought, the blue light appears and wraps around his wrist, leaving the tattoo behind.

The silence is broken by an almost violent sound of clapping. I glance around to see that even Nuala has joined in. For a second, I stay still. There's a part of me that's pissed. Sure, the prince is someone whose parents died tragic deaths when he was still a little boy. That was part of the reason he became my obsession when I was in high school. But other than that, he's had everything handed to him on a silver plate. Of course he'll be chosen for something like this. It's not surprising and therefore, it's not at all impressive.

But of course, he's the one people will clap for the most. Not some poor student who's made it against all odds. Because apparently, there's at least one thing that the Originals have in common with the humans. The fact that we don't value accomplishments. We value status.

Still, I clap with the rest of them. This is neither the place nor the time to show the world how bitter I can be about some things.

The prince walks to the other side of the Tree, where the Pied Piper is putting flower wreaths around the necks of the Chosen.

A couple of more wreaths get used and before I know it, it's Nuala's turn. I throw her an encouraging glance, not knowing what exactly to cheer for, her being chosen or not.

But when nothing ends up happening and she makes her way to the back of the crowd, where the *unworthy* are standing, I'm no longer confused about it. She has a sour look on her face that tells me she really did want this. I also realize that I kind of expected her to get chosen, despite the fact that I know nothing about her powers. Nothing whatsoever.

But I don't have time to linger on it. It's my turn so I slowly start making my way to the tree, fighting to keep my legs from shaking. I can feel eyes on me and it makes it hard not to fall apart, just the thought that his might be among them.

And I'm pissed at myself. He's *mocking* me and I'm still finding him so hot. Pathetic, Quinn, just straight-up pathetic.

To my surprise, that all disappears as soon as I come near the Tree. From a distance, it doesn't look like much. But up close, it makes me feel things I don't know how to put into words. Like it's the first thing I've ever seen. Properly at least. I lift my hand and I place my palm on its bark. I'm not even thinking about the Trials. I just want to touch it.

And when I do, I feel this soothing energy course through my body. Like there's peace beyond peace, sight beyond sight.

It startles me, that's how big of a contrast it makes to this calm energy, when I see the light appear in the hollows of the carvings. And when it wraps around my wrist, all I can do is draw in a surprised breath.

Fuck. Fuck. Fuck.

That's all that's going through my mind as I walk up to the Pied Piper, lowering my head so she can put the wreath around my neck.

There's a strange look in her eyes as she whispers, "You surprise me, little mouse."

She uses the same pet name she used when she kidnapped me to this place. But I find her ridiculously intimidating so I don't say anything. My body can't make up its mind so it does something between a nod and a shrug before I fix my gaze on where I'm supposed to go next. I join the other Chosen, turning to face the crowd, but not before I catch Faust looking at me with surprise in his eyes.

And sure, it's fine for *me* to not have expected this. But the Little Prince? How dare he.

So instead of showing how I really feel, which comes down to a mix of confusion and sheer terror, I force myself to throw him the smuggest smile I can muster. I see him shake his head slightly before he looks away. Doesn't matter. I'll make him eat his words.

"It is a fine number," I hear the Pied Piper's smooth voice boom out, "twenty four. Let us congratulate our Chosen, as well as the one I'm putting in charge of all of them." She turns to give the prince a smile. "This year's Ringleader, Andreas Faust."

My head snaps in his direction and I see his lips curl into a smile as he waves at the audience, who are now clapping and cheering like crazy. And just like that, my own smile slides right off my face.

Chapter Eight

I spend the day after the Selection in a sort of haze, my eyes darting to the tattoo on my wrist what feels like every two minutes. I keep expecting it not to be there. It's only late at night that I meet up with Nuala for dinner. And as soon as I spot her, waiting for me in front of the cafeteria, I see that her spirits are still low.

She doesn't even get anything to eat. Sitting in front of two plates, one for dinner, one for dessert, I throw her a worried glance.

"You know," I start, convinced she just needs a change of perspective, "I did some catching up with the previous Trials today, just to see what I've gotten myself into. And last year, this fae girl stepped on the wrong spot in the Arena..." I lean a bit forward, dropping my voice to a whisper. "And got spiked to death. Just like that."

"I know," she says flatly. "I was there."

"Oh, of course you were," I reply, but I'm still surprised by her reaction. "Anyway, my point is, I'd give my left tit just to be able to say 'No, thanks' to all of that."

And I finish with a light laugh, but Nuala's face just turns to stone.

"You know how many times I've heard someone say that?" she says, bitterness lacing her voice. "And you know how many times it came from someone who *wasn't* chosen? Zero."

I feel my eyebrows pulling down. "Are you seriously mad at me for being chosen?"

She just looks at me for a second. "What're you talking about?" There's no more bitterness in her voice, just confusion. "Oh shit, Quinn, sorry," she says and face-palms herself. "I mean, I don't really like it that you got chosen, but only because you yourself don't seem to be thrilled."

I just wave my hand, showing that it's all water under the bridge. "Then what?" I insist. "Do you really care about it all *this* much?"

"I *don't*," she says with a shake of her head. "I mean, it involves a lot of fighting. And believe me, I don't even like having to watch. That girl you mentioned earlier?" She leans a bit forward, as if she's embarrassed. "I *was* there, but I was covering my eyes the entire time."

"So what's the problem?"

She huffs out a breath. "You know I have six brothers."

I nod.

"Well, what you don't know is that *all* six of them," she says and rolls her eyes, "are these amazing shifters who won a lot of the Champion Titles while they were here."

"Ah," I just say, slowly nodding to show how much I get it. I lean a bit forward so I can give her a slap on the shoulder. "But you just have to keep training. I'm sure you'll be able to compete with them someday."

She shakes her head vigorously. "No, really, don't worry about it. I was just being stupid, letting these pressures that have nothing to do with my own wishes mess with my head."

She stops to throw me a grin. "And I'm sure we have much more important things to talk about," she adds as she motions at the poster on the wall to her right.

They're everywhere, not just in the cafeteria, and they're showing silhouettes of a woman and a man dancing. And when I say dancing, I mean actually dancing. Apparently, they cast spells on their posters here, just to make things a bit more interesting, I guess. And the bottom of the poster says, in large block letters, Winter Solstice Ball.

"What if I don't want to go?" I ask.

"I think you'd be the first," she laughs dryly. "And why wouldn't you want to? I mean, people will be fighting to take you."

I scoff. "Yeah, I can already see them lining up. Oh, wait, nope, still ignoring me," I finish with a laugh.

But Nuala is shaking her head. "There's an order to these things. First there's the Showing of the Chosen," she says as she starts counting on her fingers. "Although we generally just call it Showing. That's tomorrow. Then on the night of the Blood Moon, which is sometime in November, there's the Favorday, when other students ask the Chosen to the Winter Solstice and Grand Balls. And believe me, you'll have a hard time fighting them off."

I laugh. "I'm sure that will be true for the rest of the Chosen." As I say it, an image pops into my mind, of Faust being surrounded by fawning girls. "But I'll still be an outcast."

Nuala just looks at me for a second and then lets out a laugh. "It's not about popularity. It's a power grab really."

"A power grab? How come?"

"The Trials," she starts in a more serious voice, "they used to be a much bigger thing because people believed the Chosen, especially the Champion, received blessings from the Divine. But even these days, if you come out a winner, people know you're going somewhere. And there's a lot of media pomp, so even being the date of the Chosen comes with a lot of prestige."

"Holy shit," I blurt out, grabbing my forehead with my hand. "That's the last thing I need, people asking me out with media pomp on their mind."

"It'll be fun, trust me."

She says it with such a sad face that my heart breaks a little. "Can't I just pick you as my date and be done with it?" I ask with a grin.

At least that makes her laugh. "No, someone has to ask *you*," she replies, still laughing. "Not the other way around."

It's only later, when I climb up to my room, that I remember my mission. I'm reminded of it as soon as I fling the door open and find that same bunch of books waiting for me there.

At least this whole thing with the Trials has made me forget for two whole days about the fact I still don't know who left them to me.

But it also makes me pissed at myself. For being so absorbed in the books that I didn't take enough time to explore the Academy or to get myself more familiar with the way things work here, including the Trials. And I'd say I was also pissed at myself for not taking the time to meet more people, but I wouldn't even if I tried, considering how suspicious everyone's being of the 'human-bred girl'.

Still, I'm pissed enough to decide to just stop with the whole madness. I need to fucking move on and I'm fucking tired of having to hop over piles of books every time I need to go to the bathroom. And I know I have at least *some* storage space in this room.

So I get to work. I start picking them up and shoving them into drawers and closets I haven't even had time to inspect until now.

As I work, I find a few things leftover by the previous tenants. Scrunchies. Candy wrappers. Cheat sheets for everything from History to Runes.

And one really old-looking diary. Leather bound, with metal scales around the edges. I pick it up, meaning to open it and find who it belongs to.

But as soon as I touch it, it sends shivers down my spine.

And not just that. It implants in my mind the image of some girl I'm sure I've never seen in my life. I think that, by now, I can tell when someone is fae-blooded. *She* certainly is.

And by the looks of her, she's no ordinary fae. She has a rich green robe with a lighter shade shawl thrown over her shoulder. Her hair is dark brown, almost raven, and she has the most elaborate hairstyle I've ever seen, all braids and expensive-looking hair jewelry. She looks like she may as well be some fae queen from days past.

I scratch my head, wondering how a figment of my imagination can be so full of detail.

Intrigued, I crack open the diary. But before I can read a single word, I hear a female voice drawl, "Excuse me."

I drop the diary, its weight almost crushing my foot as my head snaps in the direction of the voice. There she is, the woman I just saw in my head, standing a few feet away and throwing me a funny look.

"I'd appreciate it if you kept your nose out of my *private* diary," she says, not giving a single fuck about the way my mouth drops open.

Chapter Nine

"I'm sorry," I blurt out as I pick up the diary, my mind having trouble making peace with the fact I'm apologizing to what seems to be an apparition.

"It's alright," she says, looking at me with suspicion in her eyes. "As long as you put it down."

Very carefully, I place the diary on my desk and take a single step towards the woman. The differences are subtle, but there's definitely something weird about the way light reflects off her body.

"Take a picture, why don't you?" she says dryly.

"I'm really sorry," I repeat absentmindedly, my mind racing. "It's just," I start, not really knowing where I'm going with it. "I guess I've never seen anyone…" I struggle to find words that wouldn't offend her. "Like you before."

She ignores my words. "How did you get here? Did you use the Pull?" she squints at me, barely moving a muscle as she carefully takes in her surroundings.

"How did *I* get here?" I let out a little laugh. "How did you? Are you a genie or something?"

That makes a little laugh escape her lips as well. "Genie. Seriously?"

"Sorry," I apologize, again. I take a cautious step towards her. She doesn't seem dangerous and she's actually quite young. Twenty five tops. "I don't really know much about all this crap."

"And I guess you have a foul mouth as well."

"Hey," I protest. "It's you who showed up in my room uninvited. I don't think you have the right to tell me how to speak."

"This is *my* room," she snaps back, but she says it under her breath and without looking at me, as if she's mulling it over.

I frown. "I don't get it. This room was assigned to me and it was empty when I got here."

"What year is it?" she asks as she takes a step towards me, still squinting at me like I am the intruder here.

"Twenty twenty three."

I see the surprise in her eyes. Without a word, she straightens and tries to tap one of her runes. Nothing happens. "So I must be dead then," she says as she turns back to me.

She says it in such a flat voice that I can't help but feel a weird sort of admiration for her. "Dead?" I hear my voice echo her words.

"There's no other explanation," she says as she takes another step closer to me. "What did you do?"

The tone of her voice is accusing. And that pisses me off. "What the fuck are you implying?"

"Calm down," she commands me. *Commands.* "I didn't say you killed me. As far as I know, I may have died of natural causes. But I'm almost positive that it was you who brought me here."

"For fuck's sake," I can't help but yell at her as I grab the runes hanging around my neck. "See these? I couldn't use them if my life depended on it. How the hell do you think I'd be able to make them summon some self-important ghost?"

For a second, she just looks at me. Then, to my surprise, the look in her eyes softens. I swear to god she almost smiles before she says, "Alright, no need to excite yourself."

She turns around and takes a seat on the edge of my bed. "However, I am some sort of ghost and it's obvious that you're the reason I'm here." I just keep standing there, confused as fuck.

After a moment of silence, I see her eyes lit up and she turns to me to ask, "Is there something you need? Something that might have brought me here to you?"

I frown. *This* I did not expect. "Um," I start, but then burst out laughing. "I don't know why any of it would have anything to do with *you*."

Without taking my eyes off her, I sit on the chair in front of my desk. She doesn't say anything. She just looks at me with that commanding expression on her face.

"I guess there's a lot of things I need right now. I need to learn how to use these," I start as I motion at my runes, "mostly because I need to survive the Trials."

"So you've been chosen. Alright," she drawls. "And?"

"And when I first got here, there were these books waiting for me, but I've no idea who left them to me because the magic can't be traced."

Even before I finish, I see a spark of interest in her eyes. "Really? And you found no note, nothing?"

"Nothing."

"And when you touch them, nothing happens?"

I frown and then shake my head.

"Curious," she says, tilting her head in thought. "It might be either of the two. The Trials or the books. Let's start with the books. That one might be quicker."

I can't help but straighten in my chair, excitement shooting through my body. "Really? You could help me figure it out?"

For the first time since she appeared in my room, the girl smiles. "I wasn't the most powerful fae in my generation for nothing. However..." She looks deep into my eyes. "There will be some magic involved. And you said you're unable to use your runes."

"I'll find a way," I rush to say, my voice filled to the brim with eager determination.

Chapter Ten

First thing in the morning, I rush to the House of Lycan to find Nuala. My mind is buzzing with possibilities and I can't wait to do the spell to find out who left me all the books. Moswen's instructions were clear, but I still take the diary with me, just in case we need her again. And I suck at magic and Nuala's not even a fae and I'm not what you could call a lucky person, so I'm not sure how it will all turn out, but I have to try. My friend's not in her room, so I head straight for the cafeteria.

"You're not even going to have breakfast?" she asks me when I rush up to her and tell her I need her help with something.

"Nope, too excited," I say. "Couldn't even sleep."

"In the name of Lycan, Quinn," Nuala shoots me a worried glance. "It sounds serious," she says as she gets up off her chair. "What do you need me to do?"

"Help me find the Greenhouse," I reply as I tug on her sleeve to make her go faster.

The Greenhouse is where faes have their Meditation classes. I haven't been there yet because I'm still in the more basic program. But it turns out Nuala knows exactly where it is, so I follow her down a couple of excruciatingly long hallways until one of them opens up onto a winding staircase.

At its very top, there's an ancient looking door that opens with a nauseating creak. And just like that, we find ourselves above ground, in a huge glass structure bursting at the seams from the ridiculous amount of trees, bushes and plants.

I stop for a second, looking up at the huge glass dome and inhaling a scent so intoxicating, I think I might topple over. "Holy fucking shit, this is just..."

I turn to Nuala, my eyebrows raised and my mouth open in awe, but she just stands there with her arms folded and her lips pressed tight. On our way here, I told her everything about my discovery of Moswen and her plan for my next step.

Let's just say that Nuala does *not* approve.

So I just throw her an apologetic look "Let's go find the thing," I say and start walking again. I take out the piece of paper I've scribbled the info on. "The Wynnach Thorn."

"So it's some kind of flower?" Nuala asks as she follows me down a gravel path and deeper into the Greenhouse.

"Moswen said it's a shrub," I answer, stopping to show her the image I found online. "And we only need one leaf."

"Okay," she just says, but I can still hear the disapproval in her voice.

It doesn't take us long to find it. We stumble on what seems to be a round workspace with rows of Wynnach Thorns in ornate pots. And there's a large wooden desk with all sorts of tools left lying on its surface.

"This is perfect," I almost yell out as I walk up to one of the pots, grabbing a pair of small garden shears from the table and crouching in front of the plant.

"Moswen said to be careful," I say without turning to look at Nuala. "Each leaf hides a little thorn that can be deadly if it pricks your skin. And it finds a way to prick it because, well, that's what it does."

"Maybe you should be careful about Moswen, too," I hear my friend reply. "I wouldn't believe everything that that ghost of a woman says."

I don't say anything. I simply don't want to continue the argument we had on our way here. It's enough for me, the fact that I trust her, even though I'm not sure why.

So I just clip a leaf off the stalk and jump back up, grinning from ear to ear. "Let's try it."

"I don't understand how it's supposed to work," Nuala says, squinting at my hand.

"Patience, dear Fionnuala," I drawl, the combination of her full name and my regal tone of voice making her chuckle. "Grab that bowl and pour some water. Chop chop."

While she does that, I take the stuff I brought with me out of my backpack. I place one of the books on the table and pour some ink into the bowl of water my friend places in front of me.

"First I need to do this," I say as I crack open the book and place the leaf, thorn side down, on a blank page of the book.

I feel Nuala leaning in, but my eyes are fixed on the leaf. I draw in a breath as soon as I see it start squirming, as if it has a mind of its own.

With bated breath, I keep watching until it settles. Slowly, I flip its tip over and see the thorn's managed to dig into the page. "Success," I yell out as Nuala lets out a happy squeal.

"Now what?"

"Now I do this." I take the bowl in my hand, draw in a breath and pour it all over the two blank pages in front of me. They drink it all up thirstily.

But nothing happens. I frown. "The thorn is supposed to start feeding off the leftover energy of the person who used the book. And the ink is supposed to give shape to it so we can get some kind of hint."

"I don't see anything," Nuala states the obvious.

"Maybe we need to wait."

"Why don't you try using your runes?"

I don't say anything. I just throw her a look.

"Alright, sheesh, sorry."

"Moswen said there's not a lot of spells that would work without runes, but this plant has its own magic, so I was supposed to be able to pull it off anyway." I let out a deep sigh, disappointed that nothing's happening.

"Someone just walked in," Nuala says. I look up to see her sniffing the air.

I don't even have time to turn around before I hear a familiar voice drawl, "What do we have here?"

I turn around to see Sarya walking up to us. Instead of her usual overalls, she's wearing a gorgeous red dress.

"Hi Sarya," I say flatly, hearing Nuala let out a frustrated sigh to my right.

Sarya stops and squints at the table behind my back. "Is that little Miss Chosen trying to do magic?" she asks with a mocking laugh. "Now that's something I'd like a ticket to."

I shrug, determined to ignore her stabs. "Sorry, we're all sold out."

"But seriously," she insists as she starts pacing in front of the two of us. "I'm not surprised that this one," she says, gesturing at Nuala, "*didn't* get selected..."

Before I can react, Nuala cuts in, her voice filled with anger. "Why don't you mind your own business?"

Sarya does stop pacing and turns to look at Nuala, but then just lets out a chuckle. "Have I offended you, oh powerful shifter?" she asks mockingly. "Should I be afraid for my life?"

With the corner of my eye, I see Nuala push her chest out and draw in a pissed-off breath, so I decide that we've had enough of this nonsense.

I grab my friend by the upper arm and say. "She's just being an asshole, Nuala. Let's go."

"Asshole?" Sarya gets in my face, anger filling her golden eyes. "Watch it," she hisses, making both Nuala and me freeze in place.

When she continues talking, her voice is light yet menacing. "After all, you'll be in the Trials with me and there's a lot that can go wrong in moments like those."

Fighting the need to gulp, I raise a finger of my right hand to signal to Nuala *not* to react.

"Is that so?" I ask flatly, finally daring to take a step back. I need to get the book, Nuala and myself out of here as soon as possible. But a part of my focus has to be on Sarya's hands, just to make sure she doesn't have time to use her runes.

I turn around and I reach for the book I was using for the spell. But that only draws her attention to it.

And she's fast. She's fucking fast. Before I can react, she's already slammed the palm of her hand onto the open book. "The House Olarel sigil? Where did you get this?" she asks with a frown.

My eyes dart to the book and I see that its pages are no longer blank. They have an ink stain in the shape of a black bird on them. A raven, I think. But I don't say anything. I immediately turn back to Sarya. "I'm afraid that's none of your business," I snarl, my patience wearing thin. "Let go of the book."

She just grins at me. "So it *is* something interesting?" Without breaking eye contact, she snatches it from the table.

I ball my hands into fists, but I don't manage to do anything else.

"You fucking bitch," I hear Nuala yell out as she lunges at Sarya as if she wants to knock her to the ground.

To my surprise, she actually does it. Sarya comes crashing down with a loud thump.

The book lands a few feet away from her and I jump to pick it up while I still have the chance. I hear a strange, loud noise. By the time I stand straight and turn to the two of them, Sarya is standing up, reaching for her runes, while Nuala's squinting at her, waiting for the attack.

But then a clock sounds from somewhere and Sarya drops her hand to her side.

"To hell with your fucking book," she spits out. "I was just sent to tell you to get your ass to the Main Hall. Now you've made me late."

With that, she huffs out a breath, turns on her heel and walks out of the Greenhouse, the tail of her dress trailing after her.

I turn to my friend, who's still panting slightly. "The Showing?" she asks.

"Shit, I forgot all about it."

"Apparently," Nuala says in an absent voice.

What great timing, I think to myself as I rush out of the Greenhouse. I'm definitely in the mood to be paraded around like a puppet. It's not like I have much more important shit to deal with.

Chapter Eleven

When I get to the Main Hall, I see it's been cleared out for the event. Instead of the usual bunch of armchairs, couches, desks and low tables, now all l can see is a podium with rows of high tables stretching before it. There's a huge crowd already gathered around the table with just one person seated, a guy in a fancy suit who seems to be the host having his make-up retouched. It's only after I barge in that I realize that the Showing is the kind of thing people dress up for.

Me? I'm wearing my usual jeans and sweater combination, complete with my signature combat boots. Compared to the rest of the students there, I look barely a shade better than homeless. While the girls are wearing tight-fitting dresses and ludicrously high heels, the guys are all in tuxes.

Including Faust. There's a million people here, but it doesn't take long for my eye to be drawn to him. And it knocks the air out of my lungs, how handsome he looks. For a second, my eyes linger on his waistcoat. It has the Ouroboros, the snake eating its tail, embroidered on it.

And of course, the paparazzi Nuala warned me about are all gathered around him. I take a deep breath and, fighting the shaking of my legs, I go straight for the bar. They're forcing me into this, but if nothing else, I can do it my way. Not drunk. Just tipsy enough for it to take the edge off.

I already have my hand on the champagne flute that's patiently waiting for me on a tray on the counter, when I feel the need to turn around.

It's the Little Prince himself, looking at me with that unreadable expression on his face. "I thought the text I sent out was simple enough for anyone to understand." His voice is low and stern. "To report to me as soon as any of you arrive."

I raise my eyebrows. "You were busy with the paparazzi."

I struggle not to avert my eyes, my heart skipping random beats. He doesn't reply. He just looks me up and down and says, "And that's what you've decided to wear?"

Fucker. "So it would seem," I drawl, mocking him. "Given that *that's* what I'm wearing."

There's a flash of a frown before his face goes back to doing that stupid thing where it gives nothing. "Suit yourself. But I'm putting you last," he says as he turns his back on me.

"Please, don't," I beg mockingly, but he's already walking away.

Vaguely pissed, I go back to my champagne flute. The event seems to be starting, because there's a guy who walks up on stage and gives a brief, but excruciatingly boring little speech about how pleased they were at his news station to be given the honor of blah blah blah.

With the corner of my eye, I see that most of the paparazzi stay close to Faust even as the first girl is being called to the stage to introduce herself.

Shit, will I also be expected to answer stupid questions like 'What will be your main motivation throughout the course of the Trials?'

Scanning the groups of people, I notice Professor Mistila standing to the side, seemingly alone. I don't think she'll recognize me, but she teaches History, which means she'll probably know something about the House Olarel. And just like that, the fog in my brain clears and I have my eyes on the prize again.

I take my flute with me and I walk up to her. "Professor Mistila..."

"You do realize there's such a thing as office hours," she cuts me off and looks away, taking another sip of her drink.

It's only when I'm in front of her that I notice how flush her cheeks are. I guess even vampires can get drunk off regular champagne. "I'm sorry, Professor, I just have one question."

"I swear to Lilith's blood," she says as she lets out a laugh, "if I had a penny for every time a student spoke those words to me..."

"Fair enough," I reply. "I'll leave you to it then. And I hope you enjoy the event."

I'm already turning to walk away when I see her throw me an intrigued look. "Wait," she says.

And I listen.

"You're not here to ask me what questions are going to be on the test."

I just shake my head, my lips pressed tight and my eyebrows raised slightly.

"I'm listening."

I give her a smile. "I was just wondering if you knew anything about the House Olarel."

She lets out a laugh. "Not less than what would easily fill three large volumes." She stops to look deeper into my eyes. "You do know that that's one of the more powerful fae-blooded families in all of our history?"

"What can I say?" I shrug my shoulders, hoping to charm her into forgiving me this trespass. "I haven't been among the Originals long."

"Interesting," the professor leans forward, taking me by the upper arm.

I can barely contain my excitement. She looks as if something has awoken in her, possibly the thought of finally having an audience interested in what she had to say.

"Well, first of all," she says as she takes me for a slow stroll around the Hall, "you do know that some of the Original families are so ancient, we can only guess how long they've been walking this earth?"

I had no idea, but I'm nodding vigorously.

"For example," the professor continues as she motions at the crest on the wall high above our heads, the one showing the Ouroboros, "the House Faust is one of them."

Of course it is, I think to myself. But what I say is, "And I'm guessing the House Olarel is another."

"Smart girl," she says, throwing me a wink.

I let out a chuckle. "And?"

"Given how old they are, it comes as no surprise that the earliest histories of each of those houses are shrouded in mystery. But while most scholars dismiss them as nothing more than myths…"

She stops and locks eyes with me. I just look at her, nudging her to go on. "I say even myths can be based in real life. After all, before the Brothers, the Scions thought that *we* were nothing more than figments of their imagination," she finishes with a chuckle.

I nod thoughtfully. "So what's the House Olarel origin story?"

I'm more interested in its recent history, but I'm taking my time. I want to learn everything this woman wants to tell me. And she looks more than willing, already opening her mouth to share her knowledge.

But of course, it's at that exact moment that someone taps me on the shoulder. "Quinn?"

I turn to see a girl with a name tag looking at me impatiently. "It's your turn."

"Already?" God damn it, I think to myself. Just as things were getting interesting. "Will you excuse me for just a moment," I turn to say to the professor. "I really want to hear everything you were going to say."

"Of course, dear, I'll be right here."

I let the girl lead me to the front of the Main Hall and straight onto the podium. There's a lot of camera flashes as I take my seat, but they actually come in handy because they make it hard to see the people gathered in front of me, all waiting for me to talk about myself. In part because I don't want to know if *he* is still preoccupied with his own paparazzi or if he's watching the other students' introductions.

"Tell me, Quinn," the guy who's interviewing me flashes me one of those practiced, dead smiles that don't reach the eyes. But not before he looks me up and down, judging my outfit. "Is that really your name? It's a bit unusual for a fae-blooded girl."

I let out a laugh. "It wasn't until a month ago that I found out I was a fae, so..."

"Really?" he says, throwing a glance at one of his colleagues. I feel the chatter around me die down a little. "How supremely intriguing. But you do have experience with magic? It would otherwise be difficult to imagine you being chosen for the Trials."

Oh, I hate him for asking that, but I'm definitely not going to let it show. "Let's just say I still have a lot to learn," I reply, choosing a diplomatic answer.

He flashes me a smile with zero kindness, like a predator licking his lips before his prey. "I'm sure your fellow students are helping you with that. But there are a lot of them here with skills that are simply out of this world. How do you plan to win?"

"I don't," I say, letting out a laugh. "My goal is just to survive."

I can tell he's not happy with that. He was expecting something juicier and he's prepared to work for it. "So you're not an ambitious girl, are you, Quinn?"

I look away, shaking my head as I fight to keep the smile on my face. And I already have some bland, non confrontational answer in mind, but then my eyes land on his. He's standing to the side, but he's staring at me intently. As if I'm some annoying bomb he's supposed to prevent from going off, the son of a bitch.

"I guess I believe," I hear myself say as my heart starts pounding, "there's more to ambition than trying to win an inconsequential competition I didn't even want to enter."

"Careful," I hear a warning boom inside my head. It almost makes me jump up. In the back of my mind, I notice the shift in the atmosphere that my words have caused, people drawing in shocked breaths and shifting on their feet. But I don't care, because I'm staring straight at the prince, the one who just used his powers to get in my head. And I'm pissed. I move to get up off my chair, but the journalist scrambles to keep me there.

"So your ambition, in fact, *exceeds* trying to beat the Originals of Grimm Academy?" he asks, as if it would be physically impossible to say yes. "What would it be, that noble goal of yours?"

I plant my ass back on the chair and throw him an incredulous look. "Off the top of my head," I reply, failing to keep the sarcasm out of my voice, "learning to use my powers for the greater good. Something along those lines."

Fuck, I'm fucking this up, I think as I stare into the journalist's eyes. He looks like I've just given him everything he wanted. And then some. "Thank you for the introduction," I say, trying to salvage the situation. "I'm sure you have a lot more contenders to talk to."

And with that, I get up and rush off the podium, the cameras flashing violently in my face. As I try to find Professor Mistila, I make a point not to look anyone in the eye. I'm avoiding one pair in particular.

The professor is right there where I left her, squinting at me with an unreadable expression on her face.

But before I can approach her, *he* appears right in front of me. It's so sudden, I almost bump into him. "Follow me," he snaps, his voice so commanding, I just do what he says.

He leads me to the side and when he turns to face me, his body is really close to mine and his nostrils are flaring. It's the only hint on that terribly composed face that he's, well, not pleased.

"Had your fun?" His voice is low and controlled, at least on the surface. Underneath, things are brewing.

But I guess when it comes to him, I'm insane. While my brain tells me to find a way out of the situation, *fast*, other parts of me want nothing more than to see where this would go. Just a little taste, that's all.

"I'm sorry," I reply, using my most sarcastic, condescending voice. "Have I offended you somehow?"

"Don't play dumb."

"Alright, then get to the fucking point," I hiss at him.

For a second, he just stares at me. "My *point* is..." He glances around and then flashes me a fake smile as he speaks in a low, threatening voice. "In the future, you should either respect our traditions or shut the fuck up."

My eyebrows raised, I let out a little laugh. "Yes, my prince," I say as I sweep my arms and drop my knees in a mocking bow, something like what he did to me. "Anything else you require?"

I see a flash of surprise in his eyes. But I don't wait for him to snap out of it. I just turn on my heel and walk away.

It's only then that I see a bunch of girls standing close, huffing and puffing as they watch my every move.

I don't give anyone else the chance to come between me and Professor Mistila. She looks as if she's trying her hardest not to let it be known that she too was watching my interaction with Faust.

"I apologize for keeping you waiting, Professor," I say as I walk up to her, half expecting her not to want to talk to me again.

"Tell me, *Quinn*," the professor says in a voice that's barely more than a whisper, "what exactly made you come ask me questions about the House Olarel?"

For a second, I hesitate. There's something in her tone that wasn't there before. But I don't have a bad feeling about it so I decide to tell the truth. "Someone left me these books. I don't know who and I don't know why. The only thing I do know is that one of them belonged to someone from that house."

The professor stays silent for a moment. Slowly, her eyes light up and she whispers in an excited voice, "I *thought* there was something about you."

Chapter Twelve

"What the fuck?" Nuala asks, her mouth dropping open.

Can't blame her. I myself am not just shocked. I'm even a little bit scared.

"How is that even possible?" my friend asks. "How can you be a descendant if the House Olarel is extinct?"

We're in the cafeteria, sitting in front of our plates, both piled high with burgers and french fries that remain untouched as I recount everything Professor Mistila told me.

"She says it's the *only* possibility," I reply, looking around to make sure no one can hear us. I'm not ready for it to go public yet. "Apparently, the Olarels were known for being extra protective of their stuff. And there's no fucking chance in hell anyone outside the House would ever be able to get their hands on any of it."

Nuala just looks at me stupidly.

"I know," I say under my breath. "It's fucking insane. And I understand I couldn't have just appeared out of thin air. I just didn't think my father would turn out to be a member of some all-powerful house."

For a second, I look away. I'm feeling so much all at once that I can't even begin to untangle individual emotions. *Never* in my life, not even right after I got sent those books, have I *seriously* considered the possibility that I might not be alone in the world.

"So now what?" Nuala snaps me out of it.

"I've no idea," I confess. "I guess the Archives would be a good start. Maybe I can find my family tree there or something."

"I'll come with you."

"Thanks, Nuala," I say, "but I have to warn you. I'm leaving as soon as I'm done eating, and you know how fast I can be."

She lets out a chuckle, but I can tell she's taken me seriously by the way she digs in. It takes us less than ten minutes to inhale all the food and rush out of the cafeteria.

And I know Nuala doesn't exactly like spending time in the library, but that's where the Archives are. We have to go down a gazillion steps and pass three different security checks, the Librarians waving these weird-looking wooden wands in front of us to make sure we're not carrying anything flammable or generally dangerous.

Once we're inside, I go through the main hall and straight for the plain door with the label saying Archives. I've been here many times already, so the novelty of seeing all the glass walls overlooking the inside of the ginormous cave has worn off. But it still gives me the chills, actually being able to see how deep underground we really are.

The room is just as plain as the door leading to it. From the inside, it almost looks like one of those evidence rooms you can see in crime shows. It's just boxes of files crowding rows upon rows of dusty shelves. They're all marked with names of the different houses. Byrne, de Groot, ó Maoilriain... My heart is heavily pounding as I search them with my eyes.

"No Olarel?" I hear Nuala ask.

"No Olarel," I mutter through gritted teeth. "What the fuck?"

But I'm not wasting any time. I go back to the main hall and straight for the ornate solid-wood counter where there's a shifter Librarian slapping stickers onto a pile of books in front of him.

"I'm sorry," I ask hesitantly. "I've just been to the Archives, looking for information on the House Olarel."

"You won't find it there," he says without even looking up. "It's all in the Olarel Room."

An entire room just for them, I think to myself as my lips curl into a smile. Bingo. "Where can I find it?"

"It's sealed off so we can do some restoration work," he replies, still not even dignifying me with a look. "No one's allowed to enter."

Fuck fuck fuck. I turn around to see Nuala waiting for me by the shelves. And I see by the look on her face that she's heard everything. I throw one more glance at the Librarian and go to her.

"Don't worry about it, Quinn," she whispers. "We'll come back as soon as it's open again."

Easy for her to say, I think. She's always had a family, always known her real name. And maybe it's a stupid thing to do and I'm still scared as hell, but I have to try. "No. Let's go find it."

She throws me a funny look, but she doesn't say anything. She just follows me down several hallways leading from the main hall and into separate sections of the Library. It's fucking huge so it takes us a long time to come across the right door.

I know it's the one we're looking for even before we read the tiny label saying House Olarel. It's simply because there's a huge warning sign placed on the polished stone floor in front of it.

I don't hesitate, but before I can take a single step, I feel Nuala's hand on my shoulder and I hear her whisper, "It could be dangerous. Who knows what kind of magic they used to seal it off."

My heart is throbbing. Stupid, you're being so fucking stupid, I think to myself, but I push Nuala out of the way, walk around the sign and turn the door handle.

There's a quiet click before there's silence again. And just like that, the door is open.

My heart doesn't stop pounding even as I turn to my friend and throw her a shaky smile. "See?"

But when we step inside, my mind goes blank for a second.

"Holy," I hear Nuala start and immediately break off.

To my surprise, the Olarel Room isn't a room full of books containing the information on the House Olarel. It's an empty space with ancient-looking wallpapers that have the family tree painted on them.

"Wow," my friend drawls as I walk to the left side of the room, where the tree begins.

At the top, there's the name Olarel painted on a yellowed scroll with the family motto below. Sight beyond sight, it says in a cursive so ornate, it's practically illegible.

And right below the motto, the family tree begins, featuring stylized portraits of the members of the House with numbers that seem to be too small to denote births and deaths. But then I remember what Professor Mistila told me.

"It says here," I say to my friend as I stare at the portrait of a sullen fae-blooded man, "that the first member of the House was born in 52 AD."

"52? I thought it was 53," she says absentmindedly, her voice echoing through the empty room. "But he's not technically the first. Just the first we know of."

I nod, my eyes still fixed on the portraits of people that, on close inspection, look a lot less human than I do. I take a step closer to look at the woman by the name of Namys who was born in 127 AD, died in 486 and had a forehead as tall as the rest of her face.

If I came here under any other circumstances, I'd take my sweet time and get a good look at each and every one of those ancient faces. But right now, I'm too eager. Too desperate. That these people are my family, *that* fact I'm still struggling to accept, but it doesn't make the urgency I'm feeling any less, well, urgent.

So I walk past the first two walls and stop where the family tree ends, somewhere in the middle of the third.

"Are those your parents?" Nuala asks when she walks up to me.

We're looking at the portraits of two faes, one man and one woman, who seem to be the last of their line. I draw in a breath as I read their names and the numbers telling me when they lived.

"No," I just say, disappointment in my voice. "They both died in the eighteenth century. Even if they did have a child and that child wasn't included in this tree, it couldn't be me."

"Bummer." That's all she says, but I can feel her eyes on me.

"Yeah…"

Is that really it, I wonder. Another dead end? But I can't tear my eyes away from the wallpaper. It's only when I find myself staring at the blank space where the portraits of my parents should be that I notice the pattern. Those birds that are featured on the crest of the House of Ydril. The ones that brought out a memory I didn't even know I had. The ravens.

"You know what?" I turn to face Nuala. She's just waiting for me patiently. "I don't think this can be it. I'm going to ask Moswen," I add, determined as fuck as I open my bag to dig out the diary, throwing one look around to make sure we're still alone.

"You're carrying that thing around?" my friend asks with surprise in her voice.

"Of course. It's too valuable for me to just leave it in my room. And she did tell me to open it if I ever needed her."

Nuala opens her mouth to protest, but it just stays that way when Moswen appears in front of us, throwing me an annoyed look when she sees my friend there. "I don't remember giving you permission to turn me into some spectacle."

"Nuala is my closest friend here and she won't say a word, if that's what you're worried about," I plead with her.

"That's right," Nuala nods.

"And I really need your help." I motion at the wallpaper behind me.

"The Olarel Room?" she asks after she glances around. "I swear on the Holy Word itself, if you've called me to help you with some History assignment…"

I shake my head, rushing to explain, "The books I got, they belong to someone from this House, which means…"

She cuts me off, a look of surprise in her eyes, "That you're a descendant."

"Exactly." I nod, happy that she's just confirmed what Professor Mistila told me.

"I…" Moswen breaks off as she just stares at me.

"But there's a slight problem with that theory," I add, ignoring her dumbfoundedness and pointing at the last two fae-blooded people featured in the family tree.

"I see," she replies in a voice that's barely more than a whisper. I wait for her to continue, but she just keeps staring at the wallpaper with a funny look in her eyes.

"Well?" I ask, not even trying to hide my impatience. "What do you think is going on here?"

She slowly walks up to the wall to inspect it. "I see magic residue," she says, seeming to have snapped out of it as she traces her finger over a blank spot on the wallpaper, just below the last two portraits.

"So there's something there that we can't see?" I hear Nuala giving voice to the question in my head.

I draw in a breath.

"Yes," Moswen replies under her breath. "However, the magic is too strong for you to break it," she says as she turns to look at me.

I feel my heart sink into my stomach, but I protest regardless. "I know I'm shit with my runes, but can I at least try?"

"You want to die?" she says in a tone that actually sounds scared, giving me the chills.

And all of a sudden, after finding a single glimmer of hope, I find myself in the dark again, my shoulders slumping.

"Is there nothing else she can do?" I hear Nuala ask and I turn to give her a weak but grateful smile. "She just wants to know who her parents are."

My head snaps back to Moswen, who's looking at me with such a pained expression, I'm sure she'll say no.

And she doesn't sound pleased, but she gives a quick nod. "I guess there's *one* thing you can try."

"What is it?" I blurt out, hopefulness straining my voice.

She points to a spot left of the door. "What's on this wall right here?" she demands.

"Um, nothing."

She shakes her head. "Incorrect. Look at it and think of the Mirror."

"*The* Mirror?" I ask, confusion pulling my eyebrows down.

Nuala cuts in, frowning at Moswen. "As in... the Snow White Mirror?"

Moswen nods.

"You're joking, right?" I ask, even though she looks dead serious.

"Look," she starts, ignoring my surprise, "your House was always stirring up the pot, which meant a lot of enemies…"

I raise my eyebrows, hungry to learn literally anything about them.

"So sometime in the ninth century, one of the members created a magical mirror to serve as sort of advisor to the Olarel family. One who knows all the family secrets and would never spill them to anyone else. One only an Olarel would see, of course, with the help of Sight."

"Right," I drawl, still skeptical, "so I won't just be having some mirror lie to me that I'm the fairest of them all?"

Nuala lets out a chuckle, but Moswen doesn't think I'm being funny. "No, that fairy tale grossly misinterprets what actually happened. But that doesn't matter right now," she waves at me impatiently. "Turn to the wall and try to see it."

"Alright," I mutter as I do what she tells me.

"Go, Quinn," my friend cheers me on.

And it all feels a bit stupid, but I still close my eyes and try to picture the Mirror, at least my own version of it.

"Quinn?" I hear Moswen say.

I open my eyes and turn to her.

"I'll need you to keep your eyes open for this part."

"Oh, right."

And I do keep them open, but I just end up stupidly staring at the empty wall.

"Can you feel it?" I hear Moswen ask. "What do you see?"

"I don't see anything," I reply, frustration already building in my chest.

"No," she cuts me off, but there's patience in her voice when she continues. "*You* don't, but there *is* no you. There's only the choice to see or not see. Choose the former."

I nod and I ball my hands into fists, determined to make it happen.

Seconds go by.

"And?" Moswen asks. "What do you see?"

"I don't know," I squeeze out, the effort making me feel strangely drained. "Maybe some kind of veil?"

"Alright, that's great."

"Really?" I ask, incredulous.

She lets out a chuckle. "Yes. Now all you need to do is to tear it down."

"Easier said than done," I say with a sigh, straining my eyes as much as I can.

But nothing happens.

Then it hits me. The thought makes me shudder simply because I *know* it's right. I remember the Tree, the one that made me feel like I've spent my entire life blind. And I use that memory to try to erase myself from the equation.

Almost instantly, the world around me turns sort of liquid. And everything seems to be flowing, the way that I somehow knew it was all my life, without ever becoming truly aware of it.

A part of me wants to stop to enjoy the moment. The first time I've ever successfully used Sight. But then the wall before me shimmers and a shape starts appearing, making me draw in my breath.

"It's an actual mirror," I blurt out.

"What did you think it would be?" Moswen asks from behind my back. And by the strange sensation between my shoulder blades, I know she's just tried to push me to take a step forward.

And I do. I stand directly in front of the Mirror and I ask with bated breath, "Who are my parents?"

Nothing happens. I only hear a chuckle from behind my back. I turn to see Nuala trying to suppress it with the back of her hand.

My eyes dart to Moswen, who is dead serious as she shrugs. "You know, the Mirror is a vain creature. You don't have to use any words in particular, but you at least have to address it."

For a second, I remain speechless, only my eyebrows raised. "Seriously?" I ask. Then I turn back to the Mirror and fighting the urge to laugh, I say, "Mirror, Mirror on the wall…"

The Mirror shimmers in response, making me draw in a breath. Quick, Quinn, I tell myself. "Who are my parents?" I spit out breathlessly.

As I wait for the shapes to grow clearer in the Mirror's surface, my heart threatens to jump out of my ribcage.

But it doesn't take long for me to recognize the pattern. It's showing me the missing part of the wallpaper.

And there they are, I think as I let out a shuddering breath. Syllia and Drannor Olarel, Syllia born in 1957 and Drannor 1956, no recorded year of death for either one of them.

"Holy shit," I hear Nuala say, "Quinn, those are your parents."

I feel dizzy. "What is my name?" I ask without looking away from the mirror, my voice filled to the brim with palpable tension.

This time, it shows me a piece of yellowed paper that looks like a birth certificate. It has the word Khuyin written on it. And unlike any of the countless words I've heard in my life, this one makes me want to laugh and cry, all at the same time.

Chapter Thirteen

It's a bleak morning in early November when I rush out of the cafeteria, barely saying bye to surprised Nuala. Taking two steps at a time as I climb the stairs to D7, my lips are curled into a smile.

It's been almost two months since I found out who my parents are. Now, I've spent most of that time trying to learn more.

I've gone back to the Olarel Room, but the Mirror had no more answers for me.

I've dug through both well-known and obscure books, on the House Olarel, on famous faes, on the history of the Originals...

I've never told them why I'm asking, but I've even questioned every professor who teaches anything remotely related or could have personally known them.

So far, it's all trying to convince me that the House Olarel really did go extinct. But I know the truth about the family tree, so it feels like someone tried to literally erase my parents from existence.

So in a way, I've been feeling like I can't exist either. At least not here. I've even tried to find a loophole. I know I'm required by law to be here for the next four years, but I hoped that the faculty could make an exception for me. Not a chance in hell, as it turns out.

But this morning, Nuala and I were talking shit about the professors and she got all weird when I started commenting on Professor Byrne. Telling me to chill because that man helped get her mischievous brothers out of trouble so many times, her family will be in his debt for all eternity.

That made me think. By the way he talked about things, I always thought that Professor Byrne was a newcomer at the Academy, which is exactly why I haven't asked him if he knew my parents.

But that's all about to change because I'm on my way to his class. I might even get in a bit earlier, which would mean I wouldn't have to wait for him to finish the lecture to ask what I'm dying to know.

The door to D7 is open and I can already hear the loud chatter coming from within. It's the biggest classroom because Theory of Magic is something you have to take regardless of your bloodline. Which equals *a lot* of students.

When I walk in, I see that they've all already claimed their spots at the two-seat wooden desks placed in neat rows. They're talking amongst themselves, but it's all a lot more civil than it usually is because the professor, as it turns out, is already in. He's at the pulpit, hastily scribbling something in his papers.

I smile and walk straight up to him. He raises his eyebrows as he looks up at me from his writings. "Morning, Quinn. Can it wait 'till we're done with the class?"

"Of course," I blurt out, trying to hide my disappointment.

I turn around and go for one of the desks to the left of the pulpit. I sit next to a shifter girl whose name I don't know. We nod to each other and I turn to stare at the blackboard when I hear my phone ping.

"Where are you?" the text says. The sender is just a string of numbers.

For a second, I frown. Then it hits me. Faust. I've already received a couple of his texts in our group chat, including the one he sent yesterday about some meeting that they're probably finishing right about now. But I haven't saved his contact. Out of some kind of childish spite, I guess.

But to think that he's gone and sent me a private message... It sends a rush of excitement through my body, making me feel strangely lightheaded.

I force myself to tear my eyes away from the text and lock my phone. I can't think about that right now. I have something important to focus on.

When Professor Byrne finally finishes his scribbling and greets us all, I almost thank him for the interruption. "Today we're going to have another one of our little experiments," he says.

Isn't that just perfect, I bitch to myself. It's been almost three months since I found out I was a fae, but despite all my training sessions with Moswen, I still don't know what I'm doing when it comes to Magic.

"You'll be working in pairs," the professor continues with absolutely no regard for my feelings. "Start by looking in the drawers under your desks."

I throw the girl sitting next to me a glance and we smile at each other. She opens the drawer and pulls out a plain wooden box.

"Come on, open it," the professor's voice booms. "You only have one hour to finish the assignment and you first have to figure out what it is," he finishes with a wink.

As usual, he looks amused as he starts walking between the rows of desks, watching what we're doing.

I turn to my partner, who pauses for a second and then lifts the box lid. Out floats a seemingly metal ball full of little holes. It slowly levitates to our eye level and stops.

Just as I'm about to throw my partner a confused look, a flock of ridiculously tiny birds shoot out of the holes and start circling the ball.

"Maybe we're supposed to get them all back inside?" I whisper.

Before she can answer, the door flings open and I feel the air being knocked out of my lungs. Because I see *him* walk in.

"Ah, Your Majesty, how good of you to join us," the professor cranes his neck, motioning for him to find an empty seat.

He doesn't sound sarcastic at all, despite the fact that the Little Prince is *in* this class, yet has never once graced us with his presence.

So what the fuck is he doing here, I scramble to make sense of it, watching him scan the room as he walks.

Shit, I scold myself when he catches my eye.

To my surprise, he stops for a split second and then stalks straight up to my partner, sending my heart racing. He leans to whisper something in her ear. I don't hear what he says, but he's smiling, one hand casually placed on her backrest. I see her blush and get up, walking away to find another seat. As soon as she's gone, he slides into her seat and then turns to look at me. The smile is gone. He seems to be controlling himself, but it's plain that he's pissed off. And he seems to be waiting for me to speak.

My heart still pumping wildly, I just mouth, "What the fuck?"

"Exactly, what the fuck?" he snaps, keeping his voice low, but not quite enough.

"Now that you all have your assignments in front of you..." I hear the professor start.

I turn to look at him, fighting the shaking of my treacherous limbs, but the prince doesn't let it go. "You going to pretend you didn't get my text?"

"...who can tell me..."

My finger pressed firmly to my lips, I snap my head in his direction to shush him.

"...what the House of Lycan crest has to do with the theory about types of Magic?"

But now I can feel him staring at me, trying to get me to look at him. With rushed, angry movements, I open my notebook and I write, "I'm NOT talking to you right now. In case you haven't noticed, we're in the middle of a class."

My eyes are back on the professor, but I can tell he's read it. He scoffs and leans back on his chair, folding his arms in protest. I don't react. I try to pay attention to the exchange between Professor Byrne and the other students, but he's making me so self-conscious, tapping his fancy shoes on the floor and thrumming his stupid fingers on the desk. I have to fight the urge to shift in my seat, smooth out my hair, lick my lips.

For a moment, I manage to focus on the words of the nerdy fae-blooded girl, probably about the third person trying to answer the professor's question.

"The light side of the Moon on the crest signifies the spirit and the dark side signifies the body. Some say that this is one of the earliest understandings of the existence of Physical and Mental Magic."

She goes on to talk about the uniqueness of the House of Lycan, at least from the perspective of shifters being the only ones that truly embody more than one type of Magic. And if things were different, I'd be gobbling that shit up.

But I've never been this close to him, at least not longer than three seconds. And I'm feeling just as breathless as the second he walked in. It's just that, now, I can add to that a growing ache in my thighs and between my legs, urging me to keep glancing at him. I fight it, keeping my gaze fixed ahead. But even with the corner of my eye, I can see his chest falling up and down, the muscles putting a strain on the immaculately white shirt. And whenever I look down, there are his hands, the long fingers fighting for my attention by doing that pissed-off thrumming thing with deliciously deft movements.

Snap the fuck out, I tell myself. This is a royal *asshole* you're drooling over. And just as I think that, the fae-blooded girl stops talking and Professor Byrne takes over.

"Thank you for that lovely summary, Aywin," he says. "Now, the point of all this, including the assignment, is to make you more aware of the thin lines between Physical and Mental Magic," he continues as he takes a stroll between the rows of desks. "The birds you see before you are just echoes of actual birds, but real enough for you to be able to control them as either mind or matter. And the assignment," he stops walking, pausing for effect as he so often does, "is to make them all return to their little nests at the same time, using whichever methods you have at your disposal."

The professor pauses again, throws us all a smile and says, "Go."

Almost instantly, the students around me break into a chatter as they get to work. Everyone except the two of us. I just focus on the assignment before me. I squint at the birds, hard, trying to make myself do the only thing I can. Use Sight.

Of course, he doesn't let me. He leans in and demands, "Ready to talk?"

I don't turn to look at him. I pretend I'm engrossed in what I'm doing as I say, "No. But if it'll help me get rid of you..."

"Oh spare me," he scoffs. "What was so important you had to miss the *mandatory* Trials meeting?"

I let out a deep sigh and decide I'm not letting him distract me. I turn back to the birds and I manage to invoke Sight. The scene before me turns liquid and I can see the little strings tying the birds to the ball.

With the corner of my eye, I see him snap his fingers at me.

I throw him an annoyed glance. "The text said it was a Favorday party etiquette meeting." I let my hand dart to my runes, checking if maybe I've unlocked one of them. "How was I supposed to know it was mandatory?"

"Is Favorday part of the Trials?" he demands.

"It is," I begrudgingly admit. "But I mean, really," I rush to protest, "in what parallel universe would I need to know whether to bow in front of the Archduke?"

"The parallel universe called tonight's Favorday party," he snaps at me. "In case you didn't know, sometimes parents decide to come to this event and some of those parents are really high up on the ladder. But I guess you simply don't care whether you embarrass us all."

I can't stand it anymore. The arrogance. I turn to throw daggers at him. "Not true. I just don't care whether I embarrass *you*."

He gets in my face. "Well, I don't give a fuck," he snarls. His knee is pressing into mine and sending a shock through my body, making me move to pull away. He doesn't let me. He grabs my wrist and makes me face him. "You *will* behave."

For a second, I just stare at him. "Fuck. You," I say as I break free.

I turn my eyes back onto the birds, but I can tell he's throwing daggers at me. *I'm not letting him distract me,* I repeat to myself.

I ball my hands into fists and try again. But now I'm so pissed, I can't even use Sight, let alone do anything else.

I hear him let out a bitter scoff and get up, the chair scraping against the weathered hardwood floor. I force myself not to look up as he walks away.

But then I hear Professor Byrne say, "Your Majesty, you haven't finished the assignment."

I hear said Majesty walk back to my desk and stop right in front of me. When I look at him, his eyes are already fixed on the birds.

Without so much as a frown scrunching up his face, he almost instantly makes them all stop flying. The very next second, they all get sucked into the ball. I draw in a breath, watching the light coming from the ball flicker and go out.

"There," he snaps as he turns to the professor. "It's finished."

Then, without so much as throwing me a glance, he leaves the classroom so quickly, it's like I watch him get sucked out.

After he's gone, I spend the rest of the class waiting for it to end, fuming.

As soon as the bell rings, I elbow my way through all the students leaving the classroom to catch the professor before he's finished packing up for the day. "Professor Byrne…"

He looks up and says, "Yes, Miss Longborn," in a voice that's warm but a little absentminded.

"I just have one question for you," I start with bated breath, trying to catch his eye as he goes back to shoving papers into his overflowing attaché. I catch a nod instead. "Do the names Syllia and Drannor Olarel mean anything to you?"

This gets his attention. "Olarel?" he frowns as he stops packing and straightens up, scratching his neck. "Sure, there was a Syllia Olarel who is now best known for her dabbling in Divine Magic."

"Yes," I rush to say, "but she lived in the sixteenth century. How about fifty years ago?"

The professor shakes his head. "There were no members by the name of Syllia after the sixteenth century. Or Drannor for that matter."

"No?" I ask hesitantly. But he must have known them. They had to have gone to this Academy and he teaches a mandatory class, which meant that he must have been their professor at some point. I choose to push a bit more. "They would have been students here in the late 1970s."

"No, I'm sorry," the professor just says, shaking his head with a sorry look in his eyes. "If it were any other family name, I would have told you I couldn't be sure. But the Olarels were a famous house. It wouldn't have been possible for me not to know or simply to forget."

My logic exactly, I think to myself. I nod and I say thank you, choosing not to push it any further. By the time I barge out of the classroom, Nuala is already waiting for me.

"I'm sorry, but I have to go to the Archives," I tell the friend I was supposed to go to the next class with. "You don't have to come with me," I finish with my lips pressed tight.

And I head straight for the stairs, Nuala rushing to catch up with me. "But what else is there to go through? We've scoured all the books that could have *anything* to do with your parents."

I stop walking and turn to face her. "No, not my parents," I say with determination in my voice. "Professor Byrne."

She stays silent for a moment, watching me with eyes full of surprise. Finally she says, "What? Why?"

"Because he's telling me he doesn't know who they are and I don't believe him. I think they're all hiding something from me."

"Seriously?" she blurts out, but I'm too focused on my next step to want to discuss it.

So I just give her shoulder a quick squeeze and I leave her there. I'm already stomping down the hallway leading towards the Library when I hear her yell, "Just don't forget the Favorday party is tonight."

"Can't fucking wait," I snap back.

When I get to the Archives, I'm no less miserable. The last billion times I was here, I was focused solely on the House Olarel and its members. Right now, I choose to find records of all the professors who've ever taught here. It's practically the only thing I know about Professor Byrne, but it's as good a place to start as any.

I walk down an aisle dedicated to records of births, deaths, marriages et cetera. All the most boring stuff you could ever imagine. And at the end of the row, I finally see a shelf labeled 'Grimm Academy Professors'.

Bingo, I think to myself as my eyes dart over the individual books, stopping on one titled *Grimm Academy Professors 1900-1999*.

Who knows how old Professor Byrne really is, but he should be mentioned here for sure. I pull the book out, struggling to release it from the grip of the ones surrounding it. And I crack it open, planning to start my search with the year 1900. But the book opens on 1983, where a single word has me frozen in place.

Olarel.

My mind racing, I read the first name. Drannor. And right below his name, another Olarel. Syllia.

I don't move a muscle, but my heart is beating wildly.

Chapter Fourteen

My mind is still buzzing, but more importantly, I'm *pissed*. I'm in Nuala's room in the House of Lycan and the Favorday party is in half an hour, so we're multitasking. She's trying on outfits while I'm recounting my newest findings.

"Professors, Nuala," I tell her. "My parents were professors here."

"What the fuck?" Nuala asks, stopping to throw me a confused look. "But that's good, isn't it?"

"It's both good and bad," I reply, fighting to keep myself from snapping. "It's information I didn't have yesterday, but it also makes the whole thing more complicated. More sinister. I mean, I've asked all the professors who were here back then. *All* of them. And they all said they've no idea who I'm talking about."

Nuala turns around to get a comment on her latest choice. A simple sleeveless green dress.

I give her a low whistle, smiling weakly as I say, "I think we have a winner."

"You think?" she asks, a shy smile forming on her lips.

I nod vigorously, but I'm intrigued. I myself have thrown on a simple black dress, just to avoid repeating what turned out to be such a horrid disrespect from last time. But Nuala is really putting in effort. Who is she so eager to impress, I wonder.

She takes a seat next to me and puts her hand on mine. "I know it's all weird and frustrating as hell, but we have all the time in the world to learn what the fuck is going on."

I give her a grateful smile and choose to snap out of it. I'm not looking forward to the party myself, but my only friend in this godforsaken place clearly is.

So I jump up off the bed and I clap my hands. "You're right, my dear Fionnuala. Now is the time to show those people what having fun actually looks like."

Laughing and chatting, we soon barge into the Main Hall, where the party has already started. There's a bar, a little fountain in the center, a corner with parlor games... But it's the people that draw the eye. They're all dressed even more lavishly than they were for the Showing. Me? I'm perfectly happy not standing out.

I grab Nuala and myself two pitchers of beer and we find a good spot in the center of the room, at one of the few high tables that aren't already taken. I scan the Hall, recognizing only a couple of the twenty four Chosen. A certain someone isn't here yet, or so it would seem. I down almost half of my beer, just thinking about *him* showing up at some point making me break out in cold sweat. I tug on the hem of my dress, sure that as soon as he lays his eyes on me, he'll find *something* to complain about.

"Look," Nuala jabs me with her elbow. "Sarya has been asked out by someone from my House."

"How can you tell?" I ask, squinting to take a better look at her.

"See the corsage on her wrist? That's moon vine."

"Ah," I just say, glancing around the room again. Most of the Chosen have either a corsage around their wrists or a boutonniere on their lapels. "So there's only a few that are still available."

"Including yourself," Nuala whispers. "But not for long, it seems," she adds with a chuckle as she motions at Leo staring at me intently from his table, looking handsome as hell even with the ridiculous sideburns.

I wave my hand in dismissal. "Nah, he's saving himself for Prince Charming. You've seen how they flirt with each other, I'm sure."

Nuala lets out a shy chuckle. "Even if the prince were into guys, which he's not, he wouldn't be into Leo. His type is thin, blonde, sophisticated."

"Really?" I squeeze out, my eye immediately darting to the bunch of blonde girls I saw sullenly standing near the entrance. "I see you're not the only one who knows that."

"It *is*... known, I guess," I hear her say.

For a second, I keep staring at all the blondes, natural or not, waiting for their Little Prince to show up. I don't like what I feel so I make myself snap out of it and turn back to Nuala. "And who are you hoping to ask to the Ball yourself, young lady?"

She just shakes her head and looks at the empty pitcher of beer in my hand, saying, "I didn't know you could drink so fast."

"There's a lot you don't know about me, dear Fionnuala," I reply with a grin.

It's at that exact moment that I notice a shift in the atmosphere, people's heads snapping to the entrance. I crane my neck and see *him* walk in, the blondes coming to life as they start fluttering behind him.

I can't help myself. I try not to be obvious, but I watch him walk across the smooth polished floor, dressed in a perfectly tailored casual suit. For a second, I think he'll march up to me to give my outfit an inspection or something, and my heart breaks into a gallop.

But he chooses to ignore me. He walks past without so much as a glance, joining a group of people at the other end of the hall.

I turn to keep chatting with Nuala, but she soon becomes too fidgety to lead an actual conversation. At one point, she declares that she has some business to take care of. I know she's going to ask her secret sweetheart to the Ball and she apparently doesn't want to talk about it. So I let her go without prying.

Once she's out of sight, I fight not to look, but I fail, miserably. Faust is still standing in the same group of people, but now he's surrounded by a whole host of gorgeous girls, not just the blondes. And my curiosity is getting the better of me. As I sip what's left of Nuala's beer, I find myself glancing at them, trying to figure out if there really is truth to what my friend said a minute ago, about his type of woman.

Not five minutes later, Leo walks up to me with a smirk on his face. "Well, hello," he drawls, eyeing me up and down. Now that I see him up close, there's something a bit creepy about him.

"Hello," I reply, fighting not to let my reaction show.

"You know," he says, "I never got the chance to thank you for rushing to my defense at the opening ceremony."

And his voice is sweet and what he's saying is really nice, but that look in his eyes makes me want to just... get away from him. But it's too tempting, this opportunity to dig a little deeper.

"Don't worry about it," I say flatly. "I mean, as far as I could tell, the prince was being a giant asshole."

There's a flash of surprise in his eyes. "So you don't fancy him?"

I scoff. "No." Squinting at him, I say, "But I did get the impression that the two of you have history."

He lets out a chuckle. "Our families do." He pauses before he says, "You see, it was *my* House, House Aalders, that was supposed to be on the throne."

"But then his family," I cut in, "*intervened.*"

"Exactly. But enough talking about the *prince*," he says as he takes a black rose corsage out of his pocket and holds it out for me. "Let's talk about the Winter Solstice Ball."

He wants to take me to the Ball?

"Um", I start, but all of a sudden, I have a strong feeling that I'm being watched.

I glance around nervously.

"Well?" Leo insists, licking his lips as he gives me a smile.

Now, I definitely don't want to go to the Ball alone, but I just don't like the guy's vibe and there's no helping it. "You know, I think I'll have to pass."

He looks honestly surprised and, well, not pleased, at least judging by the way the smile just slides off his face. But I don't give him a chance to react.

I turn on my heel and I go take a stroll around the hall, beginning from the end farthest from Faust and his groupies.

I don't get very far before I notice Nuala, leaning against the window closest to the entrance, looking down at her hands as she fidgets with her rings.

When I walk up to her and ask what's going on, fearing the secret sweetheart has said no, she won't say anything, but she doesn't look happy.

Goddamnit, this night. "You know what, Nuala?" I say as I take a few steps to the side, stopping a waiter to grab two shot glasses off his tray. "I think a combination of shots and darts is in order."

I make her throw back the shot with me. And then I take her by the upper arm and I drag her over to the corner with parlor games.

"Is this regular darts?" I ask without waiting for an answer. I just grab a dart and take my position. It makes me warm around the heart when I see her mouth crack into a smile.

It doesn't take us long to forget about the world around us. I make the bartender keep bringing us drinks as we laugh our heads off trying to play darts while drunk as skunks.

At one point, Nuala jabs me with her elbow and says, "There's a lot of eyes on us."

"Of course there are," I reply. "They're all being stiff and I'll bet more than half are uncomfortable in what they're wearing, while we're here actually having fun."

And I honestly don't care, but curiosity still overtakes me. As I glance around the room, I see a lot of the girls shooting us nasty looks. And just as many guys staring at me as if I were a glass of ice-cold water someone left in the middle of a desert.

One of them, a hot shifter, catches my eye and doesn't hesitate. He immediately starts walking up to us.

"I saw you staring at me," he says with a smile. "And I decided to do you a favor and introduce myself."

This makes me laugh. Mostly because I'm drunk, but still.

With a smile followed by a wink, Nuala subtly excuses herself and I let the shifter by the name of Cormac chat me up. And he seems nice and it definitely doesn't hurt that he's ridiculously hot, but my eyes still keep darting to where Faust is, surrounded by his admirers. At one point, I see him with some vampire girl. Just the two of them.

And yes, she's thin, blonde and sophisticated. He leans to whisper something in her ear and all of a sudden, I feel like I'm burning up.

"Anything I can do to make you look at *me* like that?" I hear Cormac say.

I snap my head back, frowning. "You want me to look at you with contempt?"

He laughs and takes a step closer. I'm a bit disappointed that the look in his eyes has no edge to it, but I still let him lean in to whisper, "To start, I'd settle for you letting me take you to the Ball."

While he's still saying it, I feel it again. The eyes on me. I nervously look around and I catch a glimpse of Leo disappearing into the crowd.

The feeling lingers, but I tell myself to ignore it. I shift my focus onto Cormac and I say, "Yes. I'd love to go to the Ball with you."

"What about now? Want to go somewhere with me now?" he whispers in my ear again.

I already open my mouth to say I'm with my friend, but then I see Faust walking down the hall, the blonde vampire girl on his arm and a black rose boutonniere on his lapel. Once again, he doesn't even glance at me.

So he's actually picked her as his date for the Ball.

As soon as they're out of the Main Hall, I turn back to Cormac and I nod.

He smiles, reaches into his pocket and puts a moon vine corsage around my wrist. "Just so everyone knows you're taken."

I give him a smile, I text Nuala and I let my date lead me out of the Main Hall and into one of the hallways with locked classrooms on both sides.

As soon as we walk around the corner and find ourselves alone, he grabs me by the waist and makes me turn to look at him.

I smile and he smiles too, but just as he starts leaning in for a kiss, his body tenses up and his face takes on a pained expression.

I freeze, opening my mouth to ask what's wrong, but he just lets me go, grabs my hand and pulls the corsage off my wrist.

Frowning, I watch him pull away, throw the corsage on the floor and almost yell out, "No," that pained expression still twisting his face.

Then he turns on his heel and starts *literally* running away from me.

I just remain standing there for a while, wondering if I've just witnessed someone using Mind Magic on my date for the Ball.

Nah, I finally tell myself. It must be all the beer and the shots messing with my head. But wow. The night could hardly have gone better than *that*.

Of course, at that moment, I don't realize it's not over yet. It takes me a while because Cormac and I have wandered off far from the House of Ydril, but when I get to my floor, I find something waiting for me in front of the door. A gorgeous box of chocolates with a little white envelope attached to it.

Frowning, I pick it up. For some reason, my heart is once again throbbing. I tear the envelope and inside, I find evidence that it might not have been all the alcohol after all.

A note written in elegant albeit forceful cursive.

"He would have bored you and you know it."

Chapter Fifteen

"Can't we take a break?" I plead with Moswen as she stands to my side in the graveyard, watching me pant with my palms on my thighs.

"The First Round is in less than two months," she says as she circles me, "and I know it's hard to fit a lifetime of learning to use magic in a couple of weeks, but you're barely making any progress." She stops to throw me a look that's at the same time nervous and urging. "We really need to at least get you to unlock your first rune."

I let out a deep sigh and turn back to the target in front of me. The graveyard is where we come to train because Moswen doesn't want to be seen. For fear of dark forces being at play here, I guess. But I can't say I mind. The Grimm Academy's final resting place has the benefit of total privacy, the unbelievably high hedges secluding it from the rest of the castle grounds. And it's more beautiful than any I've ever seen, with crumbling mausoleums and overrun graves creating a sort of vine- and moss-covered maze wherever you look.

"Hey," I hear Moswen scold me. "If you think I'm going to watch you just stand there like a mute…"

"Alright, no need to get your panties in a bunch," I mutter as I turn back to the statue in front of me. It's a statue of some powerful fae, at least judging by the fact he has five instead of just three runes around his neck.

But we picked this particular statue because of its tall pedestal. It allows me to place all the four Elements at eye level. A bowl of water, a rock, a lit candle and a bottle containing only air.

I muster all my determination, I activate my Sight and I try to connect with them, any of them. At least that's what Moswen says should be my first step. The First rune is always the Element rune, but just like the rest of them, it doesn't unlock until I *make* it unlock.

I stare at them like I've never stared at anything in my life, but nothing happens.

"You say I should be feeling a sort of connection with one of them."

"Yes," she cuts in. "Most faes only ever learn to manipulate one."

"But I don't see *any* difference between them."

"Don't look at the physical things," Moswen urges me, "try to get to their essence."

I take a deep breath and I try again. I try for another half hour, but it simply doesn't work. Finally, I throw my arms up and I sit with a loud thump.

"Moswen," I start, my voice deflated, "thanks for this, but I think I'd rather we try again tomorrow."

"You won't be doing yourself any favors."

"And I *will* by continuing to fail like this?" I snap at her, albeit weakly.

For a second, she just looks at me funny. Then she scoffs and rolls her eyes. "In the name of the Holy Word, quit your moaning already. You're an Olarel, which means there's power in you. You should be embracing, not resisting it."

I look up to throw daggers at her. "Sure, I'm the descendant of some fancy family, but that only makes it worse."

"Enlighten me, please," Moswen says with a quirk of her brow.

I shake my head as I look away. "I barely know anything about my parents. Even the Mirror only knows their names. But they were Olarels and they were professors here. So they must have been a couple of badasses."

And I feel stupid for feeling that way, but it just makes me doubt myself even more, at least when it comes to using my runes.

"Look," Moswen says, gliding to my side and talking in a softer voice. "I also had parents who were intimidating. So I get it. But ultimately, it's not your parents holding you back. It's just you."

I nod, lowering my head to stare at the ground.

It's only then that the thought crosses my mind, making my eyebrows pull down. "Wait," I say, looking up at her again. "When did you go to school here?"

"Why does that matter?" she asks, a frown forming on her forehead.

"My parents were professors here from 1983 to 2005. And I don't know when exactly it was that you, well..." I pause, feeling awkward about mentioning her death.

"Died," she says, in that flat voice that makes me want to kiss her and slap her at the very same time. "I can't be sure when *that* happened, but yes." She pauses before she adds, "I *was* a student here at that time."

"And?" I ask, my eyes threatening to pop out of their sockets.

"I don't remember being in any of their classes, if that's what you're asking."

"But they were the Olarel teaching duo," I insist. "You must have known about them."

"It doesn't work that way," she cuts me off.

"*What* doesn't work that way?"

She lets out a sigh, lowering herself on the ground in front of me. "I *am* Moswen, but not... all of her, I guess. The magic that keeps me tied to my diary only allows me to remember things that I've written down."

I nod, feeling stupid for even thinking it would be that simple.

"Therefore," she continues, "even if I knew them personally, but never mentioned them in any of my entries, I'd have no way of remembering it."

"Goddamn it..." I say with a sigh.

Deciding to get back to work, I get up off the floor and fix my eyes on the Element stuff again. I'm a fae, I try to tell myself. I should be able to do this, however ridiculous it still sounded to me. And however scary I found the whole thing.

Seconds go by without anything happening. I try to imagine myself doing magic. Would I be taking control of the flow of water, using air barriers to keep enemies out, conjuring fire with my hands or getting rocks to explode?

I'm deep in my visualization when I hear Moswen let out a gasp.

My head snaps in her direction and I see her staring at a hole in the hedge around the graveyard, her ears pricked up. "Did you hear that?"

"What?" I say, but she doesn't wait for me to catch up with her. She just glides away to take a peek through the hedges.

When she returns, she whispers, "Someone just saw me. A vampire."

"Did he have sideburns?" I ask, thinking of Leo and how he used fucking mind magic on Cormac just to stop me from getting a date for the Ball.

She nods.

"I know him," I say, balling my hands into fists. "He's this guy who wanted to be my date for the Ball." I don't mention the other thing. I've never told Moswen about it and I'm not planning on adding to her troubles.

"Quinn," Moswen says, pointing at the statue.

I turn around and see the rock vibrating a little. Now when I look at it, I not only see *into* it, I *feel* it. Its stable, age-old energy.

The rock vibrates a little more, moves to the edge of the pedestal and falls to the ground.

I draw in a breath, my eyes darting to the runes around my neck. One of them now has a carving of a cross with a circle at each end.

"The Element rune," I whisper, but my voice is full of nervous excitement.

"That's great," Moswen replies with an anxious smile. "And your Element seems to be Earth. But I think we better go celebrate somewhere else."

"What about my training?" I throw her a smirk. "Isn't that like the *highest priority ever*?"

"Well, excuse me for not wanting to stay chained to either my diary or you *for the rest of eternity*."

"Yeah yeah," I drawl mockingly as I pick the diary up off the ground and get ready to close it. "You better cool that enthusiasm or I'll think you're falling for me."

My eyebrows shoot up when I see that I've almost made her laugh. It feels good, I have to say. The perfect moment to close the diary shut and see her disappear.

When I walk out of the graveyard, it's still early enough to see the faint outline of the mountains in the distance, far behind the three towers shooting into the sky before me. I smile, knowing that Nuala will probably already be waiting for me in the cafeteria. And I know exactly what I'll have for dessert, the cheesecake being one of the few things in this place that I always find myself looking forward to.

All that almost makes me miss it. This weird, violently negative energy and the stench unlike any I've ever experienced. I don't know what overcomes me, but I find myself sniffing the air like crazy, trying to figure out where it's coming from.

The smell takes me down a gravel path leading from the cemetery and straight into a little grove. I walk inside and see a moss-covered bust on a pedestal.

Almost instantly, my heart starts pounding and without thinking, I take a step back.

But it's not the bust that has that effect on me. It's what I see splayed out on its crumbling pedestal.

Hearts. A blood-curdling, mushy pile of cut-out hearts. I shake my head, not even daring to think which species they belong to. But it's over. I've already pictured a pile of dead people with all of their hearts missing.

Panicked, I take the diary out of my bag and open it right then and there, despite Moswen telling me never to do it anywhere other than my room and the graveyard.

She immediately materializes next to me and I can see her opening her mouth to scold me, but I just motion to the bottom of the bust.

I guess a part of me wishes for her to use that flat voice of hers and ask me what it is that I'm so shocked by. But Moswen just stares at the hearts, the uneasiness clearly visible in hers.

"Is it just me," I start, my voice low and strained, "or is this... not good?"

"No, you're right," she says as she points at something I haven't even noticed. Drawings that have been almost completely covered by the blood. "This is dark magic. Dangerous magic."

"What is it..." I mean to say 'supposed to do', but I don't. I don't scare easily, but this keeps sending shivers down my spine.

"It's dangerous," she says, "that's what it is."

"I'm going to report it," I reply, already turning to walk as far away from the place as possible.

"Don't," she blurts out.

What? I stop midstep and squint, looking straight into her eyes.

"I think," she starts, obviously hesitating, "it could have something to do with your parents."

The shock almost makes me topple over. "What?" is all I manage to squeeze out.

"I'll explain," she replies, "but first get me somewhere safe."

I don't even say anything. I just close the diary and put it back in my bag.

I'm already out of the grove when I see Faust Senior walking out of the graveyard. His eyes are already on me, his eyebrows pulled down.

He appears in front of me, immediately making me panic. "Young lady," he starts, "you know that this part of the castle grounds is currently restricted."

"I'm so sorry, I had no idea," I squeeze out, realizing he's not talking about the... *thing* that I just saw.

But he's still squinting at me. "I thought I heard you talking to someone," he says, gesturing at the grove behind me.

Fuck. Fuck. Fuck. "No, there's no one there," I reply, choosing the present tense to avoid lying to his face.

"Good," he says, his eyes softening. "Now don't get me wrong. I'm not a stickler for rules for no reason." He pauses, throwing me a look filled with concern. "Especially with someone such as yourself."

At least my heart's stopped pounding in my chest, but now I raise my eyebrows at him.

"You're new in our world," he explains, throwing me a kind smile. "You still have no idea how much its balance depends on making sure you don't overstep any lines."

If I could do it without seeming suspicious, I'd breathe a sigh of relief. Instead, I give him a weak laugh and say, "Thank you, Your Majesty, that's solid advice right there."

I don't know what's made him amused, but he lets out a chuckle before he gives me a quick nod and turns on his heel, heading straight for the castle.

It takes all I have not to break into a sprint right then and there, especially with what Moswen told me stuck on repeat in my head. But I don't want to walk with him, so I force myself to slow down.

Luckily, despite the injury that's forcing him to use a walking stick, the old man is quite fast and within fifteen minutes, I'm back in my room. As soon as I'm there, I bolt the door and grab the diary.

"What is it that you wanted to explain?" I ask her with bated breath.

"Not explain per se," she says hesitantly.

"You're playing a dangerous game, Moswen," I reply, only half-jokingly. Because it's my very fraught nerves that she's toying with.

"I can show you," she says as she walks up to me, motioning at the diary in my hands.

"Show?"

I barely manage to say it before she places a hand on my forehead and I feel a violent jerk as I get sucked away someplace else.

It takes me a second to open my eyes, which I've instinctively shut tight at the first sign of something happening. When I open them, my room has been replaced by one of the common rooms somewhere in the East Wing of the castle. I recognize it by the Oriental interior design that can't be found anywhere else.

And there's lots of people there and everything seems okay, but there's a strange warm glow to everything that I see.

I don't see her, but I hear Moswen's voice. "You're in one of my memories," she says and somehow makes me look at one of the far corners of the room. "Pay attention or you'll miss it."

I listen, focusing all my attention on the two people, a man and a woman, sitting at a desk with a bunch of papers strewn all over it. They're both tall, beautiful fae-blooded people dressed in ornate robes. And they seem to be deep in discussion. I try to move closer, but as soon as I do, I hear Moswen say, "It doesn't work that way. You're in my body now, the echo of it at least."

And she seems to be right, because when I finally move, it's not of my own accord. I walk around the pair, in the widest possible circle, and use a free-standing bookshelf right behind their table as my cover. Because I apparently want to get close without getting noticed.

I pull a book out and crack it open, but I don't look at its contents. Instead, my eyes fix on the couple. Interesting, I think to myself.

And there's something about those people, but I don't even dare to think that they are my parents. It's only when I hear the man say, "I think it's a Blood Moon ritual," that I *know*.

"I don't know," the woman hesitates, shaking her head as she looks up, her eyes sweeping her surroundings. "That would mean..."

She breaks off, but our eyes have already met. Moswen's and hers, I mean. And for a second, I think she'll say something to her, but before I know it, I'm being sucked back into my room.

"And you said you had no memory of my parents," I say as soon as I find myself in front of Moswen once again. I'm not even trying to hide the suspicion and the anger in my voice.

She avoids my eye. "True," she mutters, only throwing me a single nervous glance. "I guess I didn't want you to see me like that. Sneaking around and eavesdropping on people to learn more about dark magic." She pauses, this time looking me straight in the eye. "Because make no mistake, the Blood Moon ritual is exactly that."

The way she says it makes the suspicion and the anger brewing inside me dissipate. But now my heart is pounding. Because it's finally dawned on me that my parents may have been involved in some shady business.

Chapter Sixteen

"They're everywhere," I mutter to Nuala as I rip off the flier that someone's taped to the inside of the Elevator.

"Of course they are," she says with a tentative smile, her words immediately followed by the opening of the door. "I don't know if you've heard, but the First Round is *tomorrow*."

As she follows me out of the Elevator, I turn to give her a smile. I'm so grateful to her for even trying to cheer me up, but the truth is, I'm scared shitless and there's nothing that can change that.

So I just keep walking, the two of us heading straight for the graveyard. The end of December is nearing and the treetops are bare, no birds singing from their branches. Moswen is insisting we do some training every day, preferably first thing in the morning.

And that's what we'll be doing as soon as we get there. But not three seconds go by that I don't subtly crane my neck to see if Leo is somewhere behind me.

"You do understand," Nuala starts as she side-eyes me, "that if he really was following you, you wouldn't know that he was doing it."

I quirk my eyebrow at her. "Nuala, Moswen told me Leo *saw* her."

"That was over a month ago and you haven't seen him at the graveyard since."

I let out a low groan. "*You* may not remember him putting Cormac under his spell..." I pause to throw her a look. "And just because I said I wouldn't go to the Ball with him... But *I* sure as hell remember."

"You can't be positive that that was him," Nuala insists.

"Sure, I can't," I say as I throw my hands up in the air, feeling helpless for being stuck in the same conversation for the millionth time. "But is this really the time not to keep all options in mind? I mean, there are so many loose ends. We still can't figure out why Moswen is even here, there's a chance that my parents were involved in something potentially dangerous and I think that something potentially dangerous is happening again."

Nuala stops for a second, making me almost topple over. She pats me on the shoulder, the look in her eyes warm and comforting.

I let out a bitter laugh and I lower my head, my eyes darting to the flier I'm gripping in my hand. The image on it sends shivers down my spine every time I see it. It's not because it's necessarily so gruesome. It just shows three people, one from each bloodline, fighting each other with deadly looks on their faces. But I don't feel any more prepared for something like that than I was a month ago. There's a chance I'll actually die, I think to myself.

"Sorry, Nuala, I'm just under a lot of stress," I finally say.

When I look up, she's looking at me as if she'd like me to vent some more, but I decide I've already had more of that shit than the situation allows.

"Would you look at those gloomy skies?" I say, choosing to pat her on the shoulder and change the subject until we arrive at our own private training ground. "It could start raining any minute now."

"Alright, let's get going then."

As soon as we get there, I pull the diary out of my bag. When I open it, Moswen appears in front of us, looking rested as usual. I know she's not even an actual person, so I shouldn't be jealous of her. But ever since she showed me her memory, my dreams have been plagued by nightmares involving my mother's eyes. So yes, I'm jealous of her.

But Moswen is looking at me with visible tension in her eyes. She's given us a quick nod and now she's getting straight to the point. Just like she's been doing lately. "Today we're going to be working on your control. You're still quite terrible at that, if I may say so."

"Even if I told you you may not, you still would," I reply, making a lame attempt at a joke.

She presses her lips tight and quirks an eyebrow at me. "I'm sorry," she drawls, "would you mind refreshing my memory? When exactly is the First Round."

"Tomorrow," I squeeze out as I pull a face at her.

"Well then? What are you waiting for?" she asks, her arms folded and the look on her face scolding.

She's acting as if I'm a child, which instantly makes my blood start pumping. Moswen and I, we haven't known each other long. But she already understands me enough to appreciate exactly how determined sheer spite can make me.

I shake my head and I work on getting into the Meditative stance. I plant my feet firmly on the ground, leaving a bit of space between them. I lower my hands to my sides and I pull my head a bit downward, so I'm looking at the straw target in front of me from an angle. I have rocks laid out before me and my goal is to use them to hit the center of the target.

As Nuala takes her usual seat on one of the moss-covered graves and Moswen stands just a bit closer to where I am, I already start feeling the effects of the pose. It's used specifically to prepare the body for channeling the flow so you're more at one with your environment.

"Moswen," I ask, making sure not to break the stance, "shouldn't I be more concerned about speed than control?"

I can't see her, but I know she's smirking. "You're actually wondering?"

"Yeah," I drawl, my lips curling into a mocking smile. "Like, for when I'm actually fighting."

"*Like*, I understand you." Moswen has gotten into the habit of mocking my 'likes', despite the fact that they rarely even occur. "But haven't I taught you anything?"

"Have *you* seen Sarya using her runes? How fast she is? I highly doubt that any of my opponents at the Trials will do me the favor of waiting around while I get into the right stance. That's all I'm saying."

"So you'd tell a child still learning to walk to *concern* themselves more with speed than control?"

I let out a sigh. "Fine. Point taken," I say as I focus on the target before me and try to feel the rock before my feet already taking flight.

And I do manage to lift it off the ground and propel it through the air. I even manage to slam it straight into the target. But it's way off center.

"God damn it," I snap at myself.

"It's okay," I hear Moswen say. "You're doing it."

I just wave at the target. "That thing is huge. If I was aiming at an actual someone, the rock would end up missing them by a whole other person."

"Maybe you're focusing on the wrong thing," Nuala says. "That's what my mother used to say."

I throw Nuala a grateful smile, but I turn to Moswen for her input.

"Try it the other way," she says.

And I do. I get into a different stance, the Lion this time, and I try to make the rock into an extension of myself. I repeat to myself that the point is to be forceful, to invoke the active energies of the universe.

This time, I don't even hit the target.

"Go back to Meditative," Moswen says with determination in her voice.

I want to groan, but I don't. Instead, I focus on following her orders. But something's still off. It just doesn't feel right, I keep thinking as I prepare to give it another shot.

So I decide to go in another direction. And I choose to keep my mouth shut because I don't want Moswen to laugh in my face because of how stupid my idea is.

Luckily, what I have in mind doesn't require me to take a different stance. I just keep a different kind of image in mind and tap my Element rune.

And I shut my eyes tight, for some reason that I honestly can't explain.

When I open them, I see the rock lift off the ground and fly straight into the center of the target.

And at first, there's silence. Then a quiet, "Wow," coming from Nuala's mouth.

I turn to grin at my companions. To my surprise, Moswen is smiling as she glides closer to me. She looks visibly relieved. "You see, I told you you just needed to keep at it. Earth can be a stubborn element, but once you understand it..."

"Oh, I didn't use Earth. I find it so rigid." I pause, scratching my head as if I was caught doing something wrong. "And Air is so much softer."

Nuala gives a low whistle, but Moswen is just staring at me.

"Let me be clear," she says, her eyes narrowing. "To manipulate the rock, you used the air around it?"

I nod.

To my surprise, Moswen lets out a chuckle. Quiet, perfectly controlled and a little sad, but still. "I'm sorry, Quinn. It's just, you haven't even mastered your first Element and now it turns out you can use a second one. It's a bit unusual, I have to say."

"Well," I start, letting out a chuckle as well. It's just that mine is a bit embarrassed. "Do you think it increases my chances of surviving the First Round?"

She nods, smiling happily.

"My dear Moswen and my darling Fionnuala," I say as I pat Nuala roughly on the shoulder and send a gentle air pat in Moswen's direction, "that's all that fucking matters."

Of course, that's not the end of this day's torture. I don't have any classes on Mondays so I keep training until my muscles start threatening to give out. But I'm happy. And I hadn't even realized it until that moment, but I've been living in constant dread of getting killed at the Trials. Of course, this doesn't mean I won't be. But my chances are a lot better today than they were yesterday.

So when I finally pack Moswen up and we leave the graveyard, I'm on top of the world. I don't even mind it when Nuala says, "The Blood Ritual. You forgot to tell Moswen that you've finished going through that last book she assigned to you."

"You know what, Nuala?" I reply, throwing her a grin. "I think I'll choose not to think about the fucking Blood Ritual until after the First Round. After all, it seems I'll actually get to see the day."

She laughs, shaking her head and opening her mouth to say something either snarky or encouraging, when we hear it. Thunderous cheering from the direction of the training grounds.

"What the…" Nuala mutters, her eyes darting there as well.

Of course, we rush to see what's going on. The training grounds are usually empty this late in the day. But now the warm, ethereal glow of dusk is falling not just on the beaten reddish ground, but on the bodies of students either sitting on the bleachers or fighting in the ring.

As we approach, I see Sarya, Harry, Zelda and *Leo* among the ones fighting.

"The Vipers," I whisper. "I didn't know Leo was one of them."

Nuala pulls me by the upper arm, saying, "Don't let them intimidate you."

But it's over. I'm coming even closer because I've already caught glimpses of several maneuvers that I don't even know how to explain. At one point, I see a swarm of daggers being propelled after a puma so large it could swallow my head without even opening its jaw. It's only after an entire minute that I realize that the daggers are actually slivers of stones controlled by Sarya herself.

"Come on, Quinn," Nuala pleads with me, "what could possibly be the point of this?"

"I'm watching because I want to know as much as possible about more than half of my opponents."

"But you know why they keep their little club exclusive."

"Sure," I say, but I'm still not turning to face her. "They play dirty or they team up. Or both."

"But they could also want you and everyone else to get the wrong impression about their powers," she says, stopping to huff and puff about it all. "You know, to throw you all off or something like that. Something not good."

"Yeah, you're probably right," I reply, hearing her breathe a sigh of relief as I straighten up and turn on my heel. "Let's go back to the castle."

We walk in silence. And only once we're in the entrance hall, right at the spot where we usually say bye, do I dare to ask. "Do you think they *know*?"

She frowns. "What? You mean what the assignment is going to be?"

I nod.

"I highly doubt it."

I nod again. I want to say something, but I just end up patting her on the shoulder before I say bye. I just want to go to my room and try to forget about everything.

And I can tell Nuala is a bit worried and a tad disappointed as well, but she doesn't say anything. She just gives me a hug and heads to the cafeteria for lunch.

When I finally bolt the door of my room behind me, I let out a deep sigh and head straight into the bathroom. There I have one of those old-fashioned tubs, with brass legs and everything, that I would've killed for growing up.

I fill it with scalding water and throw in some bath salts as well. Shea butter and wild rose, just my kind of thing. And as soon as I strip off all my clothes and lower myself into the fragrant water, the knot that's been sitting high in my throat starts unraveling, for better or worse.

Now that I've seen what I'm up against, I'm once again sure that I'm going to die tomorrow. And I've only gotten to use this tub a handful of times, I say to myself, trying to keep it light.

But it doesn't work. Because *I'm going to die tomorrow.*

That's what my mother's eyes have been trying to tell me. When they appear in my nightmares, they usually just stare at me. There are shivers in the air all around them, muffled sighs and flashes of menacingly red light. But it's the eyes that make me scared shitless.

I can't even close mine for fear of seeing them again, looking too much like the ones I've seen laid out in front of that bust. Bloody and unmistakably dead. So I push my body under the surface of the water, trying to find comfort in its warmth.

Chapter Seventeen

I wake up from that same nightmare in which my mother haunts me, but I remember something else as well. For the first time ever, Faust appeared in my dreams.

I was in the bath when he showed up, the water reflecting off him in the near darkness, revealing glimpses of his beautiful, expressionless face. He slowly walked up to me and crouched, resting his arms on the side of the tub and his chin on his hands. He didn't say anything and he didn't look me in the eye once, no matter how much I wanted him to. Tilting his head, he just slowly dragged his eyes up and down my wet, naked body. When they locked with mine and I saw the intensity in them, my nipples hardened and I let out a quiet moan. He didn't acknowledge it. He slowly reached out his hand and dipped his fingers in the water, making my legs spread for him of their own accord. The next second dragged out in anticipation of his touch with such intensity, it was bordering on painful. And just as I thought I could feel him brush my knee, he disappeared. When I looked down at the water, it had turned into blood.

It's actually great, at least that's what I think as I drag myself out of my bed. Now I don't just wish for the Trials to start because I can't stand the anticipation of my own death any longer. I also can't wait for them to start because, well, at least death should get that asshole out of my head once and for all.

Conflicted and grumpy, I get dressed and throw a glance at the clock on my wall. It's the entrance hall that all of us Chosen are supposed to meet in, so if I leave now, I'll be early.

Why the fuck did I forbid Nuala to come see me off? I guess I didn't realize that going alone would feel even more shitty than saying some awkward goodbye.

Fuck it. I'm too nervous to just sit and wait. So I draw in a deep breath and start for the door.

It's at that exact moment that I hear a knock at the door. "Miss Longborn," I hear an unfamiliar male voice call out.

I open the door to see the prince's stout vampire minion, who I've heard goes by Max, blinking at me. "Yes?" I ask.

"I'm sorry to disturb you," Max starts, "but His Majesty asked me to make sure you got to the entrance hall in time."

I inhale deeply, fighting not to let this insult get to me. I win. "Thanks, Max," I squeeze out. "You can tell him that I *definitely* will be there in time."

"You misunderstand me," he says, looking at me with sorry eyes. "I'm to escort you there."

"What the..." I just look at him for a second, but then I just shake my head and motion for him to move out of the doorway.

And I'm gritting my teeth the entire way down, but I let him. I let him escort me like some lost little puppy that his control freak of a master wishes to have brought to him.

And we're early, but by the time we walk into the entrance hall, there's already a million people there waiting for us to leave for the Arena, including Nuala. She's waving at me, a nervous but warm smile on her face. I barely have time to smile back and mouth 'Wish me luck' before I notice our very own Ringleader, the Little Prince himself.

To my surprise, he's apparently chosen to fight in his casual suit, complete with his Ouroboros waistcoat. He's towering over the rest of the Chosen, which have him surrounded like a flock of obedient children, even Sarya, Harry, Zelda and Leo.

Sniggering, they're all watching me be *escorted*. I let out a sigh and join the circle. Max just waits for Faust to give him a nod and disappears back into the crowd. And though I've just seen the Little Prince acknowledge his minion, he doesn't give *me* so much as a glance.

He just claps his hands and says, "Now that we're all here..." He motions at the Elevator behind him. So he's back to ignoring me, fucker. Fine by me.

We file into the Elevator, all twenty four of us, the contraption always large enough to accommodate the passengers, no matter their number.

"Once we're inside," Faust starts, all eyes immediately snapping to him, "take a seat and wait for your name to be called out. Is that clear?"

I nod, trying not to look at him for too long for fear of my mind filling with the images from my dream. My heart is throbbing at the very thought of what's about to happen. Once he's made sure there are no questions, Faust pushes a series of Elevator buttons that are so rarely used, they're still shiny.

The contraption moves and almost immediately stops. The door opens and we all step out, two by two, the silence and the dim lights of the Elevator being switched for thunderous clapping and bright flood lights.

I draw in a breath. I find myself in a large booth with plush chairs overlooking the inside of a huge glass dome. I walk up to the glass booth wall and look down. Ignoring the chatter of the Chosen behind me, I take time to inspect the oval-shaped ring and the bleachers rising up from its sides. There doesn't seem to be an empty seat left in the place and the guests all seem to be buzzing with anticipation.

Feeling my heart drop into my stomach, I almost curse out loud. How is it possible that I'm being forced into this and none of it is illegal?

But it's no use. I've researched the instances in which people tried to break the Bond forced onto them by the mark. They didn't just die. They died violent deaths.

My stomach in knots, I keep staring at the audience gobbling up all this modern-day Gladiator shit. When I finally notice all the screens showing our faces real-time, it almost makes me puke. Still, I keep watching, wondering why the faces of the other Chosen seem so bright and excited, especially compared to my pale and frozen one.

"Come on, people," I hear Faust say. "Take your seats."

I listen and sit next to a shifter girl that I believe is called Amra, a toned brunette in a tank top and cargo pants.

Faust comes to stand in front of us. "Right after the First Round," he starts, "we'll be having a joint interview with some of the most prestigious newspapers across the world." He pauses for a moment, his eyes sweeping over our faces. They linger on mine for a bit too long before he adds, "I expect you all to be on your best behavior. Got it?"

I see everyone nodding vigorously. "Good luck to you all," Faust says and takes his seat.

As soon as he does, I see one of the screens show Pied Piper getting up from her seat in the booth to the other side of the Arena. She approaches the glass booth wall and raises her hand, making the chatter die down.

Her voice booms from speakers all around me. "I've been told by our Scion sponsors," she drawls, her voice carrying a touch of mockery, "to drag the introduction out for the purpose of something they refer to as *building tension*."

She finishes with an exaggerated flourish of her hand, making the crowd burst out laughing. I can't help but smile as well.

"I've taken this task seriously and this is what I've come up with," she continues in her usual bored voice. She pauses for a second, sweeping her eyes over the entranced crowd. "It is my honor to welcome you all to the 176th Trials of Grimm Academy.

There will be fighting and afterwards, there will be food. Now, do you *feel* the tension?"

There's such loud cheering from the audience that I feel the urge to cover my ears. Instead, I clap with them.

"Excellent," the Pied Piper nods contently. "Then it's time to bring out our first Fighter. Let's all greet Amra of the House of Lycan."

I turn to see Amra getting up to leave our booth using a set of stairs to the left. She looks so damn focused, especially when they show her on screen, every detail of her face clearly visible.

I wish Nuala were here with me. I search the audience to catch a glimpse of her, but there's just too many people here.

What snaps me out of it is the Pied Piper drawling, "Now that our Fighter is in the ring, let's take a look at what she'll be *playing* with."

Playing? I frown. I see Amra standing in the center of the ring and a huge door right across from her opening with a loud creak.

Once they're fully open, out comes the biggest, most dangerous creature I've ever seen. I don't know what other word to use but 'giant'. To make it even worse, he seems to be wearing spiked wooden armor. The crowd roars and I just flinch, imagining the fist on that thing slamming itself into me in full force.

Fuck. Fuck. Fuck.

"You must be wondering," the Pied Piper says, obviously amused, "what this is all about. Well, you probably can't see it from that far away, but our giant is holding a teensy ball in his hand."

The screen captures it and the crowd goes ahhh.

"The Fighter's job," the Pied Piper continues, "is to take the ball from the giant and throw it... Now wait." As she says that, the screen captures the appearance of a levitating golden hoop a ways in front of the Pied Piper's booth. "Right through this hoop," she finishes, making my stomach twist at the very thought of even trying to do it.

"I also need to mention," the Pied Piper adds with a sly smile, "that you have a time limit. You only have half an hour before the clock runs out." At that, I see the image of an hourglass on the screen above me. "When it does, you're out. But if you manage to get the ball through the hoop before that time, you're a winner."

The crowd goes wild again and I hear the other Chosen around me cheer, soundly patting each other on their backs.

Nuh-uh, I think to myself. No way in hell am I focusing on anything other than surviving. I only need to manage it for half an hour and I'm done.

"And now, ladies and gentlemen," the Pied Piper says. "I think we've had enough talking."

The crowd roars once again and I see Amra get into position, leaning forward as if preparing for a sprint.

A gong sounds and it all happens so fast, I barely draw in a breath. The giant lunges at the girl and the girl lunges at the giant.

He swings one enormous, muscled arm in her direction, she evades the attack and kicks herself off the ground, shifting midair. My jaw drops as I watch her frail human body turn into the biggest bear I've ever seen, with my own two eyes *or* on screen.

With bated breath, I watch her try to attack the giant repeatedly, the creature roaring at her and flailing its spiked arms whenever she comes close. The few times she does get close enough, it rips into her bear body, spilling blood all over the ring.

Holy fuck, this seems totally inhumane. How can they do this to us?

I almost jump up off my seat when Amra's giant bear claws finally manage to land a blow. And now there's blood everywhere.

I hear the crowd yelling, but the giant seems to have more than enough fight in him to return the favor. He just lifts his hand and slams her body into the ground.

Holding my breath almost the entire time, I watch Amra squirm as she tries to pick herself up. Strangely, the giant isn't taking the opportunity to attack. Maybe he's been injured too heavily. Which is why she finally manages to push herself up off the ground and take another leap.

I don't actually see what happens. It's too fast. But I hear wild roaring coming from the giant and I see the girl shift back into her human form. The next second, she's jumping and the screen is showing the ball flying through the hoop.

The crowd breaks out into loud cheering. "And we have a winner," the Pied Piper's voice booms as I fix my eyes on Amra bleeding down there, my heart constricting in my chest.

After Amra leaves the ring, more Chosen get called to fight. Nine more win, including Sarya, Harry, Zelda and Leo. The others all lose. Hard. They also get injured so badly that the medics need to come take them away. And just as I think someone's going to actually die, I hear *his* name being called out, making my knees go weak.

I watch him walk down the steps leading from our booth and down into the arena. My eyes dart between the real him and the enlarged image of his face on the screen. He's smirking.

From the way he moves and the way he smiles, his hands in his pockets as if he's about to go to class and not fight to possible death, it's obvious that he's enjoying the attention. And I can't *not* give it to him.

"Now, this should be interesting to watch," I hear the Pied Piper say. "The prince, of course, is of the House of Lilith, which means that he could simply order the giant to give him the ball. But that's exactly why the Trial Architects have made sure the giant's skin is smeared with vampire blood."

The people around me murmur, but I don't care about that. My entire focus is on him.

Once he's in the arena, he just stops and remains standing there, waiting for the gong to sound. The screen shows him smiling as he cracks his neck in one slow, controlled motion, making the girls around me let out a giggle.

He seems so relaxed, it's making me want to slap him.

But then the gong sounds and all of a sudden, he's nowhere to be seen. Except as a blur making deft jumps around the arena, finally landing on top of the giant himself. The giant roars, flailing in an attempt to figure out what's going on, but Faust is already back on the ground, a piece of giant's armor in his hand. He takes it with both hands and snaps it against his knee, creating a spear-like weapon. Then he turns around and smirks at the camera. The son of a bitch. It makes me draw in a breath, feeling desire tingling all over my skin.

When he turns back to the giant, I see that the big guy is just about to jump at him. But Faust just raises his spear and throws it effortlessly straight into the creature's hand. The giant roars and lets go of the ball.

The prince seems to disappear. And the next time I see him, he's standing in the arena as the gong sounds to mark his victory. He's managed to get the ball and throw it through the hoop without me noticing any of it.

Holy shit.

As the crowd roars, I keep watching him as his eyes sweep over it. Oh, he's enjoying this. And for a second, our eyes meet. And his linger. I draw in a breath, my thighs clutching as the flames of his gaze lick my skin, making me go wet with desire.

Good job, Quinn, I snarl at myself. *He* is exactly where your focus should be right now.

And of course, it's at that exact moment that *my* name is called out. I feel air being knocked out of my lungs and my entire body going numb.

As if in a trance, I get up and walk out of the booth and down the steps. I can barely do more than keep breathing and putting one foot in front of the other.

Before I know it, I'm in the arena, looking up at the towering giant in front of me. He looks even more menacing from up close. And I want time itself to stop so I can figure out how to survive this, but almost immediately, the gong sounds and the giant charges straight at me.

I turn on my heel and start running the fuck away from him. Fuck. Fuck. Fuck. Only a part of my brain registers the announcer saying, "I guess there's more than one way to win," I hear the Pied Piper's smirking voice boom from the speakers.

It doesn't take the giant long to catch up to me. And I have to start climbing the arena walls to escape him, but he still manages to land a blow to my side, knocking the air out of my lungs and making me fall back to the ground.

I quickly push myself up, but the giant is right in front of me, his chest heaving. For a second, I just look at him. His eyes are filled with something that strikes me as oddly familiar.

But then he attacks again, swinging his arm at me and making me jump to my right. Alright, at least he's quite predictable, I think to myself. The very thought of having to use my magic to defend myself fills me with dread.

When he misses again, he throws his hands up in the air and lets out a long, frustrated roar. And that's when it finally hits me, what I found familiar in his eyes.

It's the same look of helpless anger my former foster brother Danny would have after Mr. Smith would leave him with more cigarette burns on his forearm.

With rounded eyes, I take another look at the giant. Holy fuck, how inhumane can this get?

He's a child. This is not an adult giant, I repeat to myself as I break into a sprint to dodge yet another one of his attacks. Suddenly feeling in control, I run as far away from him as possible and I sit on the ground.

I can hear the crowd laugh, but I don't give a shit. I keep doing my thing, just sitting there with my legs splayed out, waiting.

And the giant scratches his head in confusion, but he slowly stalks over to me.

When he's right in front of me, he sniffs the air and throws me a blank look.

I reach out my hand, gesturing at the ball in his hand and then pointing at myself.

The giant just looks at me for a second, then lets out a roar and takes another swing at me, making me kick myself off the ground and go back to running as the audience laughs.

But I've seen the hand in which he keeps the ball from up close. And it still has in it a piece of that spike that Faust threw at him.

So I circle the giant and come to a stop right in front of him. I think I'm making him confused because he's become hesitant in his attacks.

I motion at his hand again and I pretend I'm taking a spike out of my own hand, hoping he'll get what I'm trying to tell him.

He just attacks again and this time, I don't fall back quickly enough. One of the spikes from his armor catches the skin of my shoulder and rips into it.

I curse out loud and he takes a step back, watching me.

I'm panting, my heart is throbbing and pain is searing my shoulder, but I don't even try to get away. Still standing there, I ask to remove the spike for him again and I wait.

For a second, he just looks at me. Then he switches the ball from his left to his right hand and takes a step towards me.

When he finally holds out his injured hand for me, I hear a murmur rise from the crowd.

Almost without breaking eye contact, I come a little closer and I yank the spike out of his hand.

He lets out a roar and for a moment, I think that this is the end of me.

But then he calms down, bends over a little and rolls the ball in my direction.

This time, I hear gasps from all around me. I ignore them. I just pick up the ball and start running. When I'm all the way on the other side of the arena, I kick myself off the ground and I fling my hand, throwing the ball through the hoop levitating above me.

I hear the gong sound, but this time, the crowd doesn't applaud. There's a strange mix of tense silence and excited chatter as a girl with a name tag I don't bother to read comes to get me out of there. I throw her a tired albeit grateful smile.

My guide leads me out of the arena and down a well-lit hallway. And just as we're about to turn a corner, I hear *his* voice from a ways down. My breathing quickens as my ears prick up.

"I don't know what you're talking about, uncle," he says.

"You were being too smug out there," Faust Senior replies with obvious disapproval in his voice.

Faust only lets out a scoff. "I thought you wanted me to win."

There's a moment of silence before the uncle replies, "Win, of course, just without the gloating."

Oh, I think to myself, this makes me like the old man even more.

But it's at that exact moment that my guide has me turn another corner and I see them walk through an archway leading into a crowded, noisy room.

Fuck. The interview. Will this day never end?

My guide motions for me to follow them and leaves. Cameras flashing as I walk, I enter the interview room and grab a seat at the table where the remaining Chosen are already seated. It's just twelve of us now.

Once I settle down, I see Faust give one of the countless journalists seated across from us a nod. And just like that, the yelling begins.

"Tell me, Miss Longborn," a thin blonde journalist demands as she shoves a microphone in my face, "why did you choose not to fight the giant?"

"Surely," I hear Faust cut in, "you don't want to talk about the only fight that wasn't even a fight."

I shoot him a look, but his eyes are fixed on the reporter as he gives her a fake smile.

Another reporter chimes in. "What do *you* think about it, Your Majesty? After all, it's you who's been put in charge of the Chosen this year."

For a split second, I see the smile slide off his face. He clears his throat and says, "As always, our Chosen represent the best of the best. But of course, even among a select few, you can find those more worthy of the title."

He's obviously evading the question and that makes me want to slap him. But the reporters don't bite. "Does this mean you don't think Miss Longborn is an actual contender?"

Another one turns to me and asks, "Miss Longborn, was what you did some kind of comment on the Trials themselves?"

I open my mouth, but Faust is already cutting in, his voice almost threatening. "I'm sure Miss Longborn didn't think that far ahead. She..."

"Can speak for herself," I hear myself say. And despite the look of sheer fury that he throws me, I keep talking. "Why did I choose not to fight the giant? It's very simple. That giant is just a kid and whatever the Academy would want me to do, I don't fight children."

The silence that follows my words is deafening. With the corner of my eye, I see Faust staring at me, but I'm too busy feeling the onset of a panic.

I'm almost thankful to him when he finally clears his throat, gets up and says, "I think we've had enough questions for today. Our fighters, as you can see, are all wrung out and in need of rest."

No one dares to object. As I'm scrambling out of my seat, Faust is already on his way out of the room. I can't help but glance at him, the glance turning into a stare when I see him being approached by the Pied Piper herself.

She leans to whisper something to him, looking over her shoulder and straight into my eyes. She doesn't look happy.

And I can see Faust's entire body visibly tense up. His eyes dart to mine, throwing me a pissed-off look before he pulls himself together and murmurs something back to the principal. She nods and he takes his leave.

Chapter Eighteen

"You can't be serious," Nuala says as she tries to catch up with me.

"You bet I am," I have my bag with me and I'm headed straight for the graveyard.

"But you literally just finished the First Round, you're in pain and we have the Ball tonight. Do you *need* any more reasons not to go back to training just yet?"

"Nuala," I say without even turning to look at her, "I just need to blow off some steam. I don't think I could possibly be more pissed than I am right now."

My friend just lets out a deep sigh and keeps walking with me.

And I don't know if I'm overreacting, but I can't seem to control it. The anger inside me is burning bright, threatening to consume me.

But before we even get close to the graveyard, we hear screaming from the direction of the Lycan Forest. It's the deep dark woods just behind Nuala's tower.

We both stop midstep and look at each other in silence. Then we break into a sprint, forgetting all about the graveyard.

The sound of screaming leads us and a couple of other students straight into the forest. The trees there grow so close that light barely ever touches the ground.

And the screaming has died down. At first, I only see a delicate fae-blooded girl standing in the middle of a narrow path leading through the trees. Frozen.

My eyes follow the direction of her gaze. When I see it, I almost let out a scream myself.

Two bodies hung off two neighboring trees, naked and upside down. Their throats have been slit and the blood is still slowly dripping down their heads. And straight onto two candles dug into the ground below.

We all just watch in silence, just like the fae girl. No one wants to go near, but even from this distance, I can see that the candles are giving off blood-red light. One of them has a symbol of the sun carved into it, while the other a symbol of the moon.

After a couple of seconds of only hearing my heart throbbing in my ears, the fae girl whose screams led us here turns on her heel and starts walking straight back to the castle. "I'm going to go get someone," I hear her mutter.

"Quinn." I feel Nuala tug on my sleeve and I turn to her. What I see sends shivers down my spine. My friend's entire body is trembling and she has this absent look in her rounded eyes.

"Wait," I whisper.

She nods. I can tell she's in shock, but I want us to stay just a little bit longer because I need Moswen to see this. And the others urge us to go with them, but eventually they follow the fae girl out of the woods and back to the castle.

As soon as they're gone, I dig out the diary and I crack it open. Just like last time, a part of me hopes that Moswen's reaction won't be as extreme as ours. But I can tell she's fighting to keep herself under control.

"Some students have already gone to get someone," I mutter.

"Good," she says, her voice unusually shaky as she keeps staring at the sight before us. "That's good. And I think you should leave as soon as possible as well."

I don't wait for her to tell me a second time. I close the diary, I take Nuala by her sweaty hand and I practically sprint out of the forest, only one thing on my mind. To get us back to the safety of the castle.

But as soon as we're out of the woods, something strange happens. I see someone approach us, but my mind can't make sense of the person's face. I see eyes, a nose, a mouth, but it's like looking at an abstract painting. It all makes me stop in my tracks and let go of Nuala's hand.

Without saying a word, the person takes a step closer, making me take one back. Nuala follows suit, breathing heavily. My heart pounding wildly, I squint in a vain attempt to make my eyes obey.

They refuse.

Still silent, the person just raises a hand at me and the next thing I know, I lose control of my own body.

Slowly and without wanting to, I take the bag with the diary that's hanging off my shoulder and I hold it out for them.

"Nuala," I yell out, but my friend does nothing. She just lets out a long, pained wail.

I panic, trying to think of a way to use my runes without being able to control my hands.

Too late, the thought rings in my head as the person grabs the bag and starts pulling.

The very next second, the grip loosens and the person disappears. The sudden release makes me fall on my back and crash against the cold, hard ground, but at least I have the diary safely in my hands.

What the fuck just happened, I think to myself.

It's then that I hear it. "What's going on here?" the Pied Piper demands. I'd recognize her voice anywhere.

Chapter Nineteen

"Are we done?" I ask the assistant, trying not to sound too hostile. The fear that's still shaking me up and the urge to check on Nuala are making me a bit less considerate than usual.

"I'd think you'd be happy we're taking this seriously," she says as she lifts the pen off the notebook she's been writing my answers in.

"I am," I reply with a sigh, trying to remind myself that this scrawny vampire girl has only been nice to me. But I expected to be questioned by the Pied Piper herself and her assistant using her powers on me has been draining. "I'm just worried about my friend," I choose to say.

"I understand," the girl says with a smile. "But this will be the last question I have for you."

I nod.

"When you walked out of the forest, how did you feel? Apart from shaken up? Did you feel like yourself?"

As she talks, I feel the presence of her willpower in my own mind. It's like having a phantom mind inside your head. And I'd tell her the truth either way, but this makes it impossible for me to tell any lies.

"No, I didn't feel strange that way."

She just looks at me for a second. I do my best to push the thought of the diary out of my mind, but when she tilts her head, I almost let it flood me, thinking I've messed up.

"Alright," she finally concludes. "You can go."

I practically jump out of my chair, heading straight for the door.

"Your friend," I hear her say and I stop midstep.

I turn back to her with bated breath.

"You won't be able to visit her until she's released."

"Thanks," I say and practically run out of the office.

I rush to the House of Ydril, skipping steps on my way upstairs. It's already late afternoon and the Ball is in only a couple of hours. But I'm desperate to talk to Moswen, the fear that's been gripping me from before I even opened my eyes this morning finally taking a toll on me.

"And?" I ask as soon as she appears, my voice shaky with anticipation. "You think that that was an isolated incident?"

She doesn't even have to answer. The look on her face is telling me everything.

Still, I'm surprised when she says, "I'm sorry, Quinn. I thought it wouldn't come to this."

I pin her down with my stare, barely able to control the urge to shake her until she tells me what the hell is going on.

"I think it's best if I showed it to you."

I gulp and I nod, not knowing what to expect. She places a hand on my forehead and just like last time, I'm sucked into one of her memories.

This time, we're out in the garden on a clear, sunny day. I'm surrounded by a bunch of girls, all young, giddy and wide eyed. I can't really make out everything they're saying, despite how close we're standing. But there's laughter and mentions of both professors and sweethearts as people keep rushing past us, seeming to be busy with preparations for an event of some kind.

It strikes me as odd, considering how scared Moswen looked when she said she had to show me something. Odd that this would be the memory she referred to. It's then that I notice all the posters. They look a little old-fashioned, but they're basically the same as the ones we had for the First Round. It's just that, here and now, it's the Third Round that's being announced.

A shiver creeps down my spine as my eyes dart from left to right. Something's going to happen and I don't know what or when. I want to go walking around, looking for signs of trouble, but when I try, I'm reminded of the fact that I can't move unless Moswen does.

So when her eyes dart to the hedge at the far end of the garden and linger, I immediately prick up my ears. She seems to be absorbed in watching two figures approaching the castle, trying not to draw attention to themselves but obviously arguing.

My heart skips a beat. I can't help but hope it's not *them*, because whatever's happening, it can't be good. When they're almost at the Elevator door, I feel the need to curse. Is that really going to be it?

To my surprise, Moswen doesn't remain standing in her friends' circle. She excuses herself and starts making her way to the castle herself.

I admire the way she does it. Lingers in front of the castle until they've taken the Elevator. Stops to pretend to read a pamphlet in the entrance hall as she gauges which way they'll go. Makes zero noise as she follows them down a series of deserted hallways.

"If she listens to us," one of the figures starts and I immediately recognize the man who I think is my father, "then maybe we can get the Pied Piper on board."

"And if she doesn't?" the woman who I think is my mother snaps, albeit wearily. "Byrne is away. If you're wrong and she turns on us, he won't be able to protect us."

The man stops and puts his hand on the woman's shoulder. "It's irrelevant. If we're right, we've no time to waste. It's happening. Tonight, Syllia."

The woman shakes her head and lets out a deep sigh. Then she gives the slightest nod and they both keep walking, only stopping when they reach a plain wooden door at the end of the hallway.

I never get inside. They close the door behind them and I crouch before it with the keyhole at eye level.

Of course, I see absolutely nothing except a patch of candle light spilling through. And there are already words being uttered, words I can't really make out.

Fucking shit. But just as I start cursing the unfairness of the entire situation, Moswen does a little digging through her pocket and takes out a strange little contraption, long and metal, with an eye carved into the thicker end. She slides it into the keyhole and looks through it, as if she's looking through a microscope lens.

I can now see into the room on the other side of the wall. Plain as day. It looks like a study, soft armchairs surrounded by solid-wood bookshelves. And there are three people inside, all seated. My parents... and Professor Mistila.

My heart skips a beat. She looks much younger, but it's her. Right now, they're not talking because they all seem stunned, but when she speaks, I realize that Moswen's contraption isn't just allowing us to see into the room. We can hear everything loud and clear as well.

"You want me to shut down the Trials?" Professor Mistila asks.

My mother takes a deep breath and says, "Yes."

Professor Mistila lets out a chuckle as she leans forward to pour herself a drink. "I'm sorry, my dear Syllia, but I don't seem to understand what these incidents have to do with it all."

"My apologies, *veneranda*," my father chimes in. "But the hearts were cut out on the night of the Blood Moon, the corpses drained on the day of the Winter Solstice and, well... It's fresh in all of our memories what happened on Walpurgis night."

"Exactly," my mother echoes. "It's plain as day that someone's planning on utilizing the stone's power."

For a second, there's silence. Professor Mistila stays serious, but there's a touch of mockery in her voice as she says, "Syllia, I hate to have to tell you this. But the stone's powers are a thing of myth. Nothing more."

"What if they're not?" my mother demands, a bit too forcefully, judging by the way she immediately corrects her tone. "The Trials pose a unique opportunity for the thief. Are you really willing to risk a potential bloodbath?"

Professor Mistila waves her hand in dismissal. "The incidents thus far were obviously the actions of some deranged dark magic enthusiast."

"Or someone with connections in the Trials," my father throws in.

For a second, there's silence. I can see Professor Mistila squint, her entire body tensing up before my eyes. "What are you implying?" she asks in a low, warning voice.

"Professor Mistila," my mother rushes to say, "you know that he has all sorts of strange ideas. Would it be really that unexpected..."

The professor doesn't let her finish. "Not another word," she commands as she gets up off her chair with a pissed-off look on her face. "I want you out of my cabinet, now."

I hear yelling and the sounds of footsteps approaching the door and all of a sudden, I'm back in my room, Moswen staring at me with rounded eyes.

"So it's true," I mutter. "If the Third Round is held as planned, something horrible is going to happen."

And I appreciate it when Moswen comes to crouch in front of my bed. I also appreciate it when she says, "Don't worry, little Quinn. I'll protect you."

But I've long since stopped believing in fairy tales.

Chapter Twenty

As soon as I hear Nuala's been discharged, I rush to the Lycan tower. I'm so anxious to see how she's doing, I take two steps at a time. When I finally barge into her room, I find her in bed, scrolling away on her phone. She looks up and throws me a hesitant smile.

"I'm so glad you're okay." I breathe a sigh of relief and come to sit on the edge of her bed. "Wait," I say when I look into her eyes from up close. "Did they give you something?"

"I think so," she says flatly.

"But you weren't hurt," I reply, frowning. "Or was it for the mind magic?"

"It's just sedatives," she snaps a little and then looks away, her lips pressed tight. "That... person... didn't use mind magic on me."

At first, I just blink at her. Then I frown. "What're you telling me?" I ask. "That you were in control of yourself the entire time and you just stood there?"

"I think you heard me right," she mutters, refusing to look at me.

I go from concerned to pissed-off in record time. "Look, Nuala, I do understand that the thing in the woods was traumatic..." I *make* her look at me, trying not to raise my voice, but failing. "But when that fucking thief appeared, it didn't occur to you to try to help me? To stop him or her from stealing Moswen or hurting me or whatever?"

"I guess I'm a coward," my friend just says.

"You sure didn't seem like one when Sarya came to mess with us that time," I snap at her.

Nuala shrugs. "I don't know what to tell you."

"Why not the truth?"

She just looks at me for a second. Then, to my surprise, her breathing gets heavy and she slowly breaks into quiet sobbing. "That thing in the woods..."

"Tell me," I urge her, my voice growing softer.

"I used to have seven brothers, not six, okay?" she snaps and quickly collects herself, although she doesn't stop crying. "It's just, one day when I was nine, just before my first shift was supposed to happen, our town got attacked by a rival pack."

I grab her hand. "I'm so sorry, Nuala," I mutter.

"It was a massacre," she squeezes out. "And when they left, we found my brother hanging off a tree like that."

"Holy fuck," I blurt out.

"I know, but I don't want to linger on it," Nuala replies, sniffling as she wipes her tears. "I was okay for a long, long time, until today, I guess." She lets her eyes land on mine, a sorry look in hers. "I'm so sorry, Quinn. I really wanted to help, but when I saw that thing today, I just froze and when that person attacked you, it got even worse. The only thing I could do was yell."

I shake my head and wave my hand, trying to show how much I won't be holding it against her. I try to pull her into a hug, but she resists.

"No, there's more," she says, her voice sounding a lot more sober. "Now that I'm just spilling everything, you may as well know the whole truth about me."

I feel my eyebrows shoot up.

"That night," she squeezes out, "when they killed my brother, I snapped and I felt the bond between myself and my animal sever."

"What do you mean?"

She stays silent for a second. "I'm a shifter who can't shift, Quinn."

"So what?" I scoff. "We'll fix you."

She shakes her head vigorously. "No, I don't want to have anything to do with it."

"What, your choice is to... do nothing?"

"For crying out loud, Quinn," she snaps at me. "Don't you think I've tried everything?" she drawls angrily. "It's just like that for some shifters and there's nothing I can do about it."

"Fine, I'll drop it," I say as I raise my hand in defense. For now, I think to myself. "But hey," I add, smiling, "aren't you glad you got all that out of your system. I can't believe you're only trusting me with it *now*."

She shakes her head, but she also gives me a weak smile. "That's all very peachy, but the problem's still there."

"What problem?"

"Well, you know all that fun stuff happening," she drawls teasingly, "the Blood Rituals, the bloodbaths and the like? That's all stuff I'm unable to help with."

I open my mouth to tell her she's full of shit, but then it hits me. My friend knows nothing about the memory I just saw. I tell her and she listens with wide eyes and without once interrupting me. When I'm done, at first, she remains silent, thinking.

"I just don't get it," she finally says. She shakes her head and starts counting on her fingers. "There's the Blood Rituals, there's someone trying to steal Moswen, and then there's that thing with your parents, Professor Mistila and the Trials..."

She looks up at me and shakes her head. "Quinn, is it all random? Or is there a connection we're not seeing?"

"Look, that thing we just saw, and the one before it," I say, letting out a sigh as I struggle to find the words, "they're obviously identical to the incidents that happened when my parents taught here. And whoever's responsible for them, well... It'd be in their interest for no one to find out, which is one possible reason for someone trying to steal Moswen."

"So that means..." She breaks off, but she's looking at me as if she wants me to be the one to say it.

"...That we really have some kind of bloodbath to prevent, yes."

We both let the weight of the situation silence us for a second.

"If that's really what's going on," Nuala finally says, "shouldn't we go straight to the Pied Piper? Or someone, you know, who knows what they're doing?"

I shake my head. "I wish. But judging by Moswen's memory, this could be the work of someone very well protected. The kind of person no one wants to piss off. So I don't think we can risk it, at least until we learn more."

Nuala nods. "Where do you think we should start?" she asks.

"Professor Mistila," I say with determination. "She told me she didn't know my parents and that was a straight-out lie, Nuala. So it might be worth it, but I'm not happy about it being our only option."

My friend thinks for a second. "I think I have an idea."

I raise my eyebrows, nudging her to go on.

"You should join the Vipers."

I can't help but laugh. "Holy hell, Nuala."

"No, I'm serious," she insists, her eyes wide and her hand grabbing mine in excitement. "Think about it. We don't know who's responsible for all the shit that's going on. We don't even know what they want, except maybe some stone or whatever. The only thing we do know is that the Trials are somehow connected to it all." She smiles and clicks her tongue. "And who has the most inside info when it comes to the Trials?"

"The Vipers," I reply, my voice barely above a whisper.

"Exactly," Nuala says. "And they're all going to be at the Ball."

I groan as I let my body fall on the bed. "I don't want to go, Nuala."

To my surprise, she doesn't say anything. I lift my head to demand a reaction. When I see her looking at me funny, as if she's withholding something, I immediately push myself back up. "What? What's happened?"

"It's not that bad," she says, wincing, "but before you got here, I was on my phone..."

She breaks off and I jab her with my elbow.

"Just check your social media."

I whip out my phone, pull up my feed and start scrolling. "What the fuck?" I almost yell out.

Olarel House not extinct? The surviving member attacks the Dark Prince after First Round of Trials.

The mystery of the fae raised among humans: Who is Quinn Longborn and why does she claim to be an Olarel?

What's going on between the Dark Prince and the fae everyone claims is the last of the Olarels?

And so on and so forth. "When did this happen?" I ask my friend even before I manage to tear my eyes away from the screen.

"Right after the interview, so it would seem," she replies as she points at the time stamp in the corner of the first article I've just looked up online.

I throw the phone on my bed and slide my face against the palms of my hands. "Great. Now I *really* don't want to go."

"You have to," Nuala tells me with determination in her voice as she grabs my shoulder to shake me. "If you want to join the Vipers, this is, like, the perfect opportunity. And, I mean..." She pauses, forcing me to look at her. She's grinning. "You are an Olarel. I mean, at least you *claim* to be."

She's mocking me, the cursed little shifter. I just stare at her for a moment, clicking my tongue and shaking my head. Then we both burst out laughing.

"Now," I say as I get up off the bed. "It's time for that stupid Ball. Help me make myself presentable?"

She lets out a giggle and jumps up on her feet. "I'd love nothing more."

Chapter Twenty-One

The night is hauntingly beautiful, I think to myself as I steal glances through the windows we're walking by. I'm wearing an emerald green dress that's cut low on the back and I'm feeling like a million bucks. We're on our way to the Ball and yes, I'll probably be the only one there without a date, but I'm still floating because my friend proved herself to be a genius. She brought some blood gin to my room and we downed it all while getting ready, becoming giddier by the drop.

Of course, we're far from being the only intoxicated ones right now. The Ball hasn't even started yet. But long before we get to the Main Hall, we start bumping into drunk students arguing, making out and playing games out on the hallways. The men all stop to leer at me and Nuala keeps jabbing me with her elbow, giggling like a child. I pay them no mind, but I do feel the rush of a special night starting to consume me as well.

But as soon as we turn the corner and find ourselves in the entrance hall, all hell breaks loose. Flashes. People rushing towards us. All of them shoving their microphones in my face and practically yelling, "Miss Longborn!" all at the same time.

I feel Nuala grab me by the upper arm and drag me away from them. As we charge towards the archway leading into the Main Hall, I hear the reporters rushing after me, one woman's voice managing to drown out the rest. "Can you tell us if it's true? Are you really the last of the Olarels?"

Nuala pushes me through the archway and we find ourselves in the Main Hall. I turn to see if the reporters are going to follow us, but they're all walking away. So they're not allowed inside, I make a mental note to myself.

But when I turn my eyes back onto the Main Hall stretching before me, it's all I can do not to let out a gasp. There's a strange mix of classical and club music playing in the background, drowning out the chatter of the guests dressed in the most lavish gray and white outfits I've ever seen. My eyes sweep over the snowflakes covering the polished floor and the icicles hanging from the crystal chandeliers. How fitting, I think, falling in love with the Academy just a little. It's the Winter Solstice Ball and the Main Hall has been transformed into a real-life winter palace.

I turn to smile at Nuala, but just as I see her smiling back, a nervous-looking guy jumps out in front of us. "*What* are you doing?" he hisses at me, at the exact same time he throws me a pleading look and grabs my forearm. "There's a special entrance for the Chosen. You could get me fired, you know."

As he leads me out of the Main Hall, I mouth sorry to Nuala. She shrugs her shoulders, laughing as she turns on her heel. Heading for the bar, I presume. I let out a sigh, thinking how much rather

I'd just be a spectator tonight. But I have a mission, I remind myself, and that's the only thing that matters.

By the time the nervous guy leads me to the back door, I'm eyes on the prize once again, even after I hear them all chatting inside. I walk in and find myself in what I can only describe as the backstage. Almost instantly, there's silence and the eyes of the other eleven Chosen are all on me. Including *him*.

Quick, what do I do, I snap at myself as I take a step forward.

"Good, you're here," I hear a woman's voice and I breathe a sigh of relief when I turn to her and see she's part of tonight's staff. "You all need to get ready for the dance," she says as her eyes sweep over us all. "It's about to start."

I open my mouth to ask for an explanation, but she's already stormed out of the room and I'm left standing there, wondering what the fuck is going on. The others don't go back to their chatting. Instead, they take positions in front of the curtain before them. I rush to find a spot, pissed that no one fucking told me about the dance.

My eyes dart to Faust. He's chatting with the Chosen standing next to him, but I don't care. I stare at him until he notices me throwing daggers at him. For a second, he squints at me. Then he just shrugs, his lip curling into a smile that's barely noticeable. But me, it's poking me straight in the fucking eye. He did this on purpose.

"I noticed you weren't there," I hear a voice from behind my back and I snap my head in its direction to see Leo looking at me intently. "When we met up to discuss the dance. But you're in luck because I can walk you through it."

I nod, thankful that someone's going to explain it to me and not really caring who it is. It's at that exact moment that I hear a gong, followed by Professor Byrne's voice welcoming all guests to the 176th Winter Solstice Ball. The crowd claps and cheers, and I feel Leo's hand wrapping around my waist.

I flinch, but when I turn to face him, the curtain is already up and the lights are practically blinding me. "Now we're going to do a sort of waltz," he says as he leads me onto a podium with the rest of the Chosen. The music is much louder now so he has to raise his voice a little. "And after we do a couple of spins like this," he continues as he shows me, "it's on to the next partner."

"So I have to dance with *all* of the Chosen?" I ask, afraid of the answer because it would mean I have to dance with a certain someone as well.

"Yes," Leo replies as he lets out a chuckle, but the very next second, I'm out of his arms, falling straight into Harry's.

I dance with a couple more Chosen and just as I think I might be able to avoid him after all, I turn around to see Faust holding out his hand with a blank face.

For a second, I just stare at him. Then I scoff and turn on my heel, leaving him to stand there.

As the rest of the Chosen start dancing the last round, I hear Professor Byrne on the microphone again, inviting the rest of the party to the dance floor.

I myself am determined to get away, to find Nuala, to try to get some of the Vipers to talk to me. But I don't even manage to get to the steps leading off the podium, when I feel a presence to my left.

I don't even have to turn around to know it's him. His smell immediately sends my heart racing. He leans to whisper, "Give me your hand." His voice is telling me he's not joking around. "And make sure you're seen smiling."

I turn to face him. I allow myself a quick glance around the room, seeing like a gazillion eyes on us. And I don't want to be an asshole so I give him a fake smile, but I just keep standing. "I'm sorry," I say, still smiling. "I'm just not in the mood for more dancing."

A flash of anger crosses his face before he leans in and says, his voice more forceful this time. "*Take. My. Hand.* And put yours on my shoulder or I promise you'll regret it."

"You know," I hiss at him, remembering at the last second to throw in another fake smile, "I'm sure there are plenty of girls who'd *willingly* dance with you. So what the fuck is your problem?"

He scoffs as his eyes sweep the room. His voice is low again when he says, "I don't know if you're being spiteful or just plain stupid."

This makes me want to slap him, but he just keeps talking. "After the articles this afternoon, you seriously expect no one to be reading into it? You refusing to dance with me?"

I grit my teeth, but I nod. I draw in a breath and I give him my hand, almost pulling it back when I feel the rush of electricity at the touch of his skin.

Holy hell, I'm screwed, I think to myself before it even happens. I put my other hand on his shoulder, feeling the hardness of his muscles, at the same time he takes me by the waist. His hand is stiff on my back, as if he's disgusted to be touching me. Still, I feel my knees give out and a need fill my body. The need to smell him, to press myself against him, to be even closer than *this*. And when he starts spinning me in the rhythm of the music, it all becomes a little too much to bear.

So after a couple of turns around the podium, I make him stop and I pull myself away from him. Breathless and not trusting my voice not to shake, I just bow and walk away.

It's hard because my body doesn't want to listen, but I force myself to keep putting one foot in front of the other. I breathe a sigh of relief once I realize he's not following me.

Now, what I really need is my friend, but when I go look for her, I see her talking to Harry. I frown, but then I realize that he's trying to make her dance with him. And she blows him off, but then this hot fae-blooded guy cuts in and I see the two of them climb the stairs to the podium, hand in hand, while Harry watches sullenly from the sidelines.

I guess I've no other option but to get to work on plan B, that is, getting the Vipers to make me one of their own. So I draw in a breath and start walking towards Harry.

But he's not in a good mood. Once I get close, he does tear his eyes away from Nuala, but he only shakes his head at me and walks away.

Perfect.

I start strolling around the Main Hall, trying to spot the other Vipers. And there's Leo, talking to one of the professors. He looks up, catching my eye. He's already excusing himself and heading straight towards me, but I don't want it to be him, that's how much he creeps me out. If it turns out I have no other choice, sure, but until then, I'm staying out of his sight.

So I quickly turn on my heel and I almost bump into Faust's date rushing out of the Main Hall, crying her eyes out. Trouble in paradise, I guess, I think to myself. But I don't have time to linger on it.

Because there's Zelda, standing by the bar and waiting for a drink. I take a deep breath and start walking.

"Miss Longborn," I hear someone say and I stop midstep. When I turn around, I see an older vampire with a heavily scarred face towering over me. "Or should I say Miss *Olarel*?" he says with a smile.

I notice the pin on his white cloak. A black cross in a circle of rubies, the crest of the House Lilith. But the color tells me I'm talking to a Duke. I rush to bow, feeling once again that I'm being watched.

It makes the Duke let out a laugh. "No need for such formalities, I assure you." He motions at the group of powerful-looking people sitting at one of the more prominent tables. "My friends and I would very much like to get to know you."

And he's still smiling, but he's looking at me a lot like I believe a hungry cat would look at a delicious mouse. Fuck, can I even say no, I wonder. Should I try? "I'd be delighted." And as I speak, it dawns on me. "It's just that I first have to say hi to the rest of the Chosen. You know," I say with a smile, "out of courtesy at least."

There's a second of silence, during which my heart skips a beat, before the Duke flashes a smile and says, "Of course. We'll be here."

That was close, I think to myself as I walk away, even though I don't know what exactly I was scared of. It doesn't matter. Eyes on the prize, Quinn.

And I see that Zelda is no longer at the bar, but there's Sarya passing by. I practically charge at her, but before I can get close enough, Leo appears in front of me.

"You know," he says with a sly smile, "you never thanked me for helping you back there."

"Really?" I ask, frowning. "How rude of me."

"It's alright. I'm more than ready to forgive you," he replies as he leans a bit closer, "provided you give me another dance."

For a second, I *almost* say, "Sure, provided you get me in the Vipers." But I can feel it in my bones, that this is not a guy I want to be indebted to.

"You know, I would," I choose to say, "but I really have to go say hi to someone."

And I move to walk away.

He blocks me and lets out a chuckle, looking over his shoulder to where Faust is standing. He's surrounded by groupies near the center of the room.

To my surprise, I see him throw back a shot.

"Even now that you're an Olarel," Leo whispers in my ear, "you're not good enough for a prince, you know?" He turns to face me and holds out his hand. "So it might not be such a great idea for you to refuse your next best option. For the second time at that."

"What're you gonna do?" I spit out. "Keep stalking me like some psycho?" I ask, thinking about the chocolates.

With that, I leave him standing there, a flash of anger crossing his face. Damnit, now I've pissed him off and I don't really have a clue how far he's willing to go in this game of his.

And to make matters worse, he's not the only one trying to stop me from doing what I'm supposed to do. Now that everyone knows about my heritage, I seem to be the belle of the ball, I think to myself as I spot a couple of guys preparing to approach me.

The next thing I know, Faust appears in front of me, his hands in his pockets and his head tilted to the side. I frown at him. "What do you want?"

There's something off about him, the way he just looks at me. His hair is slightly disheveled and the first couple of buttons on his shirt are undone, revealing the curves of his collarbone.

"What do you think you're doing?" he finally says. It's barely noticeable, but the words are slurred.

It's then that it finally hits me. He's drunk. His skin is flushed and there's a glimmer in his eyes.

"Having fun at a party?" I reply mockingly.

"No," he says as he takes a step closer. I draw in a breath and take one back. "You're up to something. I've been watching you, I mean, you're practically a full-time job, and all this time, you've been avoiding the Duke and circling the Vipers like a cat in heat. So..."

I don't see him getting closer, but he's now in my face, crowding me so much, I can feel the heat radiate off his body. "*What* are you up to?" he demands.

Anger gets the best of me. "I know the Little Prince is used to having his way," I snarl as I move to push past him. "But *not everything* is your business."

His body vibrating with rage, he grabs me by the waist and the very next second, I'm being taken away with such speed, my vision blurs to the point of blindness.

Chapter Twenty-Two

"What did you just call me?" Faust snarls at me, his breath ragged.

For a second, I just blink at him, feeling disoriented and confused.

We're *alone* in some deserted hallway off the Main Hall and my heart is pounding like crazy. I'm pressed against the wall with his hands caging me in. He's fucking tall so I have to tip my head back to meet his eyes. They're glazed and filled with rage as he waits for an answer.

"Little Prince," I finally drawl. "Isn't that what you are?"

"You know nothing about me."

Holy shit, he's so hot when he's drunk. I fight to stay still as the need to press myself closer to him threatens to drive me crazy. "I know you like to fight kids instead of fighting *for* them."

"Yeah, what else?" he demands, his nostrils flaring.

"I know you like to stick your nose in random students' lives instead of, I don't know, making your subjects' lives better or something?"

His chest heaving with all the rage, he grabs me by the waist.

"What the fuck do you think you're doing?" I hiss at him as I try to push him away.

"Shutting you up," he growls and crushes his lips on mine, pulling my body closer to his.

I let out a moan, the desire for him overpowering me. Before I know it, my hands are scrambling to feel all the stiff muscles of his chest and back, like they can't do it quickly enough. I bite his lip and he gives off another low growl. He forces his tongue deeper inside my mouth and squeezes me even tighter, until I can feel nothing but the throbbing of his dick between my legs.

And just as I feel one of his hands traveling up my thigh, dangerously close to see just how wet he's made me, I push it away. "No," I say as I break free of his grip.

"Yes," he breathes out as he tries to take my hand. I don't let him.

I'm already turning to walk away when I hear him snarl under his breath, "Get back here, now."

Almost instantly, I feel this strange pull, my mind losing control of my own body. I start to panic, but I'm already walking back, stopping only when I'm right in front of him, his hand already wrapping around my waist. My eyes round in shock as he leans close to whisper, "Just this once. I need to get you out of my system, Quinn."

But as soon as he pulls back to look at my frozen face, a flash of surprise crosses his eyes and he quickly lets go of me. Completely. He takes a step back, but I'm so angry and I'm once again in control of my own body.

Without thinking, I tap the Element rune and I send him flying into the wall with a loud thump. My body shaking with rage, I walk up to him and ignoring the shock in his eyes, I drawl, "Don't *ever* touch me again."

With that, I turn on my heel and I walk away. By the time I'm back in the Main Hall, I feel like crying. I mean, I knew he was an asshole, but a straight-out danger?

Shaken up and pissed off, I try to find Nuala, but she's nowhere to be seen.

And just as I think about leaving myself, I'm approached by a scrawny fae-blooded guy who just blinks at me. "What?" I snap at him and immediately regret it.

"I'm sorry, I didn't mean to make you angry," he starts, visibly embarrassed but pushing through it. "I just saw that you don't have a date for the Grand Ball yet, and I'd like to be the one to take you."

Once again, I feel watched. My eyes dart around the hall and I see Leo stare at me from a distance, sending me into another fit of rage. "You know what?" I turn to the guy, bitterness in my voice as I say, "I don't think I want to go to another Ball, ever again."

To my surprise, he laughs. "Gotcha." He pauses before he adds, "And I guess you're not really in the mood to talk, so I'll be on my way."

He's so refreshingly normal about it all that I find myself stopping him. "On second thought," I start, "why don't you take me after all?"

He gives me a wide smile and says, "I'd be honored." I hold out my hand and he slides a dandelion corsage around my wrist, shyly glancing at me as he does it.

I feel my lips curl into a smile and I'm just about to ask him his name, when I notice him freeze. I frown and I take a step back. He doesn't say anything, he just walks past me and heads out of the Main Hall.

"Hey," I call out to him, but he doesn't react. It's too strange, too fucking strange for me not to follow him. So I do. And he's obviously under some spell, probably Leo's, because he keeps walking in that strange, stiff way, as if he's being controlled.

With bated breath, I follow him down a series of hallways, trying to get his attention as we go. But he doesn't stop until we reach a door at the end. He opens it and I see there's nothing below.

I gasp, thinking I'm about to see him jump. He looks over his shoulder and I can see the sheer terror in his eyes.

"Alright," I yell out, not knowing what else to do. I rip the corsage off my wrist and I ask, "Happy now?"

I see the guy's features soften as he gulps for air, his legs shaking uncontrollably as he scrambles to get away from the door.

I don't linger. He's safe so I'm already rushing to my room, desperate to see if another one of those sick messages will be waiting for me in front of my door.

And it takes me a bit to get there, but when I do, I see that my suspicions were very much founded. Panting, I reach down to grab the box of chocolates and rip the note off the fancy packaging.

"I see there's been a misunderstanding," the note starts, sending my heart racing once again. "No matter how pitiful your choice of date... you're not allowed to have one."

Chapter Twenty-Three

It's the morning of the first day of the second semester and I practically have the cafeteria to myself. I've never seen it this empty. And I guess the other students think it strange as well, at least judging by the way they keep lowering their voices.

Me? I'm trying to eat my breakfast burger, but I'm feeling quite disoriented now that I'm back at the Academy. I've spent the last month, that is, the holidays, binging my shows, going for my midnight runs and hanging out with Lisa.

Sounds pretty chill, doesn't it? Sure, if you ignore the nights, I think as I stare at one of the fountains in front of my table. Those, I spent tossing and turning, brainstorming how to prevent the bloodbath and avoiding to think about anything else that had to do with the Academy. The events at the Ball, primarily. The actions of a certain someone, most decidedly.

Of course, Nuala was with me in a way. We spent a lot of time on video calls, mostly discussing the bloodbath plans, but also chatting about everything from next semester's classes to my new stalker Leo.

I also tried, very hard, to get her to talk some more about her inability to shift. I asked questions and made suggestions, but she kept blowing me off. Then again, I still haven't told *her* what happened with the *asshole who used his fucking powers on me*. I can't bring myself to even start processing it.

When I snap out of it, I realize I'm gripping the fork so tightly, it hurts. I let out a sigh and I let it drop to the table. I've neither the time nor the energy for this shit. Especially since Nuala got stuck at home until tomorrow afternoon and the two of us were supposed to set the plan in motion. Today.

And just as I think about my friend and how much I miss her, she shoots me a text.

"Don't do anything stupid," it says. "Remember the plan and wait until I get there."

The plan, for now, is to get Professor Mistila alone and try to make her talk about my parents.

"Have you ever seen me do anything stupid?" I type back, smiling as I grab my bag and leave the cafeteria.

She sends me an emoji that's rolling its eyes at me. She wasn't born yesterday, my friend. She knows exactly how anxious I am to jump on it.

But when I barge into the hallway leading to the West Wing, where most classrooms are, I see Harry walking straight at me. And the plan to join the Vipers is just a plan B for now and I know I'm supposed to go look for Professor Mistila first... But he's here and, well, Nuala was right. If anyone knows anything about any sinister plans for the Third Round, it's a Viper.

So I make a snap decision. I lower my head, pretending I'm on my phone, and I make sure to bump into him, full force.

"Hey," he growls at me. "Watch where you're going."

"You watch where you're going," I snarl at him, fighting to look him straight in the eye, despite how menacing he looks.

He scoffs and then flashes me a predatory smile. Yes, just like that, I think to myself. "Little bird not so terrified now that she's an Olarel?"

Holy shit, could this be going any better? I give him a smile and reach for my runes as I say, "I guess I'm much more at ease with my powers now."

He bursts out laughing. "Your *powers*?" he replies mockingly. "You must be very good at hiding them then."

With that, to my disappointment, he just pushes past me and keeps walking.

Damn it. Not biting, despite my stellar performance. But at least I can go see Professor Mistila, I think to myself as I keep walking. Letting out a sigh, I start turning corners and climbing stairs as I head straight for the cabinets where the professors spend their time between classes.

To get to Professor Mistila's, I have to walk past countless others. Not all of them are occupied, but some have their doors wide open. And as I go, I see professors chatting amongst themselves, leafing through enormous leather-bound volumes and even doing experiments with strange-looking contraptions. I have to force myself not to stare when I walk past this one room where an old professor has a black vortex open right at its center, seemingly talking to someone on the other side.

But before I even reach her cabinet, I see Professor Mistila walking back with a cup of steaming-hot coffee in her hand. When her eyes land on mine, I notice her flinch for a second.

Suspicious, I think to myself, but I throw on a wide smile and I walk straight up to her. "Professor, I was wondering if I could have a moment of your time."

"Can it wait?" she says with a tentative smile. "I have a class."

Lying once again. I'd know because I've memorized her entire schedule. "Sure, I'll just come see you again in a couple of hours," I reply as I give her a wide, innocent smile.

While I wait for her imaginary class to end, I take a walk around the castle grounds. It just so happens that my general direction is the training grounds, where the Vipers can usually be found working out. And there she is, Zelda. Since I first saw her, I've found out that she's probably to blame for the death of one of her neighbors. And now she's stretching as if she's just some girl in a yoga class. What can I say? Fate just keeps bringing me to them, I smile as I try to keep my eagerness in check.

"Mind if I join?" I ask as I approach her, choosing a less explosive method than with her colleague. I don't even know where I'm going with it and it does seem a bit stupid, but hey, at least I've got her attention. She's looking up at me as she gets out of the position.

It's like freezing cold out here, but she's in shorts and a tank top, looking as if the temperature isn't getting to her at all.

For a second, I think she's going to smile, but she just frowns and walks away.

Sheesh. I'm on fire here.

Luckily, I think it's just about time to go back to chasing after Professor Mistila. I find her walking out of the classroom, chatting with one of her students.

This time, she doesn't flinch when she sees me, but I can tell she's not happy about it. "Quinn," she says when I get close. And for a second, I expect her to blow me off again. "I guess I have some time right now, if you want to go for a walk."

I nod happily and fall into step with her as she heads for the Elevator. "So what did you want to discuss? Are you interested in taking one of my classes?"

There are others in the Elevator with us so I wait until we're out to say, "Actually, I wanted to talk to you about my parents."

I don't stare, but I pay close attention to her reaction. She lets out a small sigh and asks, "What about them?"

"You helped me learn who my family is, but I still don't know who brought me into this world."

She stops to look at me. "For whatever reason, your parents aren't in any of the records. Perhaps one of them was a bastard, or they've done something unforgivable. In any case, I don't think you'll be able to track them down."

Really, I think to myself. How convenient. But when I reply, I make sure to look heartbroken. "That's fine. I just want to know who they are. Or were," I add in a sad voice. "And I thought you might help me with that."

The professor just looks at me and for a second, I think she'll finally give in. "I'm sorry, Quinn," she finally says. "I just don't know how."

And with that, she leaves me standing in the garden, near a fountain that apparently froze over the holidays, its weathered stone cracked a little on the side.

For a moment, I just stare at it, frustration bubbling under my skin. But I shrug it off because there's still one thing I can do. I don't want to, but if I have to, I will.

It's just that I'd rather wait for it to get dark. And until then, I can do some more work on trying to get close to the Vipers.

I wander around the castle grounds, stopping at a few spots to pretend I'm reading a book. But I don't run into any of them.

It's only a couple of hours later that I walk into the cafeteria to get some lunch and there she is. Sarya. And for the first time ever, she's not with Harry and Zelda.

Ugh. I hate for her to be the one I have to talk to, simply because I think she's a real bitch, but hey, it's not like the rest of them wouldn't be rated PG-18.

So I draw in a breath, whip out my phone and take a seat right next to her, even though there's like a million other empty spots all around me.

I feel her looking up and staring at me, but I just keep pretending I'm texting. I'm hoping to piss her off enough to start talking to me.

But before I know it, I'm letting go of my phone, my hands flying to my neck because the scarf I have wrapped around it is becoming too tight.

The students all snap their heads in my direction as I scramble out of my chair. I turn to Sarya to see her standing to the side of the table and raising her fingers to her mouth.

I can't speak. And I'm already panicking because, well, she's trying to fucking choke me, the bitch. But she gives a strange whistle and I feel even more terrified when Zelda appears, as if out of thin air, closely followed by Harry.

"What do you think you're doing?" Sarya asks with a sly smile as she walks up to me.

She releases her grip enough for me to squeeze out, "I was just trying to get something to eat."

As the other two glance at each other, she lets out a laugh. "Yeah, right. And what were you doing when you were accidentally bumping into Harry and Zelda?"

Goddamn it, I curse at myself. Can't believe I underestimated them like that. So stupid, Quinn, so fucking stupid. I decide the best course of action would be to tell the truth. Part of it, at least.

"To be honest," I wheeze out, "I want to become one of you."

Now they all laugh. Perfect. Sarya takes a step closer, making me flinch a little. "Sure," she says with another one of her sly smiles. "As soon as you get the Ringleader's approval, who just happens to be our leader as well." She pauses for effect. "I hear you're real-life besties."

With that, they all walk away, laughing their heads off. But that's not why I'm fuming. It neither surprises nor gets to me, when an asshole acts like, well, an asshole. But realizing that the only person who could get me in with the Vipers is Faust... Let's just say that that does get to me.

No, I think to myself as I go to my room to wait for the sun to set. If that's what it would take, I'll rather let them all die in that fucking bloodbath. After all, ever since the Ball, I haven't even been able to look at a piece of news with his name in it. Not even when they were all gushing about him taking his new girlfriend on a cruise over the holidays. Of course, I couldn't avoid seeing the pictures. And of course, the girlfriend is a thin blonde vampire girl. They all must be dying their hair to make him like them.

But as I watched him with his hand wrapped around her ethereally slim waist, her looking at him like he's some kind of god walking this earth, all I could think about was murdering him with my bare hands.

So no, I'm not exactly ready to be asking him for any favors.

By the time I realize that Professor Mistila must be finishing up with the last class of the day, I'm still pissed, but I'm forcing myself to focus. Luckily, all I have to do is use a cloaking spell, find her when she's on her way to her apartments and let Moswen take care of the rest.

It all goes smoothly enough. I sneak up on her while walking down one of the moonlit galleries, her steps echoing off the polished stone.

I dig the diary out of my bag and I crack it open, Moswen appearing before me. "I thought Nuala would be with you."

I don't tell her I've chosen to do this early. "It's time," I whisper.

It was Moswen's suggestion. During one of our brainstorming sessions, she told Nuala and myself that this was something she'd be able to do, in case Professor Mistila proved to be a hard nut to crack. We practically squealed with delight.

Still, once she actually does it, I can't help but draw in a breath. The image of her flickers before me, turning into the image of my mother, Syllia Olarel.

Without a word, she nods at me and glides over to where I can hear Professor Mistila walking. I creep closer, dying to see what happens.

Just as I thought, as soon as Syllia's ghost appears in front of her, Professor Mistila stops midstep.

"Why did you turn my daughter away?" the ghost demands.

I see Professor Mistila frown. "Who are you?" she asks in a low voice.

"You know very well who I am." I have to fight not to applaud Moswen for the way she does the spooky ghost voice. "I just wonder why you didn't say as much when she asked for your help."

There's a moment of silence before the professor takes a step closer and speaks in a threatening voice, "I said, *who are you?*"

I frown. I heard her call my mother 'my dear Syllia'. And now she's asking her *who* she is? My mind is buzzing, but I can tell that Moswen is confused as well. Shit. I quickly close the diary shut, making her disappear.

The professor is now looking around. I duck, drawing in a panicked breath. She can't see me and the spell should prevent her from sniffing me out, I tell myself.

But the sound of her footsteps is telling me she's heading straight in my direction. It's only when they stop a few feet from me that I dare to look up.

And there she is, squinting at me from above.

I slowly get up, not knowing whether to expect an attack.

"I have a sneaking suspicion..." She's frowning, but she doesn't look pissed. To my surprise, there's concern in her eyes. "That this *ghost* I just saw was your doing. Explain yourself."

"I'm sorry, Professor Mistila..." I mutter. Think, Quinn, think. Tell the truth, just not the whole truth. "I guess I wanted to entice you to talk. To be honest, I thought you were lying to me earlier."

By the look on her face, she won't be lingering on the details. "Why did you think that?" she demands.

"You seemed to be avoiding me."

She pauses for a second, lets out a sigh and gives me an apologetic smile. "Well, I was... Before I realized you had no idea."

I just blink at her, shaking my head a little to nudge her to keep talking.

"That I'm the one who spilled the news about you being an Olarel."

"Right," I say, shocked by the turn this took.

"I'm truly sorry, Quinn." The professor shakes her head and clicks her tongue as she gives my upper arm a quick, awkward squeeze. "It's not an excuse, but I had a little too much blood gin that evening and things got out of control."

"Right," I echo myself from a minute ago. My mind wants me to be elsewhere, contemplating what just happened, but Professor Mistila is raising her finger at me.

"I'm glad you're not upset, but let it be clear," she says sternly. "The fact that I myself am to blame for some of it, that's the *only* reason I'll be letting this mischief of yours slide."

"Thank you, professor," I say, my voice absent-minded as I move to walk away.

As soon as Professor Mistila is out of sight, I whip out my phone and text Nuala.

"Nuala, I just talked to the professor. And the stuff that's happening... It's even stranger than we thought," I type, thinking about what I've just learned.

Professor Mistila isn't lying about not knowing my parents. She doesn't even *remember* them.

"You did what?!" my friend types back. "I thought we agreed you wouldn't do anything alone."

I feel so lightheaded, but I almost let out a laugh. I start walking, typing some lame attempt at a joke, my eye getting drawn to the Lilith Tower, the one where the vampires reside.

I stop and just look at it for a second, its ghostly outline seeming faint against the darkening sky. Thanks to all the confusion, it didn't even cross my mind. Now that Professor Mistila is out of the picture, I only have the Vipers as a potential source of info. And they've made their terms perfectly clear.

No, I think as I shake my head, despite being all alone on the gallery. I'll cross the mythical seven seas before I come to the Little Prince with a request of *any* kind.

Chapter Twenty-Four

Bloody hell, how infuriating can *one girl* be, I think to myself when I spot her from the window of my quarters in the Lilith Tower. Going to the graveyard as regularly as other students go for lunch.

The sword still in my hand, I get so immersed in watching her, I only notice my uncle when he's already slipped the tip of his blade under my chin.

I crane my neck to look him in the eye. "I thought we were taking a break," I protest.

He shrugs, feigning innocence, but doesn't pull away. I tighten the grip on my weapon, take one clean swing and send his blade flying all the way to the other side of my newly refurbished gym. Then I trip him up and come to stand above him, the tip of my sword touching his Adam's apple.

He lets out a chuckle and motions for me to help him get up. Once he's on his feet again, he dusts himself off and says, "I can't say you're not in shape, Andreas, but we really need you to start taking the Trials more seriously."

I scowl at him. "Uncle, I'm in training twice a day, *every* day."

I turn my back to him and go to grab a bottle of water from the fridge. The sun is yet to rise, but we've already spent a whole hour training.

I hear uncle follow me. "Yes, but something is distracting you."

I gulp and I turn to him, forcing myself to look him straight in the eye. "Really? Where does it show exactly?" I ask flatly, I open the water bottle and I take my time emptying it.

I'm pretending to be clueless, but I know I'm still under the microscope for what happened at the Ball. I normally don't let my control slip that way, getting drunk and letting paparazzi take shots of me inebriated.

"Maybe it doesn't, yet," uncle admits. "But I've never seen you this… intense."

I let out a frustrated breath and I slam the empty water bottle on the counter next to the fridge. "How could I not be intense, huh? What's the point of all this?" I ask with a wave of my hand.

Uncle frowns and then takes a step closer. "You know we're not as powerful as we used to be, nephew," he starts in a gentle voice, "which is exactly why it's so important to be in control of our own image."

"I'm not talking about the bloody Trials, uncle," I snap at him and then let out a sigh. "I'm talking about my life."

Uncle peers into my eyes. "Should I be worried about you, Andreas?" he asks cautiously.

"Look, uncle," I start, "juggling being a student and a ruler takes a lot of work. And I honestly don't mind, but what does my role as a prince amount to? Being a glorified diplomat who never gets to actually do anything, that's what."

This pisses him off, I can tell from the way he's squinting at me. "Is that why I let you run things even before you're of age, nephew? So you can complain about doing your duty?"

I scowl at him. "I know how important *duty* is, uncle," I drawl, "I only wish it involved doing something meaningful."

Uncle just looks at me for a second. Then he gets in my face and says, "The faes are more dangerous than they like to let on, the shifters are constantly in search of another war to wage and the Scions are apes in possession of increasingly dangerous toys. You don't think keeping the *bloody peace* is meaningful?"

By the time he's finished, his chest is heaving.

I make myself snap out of it. "You're right, uncle. You won't hear another word from me."

He nods and straightens his shirt. "Good luck with the Count," he says, his voice back to normal.

And with that, he leaves me to get ready for the meeting.

I just stand there for a second, trying to fight it. Then I walk up to the window and look out. No sign of the girl. Uninvited, the memory of her telling me never to touch her again floods my mind, making me want to smash things.

I turn on my heel and I walk out of the gym. Who the fuck does she think she is, I keep ranting as I make my way down the hallway leading to my bedroom. Once I'm there, I get out of my training clothes and start putting on my suit. Or better yet, does she seriously think I'd end up touching her if I weren't wasted at the time?

Just the possibility of her walking around thinking that fills me with a burning rage. I've had women throwing themselves at me, gorgeous women, since before I knew what to do with them. How dare she think I'd ever even *want* to touch her again?

As I stand in front of the mirror in my bedroom, my hands are shaking, but I somehow manage to finish buttoning up my shirt. No, I snarl at myself. I won't waste another second thinking about her. I take one last glance at myself in the mirror and walk out of my bedroom.

As my assistant Max walks with me into the drawing room, I straighten up and I smooth out my shirt. I take one deep breath and we go inside.

There, the old, dried-up Count Eichel and his minions are already waiting for me. They scramble to get out of their sofas to bow. "Your Majesty," the Count immediately addresses me, "we apologize for the intrusion, but this is an urgent matter."

When *isn't* it, I think to myself as I take a seat, gesturing for the Count to start talking. The rest of them immediately follow suit. The Count is the Ambassador for House of Lilith in the Western Scion lands, which is why I have a sneaking suspicion he'll be talking about the latest occurrence of the Originals breaking the Treaty.

He does. He tells me all about the vampire killing a couple of Scions, getting caught and causing an entire avalanche of responses from the human community.

And even if it weren't the same old story told in a different way, I'd still know about it simply because I make sure to have eyes and ears everywhere. But I keep listening without letting this be known. It's something I learned a long time ago. When you're in a position of power, it's sometimes better to keep those around you clueless as to the true extent of your knowledge.

As I listen to the Count drone on, I start wondering if she's read about the incident. She probably has, a busybody such as herself. And what the fuck does she think she's doing, trying to *join the Vipers*? Does she seriously think that I wouldn't find out? That Sarya wouldn't come running to me right after? And however I look at it, I don't see a motive, but if there's anything I know, it's that she's definitely up to something.

I frown, forcing myself to snap out of it. I'm not letting the ghost of that *girl* mess with my concentration three times before I've even had lunch. But when I shift my focus back onto the Count, I find that he's once again being a complete idiot.

"He didn't even feed on those two, he just killed them," he tells me with conviction as he leans forward and presses one finger on the table, "and those fucking Lesser-"

"Scions," I cut in.

"Scions," he corrects himself, "are still demanding he be processed as an Anti-Treaty criminal."

"Let me guess," I say with a sigh. "You don't want that to happen, do you, Count Eichel?"

"That's right, Your Majesty." The Count is nodding, although it's clear that the tone of my voice is making him hesitate. "The man didn't deserve it and the Lesser-"

"Scions," I cut in, *again*.

"Yes, Your Majesty," he says with a curt nod, "the Scions are only being emotional, as always-"

"Yes, they are," I cut him off, slightly more forcefully this time, "I'll give you that." I lean a little forward, making the Count lean back. "But is their discontent with these things entirely unfounded?"

There's a moment of silence before the Count blinks at me and mutters, "No, I guess it's not."

"Shouldn't we give them what they want then, now that our primary goal is keeping the peace?"

The Count nods. "Yes, Your Majesty. I understand and I will prepare a statement accordingly."

Oh how I hate the guy and all his spinelessness, stupidity and carelessness. He moves to get up, but I raise my hand and he slumps back into his seat. I appear next to him, leaning forward as I say, "Also, it was *three* Scions and not two that the man killed."

I can tell that he's fighting to stay still, his eyes failing to look straight into mine. "If you wish to keep your position as Ambassador, you *will* have your facts straight at *all* times, understood?"

After my meeting with the Count, I have three more lined up so it's after two o'clock that I finally get the chance to take a walk and clear my head a little.

Of course, as soon as I start roaming the castle garden by myself, it crosses my mind. The option to do it again, just like I did before, twice since the incident. The option to sniff her out and accidentally find myself walking past her. For whatever mysterious reason, she wants to join the Vipers, and they've told her exactly what she needs to do to achieve that. She needs to go through *me*.

When she does, I think to myself as I focus on sniffing out her blood, that annoyingly intoxicating blend of soft and sharp notes... When she does, I'll find out exactly what she's up to. How do I know she will? By the apparent struggle I saw in her eyes when I appeared in her sight. Yes, she threw daggers at me both times. And yes, she stomped away as quickly as possible. But she also hesitated, just a little. And a little more the second time around.

I'm already on my way to the Dame Gothel statue, where her scent seems to be strongest. And the closer I get, the more those images flood my mind. The images of her as she spun around the podium with me. I strain to recall, in as much detail as possible, the way it felt to have her so close, the curve of her waist, her skin, those eyes. My heart pounds in anticipation of catching another glimpse of her.

It's only when I get close to the statue that I ask myself what the fuck I'm doing. Yes, the longing to see her makes me want to jump out of my skin. But that just makes for a very good reason not to do it. I've been under this girl's spell for too long, I remind myself, ever since I first laid eyes on her before the opening ceremony. I simply can't let her do this to me anymore.

So I turn on my heel and I walk away. I cut my lunch short, which gives me time to catch up on some classwork before a series of afternoon meetings and my last training session of the day.

But by the time I'm finished with all the endless obligations, watching news in my living room, I'm not any less restless than I was when I decided not to 'bump' into her. I soon find myself reliving, once again, the incident at the Ball. My body vibrates with rage as I imagine the look in her eyes. The *disgusted* look in her eyes before she threw me against the wall.

But it's all fine, I think to myself as I flick through the channels, because when she finally comes begging for my help, I won't just find out what the hell she's up to. I'll stare straight into those eyes and I'll turn her down cold, I will.

It makes me feel a little better, imagining the look in her eyes when *that* happens. When she realizes what refusing me actually means.

I get so lost in those ruminations that I imagine I'm smelling her again.

Only, a moment later, it turns out it's not my imagination after all. I jump up on my feet, the scent of her blood getting stronger with each second. She's close and getting closer, my heart responding with the usual tiresome pounding.

I hear a knock on my front door and the sound of her voice drifts up to me. She's talking with Max. She's here looking for me and I hear him telling her I'm not to be disturbed.

Before I realize what I'm doing, I'm at the door leading onto the foyer. I catch her just as she turns to leave. "It's alright, Max," I drawl in an effort to keep my voice from betraying my feelings, "I'll see her."

I notice the look she throws me when she turns to face me. I motion for her to follow me into the living room.

"No," she snaps. "I'd rather not be alone with you."

It makes me freeze for a second. Hot rage flooding my body, I squeeze out, "I don't give a fuck. I won't be talking to you in the foyer."

With that, I turn on my heel and dart back into the living room, leaving the door open and trying to keep my body from shaking.

After a moment of hesitation, I hear her come in and her footsteps draw close. The fact of her actually being here makes me lightheaded so I busy myself with pouring vintage scotch into two crystal glasses from the bar. I need a second to collect myself before I can face her. Especially since I sense she's pissed about me not addressing her directly, or pissed at me in general, and that fire of hers does things to me that are sometimes hard to control.

I finally turn to her, holding out a glass of scotch as I motion for her to take a seat.

She just shakes her head.

"Suit yourself," I say flatly. I put her glass away and take my own with me as I throw myself on the sofa, not too far from where she remains standing. I don't say anything. I'm waiting for her to talk and I'm going to relish it, I think as I lean back, opening my legs and throwing an arm around the backrest with the glass still in my hand.

"I'm going to cut to the chase," she starts, sounding as if she has to force each word out individually. "I want to join the Vipers, but apparently, I can't do that without *you* giving me the green light."

With that, as if she knows I'll say no, she folds her arms in defiance and a wave of heat floods me from head to toe. I fight not to let my eyes drag over her body.

"Hmmm," I say and I down the entire glass of scotch. The liquid burns my throat and I tip my head back a little, determined to look at her face and her face only. I lean forward, put the glass down and shake my head, pretending to be thinking. Should I drag it out or would it be sweeter to be blunt?

"For crying out loud," she interrupts me, her face flushed, her arms lowered to her sides and her hands balled into fists. "If you're going to say no, just fucking say it. I want no part of your lame power trip."

My skin burning and my fangs fighting to be released, it takes all I have not to jump up and *grab* her. Instead, I force my voice to remain flat as I say, "Alright. Then *no*."

She just stares at me for a second and then moves to walk away. Before I even realize it, I'm off the sofa, blocking her way out. "Why do you want to join?" I ask in a low voice.

"That's none of your business," she replies coldly.

"So it's a whim."

"No, it's not," she snaps at me. Now, that made her tick. I enjoy seeing her press her lips tight in an effort to control herself.

She hesitates for a second. "If you really need to know, I'm bad at using magic and I'd very much like to survive the Trials."

"The truth," I demand, being so close to her, especially with that flush on her face, becoming a bit too much for me to handle. "I want the *whole* truth."

"Forget it," she snaps at me and turns to walk away.

I move to grab her arm and force her to come back, but at the last second, I flinch and take a step back. "Wait," I hear myself say.

She stops, but she doesn't turn around.

"I'll tell them you can join," I squeeze out, despite the fact that it's the last thing I need, to have more of *her* in my life.

She looks over her shoulder and I see suspicion in her eyes.

"But you need to promise to respect my authority as the leader of the group."

I fully expect her to say no. It surprises me when she thinks for a second and then says, "Fair enough. I promise."

Before I can do or say anything else, she turns on her heel and walks out of the room. Once she's gone, I let out a breath and throw myself on the sofa. When I look down, I see that my hands are shaking. And all the blood in my body seems to be going straight to my dick. Perfect. That's all I needed today.

I jump up and go straight to the bathroom. I'm going to take the coldest fucking shower ever and I'm *not* going to let her inside my head again.

But they test my willpower, the images of her that keep assaulting me as water runs down my naked body. The ones from the Ball are the hardest to keep out of my head. The way that her dress clung to her body, the way that her ass felt when I squeezed it, the way that that little moan that escaped her lips made me want to rip into her until I could no longer feel anything other than *her*.

The shower doesn't help. Even after I'm out, my dick is throbbing, but I'm not planning on doing anything about it. Instead, I pace around the room, telling myself I'd sooner die than let myself fantasize about that rash, emotional, vulgar, naive, human-bred... *girl*.

It takes me a moment to realize that I've opened a hole in the wall with my fist. Pissed and tired at the same time, I yank my hand out and I go straight to bed, wanting the day to end as soon as possible.

I'm already under the covers when my phone pings, making my heart skip a beat. But it's only Amelia.

"Exactly how late do you plan on being?" the text says.

Fuck. I forgot. "Sorry, Amelia, I'm just too tired."

"But I'm wearing a super slutty dress." There's a winky face at the end.

"Tempting," I text back. "But why don't you go on without me?"

I can tell she's upset by how long it takes her to reply with a simple, "Fine." But the very thought of seeing her is off-putting at the moment.

I put my phone away and let out a sigh. Why did I do it, I scold myself. I said I'd refuse and yet, I didn't. What do I let her keep doing this to me? I roll to my stomach and I bite into my pillow, letting out a low groan.

But I know what I need to do. I'll just stop coming to the Vipers' training sessions. At least for a while, until I'm back in control. And back in control I will be.

Chapter Twenty-Five

When Nuala finally meets me in front of the Library, I'm determined not to say anything until we're already there.

As we walk, my friend keeps yawning and rubbing her eyes, thinking we're in for another couple of hours of scouring all the books that mention any type of stone, magical or otherwise.

And we are, just not where we've been doing it the past couple of weeks. And Nuala is so sleepy, she doesn't even notice where I'm taking her until we're right in front of the door.

"The Restricted Section?" she reads the sign on the smooth wooden surface, frowning as she turns to throw me a scolding look. "Quinn, we all agreed that this would be our last resort."

I don't say anything. I just look over my shoulder to make sure there are no Librarians around us.

"You do understand," Nuala hisses at me under her breath, "if anyone catches us, we're in a *world* of trouble."

"No one's stopping you from leaving, Nuala."

For a second, she just looks at me. Then she lets out a sigh and says, "Alright, lead the way."

I crack open the door and throw a glance inside. "All clear," I say, deciding to go first in case I'm wrong and there's someone lurking in the shadows.

Once we're inside and I hear Nuala closing the door behind us, I want to throw her a grin, but my eyes have gotten adjusted to the darkness enough for me to see the room we've found ourselves in. We both gasp at the very same time. It's not that I expected anything in particular, but the enormity of the space and the height which the bookshelves around us reach is simply astounding, especially coupled with the stained glass windows that look large enough to be found in some cathedral. They're casting soft light on specks of dust and weathered volumes alike.

I don't waste any time. I crack open the diary and Moswen appears in front of us. I see her lips start to curl into a smile, when she notices where we've brought her. "Quinn," she starts, her eyebrows pulling down in surprise.

But I don't let her talk. "I know what you're going to say." I'm speaking in a low voice, just in case. "But it's not like we've found anything of any use so far and we're running out of time."

Even before I'm done talking, she's shaking her head. "It's not even March yet, we still have over *four* months."

"Exactly, *only* four months," I insist, fighting not to raise my voice. "And in case you're not aware, my first training session with the Vipers is *tomorrow*."

"And that's worth risking everything?" she practically hisses at me, making Nuala squirm where she's standing.

I don't want to fight with her, but the rising fear of facing some of the deadliest students at the Academy gets to me. "The Vipers are already suspicious of me. You want me to try to get them to talk without even knowing what about?"

"I want you to be careful, *for once*," she snarls at me.

She doesn't say it, but I *know* she's referring to the time I went to Professor Mistila behind her back. It makes me let out a frustrated growl. "For the billionth time, I said I was sorry."

"Not sorry enough not to do it again, apparently," Moswen scoffs, throwing daggers at me.

I have to fight not to yell at her. "Who the fuck do you think you are, my mother?"

That shuts her up alright. And the hurt look on her face almost makes me take it all back, but then she turns her fucking back to me and says in that flat voice of hers, "I don't care what you do. However, I won't have any part of it."

My hands are balled into fists and my eyes are burning holes in the back of her head, but all I do is snap, "Fine," and close the diary shut with one violent movement.

When I turn to face her, Nuala is looking away, her eyebrows raised and her lips pressed tight.

"You plan on giving me shit, too?"

"No, ma'am," she says without a moment of hesitation.

It almost makes me laugh, but we've no time to waste. I motion for her to follow me as I venture deeper into the Restricted Section, the musty bookshelves towering over me on each side.

And there are some disturbing titles in here. I mean, I think as I scan the titles, *Blood Manipulation Level 1?*

I thumb my nose, but then my eye lands on something interesting. *Shifter Psychopharmacology.* I grab it from the shelf and crack it open, hungrily searching the Table of Contents.

"Nuala," I whisper and she comes to stand behind me, peering over my shoulder. "There are plants you can use to induce your first shift. And look, this one plant, I know I've seen it at the graveyard."

When she says nothing, I crane my neck to see her throwing me a pissed-off look. "I thought I told you to leave it alone."

"Yes, ma'am," I say with a sorry look in my eyes and I quickly go back to looking for the books for our research. Luckily, it doesn't take us long to find a decent number of contenders.

We take as many books as we can carry and find a seat close to one of the cathedral windows. "To start," I say to Nuala as I crack open the first book, "let's focus on the mystery stone. We can do mentions of the Trials later."

My friend nods and gets to work. And I know how much she doesn't like doing research, so I throw her a grateful look before I bury my nose in the book in front of me.

There are only a couple of moments of silence before I hear Nuala let out a squeal. "Ah, the Navarre stone."

I look up, my heart skipping a beat as I wait for her to keep going. "It says here that just being close to it makes you see the entire color spectrum."

I let out a sigh, cursing myself for getting my hopes up. "Yeah, I don't think so. The power that my parents talked about has to be greater. Also, I don't think it can be something we have very ordinary technology for."

It's comical, the way Nuala's shoulders slump in disappointment. "Guess you're right. I'll just keep looking."

A few hours in, we find ourselves with a bunch of notes on every kind of stone there is. Moon stone. Blood stone. The Banshee Stone. Even one stone, the Mhaenal Stone, that's been in the property of the Academy for centuries, but there's no mention of it having any powers. It's just a weird-looking stone some General brought over from the faraway lands that we today know as South America.

I let out a sigh and glance around. We haven't even scratched the surface, let alone started on researching the Trials, but I'm worried about the growing possibility of someone catching us red-handed.

Disheartened and pissed about my fight with Moswen, I suggest we leave and come back another day. Nuala seems thrilled, but once we're out of the Restricted Section and back to walking around the castle, my mind rushes to tomorrow's training session, *again.*

"Everything will be okay," my friend stops to tell me, smiling as she gives my shoulder a squeeze. "You're going to kick their fucking asses and find out everything you need to find out."

It's as if she can read my mind. "I know." I force myself to throw her a grin.

But it's not just the Vipers I'm worried about. It's their leader as well. And I haven't told either Nuala or Moswen, but I'm afraid I don't know Faust's real motive for letting me join the team and the thought fills me with dread.

Chapter Twenty-Six

The next morning, I have to drag myself out of bed. It's five AM and it's fucking cold outside, but the Vipers don't seem to like having their sessions indoors, even if it means the risk of losing a limb or two. So I let out a low groan, I pull on my clothes and I head straight for the training grounds.

A part of me hopes that this is all some kind of prank. That they've arranged for me to show up while they're all still snoring away in their respective Houses. But there they all are and they seem to have started without me.

As I approach, I breathe a sigh of relief when I notice Faust not there. But as soon as my eyes land on Sarya blasting the straw dummies to pieces with her fire magic, all that relief shrivels up and dies on me.

"Look who was crazy enough to actually show up," Harry drawls mockingly as soon as he sees me.

Before I even realize what's going on, the four of them have me surrounded. "What should we do with her?" Sarya asks as she throws the rest of the gang amused glances.

"I know," Leo says with a sly smile. "What's your record for those flexed arm hangs, Harry?" He turns to the shifter, who lets out a rough chuckle before he says, "Three minutes and five seconds."

A couple of them give a low whistle, making me frown. "I'm here to work on my magic, not do PE."

"You're here to do whatever *we* think you should do," Leo gets in my face.

Perfect, I think to myself. Now I have to suffer the consequences of pissing off my very own crazed stalker.

"Flexed arm hangs, you say?" I squeeze out, fighting to make my voice chirpy as I add, "Bring it on then."

"Perfect," Sarya says. "And remember, you're only done with your first exercise after you've broken Harry's record."

As if that's ever going to happen, I think to myself. They all laugh and go back into their positions, while I look around, blinking stupidly. "How am I supposed to do them?" I ask Sarya when I realize there are no overhead bars I could use.

She's already started sparring with Harry. She stops to look over her shoulder and points at something so far away from where we're standing, I can barely see it.

"What the," I start, breaking off almost as soon as I start.

It won't just be impossible for me to finish the exercise. It also ruins any chance I have of starting a conversation with any of them. But I grit my teeth and start walking to the far end of the training grounds, aware that anything I say in protest to their decision will only be viewed as either nagging or a sign of weakness. And I won't be giving them that satisfaction. Nope, not me.

Of course, my first attempt at doing a flexed arm hang ends up just as I expect it to. With my body coming crashing to the ground after only a couple of seconds, my arms shaking from the effort. Now, I'm not some weakling. I'm wiry and I have thighs of steel thanks to years of doing midnight runs, but my arms are a whole other story. Lisa used to joke that they have the strength and resilience equivalent to that of cooked pasta.

Still, I keep at it. After a couple of dozen tries, I manage to do fifteen seconds. Fifteen. And I actually feel proud of myself, for that one second before I notice a stir among the gang.

I drop to the ground and squint in their direction. It doesn't take me long to realize that the Little Prince himself has graced us with his presence. Goddamn it, I think to myself as I catch my breath, watching him talk to Harry. It's been two months since the Ball and I still can't even *look* at him without it sending me into a fit of rage. And it sure as hell didn't help that I had to grovel at his feet just to be allowed to be here. But of course, *that* won't be the end of my misery. Because I'm sure it won't be long before he comes to smirk at me, taking advantage of this change in our dynamic.

But he doesn't. While he's still talking to Harry, I think I see him glancing in my direction, even though he's so far away. But then he just starts sparring with the rest of them, so as I'm hanging off the bar, my entire body shaking, I can see him fighting the others and, well, wiping the floor with their butts.

Of course, it makes me want to leer. Faust is a pompous, vile, inconsiderate, privileged fucker. But that doesn't make him any less hot. And the fact that it all looks so effortless, when he manages to send someone flying to the ground... Let's just say it makes me even more pissed, which doesn't help my attempts at breaking Harry's record.

At one point, Faust leaves and I see the others disperse as well. No one throws as much as a glance at me. And of course, I haven't made a lot of progress, my new record being just shy of eighteen seconds. But as I make my way back to the castle, I conclude that I'll have to get used to it. Even if I managed to do what they wanted me to, which is absurd, they'd just come up with another way to torture me as they keep me far away from them.

And hey, at least I'm no longer actively scared for my life with them, but the entire purpose of this thing is to get them to talk to me.

That makes me want to ask Moswen for advice. And I'm in my room already, which means there's nothing stopping me from talking to her. Except the bitch version of myself from yesterday, I think to myself as I let my aching body collapse onto the bed.

But almost immediately after my head touches the pillow, I sit back up and pull over my bag. I take the diary out and I draw in a breath.

"Moswen," I tell her as soon as she appears, despite that frown still twisting her pretty face.

"What would you like me to do this time, oh exalted master?" she snaps.

I try to ignore the ugly pang of guilt that shoots through me. Sniveling apologies won't do us any good. "Moswen," I repeat, adding a touch of tenderness. "I actually wanted to apologize to you."

I see her shift a little, as if this wasn't what she expected.

But she doesn't say anything, so I just keep talking. "Look, there's been a lot going on that I'm just not used to. Don't get me wrong," I rush to add, "I'm not some delicate flower. I never had a family and the things my foster parents did to me, well, let's just say you wouldn't put them in a children's book…"

I finish with a weak laugh, frowning a bit when I see that Moswen seems to be pitying me. I draw in a breath and when I speak again, my voice is controlled and filled with determination. "But that's not the point. The point is, all this stuff that's happening, it's so different from the troubles I'm used to. And I guess I let it all get to me. But that's not what I'm sorry for…"

She tilts her head a little.

"I'm sorry for the way I treated you. I know you're not just trying to get out of this whole magical-diary situation. You're trying to look out for us as well, and I kind of made it hard for you with my shitty behavior."

I pause, happy to see her face visibly softening. "But I promise I won't let it happen again."

There's a moment of silence before she nods and says, "Apology accepted."

I breathe a sigh of relief, moving as if to hug her, only at the last second realizing what I'm doing. We both laugh.

"Did you find anything?" she asks, referring to our illegal search for info on the mystery stone. Her voice much warmer now.

I shake my head, my lips pressed tight.

"Any luck with the Vipers?"

"No, and I don't expect it to change anytime soon."

She thinks for a second. "You know," she starts, her voice much warmer now, "I really was trying to protect you. But that doesn't mean that I don't understand the urgency of the task before us. And it's dangerous..." She pauses for a second as if she's still unsure, making my ears prick up. "But there's something I'd like to suggest."

With that, she just looks at me, making me wave my hand at her to keep talking.

"I happen to know where to find Dame Gothel."

There's a second of silence, during which my eyebrows pull down in confusion. "Dame Gothel? The one whose statue we have in the garden? The witch from Rapunzel?"

"Witches don't exist, Quinn."

"Of course, I know," I rush to say. "That's just what humans used to think faes are. But however we choose to call her, how would *Dame Gothel* help us? Keeping princesses locked in towers doesn't exactly match our requirements," I finish with a laugh.

"That particular story is beyond reductive," Moswen says with an impatient wave of her hand, nipping my curiosity in the bud. "She's someone you can strike a deal with," she says with a fire in her voice. "Whatever you need, whether it's unbreakable armor or a piece of information on a mysterious stone, beings like her can give it to you."

I shake my head. "*Beings* like her? I thought she was a fae like us."

Moswen leans forward and practically whispers, "Imagine a fae that doesn't let herself be limited by our society." There's a glimmer in her eyes as she says it and her words make shivers travel down my spine. "One that has ventured so deeply into the Great Unknowns of Divine Magic that she's practically one with nature. That's Dame Gothel."

Perfect, I think to myself. As if going to Faust wasn't enough. "And *that's* who you want me to ask for help?" I ask with a feeling of dread wrapping around my entire body.

"Help?" she says with a laugh. "No need to worry about that. If she agrees to give you what you want, it'll be for a price."

"So comforting," I blurt out, wondering what the hell I'm getting myself into. But it was only a few moments ago that I decided I'd approach this whole situation with a lot more courage and determination.

So I guess this is the universe's way of saying, "Fuck you, you asked for it yourself".

Chapter Twenty-Seven

It's the dead of night and every sound you make echoes through the deserted hallways with such smug vengeance, but Nuala and I still manage to get to the Door without anyone seeing us. It's the one by the statue of the Frog King, one of only two spots on the castle grounds that allow you to use the Pull.

And it's not forbidden for students to use them, provided you do it before curfew and fill out a form, informing the Faculty of the reason for your departure, the expected time of return and so on and so forth.

And it's not like I can write 'visiting the witch from Rapunzel'. So we take advantage of the cover that the night provides.

"Sure you want to do this?" Nuala asks when we stop before the Door.

"Sure you want to come with?"

She lets out a sigh, but she nods. We approach the Door in silence. It's just a strange shimmer in the night air that you have to walk into. And if you don't want it to spit you out someplace random, you have to tell it where you want to go.

Squeezing the bag in which I'm carrying the diary, I take Nuala by the hand and we nod at each other. The woods at the edge of the world, I think to myself as I let the current drag me in.

The Pull turns out to be just as awful as the first time I used it. Once we're on the other side, I take a few wobbly steps to the side to puke my guts out. I hear Nuala doing the same.

But when I straighten up and look around, I forget all about the lingering queasiness in my stomach. The gasp that comes from Nuala's mouth tells me she's just as dumbfounded.

The woods in which we find ourselves is deep and dark, the thick, gnarly trees barely letting any moonlight through. Still, there's a strange glow to it all, as if everything around us is part of a single beating heart.

I only snap out of it when Nuala jabs me with her elbow. I turn to her, mouthing 'What'.

She points at the gigantic tree right in front of us. It's by far the largest, so large, in fact, that someone has made it their home. At least judging by one door and two windows fitted into its trunk.

And just as we stare at it, the tree starts glowing brighter and I feel eyes on me, from everywhere around me. I grab Nuala's hand, but nothing happens.

At least until a few seconds later, when I hear a creak and the door slowly opens, making my heart skip a beat. I squint to see better, but there's no one standing next to it. Or behind it.

I gesture for Nuala to keep silent. I draw in a breath and I dig the diary out of my bag. Once Moswen is in front of us, I gesture at the door, not saying a word as I do it.

Moswen takes a quick look, turns back to me and says, in a voice that doesn't seem to be hiding fear, "She's invited you inside."

"Oh."

I turn to look at Nuala, determination on my face. She seems to be just as ready as I am.

We slowly approach the house and walk inside. The interior is rough, but pleasant. There's a straw bed in one corner and a table with a single chair in the other. The center of the room is dominated by a hearth that seems to grow out of the back of the tree itself. The coals in it are softly crackling, burning with the same glow as the forest itself, just stronger. It makes me frown, thinking there's something strange going on here.

And just as I think that, I imagine that the coals have just let out a deep, soothing sigh.

The sigh turns into soft-spoken words, "My apologies for greeting you like this, little one."

My eyebrows raised, my eyes dart between Nuala to my left and Moswen to my right. They seemed to be just as surprised by the turn of the events.

But the talking coals just keep, well, talking. "Wintertime makes me tired of my usual vessel. I prefer to spend it this way. It's much more relaxing."

I muster the strength to talk. "No need to apologize, Dame Gothel." I rush to add, "If that is how you like to be addressed."

"That's of no consequence whatsoever," the coals reply, the sound carrying a note of impatience. "What have you come to ask of me?"

"I need information on a certain stone," I say, realizing that the rest of the conversation will sound even more stupid.

"*Which* stone?"

"That's the thing," I start, not without hesitation. "I don't know."

"Is this some kind of jest?" the coals ask in a voice that doesn't try to conceal the irritation.

"No, of course not," I rush to say. "I can't tell you *which* stone, but there are other things I can... divulge," I choose to say, feeling a strange need to sound more formal.

"*Divulge* them then," is the response I get.

I hesitate a bit. "I can tell you it's a powerful stone..." As I talk, I straighten up and I start using a more determined tone of voice. "A stone someone is planning on stealing during the Third Round of the Grimm Academy Trials. And I can also tell you it happened once before, in 2005, and almost ended in a bloodbath."

There's a moment of silence as the coals in the hearth burn a little brighter.

I hear a quiet chuckle. "Not almost," Dame Gothel finally says.

I frown, sensing my two companions shifting on their feet. I open my mouth to speak, but the witch or fae or whatever she is cuts in. "If you want me to tell you more, you need to pay first."

I draw in a breath, my heart throbbing from the excitement. "Tell me your price," I say.

"You," Dame Gothel replies, the coals letting out a little sigh as she does. "Stay here, bond with my home and I'll help you prevent the bloodshed."

"So there will be a bloodshed," I say at the same time as Moswen takes a step closer and asks, her voice shaking a little, "Why would you want *her*?"

The coals flicker and the light in them dies down so quickly, it makes me look around with bated breath. And sure enough, the ashes get swept into the air and before I even realize what's happening, she's towering over the three of us, a huge woman seemed to made up of clay and twigs and moss, shooting Moswen an angry look.

"You dare to inquire about my reasons?" her voice thunders, making me all but pee my fucking pants. "A price is a price. If the girl doesn't wish to pay, she may take her leave."

"I want to pay," I blurt out, my mind buzzing as it rushes to grasp everything that's going on. With the corner of my eye, I see that Moswen is throwing me a nervous look. I breathe a sigh of relief when I notice Dame Gothel returning to the form in which we found her. "I'd just like to know exactly what I'm committing to. What does bonding with your home mean and what would you expect me to do here?"

"I don't expect you to do anything," she says. "Your blood is powerful and you will be one with my home, making it easier for me to protect it from the hordes that keep coming, trying to steal my powers."

"I see," I reply, hesitant about negotiating with such a powerful being.

"Take her blood then," Moswen cuts in, her voice rushed and shaky.

I almost snap at her when I see that she's made the coal burn brighter in fury once again. But I decide it's worth a shot.

"Dame Gothel," I say, forcing myself to straighten and push my chest out, "I understand that a being such as yourself could be unjust with no consequence whatsoever. Yet you make sure that the deals you strike with those lesser of you are always fair."

I pay attention to the way the coals are reacting to my words. And they seem to be listening. "However, in this particular case, considering I'm only asking for a single piece of information, the name of the stone, I think giving you my blood would be a fair trade."

There's a moment of silence, during which I hear my heart pounding so loudly, I'm afraid everyone can hear it.

But then there's that low chuckle again and I hear Dame Gothel say, "Fair enough. Give me your blood and I will tell you the name of the stone. And nothing else," she warns.

At that, I hear a rattle coming from my right. I look in its direction and see a knife writhing against the wooden surface of the table.

Holy hell, what am I doing, I think to myself as I approach the table and take the knife in my hand. I force myself not to hesitate. The quicker I am, the less painful it will be and the sooner this will all be over, I tell myself.

So I slice the skin of my palm, wincing at the pain that shoots through my hand. It's only when dark-red liquid comes rushing out do I realize I've no idea what to do with it.

I turn back to the hearth, a drop of my blood falling on the beaten earth under my feet. As soon as it makes contact, my mind goes into overdrive. I feel being pulled in by another consciousness, my mind exploding with images of births and deaths of entire civilizations.

My heart throbbing, I snap out of it to see the coals glimmer with satisfaction.

That makes the building tension inside me loosen up a bit, but I also feel strangely lightheaded. As if someone knocked all the air out of my lungs by making me look into the depths of something I didn't even know existed.

"Thank you, this was delicious," Dame Gothel says with a slow exhale. "Now for my end of the bargain." She pauses for a second before she adds, "the name of the stone you're talking about is the Semper Stone."

I'm having trouble breathing and it seems that Nuala has taken note of it, at least judging by the way she rushes to my side and helps me stay upright. "Thank you, Dame Gothel," I manage to squeeze out. "We'll be taking our leave now."

She stops me with another chuckle. "You know, you act tough, little one, but I could taste all the fear in your blood."

I just blink at her.

"You're scared of being a fae. Scared of your own power." She pauses before she adds, "But is that really how you want to live your life?"

I frown, but she obviously doesn't expect me to answer because the door to her house opens with a thud, signaling it's time for us to leave. I have to fight to make it outside, even with Nuala's help, as the witch's words echo in my head. Not almost, she said when I mentioned the bloodbath that nearly happened in 2005. Not *almost*.

Chapter Twenty-Eight

A week after our visit to Dame Gothel, I have another training session scheduled with the Vipers. I feel like I'll only be getting myself into more trouble by actually showing up, but I don't let it stop me. I get up at the crack of dawn, again, and make my way to the training grounds with my shoulders slumped and my face taking on a more sour look with each step. It's haunted every moment of my waking life since it was revealed to me.

That my parents have probably been dead for a really long time and that it's more than likely that they were killed in some horrible bloodbath.

No wonder I get that feeling when my mother visits me in my nightmares, looking at me, without ever blinking, with eyes full of some secret anguish.

Of course, I think to myself as I approach the training grounds, it would be nice if I got something else out of Dame Gothel, other than trauma and the name of a stone that apparently does nothing at all and doesn't seem to have any connection whatsoever to the Trials. Nuala and I would know. We've searched *everywhere*. The only thing we've found is that there's another name that the stone goes by. The Mhaenal Stone, that same stone I read about weeks ago. But it's so insignificant that there's only two mentions of it, both in some historiography of Grimm Academy.

So it's absolutely delightful that on top of all that, I need to spend time among the Vipers again.

And I absolutely need to. Even if our visit answered all our questions, which it didn't, there'd still be the matter of the Second Round of the Trials, which is barely a month away, on April 30th. And as much as I don't believe the Vipers will intentionally help me get better at Magic, I'm hoping that just being around them and watching them train will improve my chances of surviving.

When I finally see them, splayed out on the only couple of benches on the entire training grounds, I breathe a sigh of relief. Their stuff strewn casually all over the low table in the center, they're laughing as they listen to Harry read something to them from his phone. They seem, well, not pissed, and they haven't started without me.

The chatter dies down a bit as they turn to watch me approach. I notice the way Leo looks at me, a frown etched into his forehead. But when Sarya says, "Who do we have here?" and the tone of her voice is not menacing, I almost crack a smile.

"*Not* someone who likes to get up at dawn, that's for sure," I say, attempting to start making friends with them. Although, I'd settle for becoming *former* enemies as well.

"We were just reading about you," Harry starts as I take a seat, forcing myself to leave *some*, not too much space between them and myself.

I open my mouth, but Zelda rushes to say, "Yeah, and it seems like you're someone much more interesting than we thought."

I've never seen her look intrigued before. It's also the first time she's ever addressed me. She's smiling at me, but I'm sensing a trap. "Really? How so?"

Harry practically barks with delight as he holds his phone up and starts reading loudly and performatively. "Fascinated by the story of Quinn Longborn, the mediocre Scion turned the only surviving Olarel? Well, let me tell you the truth that no one wants to admit."

"No, read that last bit, H," Zelda cuts in.

As he pauses to scroll, I dig my nails into the palms of my hand, trying to keep it cool. It was my choice to stay out of the loop with the tabloids, but I guess they're taking it away from me. Chill, Quinn, chill.

"So, we have a young penniless woman who claims to be of noble origin, but there are no records of her parents even existing. And then we see that same young woman throw herself, time and again, at our prince? Is that really not enough for us to see the plain truth behind all that seductive glimmer? That Quinn Longborn is just a modern-day version of the Princess Anastasia wannabe trying to play a trick on her wealthy, *supposed* grandmother."

By the time he's done, I can feel my cheeks burning from all the rage and for a second, I think the world around me turns liquid. There's a moment of silence before I manage to squeeze out, "Had your fun?"

"At least now we know," Leo surprises me by speaking, "why you wanted to join our little club." There's venom in his eyes.

I start getting up. "I don't give a shit what you know or don't know," I say to him in a tense voice and I turn to the others. "If you're done playing Gossip Girls, I'd like to start training."

"Sure," Sarya drawls, craning her neck to point at a table a ways off, strewn with all kinds of weapons. "Today we thought we'd practice a little hand-to-hand combat. See that mallet over there?"

"I think I do."

"We need you to get it here," she says as she throws me a vicious smile, "but you have to stay where you're standing."

I just look at her for a second. I hear the others sniggering. And there's no way I can do the thing she's asking me to, but I choose not to complain.

"Alright, I guess I'll get started on that then," I squeeze out as I throw them all one wide, fake smile and start getting into the right stance to use the Element rune.

I block out their sniggering and focus on getting into the right mindset. Part of my mind does register Sarya using her runes to summon a couple of other weapons so the rest of them can start sparring.

But I'm busy working on an idea. Sure, neither my Air nor Earth magic would be strong enough to get this done, but what if I use them together? If I use Earth to get the mallet out of the rack and Air to summon it to my feet?

But not a minute goes by and Leo appears to my side, breaking my concentration with his creepy stare. "You know, I could get them off your back. You only need to say a word."

"Which one? So I make sure I don't say it," I hiss at him without turning to look into his eyes.

There's a moment of silence before I hear him expel an angry breath. He grabs my arm and makes me look at him. "Maybe you're not aware of this, but I come from an obscenely rich family. My wealth actually exceeds the prince's."

"I don't give a fuck if you were the last man on earth," I reply as I yank his hand away. I'm feeling even more light-headed now and my vision changes again, so I take a step back.

He just takes one closer to me. "Right," he drawls, but I can tell he's having trouble controlling himself. "I see you're sticking to your little story, but I know exactly what you are."

"Say it," I snap at him, my voice low and threatening, even though he could break my neck without lifting a fucking finger. "I dare you."

"Gold digger."

"You fucker," I snarl as I throw a helpless punch at him.

He blocks it with ease and laughs. "So sad, how it shows that you've never had any parental guidance," he adds as he twists my arm painfully.

Fuming. I'm fucking fuming. "What did you say about my parents?" I yell at him, yanking my arm free and imagining lifting him up and throwing him to the ground like the piece of worthless shit that he is.

Dame Gothel's words rush to my mind and I decide to let it all go. I tap my Element rune.

The very next second, I see a flash of surprise in Leo's eyes before I send his body flying into the air. It comes crashing down with such brutal force that I hear bones cracking. He's on the ground, screaming in pain, and now the others are all surrounding us, throwing me funny looks.

Holy fucking shit, what did I just do?

And just as I think they'll kill me right here and now, a familiar voice booms from behind my back. "What the *fuck* is going on here?"

I crane my neck to see the Little Prince walking up to us, his face sharp with fury. I've never seen him so pissed.

"Longborn attacked Leo," Sarya rushes to say as she crouches next to him, feigning concern, I'm sure. "I saw it, he did nothing."

Nothing? I open my mouth to protest, but I change my mind. Fuck. If I want the Vipers to respect me, I can't be ratting them out to their leader. Also, I've just let myself listen to some old witch's advice and it resulted in me seriously hurting someone, so it's not like I'm without blame here.

Faust doesn't wait for me to react. When he moves towards me, I take a step back, fully expecting him to yell at me. But I just see him frowning as he scans me for injuries and then turns his focus onto Leo, who's still on the ground.

"You want me to believe that *she*," Faust points to me as his eyes sweep over the group, his voice much calmer now and carrying a touch of mockery, "managed to do *this* to *him*? Without getting a scratch herself?"

No one wants to look him in the eye, but they're all nodding away. And I want to tell him to go fuck himself, but that would be plain stupid. Just as I struggle for control, he finally turns to me and looks me straight in the eye, the intensity of his gaze freezing me in place. "Is this true? That you attacked him first? It wasn't the other way around?"

"No. *I* attacked *him*," I force myself to say. "I lost control for a second and I apologize. I won't let it happen again."

I see a flash of surprise in his eyes. And he still looks a bit suspicious, but he nods. His eyes sweep over the rest of the Vipers. "I don't care what you all think you're doing," he starts, commanding the entire group with his mere presence. "And I especially don't care what you all think of *her*," he adds, to my endless fucking surprise, "but as long as you're part of the Vipers, I expect you to act with a lot more integrity and respect for each other than *this*."

I'm so shocked at his reaction that I don't say anything. I just watch the rest of them lower their heads and nod, a couple of them throwing a glance at me before they turn to start their sparring session.

"What do you think you're doing?" Faust's voice once again makes them all freeze in place. He just quirks an eyebrow at them and says, "You've just lost the privilege to train today. You're all dismissed."

None of them don't look pleased, but they immediately start dispersing. My mind buzzing, I breathe a sigh of relief and start turning to walk away.

"Except for you," I hear Faust say.

I turn to face him, but I don't say anything.

"I need a word with you," he says, motioning for me to take a seat on one of the benches. I let out a sigh, but I listen. He takes the seat across from me. For a second, I'm busy hating how hot he looks and how good he smells.

"Look," I start, confused and bewildered at the thought of being alone with him. "I did lose control for a second, but I did say I was…"

"I'm well aware," he cuts in, raising his hand to shut me up, the fucker, "of your ridiculously short temper. But it must have been something major, that made you lose control like that. Does it have anything to do with your secret reason for being here?"

It's a stab that would normally make me instantly start fuming, but I'm still too busy processing the way he reacted to the whole Leo situation. "What's the point of this?" I choose to say. "I have classes to prepare for."

He ignores my attempt at ending the conversation. "*What is the point?*" he asks mockingly. "You think it's ridiculous for me, the Vipers' leader, to make sure they don't all kill each other over some wannabe spy?"

"I thought you at least wouldn't mind getting rid of Leo," I start, "considering how much the two of you seem to love each other."

He just looks at me for a second. "When you're a prince, you get used to people like Leo. People who think some great injustice has been done to them simply because they're not the ones in your shoes." He pauses before he says, "But you're dead wrong if you think I'm letting you change the subject."

I just look at him for a second, a strange idea taking root in my head. "Fair enough," I finally say, "I'll tell you why I joined the Vipers."

At least part of the story, I think to myself. "If you promise not to breathe a word of it to anyone," I add.

He leans back and squints at me, not saying a word. That's how much I surprise him. But he doesn't give me time to revel in it. "Alright, I promise," he says.

I squint at him suspiciously.

He lets out a sigh. "I'm sure you'd like to believe otherwise, but if nothing else, I'm a man of my word."

"Alright," I reply with a nod. I pause for a second before I ask, "You're an orphan like I am?"

Of course, I know he is. But he doesn't know that. And it seems that the question takes him by surprise. It takes him a while to say, "I'm much more than *that*. But yes."

"Well," I start, making sure to tell the truth. Just not all of it. "Just a while ago, I learned that my parents, my real parents, are probably dead."

"I thought no one knows who your parents are."

"Well, that's the thing..." I pause, trying to find the words. "I know who they are, but not even the person who knew them intimately seems to remember them. It's as if they've been erased from existence. And I think one of the Vipers, or someone close to them, may have something to do with it all."

He just looks at me for a second and then lets out a scoff. "Wow, I have to say I never would've pegged you for a conspiracy theorist."

I ignore his stab. "It's not like that. I used the House Olarel Mirror to tell me who my parents are. And no one remembering them is a fact you can easily check for yourself."

For a moment, he stays silent. "Interesting," he finally says. "You do realize that vampires have the ability to make people forget things?"

"Glamoring, sure," I reply, getting goosebumps at the very thought of it. "But, even other vampires?"

"Anyone in particular?"

"Professor Mistila."

"She the one you think knew your parents?"

I nod.

To my surprise, he scoffs. "What you're describing sounds like a minor complication," he says as he gets up. "If you don't mind one other person getting involved and if I help you circumvent it..." He pauses to throw me a look. "Will you stop with the nonsense of trying to be a Viper?"

I can barely hold in the excitement. "Yes."

He checks his watch. "I have an obligation in twenty minutes. But meet me in front of the Pied Piper's office in an hour."

I get up, rushing to say, "No, not the Pied Piper."

He stops to shoot me an indecipherable look. "The Pied Piper is among the most trustworthy people I know."

Fuck. I think for a second, but I ultimately nod. I watch Faust disappear into thin air, wondering if I'm making a mistake simply by being too desperate. But hey, that's what trying to prevent an imminent bloodbath will do to you.

Chapter Twenty-Nine

Wondering what the hell I'm doing, I make my way into the Professors' Tower and climb all the way up. I find the Pied Piper's assistant sitting at her desk in the foyer, scribbling away. When I enter, she looks up for a moment, just to say, "They'll be ready for you in a minute, Miss Longborn, take a seat." And she goes back to her work.

I do as she says, the memory of her questioning me after the incident at the woods flashing through my mind. I shake it off, fixing my eyes on the giant double door leading into the Pied Piper's office. I strain my ears, but the only sounds coming from the other side are too muffled to be of any use.

So I'm alone with my thoughts again. And I assume that it's Faust, talking with the Pied Piper, which fills me with dread. He's probably recounting what I told him. Asking for her help. But is she really someone that can be trusted, I wonder.

Or even better, is *he*? Sure, he acted pretty maturely and honorably at the training session today. But even when I put my personal feelings aside, he's mostly behaved like an inconsiderate, privileged fucker.

I let out a sigh, lifting my eyes to stare at the ceiling. The ancient-looking relief up there seems to depict some kind of battle, one side posing as the Light and the other as the Darkness itself. In real life, sadly, things are never that black and white. What the fuck does he plan on doing, I think to myself, my thoughts escaping back to the matter at hand.

But it's at that exact moment that I see Professor Mistila appear in the foyer. She spots me and gives me a nod, but then she turns to the Pied Piper's assistant and says, "I was summoned by the prince."

The assistant opens her mouth to say something, but I hear a creak to my left, my head snapping in its direction to see the Pied Piper squinting from behind the now open door. "Mistila, Quinn..." she says in a low, serious voice. "Why don't you both come in?"

Professor Mistila shoots me a funny look, but we both obediently follow de Groot into the office. Faust is already there, leaned against the window frame to my left. Despite the casual way with which he keeps his hands in his pockets, he looks very official.

"Now," the Pied Piper says as she flings the length of her cloak aside and takes a seat, motioning for us to do the same. We do as she says. "Andreas has already filled me in on all that's happened. Is that right," she adds, turning to shoot me an indecipherable look, "Miss Longborn?"

For a second, I just stare at her, panicking because, of course, it's not the whole story. There's also the matter of the blood rituals and the imminent bloodbath. But what am I supposed to do? Risk it all? So I just nod.

"My apologies, *veneranda*," Professor Mistila cuts in. "I don't seem to know what you're talking about."

I open my mouth to say something, thinking it should come from me, since I'm the one who cooked this up.

But Faust beats me to it. "There's a chance, Professor Mistila," he starts without moving from where he's standing, "that you've been glamored."

"Glamored?" she echoes, frowning. "When? By whom?"

The Pied Piper says, "That we do not know. But if you were, it was in relation to Miss Longborn's parents."

The professor throws a glance at me and then turns back to the Pied Piper. I wait with bated breath, thinking she'll start laughing or maybe even attacking us. For a second, I imagine seeing her fangs bared.

But she just says, "I see."

It makes me frown with surprise, the pensive tone of her voice. "I guess it would explain things. Primarily how Miss Longborn can be an Olarel without any of us knowing anything about her parents."

"Indeed," the Pied Piper replies as she leans forward in her chair, clasping her hands in that elegant way of hers. "So... With your permission, I'd like to try breaking the spell."

Professor Mistila nods, but I suddenly feel so afraid that I feel the urge to ask, "It won't bring the professor any harm?"

I feel all three pairs of eyes on me. I don't even want to look in Faust's direction, but my eyes dart between the Pied Piper and Professor Mistila. The former is squinting at me, while the latter is throwing me a look filled with, well, tenderness.

"Don't worry about it, Miss Longborn," she says as her lips curl into a smile. "I'll only feel slight discomfort. If you're wrong and I haven't been glamored, then nothing else will happen. And if I have been, well, it'll only make me remember what I was forced to forget."

That makes me breathe a sigh of relief, but when the professor turns back to the Pied Piper and I see the two of them give each other quick nods, it still sends my heart racing.

I feel Faust's presence, but he neither moves nor speaks. With bated breath, I watch the Pied Piper close her eyes shut, Professor Mistila's body almost instantly stiffening.

There are no words uttered, no wands waved. At one point, the Pied Piper frowns, as if she's searching for something. And the very next second, the professor's shoulders slump, making my heart skip a beat.

"Quinn," she mutters.

Sensing both the prince and the Pied Piper tensing up, I get up and come to crouch next to Professor Mistila. There's something strange about her voice and the way she holds herself. As if she's grown a decade older in a matter of seconds.

"Yes, professor?" I squeeze out.

"It's not just me," she replies in a chillingly flat voice, barely moving a muscle. "So many people, they've killed so many people and glamored the rest of us."

The shock almost makes me topple over. And then it all happens so fast.

Professor Mistila gets up off her chair, takes something out of her pocket and raises it to her neck. A knife.

I hear the Pied Piper yell out, but I don't register the words themselves because the professor jerks the hand with the knife just enough to slice her own neck in a single, violent movement.

The sight of her blood gushing out makes my knees give out and my stomach collapse in on itself.

The next moments stretch out without me barely registering any of the things that happen.

The Pied Piper's assistant barges in and starts screaming.

The Pied Piper shuts her up, sends for the doctor and starts asking me questions. What do I think Professor Mistila meant by what she said, she wants to know.

I keep telling her I don't know. I'm feeling numb but I'm frantically trying to get the blood off my sweater. She's the last person I'd tell, I think to myself, now especially.

And I guess I really seem out of control, trying and failing to unzip my bloody hoodie with gritted teeth, because Faust walks over to me and takes me by the shoulders. He says that there's been enough questioning and that I obviously need a moment to collect myself.

He takes me out into the foyer, plants me in a chair and asks me to tell him what I know.

And I do. I tell him everything.

Chapter Thirty

I don't want to leave Longborn's side, but once Nuala comes to get her, I find no excuse to stick around.

So I leave for my quarters, planning on starting the investigation as soon as possible. But when I arrive through the back entrance, I find Max wringing his hands in the living room.

I walk up to him, frowning.

"There's, like, a bunch of lords and ladies waiting for you in the foyer," he says.

"Regarding..."

"They won't say," Max replies with a shrug. "But they seem just about ready to go on a murder rampage and you weren't answering your phone so I just lied to them that you're in a meeting."

"Bloody hell," I say with a sigh and whip out my phone. When I went to see the Pied Piper, I turned it off so as not to be disturbed. And now it's showing dozens of missed calls. Frowning, I scroll down the list of names, which includes everyone from Count Eichel to Archduke Erfurt.

"Should I start sending them in?" Max nudges me, making me look up from my phone.

"No, not yet," I tell him, shaking my head. "Something's going on and I need to find out what it is before I see any of them."

Max nods and takes his leave. I pour myself a drink at the bar and go to my study to check the news on my laptop. But as soon as walk through the door, I see an envelope on my desk. The kind one of my informants uses. A new report must have arrived while I was at the Pied Piper's office.

I sit at my desk and open it, scanning page after page of official documents. The conclusion? This new drug that the Scions were testing has passed all rounds of trials. And it's about to be legalized.

And why did that bring a bunch of pissed-off vampires to my door?

Because the drug, which they seem to plan on naming Obstructor, is supposed to render people immune to Mind Magic.

I let out a sigh and I ring the bell on my desk. A couple of seconds later, I hear Max walk in. I crane my neck and say, "I need you to go out there and tell them to come back some other day."

Max hesitates so I turn my chair to face him. "I know what they're here for," he finally speaks. "I was about to come in to tell you that the Archduke has just spilled the beans."

"No kidding." I let out a laugh. "Let me guess, he wants me to form a government body that will insert itself into the Scion government."

"How did you know?" my assistant asks, frowning as he walks up to me and leans on the couch in the center of my study.

I smile at him. He's proven to be very helpful, but he's new. He's no idea how repetitive dealing with these people can be.

"Whenever there's any trouble with the Scions," I reply with a sigh, "one of them comes to me to suggest that exact same thing."

"But how can that be?" he asks, obviously confused. "It would be against all laws. That's what we agreed when we signed the Treaty. We rule over ours and the Scions rule over theirs."

"Sure," I start, talking to myself more than Max, "but it's not that the idea is without merit. For us to rule over them. I mean, we have our problems, but they're nothing compared to theirs."

Max just blinks at me, which makes me snap out of it. "Nevermind," I say as I clap my hands and turn my chair back to face the desk, "you can tell them all to make appointments, but I want them out of my quarters ASAP."

As soon as I hear him leave, I forget all about the Obstructor and the pressure from the vampire court.

It's barely been more than two hours since she told me the truth about everything. The stone, someone trying to harness its power, some bloodbath that's bound to happen during the Third Round of the Trials... But it feels like forever.

I shouldn't have let Nuala lead her away from me and back to her room. I shouldn't have done it, I think to myself as it rips into me. The image of her all shaken up, those big brown eyes looking up at me filled with guilt and worry. I want to murder someone, but there's no one to murder for it.

I decide to think about the best course for the bloodbath investigation, but I just end up checking my phone every two seconds.

Hoping to find out where she is, how she's doing, *what* she's doing. Not like I'd have anyone to find out from, I snarl at myself.

I should just stop obsessing over her. But even if I managed to do that, there'd still be the matter of the bloodbath. So however much I'd like to just make it all disappear, it needs acting on. Instead of just sitting here, I should arrange a meeting with my uncle and the Pied Piper, relate everything I've been told and ask for their opinion. I've been through countless fucked-up situations, that's what being a prince will do to you, but this is unlike any of them.

Having made my decision, I get up, whip out my phone and call the Pied Piper's assistant.

"Yes, Your Majesty," the girl answers with the usual tinge of awe in her voice, as if she can't believe she's speaking to me directly.

And I open my mouth, but picturing the assistant makes my mind flood with the image of her wiping blood off Longborn's shocked face. And then there's Longborn asking me not to say anything to the Pied Piper.

"Hello? Are you there?" the assistant asks.

"I am, Lavinia," I blurt out, suddenly changing my mind. "I apologize, it seems I've dialed the wrong number."

"That's perfectly okay, Your Majesty..."

I hang up and I just stand there for a moment. I don't think Longborn is right. I don't think it was the Pied Piper who killed Professor Mistila. I think the glamoring that was done to her included a sort of safety measure. If ever the spell is broken, the person kills themselves.

Of course, I could bring Longborn all the evidence in the world and she still wouldn't listen. She may not be as hot-headed as I thought her to be, but she is stubborn, that's for sure. Maybe it's for the best. Whatever it is that's happening, I have a nagging suspicion she's not just a pawn in it, which means she could eventually get killed herself.

A part of me screams, "What the fuck are you doing? Are you fucking stupid?" But I can no longer fight the urge to go see her. Make sure she didn't take off on her own, putting herself in even more danger.

So instead of arranging a meeting with the Pied Piper and my uncle, I leave my quarters, stopping in front of the mirror to smooth out my shirt and my hair. Then I rush to the Ydril tower, not pausing until I'm in the seventeenth-floor common room.

And there it is, 85. I heard her give her room number to someone once. I didn't want to remember it, but I did. I walk up to her door and stop.

Why am I so curious to see her room, I think to myself, but the very next second, a group of girls barge into the common room and come to a screeching halt as soon as they spot me standing there.

There's a second of silence before they all burst out giggling. I just look at them, my eyebrow quirked. Their faces flushed, they instantly go silent, disappear into one of the other four rooms and bang the door shut.

I turn back to Longborn's door, but I have to force myself to do it, my heart throbbing at the very thought of actually finding myself in there with her. And just as I'm about to raise my arm and give a sharp knock, the door flings open and I find myself face to face with Nuala.

She blinks at me and takes a step back.

"Is Longborn in there?" I ask.

Before her friend can give me an answer, the one I've come to look for peers from behind her shoulder. "What is it?" she asks, her voice low and tired.

I glance around and say, "I don't want to talk like this."

For a second, she doesn't move and I think she'll say no. But then she nods and the two of them take a step back to let me in.

Once I'm inside and the door is shut behind me, I don't dare look around. The two of them are sitting on the bed. To my surprise, the ghost that Longborn told me about is here as well, standing right beside them.

I nod at her. Moswen, I think her name is. She just looks at me with suspicion in her eyes. They're all waiting for me to start talking, Longborn and Nuala looking as if neither of them has slept in days.

I turn to Longborn. "Still don't want to tell the Pied Piper the whole truth?" I ask.

"You'd want that," Moswen cuts in, making my eyes dart to her. "Wouldn't you?"

My eyebrows pull down, but before I can say anything, Longborn waves her hand and says,

"I told you what I think happened in there. You can say what you want, but I'm not changing my mind."

For a second, I let myself look into her eyes, searching for something without knowing what. Deceitfulness, I guess. But I find none. So I nod, I let out a sigh and I say, "Alright, but even if never breathe a word of it to anyone else, the way you want me to, I'm still involved."

"I guess," she starts, letting out a sigh. "But there's nothing I can do about that now."

"There is," I say, noticing her eyebrows shoot up a little. "I hope you understand that I won't just be sitting idly by as someone tries to kill us all. So I'll be taking over the investigation."

"What is he on about?" Moswen cuts in again. She turns to Longborn to shoot her a look, instantly making my blood boil. "Like we need some kind of leader."

"I agree with Moswen," Longborn says flatly. "We're in no position to refuse help, so sure, you can help, but *taking over the investigation*? The last thing we need is for you to be pulling that alpha shit on us."

Nuala looks away, still silent and red in the face. I let out a frustrated groan. "I don't know what kind of reality *you* live in," I start as I turn back to Longborn, my voice raised a little, "but in mine, it takes a lot more sense for it to be led by someone with *actual* resources."

Moswen lets out a scoff. "Of course he'd try to buy you."

It makes me grit my teeth. What the fuck does she have against me? I choose to ignore her and I turn to look at Longborn.

She's pursing her lips just a little as she considers my words. "What would those resources be?" she finally asks.

I fucking can't believe how much convincing I have to do, but I make myself take in a breath and spit out, "A web of spies, to start with."

"That should definitely come in handy," she says to Nuala, in a voice so flat, it makes me want to grab and shake her.

"I hope you're not seriously considering teaming up with him?" Moswen asks in a voice full of bitterness. "Isn't he the one who practically assaulted you?"

The *nerve*, I think as an urge to attack her overwhelms me. I'm already leaning forward, my fangs slightly bared. But at the very last second, I stop myself.

Once I've snapped out of it, I notice Longborn studying me, her eyes darting to my clenched fists.

I loosen them up and I notice her face relax.

"Alright, you can help coordinate things," she finally concludes.

But I'm still fuming that that ghost of a woman would want to turn her against me like that. So it sounds quite aggressive when I add, "That's not all. From now on, you'll no longer be training with the Vipers."

That makes Longborn get up. "The hell I won't. In case you've forgotten, there's shit that's gonna go down during the Third Round."

"I'm aware," I say through gritted teeth. "And that's why I'll be the one training you."

Moswen immediately starts protesting. "Quinn, I think this nonsense has gone on long enough."

CHAPTER 30

To my satisfaction, Longborn just whispers, "Sorry, Moswen," and snaps her diary shut, making her disappear.

Then she turns to Nuala and says, "Would you mind leaving us alone?"

It makes my heart skip a beat. And while Nuala's grabbing her stuff and making her way out, I busy myself by glancing around. What I see surprises me. For some reason, maybe because it's been like that with every girlfriend I've ever had, I expected the room to be crammed with clothes and trinkets. This one is practically bare, only a few posters taped to the wall and a bunch of books on the shelves.

It's only when I hear Nuala close the door behind her that I force myself to face her again. All of a sudden, my mind is acutely aware of every detail on her face and body. But the bigger problem is that I've no idea what to expect.

She gets up and comes a little closer, sending my heart racing. "Look," she starts, looking away for a second, "I've heard the stories and I know how powerful you are."

It makes me melt, hearing her say that. What the fuck is going on with me?

"And I won't be stupid enough to refuse your offer," she says.

My eyebrows shoot up, but she doesn't give me a chance to react. She takes another step closer, her voice taking on a more serious tone. "But I have a condition. Outside of training, I'll want you as far away from me as possible."

Her words feel like a slap on the face, but I'll be damned if I show it. I scoff. "No need to get emotional," I squeeze out. "A simple thank you would've been enough."

She takes a step back, her face twisted in rage. "You did *not* just say that." She lets out a bitter laugh, but turns dead serious when she says, "Let me make myself crystal clear..." She practically gets in my face. "I know you're probably not used to suffering the consequences of your own actions, but until you apologize to me for what you did at the Ball, I owe you *nothing*, not even basic courtesy."

By the time she's done talking, I'm barely keeping it together. I want to tell her to forget it, I want to fucking rip into her for daring to say those things, my hands balled painfully into fists and my fangs aching for me to let them draw blood.

But I do nothing. "Tomorrow morning, at dawn" I say through gritted teeth. "Be at the training grounds."

And with that, I turn on my heel and I leave her room, slamming the door behind me.

Chapter Thirty-One

The morning after Professor Mistila's suicide, I wake up with a raging headache. It doesn't really surprise me, considering I spent practically the whole of last night tossing in my bed. And I can't remember any of it, but I have the strongest feeling that I've just been ripped out of the grip of some nasty nightmare.

It's only after I drag myself out of bed that I remember why I set my alarm to ring at the crack of fucking dawn. I'm supposed to go train with him, right now, and I've no clue what to expect from that. I'm so apprehensive, I can barely stop myself from crawling back under the covers.

Then again, it's not like I have any other choice. Training with Moswen has brought results, that's for sure, but I'm still shit at combat in general. And I've no way of knowing what's in store for me when the day finally comes, the day of the dreaded Third Round.

So I quickly get dressed, choosing long sleeves because it's still chilly outside. And I make my way to the training grounds, the silence that's still enveloping the world around me making me even more hesitant.

When I spot him, it surprises me to see he's not alone. Max is there with him, the two of them standing by the benches, looking as if Faust is dictating something.

He doesn't acknowledge me when I approach. Neither one of them does. I raise my eyebrows and I clear my throat.

Still, nothing. The Little Prince just keeps talking, making me stand there feeling like a fool. As usual, he looks breathtaking. But it's also the most casual I've ever seen him. He's barefoot, his sweatpants hanging loosely off his waist and his T-shirt revealing the curves of so many lean muscles.

"And I'll see the Baroness some other day," I hear him say just as he dismisses Max with a single wave of his hand.

Only when Max disappears does he turn to me, his face frozen in that indecipherable expression of his. I open my mouth to say good morning, because despite how annoyed he's made me with his little display of power, I'm determined to make the best of this.

But he beats me to it. "Five laps around the grounds," he commands in a voice that's like a slab of ice as he goes to sit on one of the benches and whips out his phone.

Alright, I think to myself, I could use a bit of warming up.

I walk up to the track lines and I start running. Of course, I have to try to ignore the fact that he's sitting there and that he can probably see my every move. But by the time I'm done with the five laps, I'm actually pretty proud of myself for how little I'm panting.

"Done," I say as I walk back to where he's sitting.

"Five more," he replies. And the fucker doesn't even look up.

Oh how I hate him. "Seriously?" I ask. But I'm determined to keep it civil. "Look, I'm already a good runner. I think there's plenty of things I could do that wouldn't be such a waste of time."

He looks up and just stares at me for a second. "Five laps around the grounds," he starts, making me think I'll have to keep arguing with him. "And I want you casting magic the entire time." He pauses before he adds, dragging out the words, "Without so much as slowing down."

I roll my eyes. His attitude is childish and infuriating, but at least I'd be doing something. "Alright," I say and walk back to the tracks.

I stop at the starting line, bend a little forward and break into a full sprint. After a couple of minutes of mustering all my determination, I try to use my Element Rune to knock over a straw man perched on the ground to my left.

It doesn't surprise me when I fail. After all, I can barely manage doing magic when I'm standing still. But what surprises me is the way the act knocks all the air out of my lungs. It takes everything I have to keep running.

I try again and for a second, I think I've done it. The second straw man sways a little.

But the very next second, I find myself completely out of breath so I stop running, slowly coming to a halt.

Breathing heavily, I bend over, resting my palms against my thighs.

It startles me when he just appears in front of me. "What did I tell you *not* to do?" he demands, towering over me with an intense look in his eyes.

"Stop," I squeeze out.

"And what did you do?"

"I stopped," I say through gritted teeth.

"Stand straight and try again."

I have to take a deep breath to force myself to stay calm because having to say it makes me livid. "I can't do it like that."

"Really?" he says mockingly. "I thought the more basic stuff was a *waste of your time*."

"If you got off your high horse and explained how this should help me…"

He just looks at me for a second. Then he lets out a deep sigh and slides his hands in his pockets as he starts to pace around me. "Let's see…" His voice is cold and smirking. "If, right now, you found yourself fighting in the Third Round…"

I don't like it, but my ears still prick up.

"You'd be dead in less than a minute," he finishes as he comes to a stop before me. "Isn't that right?"

Prick. "Can't say it isn't," I force myself to admit. "So what exactly are you planning to do with such a lost cause?"

"Using the one advantage you do have," he says flatly.

My eyebrows pull down. "Running?"

He doesn't even nod, but I take the silence as a yes. I frown and then I scoff. "Let me make it clear. So when I find myself in front of an opponent, you want me to *run away*?"

He rolls his eyes at me, fucker. "It's not your speed I'm counting on. You may be fast for a Scion or a fae… But you're laughably far from being a shifter or a *vampire's* match," he finishes in a low voice, his eyes darting to my neck for a second.

It makes my knees give out, their intensity.

"Fair enough," I squeeze out. "So what is it, if not my speed?"

"Breath."

I frown. "Um, what?"

He shakes his head as if I'm some child who hasn't learned her ABCs. "Part of what makes you a good runner is good control over your breathing, isn't it?"

I nod, feeling intrigued against my will.

"And the only thing you're good for right now is Air Magic, which uses the power of your breath, doesn't it?"

The only thing I'm good for? Where the fuck does he get off? He's waiting for an answer, but I'm so pissed I don't say anything. I can't even make myself nod.

"A simple yes or no would suffice," he says more forcefully.

I have to force myself to keep my voice flat. "You know, I'm here to be trained, not insulted."

He just looks at me for a second. "You wanted me to explain this to you, didn't you?" he snarls. "But I guess nothing is ever good enough for you."

I finally snap. "What the fuck are you talking about?" I practically yell at him.

"Your fucking attitude."

"*My* attitude?" I take a step closer to him, my hands balling into fists. "I'm not the one refusing to apologize for being a complete asshole and adding insult to injury by pouting like a fucking toddler."

He just keeps staring at me, but now his nostrils are flaring and his chest heaving.

But it's at that exact moment that I hear voices boom from the other side of the training grounds. The Vipers are coming for their session.

He takes a step back and squeezes out, "Good job, you've managed to waste all our time. You're dismissed."

I ignore the stab, turn on my heel and start walking towards the benches. "I'm going to watch them train."

"Suit yourself," he replies coldly.

Once I take my seat, I see that he's gone to greet them and that they've surrounded him like a waddle of ducklings. I squint. Harry's patting him on the back while Zelda and Sarya are laughing at something he said. I frown, although it's not the first time he's proved that he can be pleasant. When he wants to, at least.

It's only then that I notice Leo missing. Fucker, I think as I recall the last box of chocolates. I honestly can't believe I'm letting that guy force me into saying no to dates for the Ball. I'll really have to do something about it, as soon as I catch some free time between trying to prevent the bloodbath and not letting my royal trainer's pleasant personality drive me crazy.

I spend the next hour on the bench, watching the Vipers train. Faust doesn't join, he just cuts in with feedback every now and again. At one point, I hear him let out a laugh and it makes me freeze. He's never done that before, at least not when I was around.

The sound is rough and playful and makes me want to hear more, my thighs clenching in anticipation.

But the session seems to be over and now he's walking up to where I'm sitting, his face back to being devoid of any expression. And there they all are, running after him. I keep sitting there awkwardly as they all throw themselves on the benches around me.

And they start talking as if I'm not there, but they don't try to put a lot of space between us. They're chatting about techniques I've never heard of. Three-Legged Monster, Duncan's Lock and others with names I wouldn't even be able to repeat.

I keep sitting there hoping for a chance to cut in with a question about the Trials. But I don't expect them to include me in the conversation themselves.

"Longborn," Harry barks out at one point, making me practically jump up with surprise, "you probably know everything there is to know about the Herigast Stance."

For a second, I just blink at him, expecting them all to take his lead and start mocking me. But when I see the grins on their faces, I realize that that's not what they're doing. They're *teasing* me.

I scoff. "That one's so basic, Harry," I dare to say. "If you want, I can teach you some more advanced things," I continue, determined to see this through as I lift my hand to start counting on my fingers. "Falling Face First, Not Even Spotting Your Opponent..."

At this point, there's already loud laughter coming from everyone but Faust, but I add one more, just for the fun of it. "Blinking Your Enemies Away..."

It makes me smile, the way Harry in particular seems to be dying of laughter. The moment doesn't get ruined even when I notice Faust's eyes dart to me and linger, not even cracking a smile.

"But seriously," I say when the laughter dies down a little, "does anyone know what we'll be up against in the Third Round?"

Harry laughs. "Gotten cocky, have we?" he says. "If I'm not mistaken, you have to survive the Second first."

I smile. "Sure, but the Third is far deadlier, right?"

There's a moment of silence during which everyone seems to turn serious. I hold my breath, thinking I've made a mistake.

To my surprise, Faust is the first to break the silence. "All assignments are kept secret," he says, surprising me with the lack of condescension in his tone. "That's the only way to keep things fair."

I notice Sarya shooting him a look, her eyes darting to me first, which makes my ears prick up.

He catches it, pauses for a second and then just tips his head back a little, nudging her to speak.

"Well," she starts, "I was planning on telling you after the session. Just yesterday, I overheard my parents talking about it."

How convenient, I think to myself, but I don't linger on it.

"And?" Faust urges her to go on.

"I guess there are rumors about a donation made to the Academy to bring out some stone for the Third Round."

My eyes dart to Faust, whose eyebrows are pulling into a frown. "A donation? Made by whom?"

Sarya glances around nervously. "Leo's family."

There's a stir and then a moment of silence before Faust says, "Interesting. Especially considering he didn't even let me know he wouldn't be coming today."

"That's actually my doing," Sarya admits. To my surprise, she sounds nervous. "I found it odd that he wouldn't let us in on it... So I told him that today's session was canceled."

Faust just looks at her for a second and then nods approvingly, making her beam with satisfaction. "I wanted to talk to you before I confronted him," she adds.

"No," he snaps as he starts getting up. The rest of them follow suit and so do I. "You won't be doing anything about it," he says. His eyes sweep over us all, lingering on me for a second. "And that goes for all of you."

He waves a hand to dismiss us all and the rest of the group doesn't seem too happy about it, but they obey.

As they follow him Faust out of the training grounds in silence, I let out a breath I didn't even know I was holding in. My mind is racing so hard, I can barely think straight. It all makes sense, I think to myself as I start walking. Leo is in the Vipers and I always thought he was the one who tried to steal Moswen. Then, there's also the fact that he's an absolute dirtbag.

Of course it's him, the person we're looking for.

So I don't go straight to the cafeteria, as I'd planned. Just as the rest of the group turns left to get back to the castle, I decide to walk to the House of Lilith instead.

I stop and almost let out a gasp when Faust appears in front of me. "Where do you think you're going?" he demands.

I frown. "Wherever that vampire asshole is."

"No, you're not. We won't be confronting him directly, at least for now."

"What do you think, I'm stupid?" I hiss at him. "I'm gonna go follow his ass, not chat him up."

"Leave that to me," he snarls. "You and Nuala can keep looking for info on the stone."

I want to say no, but it actually does make a lot more sense. I grit my teeth, force myself to nod and push past him to get back to the castle.

"Same time tomorrow," he snaps after me.

I don't say anything. I don't even turn around. I just give him a quick exaggerated bow and I keep walking. And I don't see the reaction, but I know he hates it when I do that.

Chapter Thirty-Two

I'm panting heavily and my vision is blurred, making the track around the training grounds blend in with the rest of my surroundings. Still, I push through it and try to finish the third lap, casting magic all the way. It doesn't surprise me that I manage to knock over every strawman I pass by. It's the middle of March and I've been training with Faust for a while now, slowly perfecting my use of Air power.

But this time, when I try to use my other element, Earth, it almost makes me topple over when I see it's worked. I tap the rune and see the ground before me do exactly what I wanted it to do. It shakes and then cracks, opening a huge chasm right before me.

I come to a stop just in time to avoid falling in and I see a few clumps of beaten earth roll down. I barely have time to process what's happened before I see him appear on the other side of the opening, looking down into the abyss.

My lips curl into a victorious smile, but I wipe it off as soon as he looks up. There's a flash of surprise in his eyes, but I only catch it because I've gotten pretty good at reading his perpetually expressionless face. Mostly because the majority of the time he's spent training me, ever since that first session, could be described using two words. Awkward silence. But this morning, he seems pissed and is even more quiet than usual.

"I think you're ready for the next step," he finally says.

My ears prick up. "And that would be?"

He motions for me to follow him to the center of the training grounds. And then, to my surprise, he just stands there, pushing his legs apart and slowly cracking his neck. Every time I see him do that, a wave of heat washes over my entire body and I have to remind myself, once again, that this is the Little Prince I'm drooling over.

And just as I gulp, fighting not to let my eyes roam, he commands, "Try to attack me."

My eyebrows shoot up. I did *not* expect this. "You sure?"

He just stares at me.

I grit my teeth. "Nevermind," I say as I get into a position to attack.

And I know exactly what I want to do, but I hesitate. In a way, this is my dream come true. The fucker still hasn't apologized for the incident at the Ball and he's treating me as if I were some nuisance, which makes me want to kick his fucking butt so badly, I sometimes feel the need to scream. But even though he's been training me for weeks now, the very thought of embarrassing myself in front of him makes me livid.

"I don't have all day," he snaps at me.

And all of a sudden, I find the determination to wipe the floor with him. I don't say anything, I just tap the Element Rune and send a wall of air flying straight into his chest.

It doesn't seem to do anything. He's still standing there, solid as a rock, with his hands resting casually on his hips.

I ball my hands into fists, cursing under my breath, but that only makes him throw me a smirk, his head tilted in amusement. "What's that you said?"

Chill, Quinn, just chill, I plead with myself. And I do collect myself and send another, denser wall of air at him. He disappears for a second, materializing at the same spot without a hair out of place.

Grinning at me. "You know, it might be good," he starts in an amused voice, "to try to use more than one tactic to beat your opponent. Just an idea."

For a second, I just blink at him. Frowning, I dig my feet firmer into the ground and tap the earth rune with such force, it hurts. I open another chasm, right under his feet.

But of course, he just zaps himself away.

"On second thought…"

He startles me so much, I practically jump up. He's appeared to my left, looking even more amused than a second ago. "Maybe you should stick to what you know."

I just look at him for a second. Then I let out an angry growl and try to push him away with my hands.

His eyebrows raised, he just laughs, the sound rough but soft.

"You fucker, you think this is productive?" I yell at him. "I should be fighting someone my own level."

Still smiling, he shakes his head. "You think that's how the Trials will go? You'll be able to choose your opponent? Besides," he moves to follow me because I've started walking away, "I'm not even attacking you."

I stop and turn back to him. "Well, why aren't you? If we're really aiming for all this to be as authentic as possible."

He doesn't say anything. He disappears and when I see him again, he's gripping my forearm, his body so close to mine, I can only see his eyes. They're still smiling when he says, "Because I'd have to hold back."

At first, I'm at a loss for words. It's all a bit too much, his eyes, his smell and the touch of his hand. I frown and I push him away. "You're right, and this way, we can do without you touching me."

Now, that makes the smile disappear from his face. But he's not just back to his grumpy self, he seems to be seething.

"It was your idea anyway."

I open my mouth, but at that exact moment, I hear a woman clear her throat somewhere behind my back.

My head darts in her direction and I see Faust's blonde girlfriend standing a bit farther away, squinting at the two of us. "Am I interrupting something?"

My eyes dart to Faust.

"Actually, you are, Amelia," he replies, his voice as cold as it gets, "you know I'm in training at this hour."

What the fuck is going on, I think to myself.

"I do," Amelia smiles as she appears next to him and grabs him by the upper arm, stroking his bicep. "And don't get me wrong, baby cakes, I love it that you're even doing charity work now," she says as she throws me a nasty look, "but sometimes you need to live a little."

"The training's done when it's done," he snaps at her, his eyes darting in my direction before they turn back to her and linger there. "I'll come see you after."

There's tension in the air as the smile slides right off Amelia's pretty face. "Alright," she says, quickly collecting herself and moving to walk away. "I'll see you later then."

She throws me another look and disappears.

Once she's gone, there's a moment of uncomfortable silence. I decide to break it by saying, "So... what do you want me to do now?"

"Nothing," he snaps at me. "We're done for today."

And he turns to walk away.

"What about Leo? Any news?" I demand, frowning because he obviously had no intention giving me an update on the investigation, as he likes to call it.

He stops, but he doesn't turn around. "No. And I thought I said we're done for today," he snarls and disappears.

And just like that, I'm left standing there like some fool, baby cakes echoing in my mind and making me want to grit my teeth.

And still no news, huh, I think to myself as I start making my way back to my room to get changed. I guess I'll have to do this investigating thing on my own then. But just as I prepare to enter the Ydril Tower, I see a guy approach me with a nervous smile on his face.

Chapter Thirty-Three

It's been forty three minutes and Longborn still hasn't texted me back. I'm back in my quarters and I'm supposed to get ready for a meeting with the Archduke, but I can't seem to get it together. I keep pacing around the living room and checking my phone every five seconds.

After I told her we were done for the day, just before I left the training grounds, I caught a glimpse of a guy standing near the entrance, seemingly waiting for her.

And I tried to fight it, I did, but I ended up doing it again.

I pretended to leave, but I stayed behind, taking cover behind one of the oaks in the castle garden. With gritted teeth, I watched the guy sniff after her as she made her way to the Ydril Tower. And with bated breath, I eavesdropped on him asking her out to the Ball.

As I waited for her to give him her answer, I felt hot rage course through my entire body. How dare he, that little fucker.

But just as I balled my hands into fists, I saw her shake her head for no and I let out a long breath, feeling tension leave my muscles.

As fast as I could, I went back to my quarters and grabbed a card off my desk. Grinning, I wrote, "Good girl," attached the card to a box of chocolates I picked out just for the occasion and gave it to Max to deliver ASAP.

He's the only one who knows about them, my little presents to Miss Longborn. But just as I was about to enjoy visualizing her reaction once she received this one, Amelia came knocking on my door.

Pissed, she was so pissed about me forgetting to come to her as soon as Longborn and I were done with training. I don't know what came over me, but I ended up telling her it was over. She started yelling, saying I can't just break up with her and proving once again how far above everyone else she thinks she is.

"You think I'm stupid?" she finally demanded. "You think I don't know who this is all about?"

"I've no fucking idea what you're talking about," I snapped at her.

"Well, good luck," she said with a mocking scoff, "because that girl doesn't seem to choose who she'll flirt with."

Now, that made my ears prick up. I got in her face, every muscle in my body tensing up. "*What* do you mean by that?"

She just shrugged and left the room. My mind was buzzing so much, I just kept standing there. All I could think about was the guy from earlier. Did he go look for her again? Or is Amelia talking about someone else entirely?

Of course, I know what kind of person my ex is, and I did try to tell myself she's probably just making stuff up to spite me. But there was no going back. I'd already gotten so worked up about it that I eventually made the mistake that I'm suffering for right now.

I found an excuse to text Longborn. "I'll have to postpone tomorrow's training by half an hour. Would that be okay with you?"

That was fifty two minutes ago, I think to myself as I check my watch while pacing around the living room. And I did realize it was a stupid and pointless thing to do, but only after I'd already sent the bloody text.

Now I have to suffer the consequences, being unable to think about anything else other than the fact that she still didn't text me back. Or maybe she did do it in the meantime.

I tell myself this will be the last time. I grab my phone from the coffee table and pull up the messages.

Still no reply. Just 'Seen'. I never knew a single word could get me so worked up. I grip the phone with both hands and stop pacing, cursing myself for being so stupid.

And I try to tell myself not to do it, but my fingers move of their own accord. They open the chat with Longborn and type, "Not even going to dignify me with an answer?"

Once the message is sent, I just keep standing there, staring the screen down.

It startles me, when they suddenly appear, the three dots that mean she's typing.

I wait with bated breath for what seems like eternity. Then a message finally appears. "I thought you said we're done for today." I can *hear* her fucking tone.

"Well," I rush to type, "I answered your question, didn't I?"

"Are you being serious?"

"Yes, I'm being serious."

"Look, I have a busy day ahead and I really don't have time for your shit."

"My shit? Wow."

"Yes, your shit. You know, being a privileged asshole, ignoring the fact that what you do affects others... Stuff like that."

"You think you know me so well, do you?"

"If your actions speak anything of your character, yes, I know you plenty."

This makes me grit my teeth, but I keep typing like crazy. "I'm a prince in a world you still know nothing about and you have the audacity to say something like that?"

"Yes. And if I weren't onto something there, oh prince, my opinion wouldn't be making you this worked up."

"That's not what's happening here. What's happening here is you having zero manners."

She doesn't reply. For a long time, I just stare at the screen, before I throw the goddamn phone at the wall, smashing it to bits.

This makes Max walk in. "Everything alright?"

I don't say anything, I just nod. "Get me a new phone," I squeeze out as I turn to walk to my bedroom.

Still fuming, I get dressed and go into the drawing room to find my uncle and the Archduke already waiting for me.

We do the usual formal greetings and take our seats at the table. The Archduke wastes no time. He goes straight to talking about the Obstructor, the Scions planning on eradicating us and the need to put out foot down by inserting ourselves into their governments.

But I'm so distracted, I can barely hear what they're saying. The prince, I'm the fucking prince here. And I'm the strongest vampire and I have the highest grades and I have so many women throwing themselves at my feet, and she's treating me like I'm scum.

"Andreas?" my uncle's voice snaps me out of it. It's only when I look at him that I realize that I've balled my hands into fists. "Care to chip in?" he asks.

"Would you excuse me, gentlemen," I say as I get up, making them follow suit. "I understand that this is a matter of utmost importance and I'm currently not feeling well, so I think it best to reschedule our meeting."

The Archduke just looks at me for a moment, then gets up, bows and leaves the room. My uncle's not letting *me* leave though.

"You know, nephew," he starts as he appears before me, "you can reschedule all you want, but he'll just keep coming back."

I let out a sigh. "What do you think about it, uncle? They all seem to be bent on making it happen. Should I just give in to the pressure?"

He draws in a breath, thinking for a moment. "It *would* be a precedent, that much is sure. Then again, the situation is far from peaceful and you're not like others, either by birth or ability. If anyone would be justified in doing it, it would be you."

"However?"

"However," uncle echoes me, "I don't think you should bother with it. There will be better opportunities for you to assert your power and introduce positive changes."

"Thank you, uncle," I reply, "I'll think about it."

But even after he's gone, my mind is still on one of the first things he said. *You're not like others, either by birth or ability.*

Maybe I was being too big of an asshole. I make a snap decision. If she won't talk to me over the phone, I may as well pay her a visit.

I go to her room first, but she's not there.

I sniff the air. To my relief, it wasn't that long ago that she was in. I follow her scent and find her and Nuala sitting by the fountain in one of the inner courtyards.

"We're busy," she tells me as soon as she sees me.

"Busy doing what?"

Longborn looks away, but when I turn my eyes onto Nuala, she just spills it. "I heard Leo has a meeting with some Italian and we read somewhere that the stone might have been located in Italy at one point so we just want to see the guy. They're supposed to meet here."

When I turn back to her, Longborn is throwing daggers at her friend. I let out a deep sigh, making her look at me. "Follow me," I say and the two of them do it, albeit hesitantly.

I lead them to the West common room and stop at the door. "It's here they're meeting." I motion for them to take a look and they peer through the archway and into the room, where Leo is standing by a rack of suits, browsing as the Italian tailor recites their qualities.

"It's said that if you really want a good suit," I tell the two of them, "you have to have the Italians make it for you."

When Longborn turns to me, she has a victorious smile plastered on her face.

But before she can even open her mouth, I say, "He really is a tailor. His name is Enzo Russo and he's not even an Original."

The smile disappears. "So you've already checked him out?"

I scoff. "Of course I did. And you should think twice before you underestimate me like you did just now."

She just blinks at me for a second and then says, "I guess you're right, sorry."

Appeased, I open my mouth to say it's fine, but the look on her face changes. Now there's spite in it. "See what a normal person does when they do something wrong?"

That gets me instantly fuming. But I draw in a deep, long breath and I turn to Nuala. "Would you excuse us?"

I don't wait for her to leave. I nudge Longborn into one of the empty side hallways and I stand in front of her. She folds her arms, waiting for me to speak.

It surprises me, how difficult it is to squeeze out the words, especially with those eyes bearing into me. "Look," I start, unable to stop myself from hissing, "not saying you're sorry doesn't mean you're not... sorry."

She quirks her eyebrow at me.

"People make mistakes," I add because she apparently didn't understand me.

"True," she says, "but when they *do* make them, they need to apologize for them, don't you think?"

I just look at her for a moment, fuming. "Fuck you," I snap at her and turn to walk away.

She grabs me by the arm and I immediately stop. "Alright," she starts as she walks around to face me. "You say people make mistakes. Do you consider yourself to be… people?"

"I do," I say through gritted teeth. Still, her voice is softer and that's making some of the rage start dying down.

"Great," she replies. And she doesn't seem to be sarcastic. "Nuala and I aren't having any luck with the info on the stone, but we'll leave the investigation to you."

I turn to look at her, the remaining tension in me dissipating when I see that the look she's giving me has softened as well.

"And tomorrow," she starts a bit hesitantly, making my ears prick up, "maybe you could try teaching me to defend myself from whatever moves you've got. I guess I could really use the practice."

I don't say anything, I just nod and walk away. But there's warmth spreading throughout my body, the kind I'm not used to feeling.

Chapter Thirty-Four

The warm April day makes things seem so innocent, but tomorrow is casting such a shadow over everything, I'm unable to stop myself from pacing around the training grounds. When Nuala finally meets me, the sun is already setting, making the ground wet from rain glimmer in the light.

As my friend walks up to me, I see that she's confused. But I was expecting that, considering I didn't tell her why I wanted us to meet.

Once she's in front of me, I smile and say, "I thought you could be the one training with me today."

She folds her arms and quirks an eyebrow at me. "I thought Andreas specifically told you *not* to do it the day before."

"He's being stupid," I protest. "The Second Round is deadlier than the first and I really need the practice. Besides," I pause, throwing her a cautious smile, "I thought we might make it helpful for the both of us."

I see her tense up. I think she knows what I'll suggest even before I do it. But I still do. "Just today I came across these exercises shifters can do-"

"You just came across them," she cuts me off, drawling. Then she lets out a loud groan filled to the brim with frustration. "I swear to Lycan's teeth, Quinn, if you do this again, I am going to murder you with my own two hands."

As she says it, she starts walking away, but I catch up with her. "Nuala, listen to me," I rush to say everything that's on my mind, "There's a chance you didn't actually sever the bond with your animal, not completely at least. I think you're traumatized by what happened to your brother and so you're probably suppressing things you *really* shouldn't be suppressing."

She stops and turns to face me. "You know what *I* think, Quinn?" she spits out. "I think you should stop poking your nose in other people's business."

I open my mouth to say sorry, but I sense a presence behind my back and almost instantly, I see Nuala's eyes dart in that direction. I turn around and see Faust approaching us, dressed in a pressed shirt and perfectly tailored pants, his hands in his pockets in that insanely hot way of his. Goddamn him.

"So surprising, seeing the two of you here," he says, but he doesn't sound surprised at all.

"Hi, Andreas," my friend greets him, her voice weirdly strained and her face flushed.

It makes me frown for a second, but then I turn to Faust and say, "I thought you were super busy with the preparations for tomorrow." I can't help but grin at him before I add, "I didn't think you'd have time to follow us around."

He just turns to Nuala and says, "I'll take over from here."

I want to tell her she doesn't have to leave, but she already is. She throws me a glance over the shoulder, looks at Faust and, blushing, mouths, "Bye."

It makes me frown for a second, but I don't have time to linger on it. As soon as she's out of earshot, the handsome stalker takes a step closer to me and drawls, "I thought I made myself clear, Longborn."

I lock eyes with him. "You often think that and you're rarely right."

For a second, his lips twitch, as if he's about to laugh. But he just looks away, turning serious. "I don't care for your antics," he replies. "I need you to go to your room and rest."

I let out a sigh and look him straight in the eye. Ever since he sort of apologized to me, things have been a lot less hostile between us and I've actually been taking his advice. But not this time. "Just one hour," I say with determination in my voice.

"Absolutely not."

I throw my arms up. "Oh, I see, you want me to die tomorrow."

He scoffs, but doesn't say anything. He throws me a look and leans a bit forward. In that instant, I just know he's going to attack.

I tap one of my Runes and, before he manages to do anything, send him flying far away from me.

I let out a breath, but the very next second, I sense a presence behind my back. I turn around and without thinking, I raise my hands up and make all the water from the ground shoot up. It creates a barrier that he almost instantly slams into.

He stumbles backwards and I let the water come crashing to the ground. I rush to see if he's okay, but he waves his hand in dismissal and locks eyes with me.

"Full of surprises, aren't we?" he asks in a voice matching the sentiment.

I just blink at him. The reality of what's happened is still hitting me. "Did I just manage to use a *third* Element?

"Unless we're both out of our minds, yeah," he says, now squinting at me with his arms folded.

"I thought no one could manipulate more than two," I say in a hushed voice.

"Don't flatter yourself," he says with a smile. "There are even some who can manipulate all four, but that usually comes with very powerful sets of runes, like the Creator's." His eyes narrow. "And you still have only your Element rune activated, right?"

I nod, my mind buzzing. "What could it mean?" I ask.

"For now, all it means is," Faust says as he lets out a low laugh, "you're as ready for tomorrow as you can possibly be. So, today, you should just live a little."

I don't get a chance to reply. The very next second, I see Sarya, Harry and Zelda walking up to us.

I breathe a sigh of relief when I see Leo's not with them. After that third box of chocolates, I've been avoiding him even more religiously, trying to figure out a way to get back at him.

"Just the man we're looking for," Harry barks out as soon as he walks up to Faust. "Your Majesty, will you do us the honor of going to the Seven Dwarves' with us?"

Faust shakes his head, smiling. "Maybe some other time. You should all get some rest tonight."

"The Seven Dwarves'?" I cut in, frowning at Harry. "But they don't allow anyone under forty."

"They do if you come with the right person," he replies, gesturing at the real-life prince standing next to me.

"Ah," I just say, an interesting idea popping into my mind. I turn to Faust and throw him a smirk. "I think you should go. You know, live a little."

For a second, he just looks at me. Then his lips curl into a smile. "Sure, but only if you're coming, too."

He says it as if he's challenging me. I let out a chuckle. "My god," I say, feigning shock, "you want me to accompany four youngsters to some dingy bar?" I walk up to Harry, Sarya and Zelda, who are all grinning. "I don't know…" I shake my head. "Someone might steal my pearls."

Harry barks out a laugh and Faust rolls his eyes at me, but then he snaps, "Fine, let's go."

It doesn't take us long to get to our destination. Another perk of being the prince seems to be the fact that you can just use the Pull whenever you please. Once we're on the other side, I'm relieved when I see I'm not the only one to throw up. We all do, everyone except for the smirking Faust, of course.

But I don't linger on it. I've stopped feeling so worried and I now seem to be overwhelmed with a nervous sort of excitement. And the Seven Dwarves' looks just as I imagined it, ever since Nuala told me about that one time her brothers got to go. It's a wooden shack in the middle of the forest, warm light and muffled music spilling out through the cracks.

And there's no signs anywhere, no indicator whatsoever that this is the most popular bar for Originals in the entire area. Just a plain-looking double door. As soon as Faust approaches it, the door flings open and reveals a grumpy looking old woman, my ears instantly getting assaulted by the actual volume of the rock music playing inside.

"Your Majesty," the woman says when her eyes land on Faust, surprising me when her mouth cracks into a smile. "Always a pleasure to see you."

As we file inside, she throws us all suspicious looks, but doesn't say anything. And just like that, we're in.

The place is so crowded, we have to elbow our way through. Everyone except Faust, of course. For him, apparently even the Red Sea would part without so much as a moment's hesitation. Walking behind Zelda, I struggle to catch up. I have to zigzag so as to avoid slamming into dancing people and getting the beer from their overflowing mugs all over me.

But by the time Faust leads us to what seems to be a VIP lounge, I'm practically giddy with excitement. While getting settled next to Zelda, I let my eyes take the place in, one detail at a time. The light reflecting off the rows of liquor bottles above the enormous wooden bar. The collection of posters, records and other colorful shit pinned to wooden walls. And the metalwork, the magnificent metalwork all around me, like the delicate thorny branches winding around the staircase leading to the upper floors.

I lean forward in my seat and look up, trying to see exactly how many floors there are, which is why I barely even register the waiter until it's my time to order. "It's all on the house," he says with a smile.

I grin at him. "A Poisoned Apple. No, ten of them."

They just appear on the table before me. I almost fail to suppress a squeal. And for a while, I just look around, sipping the intoxicating, bright green drink and listening to the Vipers' banter. Unlike me and Faust, they can't seem to shut up. And as usual, Zelda is far from smiling, Sarya is taking every opportunity to be bossy and Harry is mostly cracking jokes.

As I look at him, an image pops into my mind of him asking Nuala to dance at the Ball. It was all so sweet, the way he shifted on his feet and avoided looking her in the eye. It strikes me as odd, that I used to think Harry was this violent guy. Sure, he acts tough, but I've never really seen him do anything of that sort and even when the Vipers still despised me, his greatest transgression was teasing me. I almost let out a chuckle thinking how the two of them, him and Nuala, would actually make a good couple.

What snaps me out of thinking about Harry and Nuala is Faust leaning in to say, his voice a bit hushed, "That book Moswen had me get for you..."

My head snaps to him. When did he switch seats with Zelda, I think to myself.

"Did it help?" he asks, locking eyes with me.

It's hard to concentrate on what he's saying when he's being so annoyingly hot, his rolled-up sleeves revealing all the glorious muscles of his forearms.

But I snap out of it and turn serious, throwing a glance at the others. They seem to be immersed in their own conversation so I just make sure to keep my own voice low as I say, "Not really. Not even a single mention of the Stone."

"I see." He looks away for a second. "But don't worry about it. Tomorrow's what matters. If the third ritual doesn't happen, we can just move on with our lives. And if it does, we'll know more."

I smile and shake my head. "That would've made me feel better if it weren't for the other thing. Leo is our *only* suspect and we still haven't even confirmed his part in it, let alone used him to find new clues."

He lets out an impatient breath. "I thought I told you I'm waiting to hear from someone. It should be any day now."

"Fine, don't get your panties in a bunch," I say as I roll my eyes at him.

For a second, I think I see his lips curl into a smile.

And then there's a moment of silence.

"You know what?" I say, shaking my head and smiling as I recognize the song that's coming on. "I actually think I'll take your advice and not think about all that stuff, at least for one day."

"Fair enough," he says as he leans forward to take a sip of his drink.

I down the rest of my vodka as I let the music wash over me. But then my eyes land on yet another girl glancing at the prince sitting next to me as she walks past. Before I can stop it, a laugh escapes my lips.

When I turn to him, he's looking at me with his eyebrows raised.

"That was, like," I start, realizing that my speech is becoming a bit slurred, "the fifth girl that's done the slow motion past our table just so she could leer at you."

"It might surprise you," he snaps at me a little, leaning forward to rest his forearms on his thighs, "but there's quite a lot of women who find me attractive."

An image pops into my mind, of Nuala blushing as she looks at him. Oh my fucking god. My friend is one of those people. She's in love with Faust.

He's staring at me, waiting for my reaction. "Surprise me?" I reply with a strained laugh, the alcohol making me say things I'd *never* say otherwise. "You're a hot, strong prince. You're basically a fantasy come to life."

His eyes are burning holes in mine. There's an urgency in his voice when he leans even closer to whisper, "Just not yours."

For a second, I just look at him. A part of me wants to tell him all about the huge crush I had on him back when I was in high school, when my life was so miserable, I desperately fantasized about someone rescuing me from it. But now I know it wasn't just me. It was Nuala as well.

My lips curl into a joyless smile. "That's the thing with fantasies," I say as I start getting up. "They distract you from actually living your life."

For a second, he doesn't say anything. He looks a bit stunned. And I'm already turning on my heel when he demands, "Where're you going?"

"Bathroom," I reply, frowning a little. "Do I have your permission, Your Majesty?"

He rolls his eyes at me and I walk away, excited about the opportunity to snoop around a little. And while my initial intention is to come straight back, on my way out of the bathroom, a ridiculously tall shifter blocks my way. He's standing next to the jukebox, smiling and holding out a coin for me. "Play something for me," he says.

I let out a squeal, grab the coin out of his hand and put on my favorite song in the whole wide world.

The next thing I know, I'm dancing with the guy as he tells me all about his latest pack and their squabbles. I'm having a great time, except for one thing. I'm afraid that when I get back, I'll find the prince in the arms of one of the girls that have been eyeing him since we first walked into this place.

But that never happens, simply because he finds *me* first. Still dancing with the shifter, I sense a presence behind my back and I turn around to see him scowling at me.

Before I can do or say anything, he appears by my dancing partner's side, making him instantly pull away from me and freeze in place. Faust leans to snarl in his ear, "Leave, now."

The shifter doesn't let him repeat himself. He throws me a scared glance and leaves the two of us alone.

"What the hell is wrong with you?" I hiss at him, my hands balled into fists.

He doesn't even look at me. "I'm taking you home, Longborn." With that, he grabs me by the arm, opens a door that I haven't even noticed and pushes me out into the cold night air.

"Let go of me," I yell as I try to break his grip.

I fail miserably, but as I throw daggers at him, he loosens it himself and I snap my arm away from him.

"Wait here until I get the others," he snaps as he turns to leave.

"No, I'm coming back inside," I say with determination as I try to push past him.

He blocks my way. "What, to that cowardly little boyfriend of yours?" he says as he motions at the bar.

"Beats having to look at *you*."

For a second, he just looks at me. Then his eyes narrow and he comes so close, I feel his breath on my face. "Now that's a lie, isn't it?" he whispers, his voice commanding and husky as he keeps staring deep into my eyes.

I find myself mesmerized, my breathing heavy and my knees buckling with growing desire.

"Isn't it?" he demands.

When I speak, my voice is a raspy whimper. "Fuck. You."

The next thing I know, he grabs me by the waist and all of a sudden, I can feel the hardness of his muscles and his cock pressed against my entire body. It's an almost uncomfortable shock of pleasure and I can't help but let him kiss me, a moan escaping my lips even before he slides his tongue between them. He slams me into the wall, his mouth devouring, his hands stroking, kneading and squeezing almost all at once.

But it's not enough. My fingers running through his hair, I take his lower lip between my teeth and I bite, hard. That makes him let out a lustful grunt and he pulls away, locking eyes with me as he gets his hand under my pants.

Without breaking eye contact, he finds the spot and slides his fingers right into me. I let out a helpless moan and I see his lips part, his eyes still piercing holes in mine.

I grab onto the muscles of his shoulders as he fingers me, the waves of pleasure making me dip my head back, close my eyes and dig my nails into his skin. His breathing ragged, I know he's watching me, silently and intensely, but instead of making me feel self-conscious, it only increases my desire for him.

And I want to tell him to fuck me right here and now, but then I remember her.

Nuala.

That's all it takes for it all to come crumbling around me. I realize I'm in some dingy bar with Faust, letting him finger me the night before the Second Round.

I have to muster all my determination to get his hand out of my pants and push him away. "No," I squeeze out, my breathing slowly becoming less erratic.

He frowns and then leans in. "Something wrong?" he whispers in my ear.

I pull away to look him straight in the eye. "Yeah. It's not like we won't see each other ever again," I make myself say, "so I really don't want to become one of your fuck-girls."

He just looks at me for a second and then lets out a rough laugh. "You've got to be kidding me."

"I'm not..." I draw in a breath, mad at myself for getting myself in this situation in the first place. "Look, you have to admit, our relationship is already weird. No need to add to it."

He squints at me, getting in my face as he demands, "No, there's something else. You need to tell me what it is."

And he's right, but I'm not ready to even think about all that, so I don't say anything. I just shake my head.

"Fine," he snaps, "then the day after tomorrow, I'm picking you up at seven and you're going on a date with me."

I laugh. "I might be dead by then."

He lets out a sigh. "Then I'll ask you again tomorrow."

"I'll just say no."

"Then say it tomorrow."

"Fine, can we leave now?"

It's at that exact moment that I hear a ruckus from inside the bar and see Sarya, Harry and Zelda barge out. I take a step away from Faust and frown at them.

"Um," Sarya says, sounding breathless, "I think we should really get moving."

"Yeah," Harry agrees. "We think we made this pack of shifters really mad."

Faust lets out a sigh and motions for them to follow him back to the Pull. Once we're on the other side, he says bye to everyone and calls me over, looking all serious. And he tells me that his spies have caught Leo getting stuff that could be used for a blood ritual.

And just like that, I'm back to being scared shitless and only being able to think about the Second Round.

Chapter Thirty-Five

The next morning, feeling bewildered and numb at the same time, I meet Faust and the other Chosen in the entrance hall. And there are so many other students gathered there, chatting away as they wait to see us off, but my eyes are searching for one in particular.

And I *do* spot her. Nuala is standing in the crowd, waving and smiling at me. A part of me thought she'd be too mad at me to come say bye, so I breathe a sigh of relief and throw her the widest, warmest smile I can muster.

Because the Second Round is about to happen, and my palms are sweating and my heart is throbbing in my chest.

I barely register taking the Elevator to the Arena, that's how absentminded I am.

This time, it doesn't take us to the booth overlooking the bleachers and the ring. Once we file out of it, we find ourselves in a room with one door and zero windows. The only furnishings are twelve plain chairs and screens hung off all four walls.

Faust motions for us to take out seats and goes to lean on the wall, his eyes directed at the screen across from him.

I follow his gaze and the very next second, the screen switches on. I see the camera catching the audience from all angles, people clapping, chanting, or just chatting away, waiting for the Third Round to begin.

Then the camera lands on the Pied Piper getting out of her seat in the central booth, instantly making the crowd go silent.

She approaches the glass booth wall, her eyes sweeping over the crowd.

"Believe me when I say I understand," she starts in her signature bored drawl, "that you'd rather I skipped the whole tiresome introduction."

I hear laughter and cheering from the audience. "However," she continues, people falling silent once again, "even the Pied Piper has obligations she cannot dismiss so easily. It is my duty to welcome you here today, but it is my utmost pleasure to tell you..."

She pauses, scanning the crowd with her mesmerizing eyes. "...that this time, I will *not* be explaining the rules to you."

I frown, my surprise echoed by the murmur all around me.

"Our Chosen will be led into the Arena one by one and it will be part of their assignment to gauge what exactly is expected of them."

What the fuck, I think to myself, glancing around to see confusion on the faces of the other Chosen. I pay special attention to Leo, but he seems just as surprised as the rest of us. Admittedly, he could be faking it.

"So without further ado," the Pied Piper continues, "I welcome you all to the Second Round of the annual Grimm Academy Trials."

As the crowd cheers, whistles and claps, Faust moves away from the wall and comes to stand in front of us, clad in his Ouroboros waistcoat and wearing a somber look on his face.

It's all eyes on him as he says, "Look under your chairs. You'll find flags with numbers on them. The number on your flag tells you when it's your turn."

I listen. I get the flag and I look at the number. Twelve. Fucking shit, I think to myself as I glance around. Leo is number three, Sarya seven, Amra eight, Harry nine, Zelda ten and Faust eleven. Lucky bastards, all of them.

And just as I think I must have angered some god in a past life, a voice booms from some heading speaker, saying "Number one."

The guy who has it gets up and goes out the only door. As soon as it shuts behind him, the screens all turn off.

"Hey," Harry yells out.

"What the hell," Sarya joins in.

"Don't we get to watch?" Amra asks, looking at Faust.

"Sorry," he just says with a shake of his head.

Fucking shit, I think to myself.

I spend the next half hour fidgeting and glancing at my watch every five seconds.

Then number two gets called out. Rinse and repeat. One by one, the Chosen keep leaving the room, never to come back.

And just as I feel the urge to start pulling my hair out, number ten gets called out and Zelda walks out, leaving me and Faust alone.

I throw a glance at him and see he's already looking at me. For a second, he stays silent. Then he says, "You'll be fine," his voice comforting.

I give him a weak smile and go back to glancing at my watch. I'm too nervous to think, let alone talk.

Soon, I hear the voice from the speaker announce, "Number eleven," and I see Faust get up and walk straight to the exit.

Just before he shuts the door behind him, he throws me a glance over his shoulder and says, "Good luck."

And just like that, I'm all alone with my thoughts. Now that I can no longer see him, I find it hard not to think about the possibility of Faust dying out there. I shake my head, focusing all my attention on the blank screen before me. If I just keep my feelings shoved down until it's all over, I'll be fine. I'll be fine.

Finally, my number gets called out and I force myself to get up. I wobble out the door and find myself in the ring, the silence of the room I've walked out of getting switched for the sound of thunderous clapping.

I don't even glance at the audience all around me. All of my focus is on the only thing before me, a rack with a whole range of weapons stacked onto it, a small pedestal with a single knife placed right in front of it.

Frowning, I walk up to the whole display and tilt my head, inspecting the items one by one. No one will tell me what I'm supposed to do, that much is clear. But what if I've no clue, I think as I feel the seconds ticking away.

It's then that I notice drops of blood around the knife on the pedestal. Squinting, I glance at the weapons on the rack. There's everything from elegant swords to clunky maces there. And some of the hilts have blood stains on them as well.

I see.

I don't hesitate. I take the knife off the pedestal and I use it to slice the skin of my palm. Then I walk up to the weapon rack and I pick out what I believe is called a scimitar, a single-edged sword with a curved blade.

As soon as I take a few swings with it, feeling that the weight should be fine, I feel a weird energy course out of the metal and straight into my body.

I don't have time to linger on it, because the very next second, I get the urge to look up and ahead.

I see a huge, levitating glass cube appear at the center of the Arena and I hear the crowd break into thunderous clapping.

I barely register it all. As I walk, all my attention is focused on the cube, which is the size of a smaller house, seems to be empty and has a set of glass stairs leading up to it.

Once I'm in front of it, I hesitate.

I look down and see a couple of trails of blood leading from the stairs and out of the ring.

Holy hell.

But I've no choice. My legs shaking, I start climbing. There are murmuring sounds all around me, but I pay them no mind.

As soon as I step inside the cube, I see a stone pillar appear at its far end. It's got flags stuck into it.

I squint, my heart pounding as I search for the number eleven. It's there. Faust made it. And by the looks of it, so did numbers three, five, seven, eight, nine and ten.

So Leo, someone who's number I don't know, Sarya, Amra, Harry and Zelda.

I blink in confusion. Am I just supposed to walk up to the pillar and plant my flag there?

But as soon as I think that, the cube shakes a little and I lean a bit forward, drawing in a breath as I prepare myself for whatever may come.

All the way on the other side of the cube, right in front of the pillar, I see a figure appear out of thin air and land on the ground with a deafening thud. Then another one and another one, until I see seven figures forming a line, all facing me.

Dark-red, stone knights.

I hear the crowd cheer and then go silent, waiting for me.

But what am I supposed to do? I glance at the scimitar in my hand. They can't expect me to attack a bunch of stone fucking knights with a blade I don't even know how to use?

My heart skipping random beats, I decide to at least start approaching.

I take a single, cautious step forward and I hear a thud to my right. Another stone knight, just dark-blue, has landed right beside me. Another one lands to my left and I lean a bit forward, glancing left and right to see four more appear to form a line on my side of the cube.

I see. I have allies, not just enemies, I think to myself.

And as soon as I do, the red knight directly opposite to me takes a step forward, unsheathes its sword and bows.

That's the leader.

I just blink at it. Then a thought pops into my head, I raise my scimitar and I bow as well, getting another wave of cheering from the audience.

And just like that, it begins. All the red knights charge straight at me and my own soldiers, making me freeze in place.

Fuck, fuck, fuck.

It's only when they're already in front of us and the red leader stops to swing his massive stone sword at me that I realize I need to get moving.

My heart threatening to burst out of my ribcage, I lunge to my right, dodging the attack and crashing into one of the blue knights.

As quickly as I can, I straighten up and get into the position to attack. I keep swinging my scimitar at the red knight in front of me, but I don't do any damage. I barely manage to dodge its attacks.

But at least now that I'm moving, my own soldiers seem to be coming to life. All around me, red and blue knights start fighting, their stone swords creating a low, thunderous noise as they slam into each other.

And my soldiers seem to be protecting me, creating a sort of barrier between me and the enemy, but one still manages to get through.

I barely have time to lift my scimitar before its sword cuts into my flesh. I curse out loud, take a wobbly step back and watch one of the blue knights cut it in half, the red stone crumbling to the ground before me.

It's fine, I think to myself as I grit my teeth and throw a quick glance at my shoulder. It's just a surface wound. I'll be fine.

As I keep dodging the attacks, each more ferocious than the last, I force myself to focus. I see three of six blue knights shattered on the ground.

If I don't do something fast, I'm going to fucking die.

I guess I'll have no choice but to use my magic.

Fuck.

Stepping behind one of my own soldiers, I stop for a second and tap the Element Rune, visualizing Earth. The idea is to blast all the stone around me to pieces and be done with it. *If* I can manage it.

But absolutely nothing happens, as if the stone isn't reacting to my magic at all. I frown, but then I see another red knight charging at me with its sword raised high.

I draw in a panicked breath and tap the Element Rune again, trying to avoid the attack by using Air instead of Earth.

Once again, nothing happens and I freeze, the knight already swinging its sword at me.

The next thing I know, one of my own lunges before me, cuts the attacker in half and comes crumbling to the ground.

I'll never make it to the other side, I think to myself as I glance at the pillar. It seems to be just as far away as it was when this started,

I'm down to only two knights and to make things worse, it seems that something's blocking my control of the elements.

That thought makes me glance at the weapon in my hand. I invoke Sight and my vision sharpens and blurs all at once. I see the blood magic in the scimitar drawing power out of my body.

So it's supposed to help *and* make it worse. Perfect.

As yet another red knight takes a swing at me, I let out an angry grunt. I try to dodge the attack, but its blade manages to slice into my waist.

I fall to the ground and I cry out, my hand darting to my waist, where I feel hot blood starting to gush out. I hear the people in the crowd gasp, but I focus all my attention on crawling away, with gritted teeth, as quickly as possible.

Pain searing the entire left side of my body, I take cover behind the last of my own knights and I try to fling the scimitar away, hoping to break the spell. But it just stays stuck to my hand.

I don't have time to keep trying because a horrifying sound makes me look up and I see the knight I took cover behind come crashing to the ground.

And just like that, I'm left alone with the five remaining red knights.

Shit, this is *not* good. I'm on my knees, panting, dizzy and in terrible pain. And the red leader is walking up to me, his sword held high.

My heart skips a beat and I close my eyes shut, imagining the sword cutting into me.

Fear threatens to overwhelm me, but instead of letting it paralyze me, I shut my eyes and take a deep, forceful breath. I sense energy align all around me, flooding me with such a tremendous feeling of connection with *everything* that, for a second, I think it's going to fry my fucking brain.

I open my eyes and just as the red leader is about to bring his sword down on me, I feel the power rush back into my body and I tap the Element Rune.

Nothing.

Without hesitation, I push myself up off the ground and start running in the direction of the pillar. I hear the sound of the sword digging into the glass floor.

And I hear the knights charging after me, but I try to drown it all out. I thought I'd get my power back if I only got rid of the scimitar and the effects of what appears to be blood magic. But there's something more going on here. It's as if none of the elements inside the glass cube can be manipulated, at all. So I think my best chance is to just try to make a run for it.

I almost get to my goal.

But just as I'm about to come to a stop and plant my flag, something slams into me and sends me flying to the ground.

Lying on my back, I see the red leader appear above me, the other four stopping behind him.

Once again, he raises his sword and I have to fight the onset of a panic attack.

At this point, I'll try anything. I close my eyes shut and I tap one of my unactivated Runes.

There's a moment of silence before I hear it, the labored sound of things being brought into existence. And when I open my eyes, I see three new blue knights appear out of thin air and land around my enemies with a loud thud.

As they take care of four of the five knights, I hear gasping from the audience all around me, but my eyes are fixed on the red leader.

Not paying the rest of his army any mind, he's swinging his sword down on me.

For a second, I feel my heart stop.

Then I tap my newly activated rune and I make a stone shield block his sword.

I don't hesitate. I push myself off the ground and lunge to my right, straight at the stone pillar.

Just as I raise the hand in which I have the flag, with the corner of my eye, I see his blade swinging at me again.

I muster all my strength and with one forceful movement, I drive the fucking flag in with the rest.

I don't wait to turn back to the red leader, but when I do, I see him and all the other knights, including mine, disappear.

As soon as they're gone, I come crashing to the ground, panting, bloody and in terrible pain.

What surprises me is that the people in the Arena stay silent. I glance up at the Pied Piper's booth. She's standing right in front of the glass wall, looking down at me.

Almost right away, I see a medic rush into the ring. Holding me up, he leads me out of the ring and into a hallway, dealing with my worst wound while walking. And I assume we're going straight to the interview because it's the same hallway I've walked before. And it's packed with people staring at me in awe, including the prince's uncle.

"Genesis, really?" he asks as we walk past him, but it's not really a question. "I have to say I didn't expect you to become so powerful so fast."

I just smile and keep walking. The worst is over, but the pain is still a lot to bear.

But just as we approach the archway leading into the interview room, the chatter of the crowd drifting through, the medic stops and just remains standing there.

I frown, but before I can ask him what's going on, I feel a switch being flipped in my head.

The next thing I know, my body starts leading me in the opposite direction, away from all the people and down a series of deserted hallways, each darker than the last. When I finally reach an old wooden door and my body stops before it, my own hand betraying me by raising to grab the handle, my heart is beating so wildly, I fear it might just stop.

Chapter Thirty-Six

My hand on the handle, I push the door open and, no matter how hard I try, fail to stop myself from walking into the darkness behind it.

But as soon as I'm through the door and my eyes adjust to the lack of light, I see it's just a large, windowless storage space with rows of crates and cardboard boxes along the walls.

I remain standing there, my heart pounding wildly and my mind racing to come up with a way out.

But it doesn't take long for me to sense a presence behind my back. I still don't have control over my own body so I can't turn around. At the same time, this makes me feel relieved and fills me with dread.

I hear footsteps and I feel a veil being thrown over my consciousness. If I could do anything, I'd scream, louder than I've ever screamed before. But I can do absolutely nothing, even as I see a person walk around me and stop right in front of my rounded eyes.

Just like that time in front of the woods, I see all the individual features of the person's face. The eyes. The nose. The mouth. But they don't fit together and the end result is a mess that my mind simply can't comprehend.

The person scoffs and takes one step closer to me.

Feeling my heart about to burst out of my ribcage, it finally hits me.

When it happened, that time in front of the woods, they tried to take the Diary away from me. And the only one who'd seen Moswen by then was Leo.

Leo.

This is Leo, using Mind Magic on me. I'm going to die now, I think to myself. I know too much and he needs to get rid of me as soon as possible. Think, Quinn, think, I urge myself, but he's already getting ready to strike, I can feel it.

I imagine closing my eyes shut and opening them again. And for a second, my Sight allows me to break through his magic and an image flickers before my eyes. The image of Ouroboros.

For a second, I feel my heart stop. House of Faust sigil. He has the House of Faust sigil embroidered onto his shirt.

Then all of a sudden, something sharp gets violently shoved into my chest, the instant wave of pain rendering me blind.

The next thing I know, I'm stumbling backwards with my hands on my chest as the door behind me closes almost without a sound.

He's left me for dead.

And I can move now, but that only makes me crash into the door and slide down to the ground, the throbbing pain spreading from my very core keeping me stiff as a corpse.

I try to scream and yell for help, but that only makes me cough up blood. I feel the life being drained out of my body, but there's no longer a single part of it I can make cooperate.

And just as my eyes start threatening to close, I force them open and I invoke Sight. I look around me, searching for something I could use to get out of this alive.

The only thing I see is this strange web of light ribbons on the ground. They remind me of blood vessels, especially because they seem to be flowing. I make my tired mind reach out to them.

I tug at one.

Nothing.

I wince, but I tug at another.

And I hear a strange crackling sound and my ears prick up, my skin feeling the ground beneath me start warming up.

"Hello, little one," I hear her say, immediately recognizing Dame Gothel's voice. "Thought you'd never notice me."

How are you here, I want to ask, but I can't reply. I can't even open my mouth.

"I could sense that you were in danger," she whispers to me as if she'd read my mind. And as she does it, I start feeling life flow back into my body. "After all," she adds, "I did taste your blood."

I open my mouth to say something, but nothing comes out.

"Yes, you owe me one, if that's what you wanted to ask," Dame Gothel says with a chuckle and disappears.

And it all hurts like hell, but blood stops flowing out of my wound and my head starts clearing up, making my mind rush to figuring out the next step.

I crawl away from the door so I can open it. I need to get out of here quickly, before everyone else starts leaving the Arena. I wince as I reach for the doorknob. I really think I shouldn't let anyone see me, considering it must be *him* who attacked me just now.

Faust. The most powerful man at the Academy. The most dangerous vampire. The leader of the Vipers. And how did I manage to not see it, that he is also the one behind my boxes of chocolates, it's beyond me.

So I slowly get up, letting out a wince with every move. I open the door, take a peek outside and rush down the hallway, checking on my wound every two seconds to make sure I haven't started bleeding again. But it's now only a surface wound and even though it's agonizingly painful, I think I won't be dying any time soon.

As quickly as I can, I make my way back to my room, which I've decided is safe enough for the time being, considering he thinks he's killed me. It seems that everyone's still busy with the interviews, because I don't bump into a single person as I go.

Once I'm there, it's like the shock dies down a little and the fear takes over. I rush to the corner of my room farthest from the door, I sit there and I pull my knees to my chest.

And just as I'm about to start pulling my hair out, it finally hits me. I whip out my phone and with shaky hands, I text Nuala to come as soon as possible.

I barely move as I wait, but my mind makes up for it by frantically running in circles. He tried to kill me. No, it can't be. But I saw what I saw.

I want to murder him. Rip his fucking throat out for making me start trusting him just so he could eliminate me as some nameless threat to his fucking image and sinister plans.

It doesn't take my friend longer than ten minutes, but by the time she barges into my room, I'm livid.

But what I see next has me tense up and push myself off the bed, my lips pressing tight. It's him. Faust is in my room with Nuala and I'm so worked up about it, I feel I won't even be able to breathe.

But his eyes are already on the blood on my shirt. He appears right in front of me, his nostrils flaring and the look in his eyes turning savage. "Who did this to you?" he growls.

I've never seen him this angry.

Clenching my fists and gritting my teeth, I throw daggers at him. What a marvelous fucking actor he is.

"What the fuck is going on?" he demands, his arms vibrating with rage. "Why won't you tell me who did this to you?"

It takes me a second, but I finally squeeze out, my voice as threatening as I can make it, "I don't know what game you're playing, Faust, but I'm not playing it with you. I want you out."

I point at the door and he takes a step back, a frown clouding his forehead. He seems as if he's struggling to regain control. "What're you talking about?"

"Get the fuck out," I command him, I tap my Element rune and I send him flying back.

The sound that his body makes when it hits the wall is a sharp thud. He almost instantly regains control of his body, but even after he's found his footing, he just keeps standing there, staring at me.

"You're fucking crazy, you know that?" he snaps at me, almost rips the door off the hinges and disappears.

Only once he's gone do I notice that Nuala is still there. I look at her and all of a sudden, I can't keep it in any longer. I let out a shuddering breath and start crying, falling into the arms she's already holding out for me.

Once we're seated next to each other on my bed, the avalanche of questions begins. Nuala knows nothing and wants to understand everything.

"Wait a second," I tell her, my voice shaky with shock and crying. I grab my bag off the floor and take out the diary.

As soon as she appears, Moswen lets out a gasp. "Holy Word," she mutters as she rushes to grab my hand.

It just passes through mine, but she doesn't even acknowledge it. "You look like you barely made it out of there alive," she says.

"It's Faust," I cut in, unable to keep it in any longer. I throw them each a look, seeing their foreheads scrunch up, but I don't back down. "It was Faust all along," I say and the rest just pours out of me like an angry waterfall.

By the time I'm done, both Nuala and Moswen look absolutely shocked.

"How scary that must have been for you…" With teary eyes, Moswen even tries to pat me on the head before she says, albeit hesitantly, "But I did tell you to stay away from him."

I almost snap at her. "Come on, Moswen, not now."

"But wait, you didn't actually see the person?" Nuala cuts in.

"No, but..."

"Then you're wrong," she cuts me off, a touch of anger in her voice.

"You can't be sure that I am," I reply, shaking my head and pressing my lips.

"Actually," my friend starts, looking as if she's trying to calm down, "I think I can."

I raise my eyebrows, but she's already turning to Moswen. "While all of you were fighting, including Andreas, I went for a walk and ended up at the graveyard."

That strikes me as odd, but Nuala is already taking out her phone and showing Moswen a picture. "This is what I found there, and what I think is, well, the third blood ritual."

I lean forward to take a look. They're stacked onto a weathered grave. The bunch of burning eyes that I'm looking at right now.

With bated breath, I look to Moswen. "Yes," she says with a sigh. "That's a blood ritual. And it seems to have something to do with Sight."

I take in a deep breath and say, "So now it's all three bloodlines. It was shifters, then vampires, now faes."

"What could it all mean?" Nuala asks.

"I don't know what the fuck it means," I hear myself hiss, "I just know who's behind it all."

"Quinn," Nuala starts, but I don't let her finish.

"Nuala," I practically growl at her. "You think *I* want this to be happening? For crying out loud, I actually started to like the guy,"

I keep going, getting more worked up with each word. "I don't know how it's happened, I mean, I *know* people, but he seems to have managed to fool us all. Of course, now it all seems so obvious. It isn't just Leo who's both a vampire and a Viper. And everything else that we eventually found out, well, Faust has a web of spies and servants, he could've planted the evidence *so* easily. Especially since we made him fucking chief of the investigation, holy fuck, how stupid we were. But we won't be making the same mistake. I mean, I did let my anger get the best of me just now, when he was still here, but I didn't actually *tell* him that I know. That I know he's tried to kill me. So we can just pretend that we don't know, which is actually quite fitting because we really need to make *him* our top priority right now. Learning as much as we can, tailing him to finally figure out what the hell's going on. So what do you think, girls, you with me?"

When I finally finish, catching my breath, there's a tense silence as both of them look at me with worry in their eyes. "Oh please don't look at me like that," I say with a sigh. "I'm so tired."

And I move to lie down, but it's at that exact moment that I hear a sharp knock at the door.

Suddenly alert, I sit up straight, I close the diary shut to get Moswen back to safety and I say, "Come in."

To my surprise, it's the Pied Piper's assistant. "Miss Longborn?" she asks and I nod. "The Pied Piper would like you to pay her a visit."

I throw a glance at Nuala and say, "Of course, I'll come first thing tomorrow."

"*Now*, if you don't mind," the girl insists.

Oh fucking hell, I think to myself as I stop myself from letting out a groan. If I didn't stop myself, I know that that groan would be full of desperation.

Chapter Thirty-Seven

As we make the climb to the Main Tower, where the Pied Piper's office is, the assistant and I only exchange a couple of words. I don't think she knows anything about what's just happened because she thinks I've sustained my injuries during the Trials. And to be honest, I don't linger on it too much. I don't even try to figure out why the Pied Piper wants to see me, that's how shaken up I still am.

When we finally enter the foyer where I last found myself on the day of Professor Mistila's shocking suicide, I I expect the assistant to tell me to wait in front of the office. To my surprise, she knocks on the door opposite to it.

"Yes," I hear the Pied Piper say and the girl nudges me to walk in.

I hesitate for a second, but then I open the door and peek inside. I don't see her, but I hear her when she says, "Come on, I don't have all day."

I walk inside and close the door behind me, surprised when I see that I've found myself in the Pied Piper's private rooms. It's still bright outside, but in here, it may as well be the middle of the night. As far as I can tell, there are no windows and the space is lit only by a couple of candles placed in sconces along the rough stone walls. I take a hesitant look around, noticing rows of bookshelves, a coffee table and a couple of easy chairs here and there. But except for those, the place is very minimalist.

"Care to join me?" I hear the Pied Piper ask and my head snaps in the direction of the voice.

I haven't noticed her because it's so dark and she's wearing her usual black dress. But she's standing next to a commode to my right, holding out a glass filled with a transparent liquid. Thinking a bit of alcohol might be exactly what I need right now, I nod and take a few steps closer to her.

But she doesn't just give it to me. She raises the wrist of her other hand to her mouth and bites into it without so much as flinching. As I watch, she lets a single drop of her blood fall into the glass, instantly making the liquid turn deep red.

"No, thank you," I say as I stop where I find myself. It would probably only take my pain away, but I'm not prepared to risk it.

She just looks at me for a second. Then she lets out a chuckle and shakes her head, stalking up to me as she says, "You know, Miss Longborn, when I first saw you, I had the feeling you weren't the sheltered pup I'm used to seeing around here. However, I never would have thought you'd be *this* suspicious."

"Does it really come as a surprise," I ask, frowning a little, "considering how we met?"

She laughs again. "If you think I'm going to apologize for that, you're sadly mistaken." She shakes her head and walks around me, stopping once she's in front of me again, as if I were her prey and she wanted to take a better look at me. "I've lived through *wars* that went on for a hundred years so I refuse to let you youngsters convince me that the way I treat you is anything less than merciful."

I scoff. "You don't have to be Dracula for me to think I should be careful around you."

She squints at me. "What about me? Shouldn't I be careful around *you*?"

"What're you talking about?" At least one good thing came out of all this, I think to myself. Any other day and I'd be terrified to speak to her this way.

Letting out an exaggerated sigh, she takes a step back, folds her arms and says, "You've been hiding things from me, little mouse, ever since you came here."

"Hiding things from you?" I reply, feigning surprise to buy time and figure out what she knows. "For me to do that, we'd have to have some kind of relationship first."

"Don't do that," she warns. "You'll only wear out my patience."

"Then tell me exactly what you're accusing me of."

She lets out a laugh. "Let's see," she says as she walks up to an easy chair and takes a seat, the tail of her dress dragging after her. "Sneaking into the Forbidden Section in the Library, for example. Lying to my assistant on the day of the First Round. Lying to *me* on the day of Professor Mistila's death." She pauses to throw me an amused look. "Should I go on?"

"It's not like *you* hadn't lied to *me,*" I protest, clenching my fists.

"When have I ever done *that*?"

"After the First Round, you told me you'd look into that mess that someone left in the woods. People were murdered, for crying out loud. And I waited, but you did absolutely nothing."

"There was nothing there," she says, her voice turning colder, "and you know it."

I open my mouth to protest, but she raises her hand to silence me. "No, I've let this go on long enough." She gets up again and walks up to me, throwing me a look with absolutely no amusement in it. "Ever since you came here, trouble has been following you, little mouse. And I've let you do as you please, even after Professor Mistila, but now that you've been assaulted, for the *second* time, if I may add, I'd like you to tell me what exactly is going on."

"How do you know?" I ask, my mind buzzing.

"That is none of your concern."

So he told her. It's only now that it's hitting me, but of course, it's a real possibility that she's in cahoots with him.

My lips pressed tight, I finally decide to say, "There's nothing going on. Can I leave now? I'm pretty beat, you know, from the ethically dubious Trials you're forcing me to participate in." I turn to face the door.

"Well," she drawls, "that's precisely the thing. You'll no longer be participating in them."

That makes me stop and turn back to her, frowning. "What? But it's too late now. I have the holy contract signed with that magic tree or whatever," I say as I lift my wrist to show her the tattoo.

"You do indeed. And it would be impossible for you to get out of it without dying…" She pauses and quirks an eyebrow at me. "But there's quite a lot that a Pied Piper can do that no one else can."

I'd lie if it didn't make me think for a second, but I almost immediately shake my head and say, "No. I have to participate."

"Really?" she goes back to that amused look of hers. "And why is that?"

I shake my head again, cursing myself for reacting the way I did and trying to think of a way out of it. "I hate not getting to finish what I started," I say with a smirk.

She just looks at me for a second. "Very well."

"What, that's it?" I ask, frowning.

She shrugs. "There *is* a way for me to get you out of the contract, but it requires you to… not struggle, let's put it that way."

I squint at her. "Lucky me. Does that mean that I get to walk out of here alive?"

She lets out a chuckle. "The door is right there, but before you leave…" She takes a step closer to me and looks deep into my eyes. "You should know you're not the first of your kind I've encountered in this life. You have a burning fire inside you and you think you can take on the world, don't you? But fire is a fickle thing and it sometimes burns the one that wields it."

"What's your point?"

"Just that it would do you good to remember that I'm keeping an eye on you."

That makes me shudder, but I force myself not to let it show. I give her a smile, turn on my heel and walk away. I don't know what she's up to, this Pied Piper of ours, but the one thing I'm sure of is that she's lying to me. And to be honest, I've fucking had it with people lying to me.

Chapter Thirty-Eight

We're out in the garden, Nuala and I, leafing through a stack of books lying next to our splayed-out bodies. The warm June sun is making the grass glisten and somewhere much closer to the sky, the birds are filling the air with their song. It's such a seemingly peaceful day and it's been almost two months since it happened. Since I got attacked with mind magic and left to bleed out in some long-forgotten broom closet.

But we've been kicked out of the Main Hall to allow the staff to get it ready for the Grand Ball, the one that's held at the end of the Third Round. Which is tomorrow. And there's someone out there who wants to use the opportunity to do something unspeakable, and that person is the guy I almost let myself fall for.

So as much as I'd like it to be, simply relaxing and enjoying the day is just not possible. My mind buzzing, I force myself to keep turning the pages in search of anything that might help us. Sure, I've managed to unlock my second Rune, Genesis, which gives me quite an advantage, but I still have no idea what the Stone really is, what it does, how it behaves...

I let out a sigh and look up from the book I currently have before me, *Geology of the Western Scion Lands*. I see Nuala scrolling on her phone.

I frown, saying, "I don't mean to be a slave-driver, Nuala..."

She looks up, her face flushing. "I know, I know." She hesitates before she adds, "But there's a lot of stuff being written about the Trials. Apparently, even the Keeper is going to be there tomorrow." She glances at her phone. "And they're talking about you again. Saying all sorts of stupid shit."

"I told you I don't want to know any of it," I protest. "Unless they mention *him* and where he's disappeared to, I don't want to hear another word."

"Alright, alright," Nuala says, raising her hands in defense and then picking up her own book again.

And I try to turn my focus back onto mine, but it proves to be impossible. Because now I can't stop thinking about where he could be. Ever since it happened, I've only been working on three things. Looking for information on the Stone, training to get good enough to be able to defeat him and trying to find out where he's been hiding.

"It just doesn't make any sense, does it?" I hear myself say and I see Nuala look up from her book. "That he wouldn't just kill me and continue as planned."

My friend presses her lips tight. "Unless he wasn't the one who did it."

"It could've been *no one* else," I insist, for the millionth time. "I honestly can't believe you're still defending him."

I pause, my eyebrows pulling down. "Nuala, do you know something I don't?"

She frowns. "What're you talking about?"

"I did think it suspicious, after the Second Round," I start, squinting at her, "when you said you went for a walk and just ended up at the graveyard."

She lets out a nervous laugh. "What, Quinn, you think *I* was the one who tried to kill you?"

I just throw her a look.

"Fine," she says with a sigh and digs something out of her pocket. Something small, wrapped in a piece of cloth and tied with a rubber band. "You're right, I didn't just *end up* at the graveyard. I went to look for this."

I take it, turning it between my fingers as I give it a closer inspection. I find that it reeks so I hold it closer to my nose. Then it hits me. "Salvia luna? One of the shift inducing plants I read about in the Restricted Section?"

My friend nods. "I guess I figured, maybe you're right, you know, when you say I'm suppressing things I shouldn't be suppressing. And who knows what this bloodbath thing will bring."

I grin. "I'm so happy for you. But why didn't you tell me about it?" I protest as I give the little package back to her.

She shakes her head and lets out a sigh. "Because I didn't want *this* to happen. I'm still not planning on using it unless absolutely necessary. And I didn't want to get your hopes up."

I just look at her for a second. I'm literally itching to tell her I think she should just try it, but I've learned my lesson. My friend doesn't appreciate being pushed into things. "Fair enough," I choose to say.

"Anyway," Nuala says, obviously wanting to change the subject, "I still think that Andreas couldn't have done it. When I found the eyes at the graveyard that day, they were still burning and he was at the Trials, possibly even in the ring."

That makes me feel frustrated with her again. "Nuala, he's a prince. He could have easily gotten someone else to do the Blood Ritual for him." I keep talking, now more to myself than her. "And let's not forget the fact that he didn't attack me just once. If we're counting the time he tried to steal Moswen."

A realization suddenly hits me and I almost jump up, making Nuala squint at me with worry in her eyes.

"What happened with Faust, the same thing could be happening with the Stone," I blurt out. She just looks at me, frowning, so I rush to explain, "For a very long time, the mistake we were making was looking in the wrong place. We were following Leo instead of Faust."

"I've *literally* no idea what you're talking about," my friend drawls, looking at me like I'm crazy.

"I just need to get one book," I say as I get up off the ground. "Meet me in my room in ten."

And it takes me a little longer than that, but Nuala has her own copy of my key so once I get there, she's already sitting on my bed, looking up at me with growing curiosity in her eyes. Probably because I'm shaking with excitement.

"It's here," I almost whisper as I drop onto the bed next to her and let Moswen out so she can hear it as well. "It's all here," I repeat myself.

Now there's two pairs of eyes looking at me without blinking. I crack open the book, hold it out and point at the title.

"The Prince and the Stone?" Moswen mutters.

"Yes," I nod vigorously, "and I know that we haven't just been looking through non-fiction, we've been scouring fairy tales as well."

Moswen's eyes are starting to round. It's dawning on her as well. "But some are still in the Fiction Section. Especially the ones not collected by the Brothers themselves."

"Exactly," I almost yell out, "this being one of them."

"So, what does the story say?" Nuala asks with bated breath. "What does the Stone do?"

I draw in a breath, making a face. "It doesn't say exactly," I start, "but if you read between the lines, I think it's pretty obvious. So there's a prince, obviously, and his father is ill and his kingdom is divided. One day, the prince leaves his kingdom so he can go steal the Stone, the only thing that can unite the three nations under his rule."

I see Nuala nodding away, seemingly genuinely interested.

"On his way, he meets a wolf, a snake and a bird. All three are in some kind of trouble and the prince saves them, you know how these stories go," I say as I wave my hand.

Moswen just nods.

"Anyway," I keep talking, "all three animals offer to repay the prince for the kindness he's shown them and he asks the wolf to give him his heart, the snake to give him his blood and the bird to give him his eye."

"And they do?" Nuala asks in a tense voice.

"Of course they do. And then there's this nonsensical part near the end, just before the prince finally finds the Stone. But once he's before it, the Stone tells him it cannot be stolen. It can only be won by the one who already has the support of all three of his clans."

"Okay," Nuala drawls, nudging me to go on.

I lift my finger and say, "But then the prince realizes he's already got it. He takes the three gifts, eats and drinks them and bonds with the Stone, getting enormous power that allows him to rule his kingdom without any objection from anyone ever."

Moswen frowns. "And that's it? What are we supposed to make of *that*?"

"Can't you see?" I rush to say, almost shaking with excitement. "The prince ends up ruling his kingdom without any objection from anyone? That's such a weird thing to say." I pause. "Unless you're talking about mind magic."

"Holy Word," Moswen blurts out. "Being able to use it on an entire kingdom, that would be unprecedented, what amount of power would the Stone have to have?"

"A tremendous amount," Nuala replies with an incredulous look in her eyes.

"But there's one good thing to be found in all this," I cut in, burning to start using this information to better prepare myself for tomorrow. "If we stop Faust from eating and drinking the stuff from the blood rituals, we've basically stopped him from being able to use the Stone."

"How do we do that if we can't even find him?" Moswen asks.

"Well," I start, albeit hesitantly, "there's only one option left. I didn't want to do it so as not to draw any attention to myself, but now I think I'll have to pay Faust's uncle a visit."

"His uncle?" Moswen echoes my words as she throws me a funny look. "I thought you said Faust had no family left."

"I did," I reply, "no family but his uncle."

It makes me frown, how pale she turns. "And his name is Baldor?"

I nod, feeling seriously confused.

But Moswen just turns to Nuala and asks, "Nuala, I'm so sorry, but could you leave the two of us alone for just a little while?"

My friend throws me a look, but she gets up and leaves me sitting there, speechless, waiting for Moswen to tell me what the fuck is going on.

"I know you're going to hate me when you see this," she finally says, "but I have to show you."

Without saying a word, I draw in a breath and give her a nod, letting her put her weightless palm on my forehead and suck me into yet another one of her memories.

This time, I find myself looking straight into her eyes. It startles me, until I realize she's in front of a mirror, brushing her hair.

And while here it's actually furnished and beautifully kept, I recognize her room. It's my room, the one I'm currently sitting in.

It's only when my eyes dart to one corner of the mirror that I see him. A vampire stalking towards me. I feel myself jump and I quickly turn around.

Then, to my own surprise, I get up off my chair and throw myself into the man's arms. He has ridiculous side-burns, but he's handsome and he's looking at me with mischief in his eyes.

"I thought I told you to stop using the passage," Moswen tells him, but her voice is so soft and not at all scolding. This is her beau, I finally realize.

"And let them keep me away from you?" he asks as he strokes her hair. "Not a chance."

It disturbs me, how familiar the features of his face are.

"But if you could only prove it to them, that it has nothing to do with you..."

"Don't worry about it," he whispers in her ear. "Soon none of that will matter. I'll have built an entirely new world, where I am king of everything the eye can see. What will your parents have to say to me then?"

She pulls away from his embrace a little. "That's when they'll start with the actual protests. Baldor," she starts, but she's hesitant.

It makes me draw in a breath. But it is him, just without the armor on his arm and the walking stick in his hand.

"You know they'll never accept it," Moswen finally says. "I know our House is ancient, but they're liberals to their cores and they'll never allow you to put everyone under your rule. They'll rather die."

"I don't care about any of that," Baldor growls a little. "I only care about you. Do *you* believe in me?"

"I do, but..."

At that exact moment, I hear a loud thud and Moswen's head snaps to her left.

And there she is, standing in the doorway with a pissed-off look on her face. *My mother,* just the way I saw her in Moswen's previous memories.

"Get out," she hisses at the man in Moswen's arms.

And then everything goes black and I find myself sitting on my bed again, looking up at Moswen, my chest heaving and my eyes narrowing. She's just standing there, waiting for my reaction with apparent unease on her face.

"What was my mother doing in your room?"

"I think you know the answer to that question," she mutters.

I can tell she's struggling not to look away. "Say something," she pleads.

"You're my fucking sister?" I yell out.

I get up, fuming. My hands balled into fists, I walk past her, all the way to the window. I look out, but I don't really see anything.

When I finally speak, my voice is full of anger and bitterness. "How funny it is, to find out, all at once, that you exist and that you've betrayed me." I turn to throw daggers at her. "That you've betrayed this entire Academy, in fact."

"I didn't realize he was alive," she insists, her voice low but forceful.

I shake my head, my lips pressed tight. "Doesn't explain why you didn't tell me about the bloodbath or your own involvement in it."

"I *wasn't* involved," she protests, struggling not to raise her voice. "And my parents, *our* parents, they did warn me about it, that I do remember, but I didn't have any recollection of it actually happening, not until you and I learned that it did."

"And then?" I demand.

"Then it started coming back to me, little by little. Something going terribly wrong at the Trials, people yelling and screaming, smoke billowing..." She pauses and then adds even more forcefully. "But it was all so vague, utterly useless."

I wave my hand in dismissal, forcing myself not to snap at her.

She takes a step closer to me. "Quinn, when we learned about the bloodbath, I honestly assumed someone else was following in Baldor's footsteps. And I didn't want you to know." she lets out a sigh. "That I'd fallen for a man like that and been so blind to what was really happening."

"I don't care about your excuses," I snarl at her. "I'm throwing your diary away and I don't care what happens to you next."

She practically gets in my face and speaks in a rushed, pleading voice. "Please, little sister, we don't know anything about the magic tying me to the diary. It might be broken once the Trials are over. I might not get a chance to talk to you ever again."

I just look at her for a second, fuming. Then I rush to my bed, grab her diary and close it shut.

And just like that, she disappears. I throw myself onto my bed, struggling to stop myself from screaming away all my shock, anger and sadness. To think that all this time, she knew she was my sister and never told me... Never told me anything about my parents, about herself, about me. It hurts like hell, especially now that I can be pretty sure that my parents were killed in the bloodbath. Now I'll never get to meet them and I'll never even get to learn anything about them.

But I've no time for that. The Third Round is tomorrow and now I'm facing an even more dangerous opponent. Maybe Faust Junior is stronger, but I was counting on my insights into his personality. Faust Senior is a great unknown to me. And I can't exactly waltz into the Pied Piper's office and ask for her help. She may be in cahoots with him. But if I don't do that, what else am I supposed to do?

And then it occurs to me.

Chapter Thirty-Nine

I hear a knock at my door and I smell my uncle, but I don't get up.

But he knocks again.

And again.

Finally, I lift my head off the pillow. "I'm asleep," I growl from where I'm lying.

But apparently, he doesn't give a shit. After a moment of silence, he opens the door and walks into my bedroom uninvited. I look up at him and slowly push myself into a seated position.

"The Archduke," he starts, breaking off to scrunch his nose up at the mess that my room is. There's clothes and empty bottles of alcohol strewn all over the floor. "The Archduke wants an answer regarding his proposal," he finishes, turning his eyes back on me.

"What, now, the day before the Third Round?," I protest, rubbing my eyes because right now even the late afternoon sun is enough to hurt them.

"That would be excellent, yes."

"Then no," I say, getting worked up about it, fast. "Remind him that there *is* such a thing as the Treaty. I don't care if he's trembling at the very thought of not being able to use mind magic on humans, I won't let anyone interfere with their right to run their own countries."

Uncle scowls at me. "Let's not be rash, Andreas," he demands. "I don't care what you decide regarding Erfurt's proposal, but I need you to give him something, anything."

I let out a bitter scoff. "So you want me sucking up to the old fart?"

He shakes his head and gives an impatient sigh. "I thought I told you, nephew, how important it is for us to have as many people of power at the Trials tomorrow."

I want to tell him to fuck off, but I know that wouldn't go too well. I let out a sigh and say, "Fine. Tell him I'll come for a personal visit the day after the Trials. He loves attention like that."

I don't wait for my uncle's reaction. I just throw myself back on my stomach, planning on going back to my initial plan, trying to sleep off my hangover.

To my surprise, uncle doesn't leave. My face pressed against the pillow, I frown.

"Andreas," I hear him say in a low yet tense voice, "I know what an Olarel girl can do to a man…"

That makes my ears prick up. I push myself back into a seated position and I stare straight into my uncle's eyes, frowning.

"But you could have any woman you want," he continues, stressing each word individually. "Why do you choose to degrade yourself like this, for *her*?"

What the fuck? How does he even know?

I guess it's the confusion on my face that prompts him to let out a laugh and say, "What, you think your uncle has no eyes? First those articles, then that incident at the Ball, then wasting your time on those little training sessions of yours..."

I feel myself start to fume. "It's not up to you to determine what constitutes a waste of *my* time, uncle," I snap at him.

Uncle just blinks at me. "I rest my case," he says. Then he comes closer, so close he's towering over me. When he speaks again, it's in a low, tense voice. "I took you in when you were five years old, boy, and I've been raising you ever since. So you should listen really carefully when I say..."

He pauses to raise a finger at me. "That girl will only ever bring you trouble."

For a second, I just look at him. "You're in luck then," I say bitterly, "because I've nothing to do with her anymore."

He gives it a think and then nods. "Good," he replies, his voice turning softer. "I'll come see you off tomorrow, but remember, if you want to come out a winner, you need to do exactly as I told you." He motions to my nightstand, where just yesterday he left me the vial with the 'special blood,' as he called it. "Understood?" he demands.

I never thought my uncle would urge me to take the vampire equivalent of steroids, but I guess he's just that scared for my life. "Understood," I finally echo him, hoping to make him stop mothering me. I need to go back to sleep and *not* thinking about things.

And he stares at me for a moment longer, but then he just taps his walking stick on the floor and disappears.

Once he's gone, I just sit in my bed for a moment, my mind buzzing again. Great, I think to myself as I get up, now it's going to be impossible to get back to sleep. I've only managed to get her out of my head and now he's put her back in.

I pace around the room, trying to shake it all off, but it's not working. Before it all happened, the Second Round and all that, there were things brewing under the surface. She was looking at me differently and it was making me feel this...

But then it happened and it all turned to shit. I was so full of anger at whoever did that to her that it didn't occur to me right away.

That her kicking me out of her room meant that she thought it was *me*. That she'd seriously think I'd try to fucking murder her.

I stop to look out the window. I haven't gone out much since it happened. Just a meeting now and then, mostly with the spies I hired to find out who did it. The rest of the time I spent in my quarters, coming up with the most painful ways to kill someone. It was comforting for a while, imagining being able to hurt the fucker who did it to her.

Now, the only thing comforting me is that the day will soon be over, the late afternoon sunlight slowly getting swallowed by darkness.

And just as I turn to go back to bed, I imagine that I've caught a whiff of her scent. Perfect, I think as I grit my teeth, furious at myself for still allowing her so much space in my head.

But then I hear a quick knock at my door and I see Max stick his head in, saying, "Longborn was here, asking if I knew where to find you."

Drawing in a sharp breath, I ask, "What did you tell her?"

He frowns a little. "Nothing, of course."

Despite my mind telling me it's a seriously bad idea, I hear myself say, "Go get her."

He just looks at me for a second, nods and leaves. I rush to the mirror, my heart racing. My reflection shows a stubble and dark circles around my eyes that I can do nothing about right now. But at least I can put on some pants and smooth out my hair a little.

When I walk out of my bedroom and into the living room, she's already there, standing near the doorway and looking at me with a funny look in her eyes. "I didn't know where else to go," she says in a hushed voice.

It does things to me. My heart tightens in my chest and I move towards her. Despite all the anger that I'm feeling, all I want is to fix things for her.

But once I'm in front of her, she takes a cautious step back.

My heart breaks and almost instantly, all the anger comes rushing back. To hide the whirlwind of emotion, I walk up to the bar and pour myself a drink.

"Your only option was the man who tried to kill you? Must be serious," I say and I down my whiskey, slamming the empty glass back onto the bar.

"Actually," she starts, flat-out ignoring my stabs. "That's something I need to apologize for. I know it wasn't you."

That surprises me, but I choose not to show it. I lean on the bar behind me, fold my arms and ask, "Really?" I'm barely managing to keep the bitterness out of my voice, but I don't care. "Warms my heart to hear you say it."

She lets out an exasperated breath, her hands balling into fists in that incredibly annoying way of hers. "In my defense, what else was I supposed to think? First of all, the person who attacked me did use mind magic on me..."

"Just like *I* did," I cut her off, my voice shaky with anger. I appear right in front of her, making her lips part and an almost inaudible gasp escape them. "Do you know the things I've done for you?"

"Oh, I know all about the chocolates," she starts, waving her hands and raising her voice a little. "What, you thought I'd never figure it out?"

"Things to keep you *safe*, goddamn it."

"And now I know you're telling the truth."

I get even closer, so close, I can only see her face. "It's too fucking late," I growl through gritted teeth. She's looking up at me in silence, those big brown eyes casting their usual spell. I want to make her stop with all this nonsense so I can plant an angry kiss on her lips, slam her against the wall and eat her out.

But I know better. "One second, Quinn," I whisper. "I lose control for one second and I fall all over myself to make up for it and you still end up thinking I'd try to fucking *murder* you? Is that really what you think of me?"

The very thought makes me want to rip my own heart out.

"No," she starts, a sorry look in her eyes. "Look, we don't have time for that right now."

"I see," I say in the flattest voice that I can muster, and I move to turn so I don't have to look at her.

"Faust," she rushes to say as she walks around to face me. "I didn't just realize it wasn't you who tried to kill me. I found out who it really was."

I just look at her for a second. "Tell me," I command, already fuming.

"I need you to stay calm."

"Calm?" I growl at her, my entire body vibrating with rage. "I am calm," I squeeze out as my mind floods with images of throats being ripped out. "Now spit it the fuck out."

"Alright," she says, but she looks even more hesitant than before. "Moswen showed me one of her memories, where I heard, well, the killer, talk about his plans just before the bloodshed happened. And when he came to kill me, I couldn't see his face properly, but what I *could* see was the sigil embroidered onto his shirt." She pauses, throwing me a funny look before she adds, "The Ouroboros."

Her words make me frown and pull away a little. "You're saying it's my *uncle*?"

She doesn't answer, she just presses her lips tight.

"You can't be serious," I say with a scoff.

She looks away for a second. "I think it's perfectly normal for you to have a hard time accepting it…"

"Hard time accepting it?" I mutter, not believing the words that are coming out of her mouth. "Tell me," I start, forcing myself to snap out of it, "is that all you're basing these grave, *grave* accusations on? Some dead girl's memory and stitching on a shirt?"

She draws in a breath and says, "Your uncle seems to want power, Faust. The Stone, as it turns out, amplifies mind magic so much, you could use it to control an entire country." She throws me a look filled with pity. "And he is out to get it."

I throw my hands up and take a few steps back, letting out a bitter laugh. "Are you even listening to yourself?" I demand. "If my uncle wanted the Stone, why didn't he just steal it the first chance he got? Why would he wait for the Trials?"

"Because it cannot be stolen, it can only be won," she rushes to say. "So instead of stealing it, he made the donation to have it brought out for the Third Round." She gets a little closer to me and looks at me with pleading eyes. "Faust, listen to me. Literally everyone will be at the Trials tomorrow. If your uncle's plan backfires, there'll be a bloodbath. And if he goes through with it, he'll put us all under his control. But that's where you come in. If you only stop him from attending…"

I just stare at her in silence. It feels as if my heart is shattering into a million tiny pieces. But it's no wonder really. After all, she *has* been toying with it ever since I first laid eyes on her. I turn my back to her and I say, "My uncle was right. You only ever bring trouble."

She stays silent for a second. "I knew you wouldn't want to help."

"Not another word." I don't turn to look at her. I wouldn't be able to bear it. "Leave, now."

For a second, there's silence. Then I hear her leave the room and close the door behind her.

Once I find myself alone again, I find my phone and I text uncle to give the Archduke the green light. And then, unable to contain myself any longer, I walk up to the bar, I grab the first bottle I see and I smash it against the floor. It doesn't really help, but I smash another. And another. And if I could, I'd set the world on fire, I'd take a seat and I'd watch it all burn to the ground.

Chapter Forty

I let myself be led out of the Elevator and through a hallway opening up onto the ring, for the third and hopefully last time ever. As we walk, we're greeted by an instant and violent flash of cameras. I throw a glance at the other Chosen. There's only seven of us left. Sarya, Harry, Zelda, Leo, Amra, Faust and myself. Their faces are pale and their bodies stiff.

The journalists lining the walls all swarm around me, pointing their microphones at my face as they shout out their questions. They want to know whether the thing I did last time was real and which tricks I have up my sleeve for this round. My eyes automatically dart in his direction, but Faust doesn't step in to save me from their greedy grip.

And I know why. He's still pissed at me, more pissed than ever. So he just throws me a glance and keeps leading the rest of the Chosen out into the Arena. It makes me feel sad and murderous all at once.

Letting out a sigh, I elbow and curse my way through the vultures and rush to catch up with the others.

We walk through a huge double door and the enormous space of the ring opens up before us. The crowd cheers more than ever and I see that the screens aren't just showing our faces. The cameras are turning their spying eyes onto the audience as well.

As we come to a stop somewhere around the middle of the stretch of beaten earth, I watch with bated breath as they show some of the fiercest and most famous Originals of our time. The leaders of all three noble Houses. The alphas of the independent shifter packs.

And yes, even the Keeper, I think to myself as I squint at the booth right next to the Pied Piper's. So far, I've only seen her in pictures, the blonde, fae-blooded Nikky. And right now, in the midst of all the buzzing anticipation, she's smiling as her equally gorgeous shifter mate is whispering something in her ear. But I've read things about her and I know she's just as dangerous and passionate as she is beautiful.

She reminds me of what I've come here to do. Not to participate in some outdated form of the eternal search of glory, but to try to save all these people from getting killed today.

What snaps me out of my ruminations are the looks that the Chosen are throwing each other. It's only then that I realize that the Trials should've started already.

And just as my eyes dart to the Pied Piper's booth and see that it's still empty, Baldor Faust himself rushes in and takes her seat.

I *cannot* fucking believe it.

"Welcome, everyone," his voice booms from the speaker, "to the Third Round of the annual Grimm Academy Trials."

The crowd cheers loudly and Faust Senior raises a hand to ask for silence.

"The Pied Piper won't be with us today, but not to worry," he exclaims. "Our Chosen are all here and ready to fight for the title of Champion!"

I'm barely registering the crowd's response. My mind is elsewhere, wondering why the fuck the Pied Piper's not here and what it could mean for me, what it could mean for us all. Is she out there somewhere helping him execute his plan?

"But before I tell you what the Third Round will entail," Faust Senior continues, "let's first greet all of today's special guests, starting with the Archduke of Erfurt."

I roll my eyes, tapping my shoes on the floor. As he drones on, I fight the urge to glance at Faust. He's made his choice and though I can't say I can blame him, I can't count on him either.

It's only when Faust Senior has finished sucking up to all the esteemed guests that I make myself snap out of it.

"Now," he says teasingly. He seems to have slowly gotten into his new role as the announcer. "You're probably all eager to find out what kind of test we'll be putting our seven heroes to."

The crowd responds by breaking into thunderous cheering and clapping. It's deafening, but as soon as I notice the other thing, my focus becomes undivided.

I fix my eyes on the ground before me, feeling it tremble under my feet and hearing a low, pained sound.

And just as the six of us start throwing glances at each other, the ground cracks and moves, revealing a set of stairs leading down into the darkness.

The crowd murmurs in excitement. My heart breaking into a gallop, I squint and I look up at Faust Senior, waiting for an explanation.

"Wondering where they lead?" he asks the crowd, his voice low and full of suspense.

Um, not more than *I* am.

But he only pauses for a split second before he says, his voice barely above a whisper, "Only to the very Heart of The Castle That Isn't..."

The crowd murmurs. I throw a glance at Harry, mouthing "What?"

But before he can do anything but raise his eyebrows, Faust Senior keeps talking, "Yes, you seem to know what I'm talking about. The usually entirely inaccessible part of Grimm Academy, its ancient core that to this day holds secrets of divine magic." He pauses before he adds, lowering his voice, "Magic so dangerous, the Pied Piper had to get a team of professors to prepare the extremely inhospitable terrain."

Great, I think to myself, my palms already sweating.

"As for our Chosen," Faust Senior continues in a low voice, "they only need to climb down, get to the farthest point, grab the Stone that's waiting for them there and come back to us."

That's all? No biggie, I tell myself in my most sarcastic inner voice.

But then a gong sounds and I find myself walking up to the stairs with the rest of the Chosen. Once we're right in front of the opening, Faust Senior yells out, "Let the Third Round begin."

And just like that, accompanied by yet another round of deafening cheering, the others start rushing down into the darkness.

I, on the other hand, choose caution. I take one step at a time, inspecting things as I go. But there's only raw earth around me, the stairs seeming to have been carved into the ground using only Earth Magic.

Still, the deeper I go and the fainter the sound of cheering becomes, the more my heart throbs in my chest.

By the time my feet hit the landing, I'm all alone in near darkness and I can no longer hear the people outside.

At first, my mind thinks there's only silence. But only for a second, until it starts noticing all the sounds. The flowing, the rustling, the pounding.

With bated breath and eyes open as wide as humanly possible, I take a few more steps and realize that I've found myself in a sort of cave. But instead of being carved into stone, it's a tangle of roots, branches swinging off the ceiling above me.

I move carefully, glancing left and right before every step I take. I look around and see another opening, darkness lurking behind it. It's the only way ahead and the others must have taken it as well.

And my intention is to keep walking carefully, but the energy of the place makes me rush myself.

Once I'm nearly through the opening, I feel something tugging at my ankle, making my heart skip a beat.

I look down to see one of the roots has wrapped itself around my leg. And it's moving fast, already climbing up my thigh.

I lunge forward, trying to pull my leg out, but it doesn't budge. Quickly, I tap my Element Rune and have the roots get sucked back into the ground. I don't hesitate. I run out of the place, throwing one last look back to see a gazillion other roots shooting into the air after me.

But as soon as I take a few more steps away from them, they go still and then get sucked back just like the first one.

Leaning forward and resting my palms on my thighs, I let out a shuddering breath. And just as my heartbeat goes back to normal, I hear a scream from somewhere behind me. A woman.

Blood curdles in my veins. Is it Sarya or Zelda or Amra or someone else entirely? I straighten up, turn on my heel and squint ahead, my ears pricked up. The space I'm in right now is a wide, dark tunnel carved into the ground. And it's a winding one so I can't actually see where it's going.

Hesitantly, I start walking down and straight at the source of that scream. What other choice do I have, I think to myself as I keep my hand raised to my Runes. Just in case.

But just as I see light somewhere in front of me, I hear it again. The same voice screaming, only more drawn out. I stop, my ears straining.

A part of me wants to turn around and run away, but if I want to save everyone from dying horrible deaths, I absolutely have to keep moving forward. So I force myself to pick up the pace, walking straight towards the blood-curdling sound.

As I make my way down the seemingly never ending tunnel, I try to drown out her screaming by humming things to myself. It won't help, me being scared out of my wits before I even lay eyes on her.

As I walk out of the tunnel, the light almost blinds me, making me raise my hand over my eyes. I'm squinting and I can't see her yet, but I can hear her loud and clear. "Please," she's sobbing.

I recognize Amra's voice. "Wait there," I yell out, "I'm coming to you."

I hear a crack and a thud and the sob turns into yet another scream.

My eyes finally get adjusted to the light, I lower my hand and I see exactly why it's so blinding. I don't know where it's coming from, but it's reflecting off the countless walls of crystals all around me. And right in front of me, suspended in the air, I see Amra. Except for her head and one hand, she seems to be completely encased in one of the crystals.

I rush to her. Obviously struggling to break out, she looks at me with pleading eyes. "Help me," she says and looks at the floor below her, where I see a piece of crystal with her hand in it.

Her fucking hand.

That was the crack I heard.

My hand darts to my mouth and I'm glad of it, because I don't want to make her panic even more. I quickly tap the Element Rune, hoping to get the crystals off her, but it doesn't work.

"Stay calm," I mutter as I come closer to inspect things. I've never seen anything like this stone and my Sight tells me it's not the kind of material I could manipulate.

What the fuck am I supposed to do? And just as I think that, she lets out another scream and the crystal that's got her trapped cracks along the middle.

I panic. I tap my Element rune, even though I know it won't work.

For a second, I think I see the crystal shrink.

Amra goes quiet and it makes me hold my breath in.

Then, just like that, I see the lower half of her just fall to the ground, her eyes rolling back in their sockets.

Holy shit. Holy fucking shit, I think to myself as I sit down with a loud thump. Maybe I just want to make sure it's real, what happened, so I grab her free hand, now lying there on the floor next to me. I pull my knees to my chest and I just sit like that, rocking back and forth. Her hand remains dead in mine. We're going to die, that's all I can think, we're all going to die.

Then it happens. The crystals still encasing Amra's hand start coming to life and creeping up my own skin. They're threatening to swallow me as well.

I jump up off the ground and try to shake them off, fighting not to let panic overtake me. If I can't control them, there's only one thing I can do. I can try to shrink them.

And I still only have my Element rune activated, but this is a matter of fucking life and death, I think to myself, gritting my teeth as I stare at the crystals.

Nothing seems to be happening.

And they've already reached my fucking elbow. Fuck.

I strain my eyes even more and I see them shrink.

It almost makes me cry with relief when I see them disappear.

I don't hesitate. I rush straight for the next opening, only throwing a glance at my runes to see that I really did just activate the third one. The Growth rune.

But she's dead, Amra has just *died*, the thought echoes through my mind. It all feels so unreal, but I have to keep going, keep going until I can't keep going any longer, otherwise…

Otherwise who knows what will happen, but it sure ain't going to be pretty.

So I make my way through the next opening. What's waiting for me on the other side looks like a regular cave. I walk through it and I find myself in another one.

I keep walking through cave after cave for what seems like an eternity. Every now and then, I hear blasts, yelling, sometimes even more screaming.

When once again I walk out of a cave only to find myself at the entrance of a seemingly identical one, I stop to come up with a plan.

Because I really need to speed this up. The more time I lose, the more time Baldor and the Pied Piper have to get the Stone.

So I take a closer look around. I'm breathing heavily, my mind buzzing as I look for clues on what the hell is going on.

I invoke the Sight, but it doesn't show anything I haven't already seen.

I let out a frustrated groan and stomp my foot on the ground. It's then that it occurs to me. I look down.

I look down and I see a trail on the ground. Tiny footsteps.

Drawing in an excited breath, I rush to follow them.

They start leading me down a series of tunnels, twisting and turning. And there's something strange about them. I feel them as if they're living and breathing things. Or a *single* living and breathing thing.

I stop and prick my ears up. And sure enough, the sound isn't crackling, but pattering. But it's still her.

"I'll start thinking you have a thing for me," I say, "Dame Gothel."

Her chuckle sounds as if the earth itself has produced it. "Don't flatter yourself, little one," she says as she makes the ground before me move, rise and form an enormous woman made of clay and twigs and moss.

The woman, Dame Gothel, looks down on me from high above and almost whispers, "I have a soft spot for all orphans. Always have and always will. Especially the ones with a lot of fire in them."

It makes me frown for a second, because it brings Hansel and Gretel to mind, when Dame Gothel is the witch from Rapunzel. Or could there be more than one story told about her? It sends shivers down my spine, but I've more important things to think about. "If that's really the case, will you help me find my way?"

Dame Gothel smiles, goes back to her incorporeal form and whispers, "What else am I here for? Just follow my footsteps and you'll get out of here soon."

"But this place seems to be huge. Do you know where I'll find the Stone?"

"Where will she find the Stone?" She laughs so hard, it makes me a little sore. "Do I need to spell everything out for you, little one? It's a *fairy tale* stone, for crying out loud."

With that, I sense her disappear.

And the very next second, I hear more screaming. Shit, I've been dragging my feet, I curse myself as I keep running where the tiny footsteps are leading me.

After only a couple of more turns, I barge onto an enormous clearing with seemingly no ceiling at all. Sprawled in front of me, I see what seem to be the ruins of some ancient castle. The air is heavy with mist and that mist feels so strange that I don't even register the movement until it's already happening.

A dark specter lunging straight at me. It grabs my waist and yanks me away from the ground, making me let out a muffled scream.

With my body in its firm grip, the specter starts circling the air high above the ruins below. I see towers, a throne room, houses and streets around the castle. I try to break free, planning to use Air Magic to help myself back to the ground. But the specter's grip is so strong, I can't even break my hand free to use my runes.

Just as I wonder what the fuck this thing plans on doing to me, I notice where it's taking me. To a nest atop of an old tower, filled with bones of other creatures it's killed.

My heart swelling in my chest and leaving me breathless, I start thrashing like never before in my life. I thrash and thrash, but it's not helping. And just as I'm about to be lowered into the nest, I see a shadow, as quick as lightning, dart through the air in front of me.

It takes a swing at the specter holding me, making it let out an ear-piercing screech and start flying away from the tower in a desperate attempt to save itself.

The next thing I know, I'm falling to the ground, trying to tap my Element Rune so as to avoid breaking all the bones in my body.

And I manage to do it, at least for the most part. When I push myself off the ground, panting and trying to stop myself from letting out a pained moan, I realize I've only broken a couple of ribs.

I quickly look around. The specter is nowhere to be seen and it seems to have dropped me onto one of the streets far from the castle.

To my surprise, the very next moment, I see Faust landing on the ground before me. He's hurt, blood drenching his torn-up shirt.

I let out a quiet gasp and I move to get closer to him, but he just gives me a once-over and disappears.

And of course, I'm relieved that I'm still alive. But there's also a part of me that's scared that he's dying and another part that's pissed that he's had to save me.

But to be honest, I've no time for feelings. I dust myself off and I go after him, pain making me wince with every breath of air I take. I can't be sure where he's disappeared to, but it seemed to me that he went straight for the heart of the castle.

And when you think about it, isn't *that* where a fairy tale stone should be hidden?

Holding my hand to my bruised chest, I start down the deserted streets leading in that direction. As I make my way, I keep looking out for another one of those specters, but I neither see nor hear any.

To my misfortune, I do see *bones*.

Bones all around me. Animal bones. Human bones.

It makes shivers run up my spine, but I've no choice. I have to keep going.

It's only when I enter the castle grounds, crumbling walls shooting into the sky around me, that I see them.

Zelda and Leo.

Lying on the ground, their bodies mutilated by what would have to be either a shifter or a ginormous fucking animal.

For a second, I just stare at them, my chest heaving and my breathing erratic. With the corner of my eye, I spot Sarya and Harry, both covered in wounds, disappearing down some kind of cellar to my left.

I fight not to look at Zelda and Leo again. It won't do me any good, to stare into their dead eyes. But I still do. I walk up to them and just keep standing there, fighting the onset of a panic attack.

To think that I used to think that this guy lying in front of me was behind all this...

Then I hear it. The snarl.

My head snaps in the direction of the sound and I see a huge armored lion stalking straight at me.

My heart racing, I tap my Element rune, but it only makes the earth below me tremble a little.

The lion leaps and swings a paw at me.

All of a sudden, I'm on the ground, my arm all bloody and a lion growling at me.

I use my Element rune again and I send him flying back.

He falls to the ground a ways off, but quickly gets back on all fours.

Adrenaline flooding my body, I yell out as I tap my rune and make the Earth swallow him whole.

Once I see him get sucked in, I let out a breath I seem to have been holding. Now panting, I push myself off the ground and I keep moving. For a second, I consider going after Harry and Sarya, but underground? I don't think that's where the Stone would be, so I choose to keep following Faust.

Soon, I start finding trails of fresh blood and dead armored animals all over the place. In an inner courtyard, in a reception room, in a kitchen.

It's only once I get to the throne room that I see him again. Faust, standing in front of the massive stone throne and next to an even bigger armored bear.

The bear is all bloody and so is Faust. He's swaying on his feet and has one hand pressed to his chest.

Suddenly panicking, I run to him and start inspecting him for wounds.

And holy shit. He's so wounded, I'm amazed that he's even standing.

Seemingly not even recognizing me, he just slaps my hands away. "Let me be," he mutters, takes something out of his pocket, a vial, and downs its contents.

But it's only when he turns around, however shakily, and starts walking straight to a pillar in front of the throne behind him, that it hits me.

I let out an actual gasp and open my mouth to tell him, but there it is. Resting on the surface of the pillar. Glowing. *The* Stone.

And Faust is already reaching for it.

"Don't," I yell out.

Slowly, he turns to look at me. "Why not?" he squeezes out, his voice pained.

"It's exactly what your uncle wants you to do," I blurt out. "I don't know why I ever thought he'd come win the Stone himself," I say with a shake of my head, "when he can just send you."

He just blinks at me and then lets out a weak, pained laugh.

"Did he give it to you," I insist, "what you just drank? You know what it is? The remains of all the Blood Rituals. The only way for you to unlock the power of the Stone."

This time, he squints at me angrily. "You're really something, you know that?"

He doesn't let me answer. He turns back to the Stone. Before I can do anything, he's already grabbed it and I know that it's too late when I see his body start to emit that same glow and I hear a chuckle sound behind my back.

Chapter Forty-One

I turn around and see Baldor Faust strolling up to us, smiling and tapping his walking stick on the ground.

"Uncle," I hear Faust mutter.

My eyes fixed on Baldor, I want to tell his nephew 'I told you so,' but I know better than that, I remind myself.

The uncle closes the remaining distance between them. "Andreas, you've been amazing. But what I want you to do now is take the Stone with you," he says as he points at a door behind the throne, "walk out into the Arena and make everyone bow to you."

"Why are you doing this?" his nephew asks, looking as if he's been struck by lightning.

I just stand there. What I really want is to attack, but I owe it to Faust to let him try to deal with his only remaining family by himself.

Baldor lets out a chuckle and says, "You know the answer to that question, nephew." He starts pacing up and down, one hand on his back and the other on his stick. "The balance of our world is hanging by a thread. Imagine being able to fix *everything*. That's what the Stone allows."

"Is that why you didn't care about the Archduke's proposal?" Faust asks in an accusing voice. "You had bigger fish to fry, didn't you?"

"Think what you will," Baldor says. "The first time I tried to get the Stone, it rejected me," he adds as he looks down at his injured left side. "But it didn't reject *you*. And each in his own way, you and I are special. If we put our minds and hands together, we could make the world a *much* better place."

My eyes dart to Faust. With bated breath, I watch the struggle on his face. "Maybe if I made it temporary, just long enough to-"

And just like that, I can't take it anymore. "Are you fucking kidding me?" I yell out, making both men turn to look at me.

"Longborn," Faust starts.

But his uncle cuts him off, looking pissed. "Andreas, compel her or I will do it for you."

"What kind of monster are you?" I demand.

"What did you call me?" Baldor hisses as he appears right in front of me. "Would a *monster* delay getting rid of you for as long as I have?"

I open my mouth, but I don't manage to say anything.

I see Faust lunge at his uncle and get in his face. "So you admit it?" he snarls at him. "That you went and tried to kill her?"

Baldor doesn't say anything. He just raises one hand and I see Faust's entire body tense up, his face taking on a pained expression. "Stop it," he yells at his uncle, but he makes him take a step back and just keep standing there.

I snap. Quickly, I tap the Element Rune and send rocks flying straight at him.

He just dodges them and looks deep into my eyes, raising his left hand at me while his right is still busy trying to control his nephew.

"Leave her the fuck alone," I hear Faust growl at him.

I try to stop it, but Baldor manages to assert his control over me, making me freeze in place.

He turns to his nephew. "Now go out and make them bow to you," he commands.

I myself can't move an inch, but I see Faust struggling not to listen. "Uncle, I'm warning you. If you don't stop, I'm going to use the Stone against you."

Baldor just shakes his head. "I'm afraid you wouldn't be able to. I put a drop of my own blood in the mixture I gave you. A failsafe of sorts, in case you chose... not to cooperate." He pauses for a second before he adds, "Now stop resisting and get out there. The people won't be waiting forever."

For what seems like an eternity, Faust keeps struggling, the veins on his face bulging, but then he lets out an exasperated breath and moves for the door behind the throne, stiffly and without a word.

"Good boy," his uncle says as he follows him.

Once again, I try to move and I fail miserably. It's over, I think to myself as I watch them leave without being able to do anything to stop them. And they manage to go through the door, which seems to lead straight back into the ring, and all of a sudden, I find myself alone, my mind racing and my heart pounding.

I hear the crowd cheer and start preparing for the worst.

But the more he controls his nephew, the weaker Baldor's grip on *me* becomes.

As soon as I feel my body as my own again, I tear my feet off the ground and run after the two of them, through the door behind the throne and up the stairs leading onto the ring.

I barge outside, raising my hand in front of my face. After the darkness below, the light outside is blinding. As my eyes adjust to it, there's only silence. I squint and I see everyone in the audience standing still with their heads bowed down.

Nuala, I spot Nuala among them.

I panic and my eyes dart to Faust, who's standing to the other side of the stairs we've just climbed, his uncle by his side.

His uncle who's spotted me and is now squinting in my direction, preparing to do something about it.

Without hesitation, I tap the Element Rune and send a wall of dense air flying straight into him.

He just dodges it and lands right in front of me, his nephew turning to me in one swift but awkward movement, his eyes filled with so many emotions, I can't even begin untangling them.

"So you're fine controlling everyone else, but not her?" his uncle spits out.

"Let him go," I yell out as I shoot another, denser and angrier wall of air at him.

He dodges it, but pretends as if he didn't hear me. He lets out an exasperated sigh and says, "Fine. I guess I'll have to find another way to deal with her."

All of a sudden, I get the urge look up. I see people from the audience staring at me as they get out of their seats and start making their way down the bleachers and into the ring, all of their movements perfectly synchronized.

I draw in a breath, taking a few quick steps back as my mind scrambles to find a way out of it.

But I don't have time to think, because I see the Keeper walk into the Arena, throw one of her arms back and lunge at me with a ball of lightning in her hand.

Holy fuck. Breath held, I stumble backwards and I tap the Growth Rune, making the ball of lightning in the Keeper's hand expand until it swallows her, sending a shock through her body that has her collapse to the ground.

I fall to my knees, air knocked out of my lungs. When I finally manage to catch my breath, I see the rest of the crowd start to walk over her body and keep coming for me.

I tap my Element Rune and make an air bubble around my entire body, stopping them from getting too close. It's at that exact moment that I hear someone yell, "Make them snap out of it."

I turn around and see the Pied Piper charging through the double door and into the ring, visible signs of fight on her dress. She's making her way through the crowd by throwing merciless blows at everyone around her. Who was she talking to?

As the mind-controlled crowd keeps pushing at the barrier of my air bubble, I turn my eyes back onto Baldor. He doesn't look fazed. His eyes sweeping over the chaos around us, he chuckles and makes his nephew send some of his creatures at de Groot. I want to help her, but maintaining my air bubble is quickly draining my energy.

Among those attacking the Pied Piper, I spot the only two remaining Vipers, Sarya shooting rocks at her and Harry shifting into the biggest grizzly I've ever seen.

I draw in a breath as I watch de Groot let them get closer. Once they do, she just slams them into the ground with a couple of blows of her hand. Fuck, she's strong.

But then the Keeper attacks her by making the ground beneath her start crumbling.

De Groot jumps up in the air, lands right in front of her and sends her flying to the ground.

It feels so fucking good to know that she's on my side. I turn back to Baldor and decide to grit my teeth, stop wasting my energy just defending myself and take the opportunity to attack.

As soon as I let the air bubble burst, the people almost come crashing into me. I jump up, quickly tapping the Element Rune. I make the air below me dense so when I land on it, I remain hovering high above the ground. Looking down at Baldor, who now seems to be fighting the Keeper, I lift my hand to my Runes.

This time, I won't be showing any restraint. I send a huge wall of earth flying straight at him.

He just dodges it and charges at me. With the corner of my eye, I see Faust standing in the middle of everything, his body vibrating with the effort to break free of his uncle's magic.

Raging inside, I turn back to Baldor and raise my hands to send another wall of earth at the old prick's chest.

To my surprise, that's not what ends up happening. Instead, I knock him over with an angry ball of fire shooting out of my palms.

My Air Magic failing me, I fall down to the ground, making the people below me disperse. What the fuck just happened? Since when can I use Fire?

I quickly push myself up. When I look at him, I see Baldor lying on the ground, heavily burned and panting. But when his eyes meet mine, they don't linger there. They dart to something behind me.

The next thing I know, a knife gets stabbed into my back, right above my heart, and I let out a pained scream and come crashing to the ground.

As I lie there, I watch Baldor dodge attack after attack. And the people that keep charging at him are the ones whose asses de Groot kicked when she arrived.

Then it hits me. When she said to make them snap out of it, it was me she was talking to.

My eyes dart to Faust, who's still under his uncle's spell. And there's the Vipers, the Keeper and the Pied Piper trying to take down Baldor, but there's still so many of those that are under the prince's control and things are getting out of hand, people yelling and attacking each other all around me.

One of them being Nuala. I see her getting beaten up and I rush to her, knocking over both her and her attacker with a wall of air. As soon as I do it, I see them snap out of it, my friend pushing herself off the ground to give me a quick hug.

So there really is only one way to do this. "We've no time to waste," I tell Nuala. "We need to make everyone snap out of it."

She nods and as I turn to look around, to see exactly how to go about it, I notice her dig through her pocket and pop something in her mouth. I frown at her, but she just says, "I'll have your back."

Quickly, because Baldor is sending more people in my direction, I tap the Element Rune and squeeze my eyes shut, making the earth below me tremble.

And it's all terribly loud, but nothing really happens. People just keep attacking each other.

Just as I let out a frustrated groan, I hear someone charge at me from behind and I turn to defend myself, when I see my friend shift, right before my own two eyes, into the biggest, most beautiful white tiger I have ever seen.

The tiger knocks the attacker out cold, stalks back to me and, well, gives my face a thorough lick before she turns back and goes to run after Harry's grizzly.

The next thing I know, I hear Faust groaning from exertion. My eyes snap in the direction of the sound and I see him standing in the middle of it all, blood running down his eyes from all the effort he has to put in fighting his uncle.

I feel hot rage coursing through my body. What's enough is enough, I think to myself, I shut my eyes and I tap the Element Rune.

Once I open them, I see fire swallowing the bleachers all around us and drawing everyone into the center of the ring.

Within a minute, all that wood and metal comes crashing to the ground.

I drop to my knees, the sudden silence around me thundering. I see people snapping out of it and Baldor trying to get up off the ground.

My eyes dart to his nephew, who seems to be regaining his control as well, fire burning in his eyes.

The next thing I know, he's grabbing his uncle by the neck, lifting him up off the ground.

He growls, "I'm going to kill you with my own two hands."

And as the rest of the crowd watches in silence, he tightens his grip, making his uncle's face start turning purple.

"Andreas," he squeezes out, "you know this is right. Just yesterday, you told me to give the Archduke the green light-"

"I can't believe I didn't see it," Faust snaps at him, his body vibrating with rage, "that family and duty are just excuses to you for your own ambition. I'm going to enjoy watching the light go out of your eyes."

"Don't you dare, boy," Baldor snarls back, "if you lose me, you lose *everything*, family and position, and you know it."

"I've never cared about position and I no longer have a family," Faust growls, "but at least I'll have peace of mind knowing I chose to do the right thing." And with that, he starts tightening the grip.

I push myself off the ground and run to him. "No," I command, "don't."

He turns to look at me. "He tried to kill you, Quinn."

There's such pain in his eyes, it makes me go silent for a second.

"I know, but trust me, Andreas," I finally tell him.

He loosens his grip and lets his uncle's body fall to the ground. I hear rushed footsteps and angry yelling as the Pied Piper takes control of Baldor, but my eyes are still fixed on his nephew's. I reach out my hand, but he just turns on his heel and walks away, dropping the Stone onto the bloody ground below.

Chapter Forty-Two

We're sitting in my room, drinking in preparation for the Grand Ball. Nuala is giddy with excitement and I'm wearing the most beautiful dress I've ever had the chance to wear, about to be paraded around as one of the two Champions of this year's Trials.

But how can I feel good about any of it when it's only been two weeks since it all happened? They've treated the wound that was apparently about to kill me, but I've got fresh cuts and bruises all over my legs and arms. I'm thrilled for my friend being freshly in love with Harry, but that means that I'll be attending the Ball by myself, *again*. And it's not like I won't be drawing attention.

Now that everyone knows who my parents were and what happened to them that year when Baldor Faust first tried to get his hands on the Stone, I'm even more popular with the press. It doesn't help that both the Pied Piper and the Keeper have taken a special interest in me, trying to teach me to improve my magic. Apparently, Creators, that is, faes that can create things out of nothing, not just manipulate the world around them, are hard to come by. And that makes me proud, sure, but it also makes me terrified.

But what's worst of all is that I still can't stop thinking about *him*. I wonder if he's going to come to the Ball at all. He should. If nothing else, to allow them to crown us as winners.

That's what princes do, right? Show up for stuff like that even if they don't feel like it? Even if their entire world has just crumbled to the ground?

"Quinn?" my friend calls out, snapping me out of my ruminations and making me look at her. "I don't know what you're thinking about, but I'm sure it goes against your promise."

Ah. My promise to have fun tonight, yes. I give her a weak smile. "Nuala," I start in a low voice, "do you think I should talk to her after all?"

"I support you whatever you decide," she replies with determination in her eyes.

I let out a chuckle. "I know, but what do you really think?"

"I think you should talk to her, yes," she rushes to say. She's obviously been wanting to. "She's your sister, after all."

I think for a second. "Would you mind leaving the two of us alone then?"

"Of course," she says with a warm smile.

"You're the best friend a girl could ever have."

"And you're the sappiest."

We stick our tongues out at each other and she leaves my room, closing the door behind her.

Letting out a sigh, I grab the diary off the bed and I crack it open.

"Just so you know," I say as soon as Moswen appears, "there was no bloodbath and we all made it out alive, no thanks to you."

She just looks at me for a second. "I guess I deserve that. But once again, Quinn, if you knew how very sorry I am... About all of it..."

"You don't get it," I insist, pressing my lips tight, "how much I just can't believe you'd rob me of that. Knowing that we're family, getting to know you, asking you questions..."

"Sometimes people do stupid things," she cuts me off, her voice heavy with remorse and sadness, "but that doesn't necessarily mean they don't care. I know it wasn't the case with me. But listen..."

"Yes?" I demand, noticing her becoming anxious.

"The magic keeping me here," she rushes to say.

But I cut her off. "It's waning."

"It is," she nods. "I don't think we have much time. So listen, Quinn," she says as she crouches before me and looks deep into my eyes. "You had two parents who loved you more than anything."

I feel tears welling up in my eyes.

"Your father loved reading to you and your mother never went for a walk without you. He was the grumpy one, stubborn and focused on his studies, while she was the ray of sunshine, relaxed and always up for a little mischief."

I wave my hand, trying to stop myself from crying. "Thank you, but I want to know more about *you*."

I choke on my words because it's at that exact moment that I see her becoming fainter. I reach out my hand and I open my mouth, but she stops me.

"It's alright, Quinn," she says with a sad smile. "None of it really matters. You're my little sister and my soul will always know yours."

And with that, she disappears. For a second, I remain sitting there, frozen in place. Then a gush of tears bursts out of me, shaking me to my very core.

I've lived through it all and for what? To lose a sister I've only just found? To cause *him* to lose the only family he'd ever had? And I know that none of it is my fault, but it still feels that way.

I force myself to stop crying and I look at the clock on the wall across from me. The Ball should be starting any minute now, but I don't know if I want to go.

And I don't think I will.

At least not until I've had one thing taken care of.

So I get up off the bed and leave my room, heading straight for the Lilith Tower.

And sure, he's there. When I ask for him in the foyer of his private fucking quarters, I hear his voice from the other side of the wall saying, "Let her in."

I take a deep breath and barge into his living room, where I last found myself when I came to ask him to let me join the Vipers.

He's sitting on the couch, his back turned to me. His left arm is thrown over the backrest. "Come to fuck up my life some more?" he asks, his voice strangely flat as his eyes stay fixed ahead.

"I'm not here to ask favors," I say as I walk around the couch to face him. He's clad in a gorgeous suit and has a glass of whiskey in his other hand.

He looks up and drags his eyes down my body. "Ah, I see," he says and downs his drink, "you've come to rub more salt in my wound." And with that, he gets up and looks away, walking up to the bar.

I follow him. "I don't know what you're talking about," I protest, suddenly fuming. "I've come to say I'm sorry about your uncle. You never gave me the chance."

He stops and turns to face me. "I never thought you cared," he snaps back, his voice a slab of ice.

"How can you say that?" I reply, frowning.

He groans and waves his hand in dismissal. "What're you really here for?"

That makes me think for a second. "I guess I'd like us to stop being enemies. You know, move on."

He lets out a bitter laugh. "Move on?" he says as he takes a few steps closer to me, his nostrils flaring and his voice brimming with tension. "I'm afraid that you and me moving on would be the end of me. But I'm sure you'd love *that*."

"Really?" I ask, not believing the words that are coming out of his mouth.

He gets in my face. "Really," he snaps back.

I let out a frustrated groan. "You're infuriating, you know that?" I say as I turn to walk away.

He appears in front of me, blocking my way out. "Not nearly as much as you are," he growls in my face, so close, I can only see his eyes.

For a second, we just stare at each other, fuming. Then he grabs me by the waist and crushes his lips on mine. I throw my arms around his neck and he pulls me even closer, until I can feel all the hardness of his cock. He slides his tongue between my lips and starts dragging his hands all over my body, making a wave of pleasure come crashing down on me.

How dare he feel this good, I think as I pull away to look at him. His eyes glazed, he frowns and leans back in, demanding another kiss, but I bite his lower lip instead. He lets out a low growl and bites back. His arms wrapped tightly around my waist, he makes me take a few wobbly steps backwards and slams me against the wall.

There, he starts fumbling to pull the fabric of my dress down and around my breasts. And just as I lift my hand to help him, he lets out a low groan, pulls away a little and tears the whole thing off with a single jerk.

It makes me let out a shuddering breath, when his eyes start dragging down my body. I let him look, his breathing becoming more erratic as he runs his hands all over my breasts, my stomach, my ass, until I can't take it anymore.

Slick with desire for him, I let my hand dart to the zipper on his pants.

He blocks it, grabs my chin and makes me look him in the eyes. "Don't tease," he says in a low, thick voice.

"I'm not," I say defiantly.

"What about that date?" he demands.

"Fuck the date."

He just looks at me for a moment, tightens his grip on my waist and whispers, "I don't think you know what you're getting yourself into." He leans closer, his lips touching my ear. "I've been waiting for this moment for a very long time, Quinn. I've a long list of things I want to do to you."

That makes me so hot, I just say, "Mmm."

"Are you going to be a good girl and let me?"

"No," I say and I pull away to look him in the eye.

"Quinn," he growls, frowning.

It almost makes me laugh. I lean in to whisper, "You'll have to make me."

I feel him tense up. "Fuck," he drawls, his breathing ragged as he tips his head back to look at me, burning holes in my eyes.

"Bite your lip," he commands.

He fixes his eyes on my mouth and watches me do it.

"Harder," he demands.

I bite into the skin, making a drop of blood wet it. He stares for a second, a savage look in his eyes. Then he crushes his lips on mine and shoves his tongue deep inside my mouth.

A vampire's kiss.

Almost instantly, I feel a connection of the kind I've never experienced before. As if we're one and the same, him and I. He's kissing me and I feel exactly what the touch of my tongue does to him, how my smell drives him crazy, how his dick throbs whenever I squeeze the muscles of his shoulders. I feel his pleasure and I know he feels mine.

But it's only when he pulls away that he puts me under his control, the tendrils of his mind wrapping around my entire body. Then he pulls away and takes a seat on the couch, his legs wide open and one arm thrown over the backrest.

For a second, he just soaks me up, naked and standing right in front of him. Then he motions at an easy chair to my right and says in a thick, commanding voice, "Sit over there and touch yourself."

My body moves of its own accord. Throbbing in anticipation, I slowly get settled, spread my legs wide and start sliding my hand between my thighs. It gives me so much pleasure, the way he leans forward and fixes his eyes on me like a hawk.

It's only when my fingers start brushing against my clit that I realize this is something else entirely. I let out a helpless moan. It's my own hand, that I'm sure of, but the connection between us makes it feel like his. Like he's the one using it.

Without breaking eye contact, he makes sure he's got me wet enough, finds the right spot and pushes my fingers deep inside me, making me let out another moan. As soon as I do, he appears closer to me, his look even more intense and his breathing more ragged.

Slowly, he starts sliding my fingers in and out of my pussy, making my chest heave and my face blush.

And every time I let out a moan, he comes a little closer. This time, he gets on his knees in front of my pussy and leans over me, dragging his hands up and down my naked body. As he fucks me with my own fingers, he uses his thumb to stroke and knead my clit, just to drive me crazy.

Pretty soon, he has me panting and as wet as I can be, the anticipation of his touch almost making me whimper with desire.

But just as I'm about to come, he pulls both our hands away. I open my mouth to protest, but then he whispers in my ear, his breathing ragged. "Now bend over."

I do as I'm told, getting up and turning to plant my knees and my palms onto the easy chair. "I'm going to fuck you so hard," he says as he walks up to me and starts running his hands up and down my body, squeezing and kneading as he goes, "you won't be able to walk for days."

"Yes, please," I squeeze out, my own voice raspy and filled with desire.

I hear him unzip his pants and feel the hardness of his cock press against my ass. And all I want is to rub against it, but he doesn't let me. He teases me with it, sliding it up and down my slick pussy.

When he finally pushes it in and starts slamming into me, it makes my eyes roll back in my head and a moan escape my lips. He keeps fucking me, harder and faster. And I want it even harder and faster, but he's not allowing me any control of my own body, my ass remaining just where he's planted it, despite all my yearning for his cock.

"Oh fuck, Andreas," I groan and he grabs me by the hair, pulling me away from the easy chair and closer to him, so the entire length of his chest is pressed against my back. Feeling the hardness of his muscles, I hear him pant in my ear, "Now you'll come for me like the good girl that you are."

And with that, he starts thrusting inside me faster than I thought was possible, making my pussy clench around his cock.

I don't answer him, I'm too busy moaning, but I do come for him, I come for him hard, at the same time he comes for me, biting down on my neck as his thrusts start slowing down.

For a while, we just stay that way, his dick still inside me and my back still pressed to his chest. Then he pulls out and turns me to face him, his mind tendrils letting go of my body.

I hear a knock at the door.

"Not now," Andreas growls, glancing over his shoulder to scowl in the direction of the sound.

There's a weird look in his eyes.

I just tilt my head and shove at his chest.

"Remember when you said you didn't want to be my fuck-girl?"

"Well," I say in a soft, flirty voice as I start unbuttoning his shirt.

He grabs my wrists and pulls me closer. "I'm done playing games, Quinn." The way he says my name makes my heart skip a beat. "If you wanted this to be a one-night stand, fine. You've had your way with me and you can leave, no strings attached. But I'm warning you..."

I have to suppress a laugh. "Yes?" I just say, trying to keep a straight face.

"If you stay, you're *mine*."

The intensity of the look in his eyes makes me turn serious. I don't say anything. I just pull away from him, stand up and, feeling his eyes on me the entire time, slowly walk over to his bed. I get on it, lie on my side and throw him a smoldering look.

He appears before me in a heartbeat. "Spread your legs for me, Quinn," he commands in a low voice.

"Not before you finish taking *all* your clothes off," I tell him.

His lips curl into that sexy smirk of his and his hands move to obey, but the very next second, there's more loud knocking at his door. We both freeze and he lets out a frustrated sigh, shaking his head.

"What did I tell you, Max," he growls without taking his eyes off me.

"I'm so sorry to disturb," I hear Max say, "but there's a lot of people asking if you're even coming to the Ball."

I get up and start looking for my dress. "We really should get going," I say.

Andreas lets out a groan and leans in to give me a long, passionate kiss.

"Fine," he says when he pulls away. He walks up to his dresser and starts rummaging through his stuff. "But you're coming as my date," he says as he stalks over to me and slides a black rose corsage around my wrist.

I let out a chuckle, saying, "You know that's against the rules. The Chosen taking each other to the Ball."

"Fuck the rules," he says with a smirk.

I can't help but smile, warmth flooding my chest and making me lean in for another kiss.

By the time we arrive at the Main Hall, everyone's already there. And they all seem to be craving our attention, especially once their eyes dart to my hand in his. He doesn't let go of me for a second.

And as we walk around, greeting everyone we meet, I can't help but wonder how strange life can be.

Less than a year ago, if someone told me I'd find a life among the Originals of Grimm Academy, I'd laugh and tell them to shut up. And what ended up happening is far more unbelievable than *that*.

Enjoyed House of Ydril?

There's more! - Don't miss out!

Review, newsletter signup, socials, it's all here!

Or visit lyraforger.com

ORIGINALS OF GRIMM ACADEMY

FULL SERIES AVAILABLE

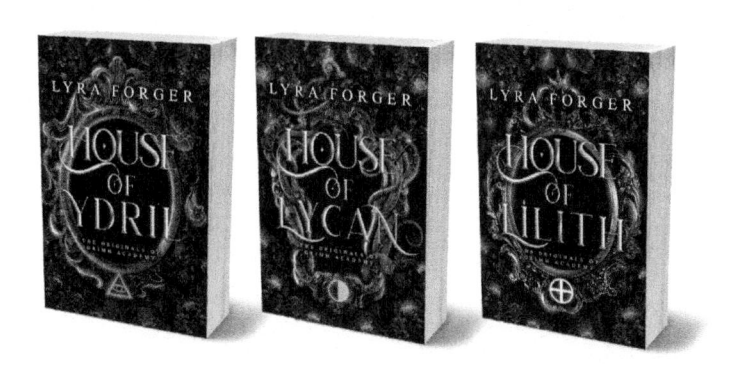

Printed in Great Britain
by Amazon